**Blood . . . bright red . . .
steaming under the light of
black wax candles
and torches . . .**

He was both priest and victim. Holding the knife and
wearing the black robes of a High Priest, he stared
down at the naked and bound form on the altar stone.

And he looked up, straining against the bonds, the
sacrificial victim, feeling the cold from the engraved
concrete altar biting into his back. The wide blade of
a rune-carved knife rose, catching torchlight on its
tip. He didn't feel the tip of the sacrificial knife pierce
his chest. The chant filled his head, filled all the
heavens. A brilliant blackness exploded outward from
his heart and brain. . . .

Resurrection, Inc.

Kevin J. Anderson

A SIGNET BOOK

NEW AMERICAN LIBRARY

For John Postovit and Kristine Kathryn Rusch,
who have been with me
through all incarnations of this story.

And also to Neal Peart, Geddy Lee, and Alex Lifeson
of RUSH, whose haunting album
Grace Under Pressure inspired much of this novel.

NAL BOOKS ARE AVAILABLE AT QUANTITY DISCOUNTS
WHEN USED TO PROMOTE PRODUCTS OR SERVICES.
FOR INFORMATION PLEASE WRITE TO PREMIUM MARKETING DIVISION,
NEW AMERICAN LIBRARY, 1633 BROADWAY,
NEW YORK, NEW YORK 10019.

Copyright © 1988 by Kevin J. Anderson

SIGNET TRADEMARK REG. U.S. PAT. OFF. AND FOREIGN COUNTRIES
REGISTERED TRADEMARK—MARCA REGISTRADA
HECHO EN CHICAGO, U.S.A.

SIGNET, SIGNET CLASSIC, MENTOR, ONYX, PLUME, MERIDIAN
and NAL BOOKS are published by NAL PENGUIN INC.,
1633 Broadway, New York, New York 10019

First Printing, July, 1988

1 2 3 4 5 6 7 8 9

PRINTED IN THE UNITED STATES OF AMERICA

Contents

PART I

Resurrection

1

The two Enforcers found the dead man in the street, long after curfew. The city's night hung around them, tainted with a clammy mist caught between the tall and dark buildings. The smell of fresh blood and the sweat of close-pressed bodies drifted upward into the air.

The slain man was naked, spread-eagled inside a geometrically perfect pentagram drawn in blood. At each of the five corners of the pentagram, candles of black paraffin burned, made to look archaic with artificially molded runnels of wax along the sides. A wide knife wound hung cleanly open in the center of the victim's chest, like an appalled extra mouth.

With a throb of its rear jets, the Enforcer's armored hovercar descended to the flagstones. As the engine purred its way into silence, Enforcer Jones, a tall and thin black man, emerged from the craft. He hung back uneasily, remaining near the hovercar. "Neo-Satanists again!" he muttered under his breath.

The other Enforcer, Frampton, agreed. "Yeah, they give me the creeps." But he went eagerly forward, amused and confident.

Weapons bristled from pockets and holsters on the Enforcers' body armor; a tough helmet with a laser-proof black visor covered their faces. In the mercifully brief four weeks Frampton had been assigned to him, Jones had never seen Frampton's face, but somehow he imagined it would wear a stupid boyish grin, maybe some scattered pimples, maybe curly hair. Frampton thought all this was fun, a game. It didn't matter—they weren't friends, nor would they be. Other Enforcers had a real camaraderie, a team spirit. But this would be Jones's last night patrol anyway.

"Think I should put out the candles?" Frampton asked.

Jones moved away from the hovercar, shaking his revulsion of the pentagram, the blood sacrifice. "No, I'll do it. You see to his ID."

Frampton retrieved some equipment from the hovercar

while Jones stepped forward, methodically squashing each of the five black candles with the heel of his boot. In the distance, between gaps of the massive squarish buildings, he could see the running lights of another patrol car moving in its sweep pattern.

Frampton made a lot of noise as he carelessly tumbled the equipment onto the flagstones within the pentagram. He picked up one of the scanner-plates and pushed it flat against the dead man's palm. The optical detectors mapped the swirls and rivulets of the man's fingerprints, searching for a match in the city's vast computer network.

"Nothing on The Net about him." Frampton double-checked, but came up with the same answer again.

"Figures," Jones said.

"Ever wonder how the neo-Satanists *always* manage to get people who aren't even on The Net? Weird." Frampton sounded breathless. He was always trying to make conversation.

Jones turned an expressionless black visor at his partner for a long and silent moment. He wanted to act cold, wanted to be gruff with the other Enforcer. It was too late to make friends now—better just to keep up the act. "How do you know they don't just alter the data on The Net?"

Frampton considered this in silent amazement. "That would be awfully sophisticated!"

"Don't you think *this* is sophisticated?" Jones jabbed a hand at the body, the candles, the pentagram. "Enforcers sweep this area every five minutes after curfew. You know how strict it is, how closely patrolled—and the neo-Satanists *still* managed to get him out on the street, light the candles, draw the pentagram, and then vanish before we could get here."

Only members of the Enforcers Guild were allowed on the streets of the Bay Area Metroplex between midnight and dawn. Jones didn't fully understand the actual reasons for the curfew—some rumors mentioned a war taking place somewhere, but he had yet to see any signs of battle. Other, more sensible people cited the occasional violent riots caused by the angry blue-collars who had been displaced from their jobs by resurrected Servants.

Jones himself had participated in some of the after-dark mock street battles staged by the Guild. Nobody really got hurt—only a few blasted palm trees, a few scorched tile rooftops, and a lot of noise in the streets. But it all sounded terrible and dangerous to the general public cowering in their living quarters, and they would always feel grateful for the protection the Guild offered. Besides, it gave all the Enforcers something to do.

Earlier in the night, Jones and Frampton had captured a chunky Asian man cowering under the overhang of a darkened business complex. The man had been trying to hide, not knowing where to go, as if he had a chance of avoiding the Enforcer sweeps.

Frampton had pulled out two of his weapons, striding toward the cowering man, but Jones restrained his partner and listened while the chunky man babbled an explanation. He and his wife had argued, and he had stormed out of their apartment, either forgetting about the curfew or not caring. Now his wife wouldn't let him back in, and the man had been trying to hide until dawn.

Sheepishly the Asian man keyed his Net password into the terminal mounted in the armored hovercar; his ID checked out.

"You know what we have to do now," Jones said from behind the visor.

The man swallowed and hung his head in dejected horror. "Yes."

"All your Net privileges revoked for a week. Sorry. Curfew is curfew." The Asian man sulked behind the restraining field in the back of the hovercar while Jones and Frampton escorted him home.

Without The Net recognizing his identity, the man would be effectively a non-person for an entire week; he could not buy anything, or make person-to-person Net voicelinks, or call up entertainment on The Net itself; he could not get into his own home unless someone else let him in.

The man's wife looked frightened but not surprised when the Enforcers arrived to escort her husband back into the dwelling; she didn't look pleased to see him, and the prospect of having to do everything herself for the next seven days seemed to make her even angrier yet. . . .

"Give me a hand here?" Frampton opened the refrigerated, airtight compartment in the back of the hovercar and returned to the slain man in the pentagram.

Jones bent to take the body's feet while the other Enforcer tightened his handhold under the man's armpits. Jones could feel the rubbery dead flesh of the victim's ankles even through his flexsteel-mesh gloves.

Frampton pursed his lips and grinned at the mouthlike wound in the dead man's chest. "Well, it's off to the factory for you, my boy. I bet you're going to miss all this, Jones."

Transfer generally equated with punishment in the Enforcers Guild, and Jones had screwed up several days before, during a daytime stint on the streets. He had frozen for a moment, let his conscience whisper a few words in his ear, when he had seen a rebel Servant break from her routine and run.

All Servants were reanimated corpses, dead bodies with microprocessors planted in their brains to make the bodies move again, to let them walk and talk and do what they were told. It was much cheaper than manufacturing androids from scratch for doing menial and monotonous tasks.

But even with her head shaved, the lifeless pallor to her skin, and the gray jumpsuit/uniform of all Servants, Jones had difficulty convincing himself that the rebel Servant wasn't human, that she was already dead and merely reanimated, that she didn't matter.

The Enforcer found his reprimand ironic: Starting tomorrow, he would be taken from his easy post-curfew beat for full-time service at Resurrection, Inc. to escort newly resurrected Servants to their assignments.

But at least it would get him away from Frampton and his constant inane chattering.

They placed the slain man in the back compartment of the hovercar, folding his arms and legs neatly to fit him into the cramped space. Frampton stood with a miniature Net keyboard in his hand, punching in data about the discovery. "Verify cause of death," Frampton said. "Single wound, no other apparent bodily damage, no identity information on The Net."

Jones glanced at the wound in the man's chest. "Verified."

"To Resurrection, Inc., right?"

"Yeah."

Frampton dropped his voice slightly. Because of the dark visor, Jones could read no expression on his partner's face. "Man, I hope that never happens to me."

Jones closed the compartment and set the controls for

quick-freeze. A hissing noise filled the air. He knew exactly what Frampton meant, but he asked anyway, "What? Being a neo-Satanist sacrifice, or becoming a Servant?"

"Neither one."

2

On the sixth underground level of Resurrection, Inc., the technician placed the body from Vat 66 onto a clean inspection table. The body's arms moved loosely, still dripping, almost cooperating, as the tech rearranged them. Four days of conditioning had left the muscles free of rigor and the dead brain ready for imprinting as a Servant. The room smelled strongly of chemicals, making the tech's eyes and nostrils burn, even after his two years of working there.

On the pocket of the tech's non-porous lab smock, he had carefully stenciled his name, "RODNEY QUICK," so no one would steal it. Yet Rodney Quick was generally the only human to spend an entire shift on Level Six anyway; the rest of the workers were Servants—bald and dressed in their characteristic gray jumpsuits—and certainly no *Servant* would dream of stealing his lab smock. But the stenciled name made Rodney feel important and easily recognized by anyone who might take notice of his work.

Rodney straightened the body's pliant limbs while drops of vat solution trickled into drainage grooves cut in the polished table surface. The tech hummed to himself as he found a roll of shredded duo-sponges and dabbed the remaining solution from the body.

Thick but limp brown hair hung straight down from one side of Rodney's head, while on the other side the hair had been tapered drastically back, leaving the area above his ear shaved clean. He stood a few inches shorter than anyone who had ever tried to intimidate him, and his watery blue eyes somehow always carried a look of fear. The gold-plated stud in his left nostril and the two silicon fingernails on his right hand should have been stylish.

Adjusting the bright overhead lights, Rodney let the glare wash down on the naked body, illuminating the open wound in the center of the man's chest. Beneath the inspection table, sharp-angled shadows crowded on the floor, responding with grotesque exaggerations to

14

Rodney Quick's every move. He was reminded of the monsters he had imagined under his bed-unit when he was a child.

The pre-Servant from Vat 66 had finished several days of initial prep for resurrection, soaking in a solution of scrubber bacteria that removed all the lactic acid from the muscles and purged the dead body of waste and undigested food. As a last step before bringing the body to the inspection table, Rodney had drained all the blood vessels and refilled them with saline solution in preparation for the synBlood.

Rodney slipped a pair of magnifying goggles over his eyes and bent down to inspect the wound in the man's chest. His own shadow lurched across the prone body, but Rodney didn't notice with his drastically reduced field of view. The tech could see that the wound was clean; the tissue had been hacked and the veins and arteries roughly severed, but Rodney didn't think it would be difficult to make repairs.

He measured the body's chest cavity and, leaving the table unattended, went searching for an appropriate synHeart. In the resurrection room other Servants wandered about, performing pre-programmed tasks, checking dials and monitoring other vats, meticulously jotting down information. Rodney always felt the irony of having Servants assist him here on Level Six—it seemed like having cattle help out in a slaughterhouse.

The technician stopped at the door to the organ-supply room, keyed in his request to the Net terminal mounted by the door. Moments later, in a puff of cryogenic mist, the door slid open and a flashing light indicated the location of an appropriate cardiac pump. Rodney removed the synHeart and, as he walked out of the clammy-smelling storeroom, he was tempted to toss the organ up in the air and try to catch it when it came back down. But he restrained himself—as always, Supervisor might be watching.

"Out of useless death, we create Service to mankind," said the inscription above the elevator doors—a quote attributed to Francois Nathans, the magnate of Resurrection, Inc. Rodney suddenly noticed the quote again after two years of working in the lower levels, and he wasn't quite sure whether to take it with a liberal dose of seriousness or irreverence.

Certain criteria had to be met before Rodney could

even begin the resurrection process, and the Enforcers didn't always know what they were doing when they brought the bodies in. Rodney rejected some of the pre-Servants if they had been too badly mangled, or if rigor had set in too firmly. A potential Servant generally had to be the victim of a sudden death—if a person died from a debilitating disease or old age, the machinery of the body would already be damaged. And Rodney Quick was not about to spend all his waking hours restringing ganglia, growing compatible muscle fiber, popping in a junkyard of synEyes, synLivers, synLungs—no thank you, the company wasn't quite *that* desperate for pre-Servants. Besides, the whole process had to be cost-effective or it wouldn't make good business sense.

Any death from an accident, or poisoning, or even cardiac arrest was fair game, though. The Enforcers brought in even marginally adequate bodies, anyone they found dead, whether after the curfew or during the daytime, whether dead in bed or killed during one of the street riots. Sometimes Rodney wondered what kind of hold Francois Nathans had on the Enforcers Guild to make them cooperate so easily, especially when Nathans publicly despised the Guild for forcing its "protection" on all of them.

The inadequate pre-Servants, along with other discarded bodies, were shipped off to be converted into animal feed for the great Midwestern agricultural wasteland. Oh, sometimes the family whined about not having the body of their loved one for whatever funeral rites they desired, but Nathans and his partner Stromgaard Van Ryman had won a major victory by battling—both legally and morally—to convince the public that the dead were a major resource to be used for all mankind. What a terrible waste, they campaigned, to stick a body uselessly into the ground just so a few family members could cry a lot over it.

Rodney brought the synHeart back to the table and, adjusting the local room temperature to keep him from perspiring, took a deep breath. He lowered his magnifying goggles and arranged his tools, then set to work. He used arterial sealants, capillary grafts, cellular cement to lock the cardiac pump firmly in place. His crouched back sent him stiff pains every half hour or so.

The technician worked alone, in silence, and when he finally eased the tiny battery pellet into the synHeart's chamber and made ready to close the chest wound, he mused to himself, amazed at how easy it had been for him. His spine ached, and his fingers felt stiff, but he felt good, proud at proving his skill again. Let Supervisor try to deny that he was one of the best damned technicians in all of Resurrection, Inc!

Though both of Rodney's parents had been blue-collars, he himself had fought above all that. It could be done, if you had the ambition and the drive. He had spent his teenage years in terror, knowing that he was doomed to follow in his parents' footsteps of manual labor, tedious blue-collar work that required no brains, no skill at all. Then even that bleak future had been stolen from him by the Servant revolution.

But Rodney had had enough years ahead of him to plan a little, to realize how he must adapt to survive in a rapidly changing new world. He had pored over the resources of The Net, isolating himself, focusing his teenage world on the bright pixels that offered him a window into humanity's greatest collection of data. He expended all his effort to climb a few rungs higher on the ladder of success, finally reaching a position where he could feel important—Main Technician on Lower Level Six of Resurrection, Inc.

But now, with Servants rapidly replacing many blue-collar jobs, all the lower rungs in the ladder of success were also disappearing—and Rodney Quick found himself back near the bottom again through no fault of his own.

Rodney's father, who had worked in a factory that manufactured shampoo and other soap products, was killed in one of the early anti-Servant riots on the streets, receiving the full force of an Enforcer's scatter-stun. Rodney's mother, tossed out of her job as a dishwasher at the Sunshine cafeteria, now lived off the blue allotment, a special fund garnered from a tariff on the purchase price of Servants. His mother now wandered the streets with the other aimless and apathetic blues who had no training and no hope for any other type of employment. Competition was vicious for the remaining jobs, and Rodney's mother didn't have the stamina or the enthusiasm to fight for something she had always thought would be hers by default. Nor would she have anything more to do with her son, claiming that the stink of Resurrection clung to him and that it reminded her of her husband's blood.

17

Rodney finished the synHeart operation on the pre-Servant and sealed the dead man's chest, taking care to make certain the skin seams matched. He then rigged up a slow-pump that began the long and delicate process of refilling the blood vessels with synBlood.

Rodney clasped his hands behind his back in a Napoleonic pose and walked away from the pre-Servant on the table, leaving the pumps to do their work. He inspected the entire resurrection room like a commander surveying his troops. Occasionally he had other human sub-technicians to assist him in some of the inspections and operations, but most of the time Rodney remained the only human on the floor, with only a few other Servants to handle the uninteresting tasks.

Seventy different vats rose from floor to ceiling, dispersed in perfect geometrical order around the room. Some of the vats were for the initial bath of scrubber bacteria; others were for the solution of genetically volatile bacteria to perform the finishing touches before reanimation. Intermediate holding chambers of mud-thick silvery paste were sunk into the floor between some of the vats. At any one time Rodney could prepare over a hundred different Servants for resurrection.

While grooming himself for a position at Resurrection, Inc., Rodney had reached out through The Net, uncovering the scattered history of Servants and the corporation. After many abortive attempts to build a serviceable, human-looking android, researchers had given up in despair at the incredible task of manufacturing something as sophisticated as the human body. Even the few almost-successful android attempts would have been prohibitively expensive to mass-produce—and if android labor was going to cost more than even Union workers, why bother at all?

But fifteen years before, Francois Nathans had realized that a nearly inexhaustible supply of almost-androids lay waiting to be used: the perfect machine of the human body, discarded at death but often still completely serviceable after only a few minor repairs. Rather than trying to recreate out of inanimate materials, and then mass-produce, the delicate interconnecting mechanisms of neurons and muscles and bones and tendons and sensory organs, Nathans argued that it made more sense to find a new "engine" to put into these already built—but no longer functional—machines, instead of doing everything from scratch.

The sophisticated microprocessor embedded in a Servant's head linked into the existing contours of the brain, simulating life. Attached to the proper ganglia, the microprocessor acted as a controlling motor, a new engine for the discarded machine. A special "Command" phrase bound all Servants and made them obey, locking their reflexes and forcing them to follow instructions.

As far as Rodney was concerned, Servants weren't real people; the tech couldn't begin to think of them as such. Sure, the bodies moved, and Servants could respond when you talked to them, but no way did a real *person* live inside. Servants retained their language skills, and some basic knowledge—pretty much anything that happened to be residing on the surface of the temporal lobe. Servants varied—some were like blundering zombies who needed explicit instructions for almost everything, but others held a residue of intelligence and could actually respond almost conversationally.

But no Servant had a memory of its past life—all of that had been erased either in death or in the resurrection process . . . or maybe the microprocessor just couldn't reach deep enough to catch hold of those memories. It didn't matter—despite the artistry Rodney Quick put into the creation of his Servants, they were all just pieces of equipment, machinery, appliances. Certainly not people.

Rodney stopped and gawked at the body of a well-proportioned young female floating in one of the final baths, weighted down by heavy spheres tied to her waist, wrists, and legs. The front panel of the vat was transparent, and she hung suspended in the thick golden-colored solution, but Rodney could imagine all her details to perfection. She had already been shaved and trimmed, but Rodney still remembered when she had come in, dead from self-inflicted poison. She'd had thick red hair, beautiful, almost the color of blood. Rodney kept records of all such details.

It seemed that every time he tried to start a relationship with a woman, an honest-to-goodness human being, she always broke it off. According to one of his Net database searches, handlers of the dead had been despised and shunned throughout history, though in later years men claimed to be enlightened about such things. Undertakers and morticians, sextons during the Black

Death, gravediggers, the *eta* in Japan, "resurrectionists" in the nineteenth century illicitly providing dead bodies for medical research. . . . How the hell was he supposed to fight against leftover cultural sentiments?

Rodney sometimes wondered if spending his teenage years sweating over a Net terminal, trying to escape from the other jobless blues and into a *real* job, might have left him socially inept. Not quite able to relate to others in a meaningful way? He dressed stylishly, according to illustrations in all the Net periodicals. He tried to be funny, compassionate, interesting—yet women seemed so volatile, so unpredictable, with so much capacity for *hurting* in them.

But Servant females never said a harsh word. Rodney placed his fingertips against the warm glass of the finishing vat, staring at the naked body of the once redheaded female, watching as she moved slowly in the gradual convection currents of the amniotic fluid. His own breath began to condense fog on the side of the glass.

"What, exactly, are you doing, Mister Quick?" A woman's voice: deep and thick, uninflected but carrying a symphony of overtones that made Rodney's blood congeal.

Supervisor crossed her arms over a deep-purple sleeveless tunic edged with random lines of silver thread. She stood nearly Rodney's height, built somewhat stockier, but seemed immensely tall in her own personal presence. Her long bluish-blond hair had been pulled into three even braids, neatly splayed and pinned to the back of her purple tunic. A primary Net keypad had been tattooed on the palm of her right hand. Supervisor's eyes had a pearly, distant look to them, but hard lines on her brow and around her lips quickly destroyed any dreamy look she might have worn. Though she stared directly at him, Rodney felt as if Supervisor watched him with many more eyes than just the two on her face.

One of the few humans who could act as a walking Interface with The Net, Supervisor lorded over all the lower levels of Resurrection, Inc. Her brain carried a remote gateway processor, implanted so that she could directly connect to The Net. Interfaces were rare and highly valued, so Francois Nathans had arranged to effectively *own* Supervisor, protecting her and doing everything to keep her happy. Consequently, Supervisor encountered no interference when she acted out her managerial fantasies on her human underlings.

She enjoyed harping on Rodney in particular, or so it seemed to him.

"I asked what you are doing, Mister Quick." The flatness of her voice didn't change, but Rodney could hear a thread of surprise that he had not immediately answered her question.

"I am inspecting the vats, madam. To be sure the Servants haven't made mistakes in their tasks."

"Servants do not make mistakes if their instructions are clear," she said.

"You're right, madam. I was making sure my instructions were clear." Rodney clenched his fingers into a fist.

"Why aren't you keeping careful watch on the pre-Servant in Vat 66? Everything is routine?" Supervisor's voice had the barest lilt at the end, only enough for him to guess that she had been posing a question.

"Yes, um, everything's routine, madam. I'm pumping the synBlood in right now, and then he'll go to the secondary vat. You're welcome to inspect my surgery—you can see I took great precautions while installing his new cardiac pump. I'm sure you'll find everything satisfactory."

"Since *you* are involved, Mister Quick, I expect nothing more than 'satisfactory.' You are incapable of better.

"The pre-Servant in Vat 66 now has a new designator, a name. You will henceforth refer to him as 'Danal.' " She paused, and then spoke again; her gaze bored into him. "I will give you a warning, Mr. Quick. Francois Nathans himself has expressed an interest in this particular Servant. After resurrection is complete, Danal is to be presented to Vincent Van Ryman."

"Van Ryman? But . . . isn't he the neo-Satanist priest?"

"That is his business, not yours," Supervisor snapped, raising her voice only a little, but the relative difference was enormous. "Your point of concern is that Mister *Nathans* is extremely interested. Therefore your performance on this resurrection will have a direct bearing on your own future existence. Think on that carefully, Mister Quick, before you become distracted by female anatomy."

Rodney swallowed. "Yes, madam. I, um, understand perfectly. I won't let you down."

"I have no confidence in you whatsoever. You cannot let me down." Supervisor turned curtly and walked across the room to the elevator shaft, seeing yet not seeing with her pearly Net eyes.

Shaken, Rodney retreated from the female's vat and hurried back to the inspection table, where the slow-pump droned as it continued to exchange the inert saline solution with artificial blood. Rodney used his magnifying goggles again to carefully check for any minute leaks around the seal of the chest wound. Satisfied, he removed the goggles and stepped back to look at the pale and motionless body stretched out under the harsh glare of the overhead lights.

He hated this place, but he couldn't think about leaving. Sometimes, though, he had to unleash his rebellion in little ways. Smirking, Rodney patted Danal's cold cheeks in mock paternal affection. He muttered to himself, "Such tender loving care for a corpse!"

He swallowed in a dry throat, looking around to see if Supervisor had seen him. She always moved silently, maliciously, spying. He didn't see her, but that meant nothing—when linked to The Net, she had all the ears and eyes of the entire network.

The other Servants moved about their mindless tasks. The vats bubbled and the slow-pump hummed, but everything else was quiet. Lower Level Six seemed suddenly alien to him, and Rodney felt vulnerable and alone.

3

Jones carefully arranged the pieces of his Enforcer armor on the spongy bedroom floor, and then aligned all his weapons on the bed-unit. He yawned and stretched before beginning the laborious daily process of assembling his uniform.

He slipped the torso guard over his shoulders and mounted the pelvic plate, making sure everything fit properly before fusing the seams. Then came the arm guards and several segments of leg shielding. The armor was made of lightweight flexsteel fibers, dura-plated around the joints, making for a flexible and comfortable suit, but completely protective.

Last, Jones picked up the high-impact fiberglass helmet and stared for a moment at his reflection in the polarized black visor. The visor could withstand even a laser strike full in the face, but it didn't allow so much as a glimmer of feeling to show through. Jones narrowed his dark eyes, trying to make himself look tough but not quite succeeding. His thin moustache had never grown quite full, though he hadn't shaved it in years. Jones was tall, well built but not massive—yet every Enforcer looked the same behind all that armor.

He picked up his weapons in order, slipping them into the appropriate sockets on his armor. Heater-knife, club, grenade, smoke bomb, two projectile weapons, a fully charged scatter-stun, and a pocket bazooka. Bristling with death, every day: instead of filling Jones with power and confidence, it made him feel small and dependent. Not a policeman, according to the official description on The Net, but one of the "conformance assurance personnel," or perhaps even "a modern-day knight against the dragons of social unrest."

His personal Servant Julia stood at the doorway, watching him, waiting for him to speak.

"Good morning, Julia." He consciously gave her a warm smile.

"Good morning, Master Jones," she said, like a re-

23

cording. She still wore the long blond wig he'd bought for her, but then he remembered with some sadness that he had just never told her to take it off. According to the scant information he had been able to get from Resurrection, Inc., Julia had had blond hair during her life; and apparently Julia had been her real first name. But they told him nothing else about her.

She was small and trim, and would have been attractive—though not beautiful—if it had not been for her baldness and the unnatural pallor of her skin. The transparent synBlood did nothing to give a flush to any Servant's skin. Servants didn't need to sleep, though they could sit motionless and pass hours without flinching. Julia's hair would never grow, nor would her fingernails.

Jones strode to the door of his quarters. She didn't move. "Wait for me, please, Julia. You can do whatever you want during the day, and I'll see you when I come back home." He spoke gently, as if it mattered to her.

Julia sat down on a chair facing the doorway. "Yes, Master Jones." Her blond wig had shifted on her head, but she made no attempt to fix it. He knew full well that she'd be there, unmoved, when he returned in the evening.

He was trying so hard, hoping, but he began to confess that nothing would make her seem more human, like a real companion. Jones had bought her the wig and some real clothes in place of the gray Servant jumpsuit, but the clothes made her look pathetic—she wore them like chains, though perfectly willing to oblige. Somehow Jones felt as if he had tried to dress up a dog or a monkey in some ridiculous costume. Julia was not meant for a dress, or for any sort of human trappings, because she was not—he knew he would eventually admit it to himself—she was not human.

Jones rarely went out even to entertain himself, and he made almost no effort at all to join the camaraderie with others in the Enforcers Guild. He just didn't remember how to make friends anymore, and all he had to comfort him were the scars of an earlier friendship.

People felt intimidated by Enforcers, and Jones suspected that the Guild itself fostered that attitude. He doubted if anyone would want to have an Enforcer as a true companion. Even female Enforcers were few compared to the males, and any Guildswoman snapped up a male companion of her choosing.

A month before, everything had finally reached its peak, but Jones had covered it up well. He had become completely exhausted from staring at the walls, the ceiling of his apartment, alone, blinking at the vapid Net entertainment channels. Enough. A few more nights like this, and he would have to squeeze back tears, or else run yelling through the empty after-curfew corridors.

Jones had surrendered most of his merit earnings to purchase a Servant, compulsively, before he could think too much about it. Though only an inexpensive, marginally responsive Servant, Julia had brought him to his knees in debt. For what? He didn't know. Few people like him ever had a Servant; he wasn't so sure he even wanted one. Ever since his transfer to become an escort for Resurrection, Inc., Jones had been required to guard and protect emerging Servants against the angry people on the streets. But he himself had a knee-jerk reaction of dislike and uneasiness toward Servants. Why in the world did he want one for himself? What was the point?

Sure, he had convinced himself he needed someone to sweep the floors, to cook and clean and do other routine things a Servant would be expected to do—but Jones also wanted someone to talk to, a companion, a friend. Okay, so he was lonely—bring out the violins, he thought bitterly. It wasn't his fault, but he just didn't have it in him to lay his friendship on the line, to risk everything. Friends were unpredictable—they died. . . . And it was easier to buy a Servant, a surrogate companion—that's me, he thought, good old path-of-least-resistance Jones.

With unrealistic expectations and barely restrained hope, Jones always treated Julia as an equal human. Though Julia rarely responded with more than mechanical gestures or words, still he talked to her, *asked* her if she would do things. He wanted to be a friend, and have a friend in return. He wanted to console himself by having someone else around. He talked and she listened attentively, apparently interested regardless of the subject matter, and Jones felt relieved just to have his bottled-up words falling on open ears, Servant or otherwise. But he knew deep inside that Julia was not interested, and he doubted if she even understood what he really felt.

Jones had tried to make love to her, once. She had been fully cooperative, even though he found himself reluctant to give her the explicit step-by-step instructions she required. He sensed absolutely nothing spontaneous in their lovemaking, no feeling and no compassion on her part—Julia had been simply doing a task, like any other—and Jones abhorred himself afterward.

Often, when he couldn't sleep, he repeated to himself that he had purchased a Servant, not a friend, barely even a pet—an *appliance*. But still he couldn't abandon hope completely. Jones continued to search for something, a flicker behind her eyes, or something responsive to his words and gestures, something to let him know she was aware of him as a person rather than as "Master."

It was probably an echo of that hope that had damned him, that had forced his punishment and transfer to Resurrection, Inc. He had hesitated a moment too long on the streets when a renegade Servant had come running down the thoroughfare marked for pedestrian traffic only. Jones was in full armor, patrolling the streets, keeping the numerous sidewalk vendors and craftsmen cowed, watching the vagabond singers, the jugglers. Then the female Servant had gone running by, her eyes glazed with fear, her skin looking almost flushed. Her loose gray jumpsuit fluttered with the speed of her flight—Jones had never in his life seen anyone run so fast.

But something traveled through the crowd even faster, an almost telepathic warning that passed from person to person, sensing something amiss with a flash of mob insight. Their tinderbox mentality ignited upon seeing something unusual, alien—a Servant with fear on her face, with life in her eyes, fleeing from shouting men. The rest of the crowd began to converge, blocking her way.

Momentarily Jones felt his body freeze with shock and surprise. The female Servant seemed to have stolen some small pieces of equipment—a Servant had *stolen* something, and Jones's amazement grew even greater. He mechanically pulled out his scatter-stun.

The people saw the Enforcer and seemed to hesitate for a breathless moment. They wanted to see blood. Jones could feel it.

The female Servant knew she was trapped. Jones was appalled and did not look directly at her as he pointed the scatter-stun; he had the setting turned low. The Servant looked at him for a microsecond, pleading with her eyes, as if she could understand something in his flickering hesitation. But she could never have read anything through the black polarized visor that covered most of his face.

Before he could fire, the Servant leaped to the side of the street in three great strides, still clutching her precious equipment. Too late, Jones saw the KEEP OFF THE GRASS patch like many others scattered at random places on the city streets—a square of lush green lawn bounded by a low barbed fence; everyone knew that the patches of greenery were covered with a disintegrator blanket to vaporize anyone who dared to step on the perfect grass.

Jones knew immediately what the Servant intended to do, and fired a burst of his scatter-stun, catching and stunning a few others in the crowd standing too close to him. The Servant leaped gracefully over the barbed fence and plunged without a ripple through the green grass, vanishing instantly. A thin smell of ozone drifted upward, but Jones only stared. The disintegrator and the lush grass had swallowed her up completely. A Servant who perhaps had somehow awakened to her own humanity again . . . but now he would never know.

Then the crowd had turned ugly, deprived of their entertainment for the moment. Other Enforcers eventually arrived, subduing the disturbance; a dozen people had died. Jones felt invisible fingers pointing at him.

But the Enforcers Guild didn't punish its members openly, didn't believe in public disgrace—the Guild protected its own. But there always remained transfer—yes, the Guild protected its own, all right. And he had been pulled from his curfew beat to the much more unpleasant job of guarding Resurrection, Inc.

Now he wondered if it had been worth his mammoth effort to get into the Guild six years before. Jones had to either buy his way in, or be chosen by someone important in the Guild—or he could be sponsored.

Jones had been sponsored by a friend, Fitzgerald Helms. Actually, the word "friend," with its flat single syllable, was completely inadequate to describe the complex and trusting relationship he had had with Fitzgerald Helms. It was the sort of thing that happened no more than once in a lifetime—a friend who made you know what it would be like to have a clone, because only a carbon-copy counterpart could be so much like yourself.

Jones and Fitzgerald Helms had been on the streets together during their teenage years, when they could look at the jungle of the city with exhilaration rather than confused fear. Helms was a mulatto, pale enough that he could disguise himself if he wanted to, but he never wanted to. He let his reddish scouring-pad Afro grow out in wild directions, while Jones himself kept his wiry black hair trimmed tight against his skull. Neither one of them could grow much of a moustache, but both had tried relentlessly since they were fourteen.

Both Jones and Fitzgerald Helms avoided their listless parents, business and technical people so wrapped up in their jobs that they had no ambition to *do* anything. Jones and Helms had not been interested in education or the rat race of the corporate world. They blithely accepted a blue-collar future without qualms, confident that they would find a job working in one of the larger manufacturing plants, or as gardeners, mechanics, whatever—the possibilities seemed endless. But then had come the Servant revolution, and the two young men found themselves in a generation slice that was too old to learn the new tricks necessary to cope with a changed world.

The younger kids—the smart ones, at least—had nearly enough time if they wanted to launch themselves into feverishly learning Net skills, or some profession that required mental ability rather than just movable arms and legs. But Jones and Fitzgerald Helms both found themselves out of that game. They had been athletic and active outside, surviving more than their share of street fights, but neither one of them was good enough to fantasize about a career at athletics or the other violent entertainment modes. After nearly a year, they could no longer avoid facing their only remaining option, a dark option they both hated to consider. Enforcers. The Guild would take care of them. If they could pass the incredible tests required of outsiders before they could be allowed to join the Guild.

He and Helms had primed themselves for weeks ahead of time, training, fighting, running, even studying various weapons capabilities as described on The Net. First Fitzgerald Helms would beat Jones, then Jones would beat Helms. They were perfectly matched, reflections of each other.

But on the day of the brutal, *real* tests in front of the

Guild echelon representatives, Helms had succeeded, and Jones had failed—both of them by a hair.

Fitzgerald Helms immediately designated himself as sponsor for Jones, but neither one of them wanted to contemplate that as a possibility. Jones could only admire the shining armor, the weapons, the confidence his friend gave off even behind his polarized visor.

A year later, Helms was killed at the end of a vicious game of Dodge the Enforcer. Some out-of-work blues driven nearly insane from the boredom, the frustration, the hopelessness, became almost suicidal. They made a game of provoking an Enforcer to the point of outrage, and then tried to escape before the Enforcer let loose and killed them. Helms had been caught up in a surprisingly elaborate plot staged by several starving former restaurant workers; the ringleader, a thin and wild-eyed dishwasher, proved to have a brilliantly logical and manipulative mind—a mind that would surely have gotten him a job working with The Net if he had so much as tried.

He had directed a game that looked so childishly desperate and simple, but Fitzgerald Helms had fallen prey to its complexity and found himself trapped in a cul-de-sac with the laughing wild-eyed dishwasher. The dishwasher had looked on the point of orgasm when he detonated the chunks of explosive taped to his own body, leaving no portion intact to resurrect as a Servant, and not much of Fitzgerald Helms either.

The other accomplices in the game were immediately rounded up, cleanly executed, and shipped off to Resurrection, Inc. Before killing each accomplice, the Enforcers took great pleasure in informing them that, as Servants, they would be used exclusively for Guild labor.

And, according to the rules, Jones took the place of his sponsor in the Guild when Fitzgerald Helms was killed in the line of duty. Jones had not looked forward to the day when he could claim the benefits of sponsorship, but he had known it would happen sooner or later. Rumor had it that Enforcers on the street didn't live long, despite their weapons and armor.

Jones was even offered a reduced-price option on the Servants resulting from the executions, but he had declined. He hadn't even considered purchasing someone like Julia until much later.

And now he was in the Guild, comfortably set for life.

He had to do his best, make a clean effort, in honor of Helms. All he could do was sit and hold the memories, over and over again. Jones knew he could never find another friend like Helms, and he didn't bother to try.

He stood at the doorway of his living quarters and took a last look at Julia, sitting on the chair and watching him with rapt attention. She hadn't moved a muscle.

The dawn light cast deep shadows from the buildings onto the street, throwing everything into an exaggerated black-and-white relief. Beneath his visor Jones could catch the faint damp tang of salt in the air. Pigeons and seagulls had begun to stir, looking for any scraps of garbage they had missed on the streets the previous evening.

Jones stood in front of the mammoth headquarters of Resurrection, Inc. The towering gray structure looked like a tombstone for all humanity—and the unseen underground complex below was several times the size of the administrative offices above. Two sets of revolving doors waited to receive the visitors and workers. A great marble plaque engraved with the words "Servants for Mankind—Freeing Us from Tedium to Pursue Our True Destiny" stared from the front of the building.

People had just begun to venture outside, freed from curfew for another day. The streets were quiet now, but they would start to get ugly later on. They always did. And Jones would have to march back and forth, escorting Servants to their assigned labor, making certain nothing got out of control.

Francois Nathans, the head of Resurrection, apparently professed a great dislike for the Enforcers and their Guild; but he was forced to keep a pool of Enforcers around his corporation due to the very nature of the work he did and how much the public disliked it. Jones tried not to think about it, afraid he might somehow get into trouble, but he found it ironic that the one man in the Metroplex powerful enough to seriously damage the Enforcers Guild had his hands tied, forced to use the services of the Guild more than almost any other private corporation.

Jones stopped for a moment, staring at the huge poured-stone building, the one structure that was almost single-handedly reshaping society. "First the discovery of fire. Then the Industrial Revolution. Then Resurrection, Incorporated." That had been one of their more successful slogans.

"And then what?" Jones thought.

Several people pointedly avoided Jones as he pushed his way through the gleaming revolving door.

4

The body named Danal hung suspended in the final purging bath of amniotic solution. Faint smells of chemicals wafted up from the open vents at the top of the vat. Rodney Quick wished his nostrils would become desensitized once and for all.

A long, colorless scar ran down the center of Danal's chest where Rodney had implanted the synHeart, a scar that would never fade because a Servant could not heal itself. Danal's body had been shaved and his nails trimmed back; he hung in the amber nutrient bath, drifting, held submerged by weighted spheres attached to his arms, legs, and waist. The pre-Servant's eyes were closed beatifically, as if enjoying his last peaceful taste of death.

An involuntary shudder traced itself down Rodney's spine, but he managed to hide it from any invisible spying eyes. Seventy other vats functioned in the large room, creating Servant after Servant. Each day new pre-Servants arrived, and resurrected bodies walked out under their own motor power. Have microprocessor, will travel. The entire system was too efficient to be openly ugly, and perhaps that was why it had fooled him for so long.

The bright harsh light of Lower Level Six seemed colder every day. Death surrounded Rodney, and the stink of resurrection chemicals hung about him like a cloud, a breath from the Grim Reaper, clinging to him even when he walked away from work and tried to slip into a normal life of his own.

The odd feeling of low horror had been growing steadily within him for days now, making it difficult to do his job. Only now, after all the time of working for Resurrection, had he finally come to face his own mortality, the very real possibility of his own death. The knowledge slowly turned his nerves to jelly.

Supervisor breathed down his neck like a vampire, making his job a nightmare. She seemed to have singled Rodney out for career destruction, just at a whim. Rodney knew of other humans who had worked for her, filling various jobs—including the one he himself now held—and those others had disappeared, with no explanations and no excuses offered by management. As a living Interface with The Net, Supervisor knew full well how valuable she was to Resurrection, Inc. She seemed sickeningly confident that no one would call attention to anything she might do. Rodney felt trapped in a cat-and-mouse game, unable to do more than panic. He continued to do his job, hoping that it wouldn't be today, not today. But he didn't know how much longer he could grovel and use excuses to fend off Supervisor's increasingly more elaborate accusations.

The worst part had been recognizing some of the new pre-Servants that came in just after the unofficial disappearances, Supervisor's previous victims. The records claimed that these cadavers were other people entirely, and The Net denied any correlation with the missing humans. But Rodney never forgot a face. Not even a waxen grimace of a death could make him doubt the identities of the bodies going into the resurrection vats.

And being turned into a Servant must be worse than dying in the first place.

What alternative did he have? When people died clean deaths, they ended up as Servants; Rodney, of all people, knew the criteria for acceptance. Was he supposed to hope for a long, debilitating disease to ruin his body . . . or a messy enough death that no technician would bother to reassemble the pieces?

The more he thought about it, the more Rodney felt a gnawing helplessness—he could do nothing to save himself if Supervisor finally chose to destroy him, and he could do nothing to protect his own body afterward. What option did anybody have?

Yes, he did know of an option, but he barely dared to whisper it in his own thoughts. *Cremators.* Even the idea frightened him, but he knew it had to be true. He *believed* in the Cremators. The need was too great for it to be just another rumor.

More than ever before, people had become preoccupied with, and terrified of, death—caused in great part by the brooding and listless presence of Servants. But Rodney had heard of a mysterious group of militants—the Cremators—who, if you formed a contract with them, would do everything in their power to destroy your body after death, guaranteeing that you could never become a Servant. Ashes to ashes, dust to dust, with all the ritual. Real information about the outlaw Cremators was hard to come by, though, and The Net swallowed up any actual reports of their activities.

Francois Nathans himself had frequently publicized enormous rewards for any information about the Cremators. Nathans seemed to be nervous, perhaps even frightened by them—and if it was all just a fabricated rumor, why would such a powerful man care? The Enforcers Guild turned every suitable dead body over to Resurrection, Inc.; Rodney didn't know for sure if the law required it, or if the corporation paid well for them, or if Nathans just twisted the thumbscrews on the hierarchy of the Guild. But if the Cremators were snatching suitable pre-Servants out from under Nathans' nose, then the man would be hard pressed to ignore the challenge.

Rodney didn't know if he dared attempt to contact the Cremators, but it would have to be soon. Would they even meet with him, knowing that he worked for Resurrection, Inc? He became jittery again. Rodney didn't have the slightest idea how to begin his search. What if someone found out?

"I like to see a man contemplating, thinking."

The man's voice seemed to echo off the walls, and Rodney whirled, looking for its source. For a terrified moment he was disoriented and did not notice the three others standing in the maze of vats and tables.

"That's one of the reasons why I worked so hard to create Servants," the man continued. "To free more of man's time for philosophizing."

Then Rodney saw Supervisor's purple sleeveless tunic and her cold, half-focused stare, but he realized with some relief that she seemed cowed by the two men standing beside her. The taller of the two men was much older, thin, but with a fire of knowledge behind his eyes that made even Supervisor's gaze seem harmless. The older man was immaculately dressed, and his steel-blue hair had not a strand out of place. The other man seemed much younger but he carried himself with an uncharacteristic weariness and uneasiness. The younger man had gleaming dark hair and a shadowy complexion that spoke of possible Asian or Indian ancestry deep in his genes. He stood a few inches shorter than the older man, but his shoulders were broad and he radiated an animalistic strength.

The older man arched his eyebrows as he looked at Rodney, and he spoke again without taking his gaze from the technician. "Don't be rude, Supervisor. Please introduce us."

"Yes, sir," she said, looking surprised. "Mister Nathans, this is Rodney Quick. Rodney, this is Francois Nathans, and the gentleman with him is Vincent Van Ryman."

Neither man reached forward to shake his hand, and Rodney had all he could do to keep his own composure. He had never before seen either of the two men: the head of Resurrection, Inc. and the supposed High Priest of the neo-Satanists. What did they want with him? What had Supervisor accused him of now?

Rodney became suspicious again. He didn't know what Nathans or Van Ryman looked like. He felt his heart beating harder, hammering the blood through his veins with such force that it squeezed cold sweat out of his pores. This could be a trap. This could be some twisted trick for Supervisor to make him drop his guard in awe at the distinguished visitors . . . and then she would do something to make him cause his own downfall.

But what if these two were the real Nathans and Van Ryman? Then Rodney would probably act like an idiot and cause his own downfall with no help from Supervisor whatsoever. He had no way of telling. Rodney knew little more than a scattered collection of half-truths and legends about famous people. He did have a sixth-level Net password, but that didn't allow him access to the most confidential databases.

Rodney knew, though, that Francois Nathans had founded Resurrection, Inc., as a junior partner to Stromgaard Van Ryman—Vincent Van Ryman's father—who provided most of the financial backing for the new corporation. Stromgaard Van Ryman had apparently shown an adequate business sense, but Nathans was far superior in vision, charisma, and political savvy. Eight years after the formation of Resurrection, Inc., when Servants had begun to make major inroads on the work force, Nathans had assumed his role as head of the corporation, and Stromgaard Van Ryman had sold his portion of control. About the same time, Stromgaard was apparently involved with the inception of the neo-Satanist movement, but two years after the new religion had taken root, Stromgaard mysteriously disappeared. Rumor said he was sacrificed by his own cult. His 21-year-old son Vincent had emerged as the High Priest of the neo-Satanists shortly thereafter.

That had all happened several years before. And now Rodney knew the Servant from Vat 66—Danal, he corrected himself—was somehow special. Vincent Van Ryman supposedly had something important in mind for him. But why was Nathans interested, too? Just out of camaraderie with the son of a friend? Or just to make certain his important customer went away satisfied? Or did Nathans have something to do with the neo-Satanists, too?

"Mister Nathans and Mister Van Ryman would like to see Danal now. They want to make sure everything is satisfactory." Supervisor's flat voice held many subtle overtones, and Rodney heard each one of them like an icicle on his eardrums. Van Ryman still had not spoken.

"I saw you inspecting our Danal as we came in," Nathans said. His voice was rich and friendly but somewhat distant, as if he spoke through a mask over his own personality. "It's good to find such diligence, especially in one of our own workers."

Rodney finally found his own voice, using instinct to switch into a self-defense mode, smoothing the stutter from his words before he spoke them. "Yes, sir. Supervisor hinted at how important this Servant is to you, and I've been watching him very carefully. I'm sure you can see that everything is perfect. The surgical work installing his synHeart is the best I've ever done."

Nathans smiled. "I'm very pleased to hear that, Mr. Quick. May I call you Rodney?"

He nodded quickly, feeling terribly conscious of his hair, wondering if it was out of place, if his gold nose stud was tarnished, if the beads of sweat were showing on his forehead.

Van Ryman went close to the tank, fascinated by Danal's body submerged in the golden solution; he seemed unable to tear his eyes from it. The dark-haired man pressed his face up against the glass to see more clearly.

"Supervisor, leave us," Nathans said abruptly.

Supervisor looked surprised and rebuffed at the dismissal, but she turned without a word and left. The simmering noises of the vats swallowed up the rustle of her clothes. Rodney could barely contain his satisfaction as he watched Nathans's offhanded manner with her. Rodney felt important, raised back up to the level of a human being again. He had to consciously restrain himself from strutting like a bird.

Nathans reached out and placed a paternal hand on Rodney's shoulder. The tech stiffened a moment, but allowed himself to be turned aside as the older man began to walk slowly along the row of resurrection vats. Rodney followed closely, and Francois Nathans began to speak to him in a hypnotic voice, making him feel warm and confident in himself, saying all the right things, pulling all the right strings.

"Rodney, we've been watching your work for a long time. You have a special touch with the Servants, and you know the resurrection process inside and out. It's unfortunate that Supervisor's been slipping your name to us frequently, placing the blame for certain minor things on your shoulders, but *we* haven't seen any decline in the quality of your work. I'm tempted to think that she's just playing another one of her games, pin the tail on the scapegoat. She does that, you know. Remember, she's not quite normal, not like you and me—she gave up a lot to become an Interface with The Net. The company needs her services, but sometimes she overestimates her own importance. I don't think you have anything to worry about." Nathans smiled broadly.

"She sure knows how to make work miserable for me," Rodney said quietly. Internal ropes hindered him from opening up to the man's friendliness. He still wondered why the two men had come to him, what they had in mind. As Rodney and Nathans passed a row of recently emptied vats, the tech noticed that Van Ryman had remained behind to stare through the glass walls at Danal in the resurrection solution.

Nathans interrupted his thoughts. "You might wonder why I'd take the time to come talk to a mere technician." He paused. Rodney didn't dare acknowledge the suggestion with a nod.

"Well, because I firmly believe that the future of any corporation begins at the roots. The future managers are today's technicians, if you don't mind my being frank, and I always like to keep a pool of candidates under consideration for possible promotions."

Rodney's heart fluttered; none of this seemed possible. Then, out of the corner of his eye, he saw Vincent Van

37

Ryman do something to the vent at the top of Danal's tank. He turned quickly and suddenly felt Nathans's grip tighten on his shoulder. Summoning up his courage, Rodney turned back to face the head of Resurrection, Inc.

"Thank you for your confidence in me, Mr. Nathans." Rodney forced a calm expression onto his face. "I'll try not to let you down."

Nathans smiled at him again, this time with dazzling sincerity. Vincent Van Ryman came up to join them, and Rodney was alarmed to see a heavy expression of near tears on Van Ryman's face.

"I think everything's satisfactory, Mr. Quick," Van Ryman announced; his voice was rich and mellow, but with a curious strained edge to it. "You certainly know your work."

Rodney averted his eyes, trying to look embarrassed at the compliment. "It was just a routine resurrection. I'm sure you'll be happy with your Servant."

Things seemed less certain now. At least Supervisor was straightforward in her psychological warfare. Was Nathans truly the compassionate boss he seemed to be?

Rodney *had* seen Van Ryman meddling with Danal's tank, he was certain of it, though he couldn't imagine what possible sabotage the dark-haired man could have performed. If Van Ryman was indeed the High Priest of the neo-Satanists, perhaps he had some other ritualistic purpose in mind. And in that case, though it might give him the jitters, Rodney didn't particularly care. Mumbo-jumbo and superstition were weapons against the uneducated blue-collars.

But if Van Ryman *had* done something, should Rodney mention it to Nathans? Or might that be worse than not saying anything, if Nathans ended up being part of it? After all, Nathans had carefully led him away from the tank, distracted him, so Van Ryman could have time alone.

Or maybe Nathans had been deviously sincere about looking for new management recruits, and this was some sort of test to see how dedicated Rodney was to the successful completion of his job. If so, if he suspected sabotage from anyone—even a person as powerful as Vincent Van Ryman himself—then he should report it to Nathans. But he should also be willing to trust his ultimate boss, Francois Nathans, in all things. And if Nathans was obviously involved with this staged tampering perhaps Rodney was supposed to see the attempt, but to trust Nathans to intervene if anything absolutely needed to be stopped. Should he say anything or not?

Rodney's head was still spinning when Nathans patted him on the back, and Van Ryman shook his hand, thanking him for the preview of his new Servant. The technician convinced himself to make a parting comment. "Thank you both for coming. I very much enjoyed meeting both of you. I hope I haven't disappointed you."

"Of course you haven't, Rodney. I'm sure we'll be talking again." Nathans nodded and then motioned for Van Ryman to enter the lift compartment first. The doors whisked shut and swallowed up the two men.

The instant the lift doors had closed, Rodney rushed back to the vat that held the Servant named Danal. Carefully he inspected the vent openings, but could not tell if they had been moved. He sniffed the air, trying to detect any unusual smell, but found none. A smudge on the transparent wall showed where Van Ryman had touched the glass, but that proved nothing. He squinted into the yellow amniotic fluid, trying to detect any changes. Was it murkier now than before? Did he see any difference?

Supervisor wouldn't hesitate for a moment if Rodney did anything to jeopardize the successful resurrection of this particular Servant. The scrubber bacteria in the final bath, the solution in which Danal now hung suspended, were genetically volatile, easily mutated, and more than once a mutated solution had adversely affected the physical or mental condition of a reanimated Servant. Sometimes the motor control seemed skewed; sometimes the mental faculties were dulled or sharpened—and an unusually intelligent Servant caused more concern than a totally stupid one. What if the original memories of the individual somehow came too close to the surface? But without the final solution to do one more scouring and to replace the electrolytes in the brain, the microprocessor would not function properly.

Rodney could think of no way to verify any tampering, short of taking a sample of the amniotic solution to the analytical lab. But then he'd have to explain his suspicions, and that might cause him as much trouble as he was trying to avoid.

The more he thought about it, the more he convinced

himself that Nathans had devised a test for him. Or perhaps it was Supervisor's doing after all. But even the major fact of knowing this was a test didn't help him at all. Nor did he know what the penalty for failure would be.

5

"Command: Open your eyes."

The Command phrase sent the microprocessor into its override mode. Synapses fired, reforging old links through ganglia. The microprocessor tagged and identified the proper muscles, then caused them to contract.

Danal's eyes fluttered open.

Light bombarded his retinas, and the microprocessor immediately directed the irises to constrict, stepping down the glare. Danal blinked a second time.

Sensations began to fill his mind like wildfire; each cell in his body awoke with a scream of exhilaration. Danal sensed that his body was slick and smooth, hairless. He could feel every nerve ending like spiders on his skin; he could almost feel the light from the harsh overhead panels striking him.

A man filled his field of view, and Danal drank in every detail without looking elsewhere. The technician stood slightly shorter than Danal, and his face seemed wildly asymmetric with brown hair hanging long on one side of his face, cropped short on the other—one eyebrow shaved, the other enhanced by eyeliner—a single gold nostril stud reflecting the light. Danal stared without moving, and the descriptor words and concepts congealed in his brain, reassigning mental labels to the images his retinas conveyed: "brown," "gold," "eyebrow."

The microprocessor frantically scanned Danal's temporal lobe, accessing any information that had survived the journey through death and back, scribbling on the newborn tabula rasa. Danal noticed black symbols across the pocket of the tech's white lab smock, but for a moment they meant nothing to him. Then suddenly, like a light bulb flicking on inside his head, the symbols snapped into focus and became words, RODNEY QUICK.

"Can-you-understand-me?" Rodney said in careful syllables.

Danal heard the question, digested it, and searched for the appropriate response. Slowly, still uncertain of his

41

specific muscle control, he moved his head down and then up, hesitantly at first, and then nodding deeply and confidently.

"I want you to answer me with your voice," Rodney said quickly. "Command: Answer."

Danal dredged up the word from deep under his subconscious, peeling back the wrapper of information stored there. Other words, phrases, idioms poured forth, filling the empty pockets of his resurrected brain. He exhaled, setting his vocal cords vibrating with specific and careful control. He moved his jaw, his tongue, his lips, shaping and forming the sounds in the immensely complicated task of speaking:

"Yes."

The nutrient solution still trickled out of the tank from which Danal had emerged, running through grates in the floor to holding vats even farther beneath the ground. Danal stood like a statue. Solution dripped down his slick skin. He noticed that the yellow droplets had a decidedly pinkish tinge, and something buried at the back of his mind told him that the different coloration was a sure sign of mutating bacteria in the final bath. . . .

Rodney quickly hosed the remaining liquid into the grate, washing away any incriminating pink tint, although the anomalous color was already fading as the mutated bacteria died upon exposure to the harsh outside world. For good measure, Rodney turned the high-pressure hose and blasted the motionless Servant, rinsing the last of the solution from the Servant's skin.

Some of the exterior nerves on Danal's body shut themselves down as the icy water drenched him. His fragile muscle control, still not completely activated, went haywire. Danal fell backward, collapsing to the floor. Too late, his arm reached out to break his fall, but he twisted awkwardly and struck his head on the side of his emptied vat. Half an instant later, he identified the sensation of pain.

Danal lay crumpled and helpless—but completely awake—on the cold, wet floor as the tech stood over him. Danal stared at a droplet of water barely half an inch in front of his unblinking eye, fascinated by the play of light on its surface.

"Oh, brother!" Rodney snorted, "Command: Stand up."

The microprocessor reached out again for the right

nerve ganglia, activating Danal's Servant programming. His muscles awakened, and he climbed stiffly to his knees, barely keeping his balance and barely able to stop the landslide of sensory input pouring into his undead eyes. He coughed the nutrient solution out of his lungs, then regained control of himself. An impulse made him want to smile blithely, but somehow the subtle facial muscles remained frozen, leaving Danal filled with awe yet expressionless.

Without turning his head from the tech, he used peripheral vision to focus on the room around him, the vast resurrection chamber with its rows upon rows of different vats and chambers, inspection tables, other Servants going about their tasks. Danal found it fascinating.

Rodney narrowed his eyes and looked furtively over his shoulder, then turned back to the newly resurrected Servant. "Command: Dance!"

Jerkily, without thought, Danal tried to lift one leg, then the other. He somehow managed to hop back and forth, looking ridiculous. He stumbled again, but regained his balance. His muscle control spread rapidly, and with the speed of the microprocessor Danal seemed to have a longer time to compensate and shift his balance. The Servant achieved a subtle mastery of his body, like a precocious child rapidly putting together all the pieces of a jigsaw puzzle.

Rodney gave a little superior-sounding laugh.

"What are you doing *now*, Mister Quick?"

Danal watched as Supervisor came up silently from behind. She moved as if partially in a trance, floating between the vats, but with a presence about her that made her seem to emanate from the walls, the floor, the lights, everywhere The Net could see.

Rodney jumped, and Danal could see the color drain from his face. But the tech composed his face into a serious expression without missing a beat and turned to face Supervisor. "I'm testing his muscle reflexes, madam. He seems to be coordinating well."

"Bullshit." Her voice carried no excitement, no anger, just a flat statement that exposed the technician as a liar, allowing no room for question. "Mister Nathans said to give Danal special treatment. If you fail, I am going to destroy you."

The tech spoke defensively. "This Servant is my very best work, madam! Look where I installed the synHeart

43

unit: only half the scar you'd expect. You saw the wound where the neo-Satanists hacked out his heart!"

"Just do your job, and do it adequately, Mister Quick." Supervisor smiled at him, "Try to survive as long as you can."

Rodney made no comment, but Danal noticed faint beads of sweat begin to pop out of the tech's visible pores.

At the mention of the scar, Danal stared at his body, looking at the white line at the center of his chest where the—knife—had cut. His past seemed to be swathed thickly in cheesecloth, hidden from his view, and he wondered—but any answers rising in his memory melted like snowflakes in a fire. He wanted to reach out and finger the scar, but his muscles could not find the volition to do so.

Supervisor stood in silence for a long moment, apparently to let Rodney fidget and sweat for as long as possible. "Well, Mister Quick? Is he ready?"

"Yes, most certainly. As always, promptly on the deadline. A routine resurrection, madam."

"We'll see, won't we?" Supervisor held out her right hand, running her fingers along the primary Net keyboard tattooed on the palm. Ten keys, each with five functions coded to the five specific fingerprints on Supervisor's left hand, made it possible for her to type fifty different characters. She input the proper sequence that linked her to the vast resources of The Net. After she had reoriented herself to her new position as a small blip in the enormous computer database, Supervisor activated the Net-compatible scanners implanted in her eye. Danal endured her inspection as she looked at him through machine eyes.

"Glycerin levels all wrong. And I see a glitch in his brain-wave pattern. Dammit! The bacteria mutated—you weren't watching him, Mister Quick." She seemed unaccustomed to using an angry tone of voice, and the words came out awkward, but still threatening.

"Yes! Yes, I was, madam! The nutrient bath was as clear as can be—yellow like chicken soup!" One, and only one, drop of sweat ran down the side of Rodney's forehead.

"I somehow doubt you saw nothing unusual. Even you aren't quite that stupid. You've been licking the glass on the female tanks again, haven't you?"

"No, madam!" He sounded indignant. "You know how attentive I've been, especially with this Servant."

Supervisor abruptly ignored Rodney and turned to the placid-looking Servant who stood damp and naked under the harsh lights. "Danal, what do you remember from your past life?"

Danal wrinkled his forehead a little, but stood silent.

"He's brain-damaged! Aww, shit!" Rodney gasped to himself. Nonchalantly, but with amazing speed, Supervisor boxed him in the ear to silence him.

"Nothing," Danal finally answered. "I don't remember anything."

Supervisor paused, looking somewhat surprised. Rodney breathed a loud sigh of relief and put his hands on his hips, trying to regain a semblance of control. "Why did you take so long to answer?"

"I was thinking." The words flowed easily through his vocal cords now. After an oblivion of rest, he wanted to stretch his voice, to shout, to sing. But his body didn't move. He stood and waited, like a mannequin.

Supervisor and the tech looked at him strangely for a moment.

"Servant, Command: Input Mode." Supervisor's fingers raced across the tattooed keyboard on her palm.

Danal's body responded of its own volition, controlled by the microprocessor. His arms and legs snapped to attention, and he opened his mind to receive.

In less than a second The Net scanned Danal's new identity and confirmed his name and the name of his Master, Vincent Van Ryman. After a short pause, short even for the microprocessor's view of time, bytes of information filed onto his memory, and his parched mind rapidly absorbed the data.

The Net gave him nuggets of his Master Van Ryman's history and habits, presumably so Danal could be a better Servant for him. All at once, and without time to sort through the facts and arrange them in any order, Danal learned that Vincent Van Ryman lived a comfortable life from the profits of when his father Stromgaard had sold his share of Resurrection, Inc. to Francois Nathans. Protected by elaborate Intruder Defense Systems, Van Ryman lived alone in an eccentrically antique home.

Julia? Danal wondered. The thought had come to him from the far reaches of his mind, whispering at the corners of his ears like memories shouting at him through miles of dense fog. The thought came with no explanation, no further details—who was Julia? Other memories, a seething pot of déjà vu boiled far beneath the surface of his brain, out of the microprocessor's reach.

Another pause in the microprocessor's slowed-down time—Danal felt The Net picking around in his mind, double-checking, making sure of his identity. Danal kept his thoughts vividly aware, though he didn't know what to expect, or how he would know if something went wrong. His core-programming penetrated deeper than instinct, molding his life, making him know that he was not to ask questions, not to think, not to feel.

He suspected that he already knew as much as a Servant should know about his Master, but The Net divulged yet another file, this one coded for a much higher-level password.

Vincent Van Ryman was the leader of the neo-Satanists,

not anymore!

a secret society that had adapted ancient Satanism to the context of modern technology. Van Ryman had, however, denounced his connections with the group, and had become one of its strongest opponents—but recently he had returned to the fold again, with a zeal and vehemence that overshadowed even his initial fervor.

impossible!

Danal's head swam with a whirlwind of conflicting thoughts, ghosts of memory fleeing like shadows whenever he tried to focus on them. He was a Servant. His mind was a clean slate, polished smooth by passage through death and back. He had nothing of his past.

Or, more likely, he was not able to access the memories . . . but he knew they existed, closeted away somewhere. And these spurious glitches of thought jumping out helter-skelter onto his forebrain—did they flash back to a life that never existed? Who knew what dreams and fantasies a brain could summon and create during the deepest sleep of all?

By the time Danal had assimilated all this, Supervisor's finger still hadn't had enough time to lift itself from the keypad on her palm. "Completed," she said to no one in particular. "Servant: What is your name?"

"My name is Danal."

"Who is your Master?"

"Vincent Van Ryman."

"See, I told you he wasn't brain-damaged," Rodney interrupted. "I watched him like he was my own baby."

Supervisor ignored him completely. "What is the square root of 49?"

"Seven."

"Spell the word 'Rhinoceros.' "

"R-H-I-N-O-C-E-R-O-S."

Supervisor tested him with the standard questions, assessing the baggage of knowledge he had managed to carry over from his first life.

"He tests out quite high," she commented after she had finished. Rodney grinned broadly, as if barely able to control himself from giggling now that the terror and uncertainty had passed.

Danal said nothing. He waited, wishing he had some tool to dig deeper into his memories and bring them into the light—or cauterize them and seal the images below his consciousness forever.

6

Danal stared out the narrow window of the Enforcer's hovercar as the Metroplex rushed by below. He sat back in the detention/cargo compartment, saying nothing. The Enforcer escort seemed to ignore him.

The elevator had taken Danal up from the lower levels of Resurrection, Inc., leading him to the lobby. Most of the reception area had been decorated with deeply grained clonewood, giving it the rich, somber appearance of an old-time funeral parlor. Danal had stepped out of the lift and, without moving, stared at the carpet, the ornaments, the light-fountain, the receptionist. Only a moment later, one of the Enforcers came and took him to a waiting hovercar, commanding him to wait in back.

They rose over the crowded streets. The monotonous buzzing of the pedestrians seemed to interfere with itself and left an eerie type of silence in the air. Barely heard, smog scrubbers mounted on the sides of taller buildings added their background drone, filtering the air to recover valuable chemical particulates. Apartments and business complexes stretched into the sky, and endless blind eyes of windows gaped at the world.

As they flew, the Metroplex seemed to stretch out, clean and repetitive, like a vast computer chip from the air: street after street, section after section, all arranged in geometric order. The larger industrial centers could be seen in the distance, but all around them lay the spreading shopping zones intermixed with residential areas.

As the hovercar approached its destination, Danal spotted the vast Victorian mansion looming in front of them, an anomaly among the crowded condominium complexes. The gabled house seemed to command the entire area, standing alone at the end of the block, surrounded by a small lawn of carefully groomed green vinyl sod.

Van Ryman's bizarre home bristled with odd angles, sharp gables, and black and peeling shutters. One of the

48

gutters hung carefully askew, as if it had been mounted purposely off balance to provide a calculated effect, dramatically decrepit. A weathervane driven by a random motor sent the silhouette of a capering demon in drunken pirouettes. Leering gargoyles squatted on the gables, somewhat brighter and more polished than the rest of the structure, as if they were new.

> *But the gargoyles were removed.*
> *Stricken from the home in disgust.*
> *Why are they back?*

Danal stumbled slightly from the throbbing flashback as he tried to keep a placid expression on his face, a Servant's expression. He grasped at the fleeing thought that had soared outward from his mind's core, slipping through his mental fingers. Ripples in his memory died away, leaving a blank hole and no more of an answer.

Another bubble had popped deep in his subconscious— the spark of a buried memory from beyond the wall of death, like an outstretched hand from the grave. The first such explosion of unbridled memory still burned bright in his mind from when he had stood, still dripping, newly awakened from the resurrection vat. A name, a concern— *Julia*—but no face, no other details arose to fill in the gaps. . . .

So many sights, sounds, smells, experiences had poured into his starved sensory organs, and everything fell neatly into the empty pockets of his memory, stocking the shelves, filling in the gaps. Danal felt ready to burst after a scant few minutes, and he rapidly learned how to filter what he experienced, to weed out some of the extraneous detail no matter how much it saddened him to have to ignore any part of his new life.

He wondered if all Servants felt this way.

The Enforcer unsealed the detention/cargo compartment, allowing Danal to step methodically out of the hovercar. The Servant stood next to the Enforcer in front of Vincent Van Ryman's mansion, waiting. The Enforcer seemed uneasy, jittery. Danal felt himself churning with doubts, curiosity, perhaps even rebellion. Part of him *knew* what Servants were like and what they were supposed to be like. But something was wrong. And that frightened him.

The Enforcer finally stepped on the walkway to the

porch, in front of a faintly shimmering wall of air: the deadly force field of Van Ryman's Intruder Defense Systems.

"Vincent Van Ryman!" the Enforcer called, afraid to go any nearer to the house. "I have escorted your Servant Danal." The Enforcer fidgeted. Danal stood perfectly still, expressionless.

The spangles in the air faded, and Danal sensed that the field had been switched off. But the Enforcer did not seem eager to proceed. He cleared his throat. "You go first, Servant. Command: Walk."

The Enforcer motioned him ahead, and Danal strode calmly down the walkway to the porch. The sidewalk was poured from black textured concrete and clean, without weeds. Danal kept walking, his legs mechanically moving him forward as the Servant programming forced him to follow the Enforcer's Command. Uneasiness grew in him, but he didn't try to smother any new visions rising to the surface, where the microprocessor could grasp them and hold them up for inspection.

Déjà vu. The phrase suddenly clicked into his head, and somehow it felt right.

He mounted the creaking steps of the porch, where the rail appeared splintered and weathered, but when he focused his attention on it for an instant, he realized that it had been painted and textured to appear so. Everything here had the tinge of familiarity to it, and the part of him that wasn't frightened wanted to see what lay hidden inside Vincent Van Ryman's home.

Apparently relieved at seeing his charge delivered safely, the Enforcer saluted the unseen monitors in Van Ryman's house, then turned and walked quickly back to the hovercar. Danal watched him for an instant, puzzled, and then faced the door.

"Your Servant Danal reporting for duty, Master Van Ryman." He remained on the porch, drinking in the details of the wood, seeing an artificial hornets' nest carefully mounted under one of the eaves. He stared at the ornate door knob, at the hideous brass gorgon's head that gripped a door knocker in its fangs.

A voice struck at him from a speaker hidden in the gorgon's jagged mouth. "Open the door and come in, Danal."

The interior hall was dimly lit by a hanging chandelier that left the corners in a deep murk. Plush purple carpeting cushioned Danal's feet as he took another step forward, and stopped. His Master Van Ryman stood in shadows at the end of the hall.

"Welcome, Danal." His attitude seemed to show an irregular mix of excitement and terror, masked by an effort to seem calm.

Danal voluntarily used the microprocessor to think and examine with greater speed, filing the details in his growing mental database. Van Ryman was almost exactly the same size and build as Danal, but he had dark, lanky hair grown long and square about his shoulders; his face was wide and somewhat rough, but receptive. A rich green robe loosely covered his tight-fitting black clothing. Van Ryman's forehead was damp and glistening clean, reddened as if he had just scrubbed it vigorously.

They stood frozen, staring at each other, and Danal felt oddly like an animal squared off at a territorial boundary. Van Ryman's face sparked a strange reaction in the Servant. He seemed familiar, oddly so. Danal wanted to ask a question, but he felt queasy inside, uneasy, even though his synHeart carefully regulated his pulse. Without the subtle control of his facial muscles to show and release his anxiety, the turmoil reflected back into his mind.

To break the frozen moment Danal reflexively turned away to close the heavy clonewood door.

Vincent Van Ryman chuckled to himself and took two steps closer; Danal could hear his quiet sigh of relief like thunder in the muffled silence of the house. Under the better lighting of the chandelier Danal saw his Master's eyes, and realized that *they* had struck a lance of disorientation in him, *the eyes*—somehow wrong. Something didn't fit, but Danal turned his mind inward and beat down the feelings, uneasily desperate to keep his identity as a Servant.

"Once again, let me welcome you into my home, Danal." Van Ryman's gaze was marginally fearful, flicking over Danal's face, penetrating, as if waiting for some reaction. The Servant fought to keep from staring at his Master, at the man's familiar features, at his unfamiliar *eyes*.

Van Ryman surprised him by stepping forward to grasp his gray Servant's jumpsuit, pulling it open at the chest. With a discernible shudder of excitement or revulsion, Van Ryman touched the lumpy pale scar of Danal's death wound on his pallid skin. The man smiled to himself, nodding. Incapable of resisting, the Servant stood motionless for the inspection.

In the close light Danal could see nearly invisible red pinpricks clustered behind Van Ryman's ears and dotted unevenly along his jawbone. They would have been indistinguishable in less dramatic lighting, with less intensive observation. Danal noticed similar pinpricks on the tips of his Master's fingers.

Van Ryman pursed his lips and placed hands on his hips as he stood quietly, staring at the Servant with a faraway look in his eyes. Then, nonplussed, he straightened Danal's gray jumpsuit again as if nothing had happened and rubbed the palms of his hands rapidly together with a scouring sound.

"Please, won't you come into my study? Command: Follow." He spoke cordially but firmly, with enormous self-confidence. Van Ryman started down the hall, then turned to keep his eyes on Danal, as if uncomfortable at having his back to the Servant. They passed a small control room for the Intruder Defense Systems and a bathroom. Danal followed, wide-eyed again, gulping in the details of the house as he walked.

He felt a sense of skewed antiquity in the dark elegance: many things old and valuable, but with no common focus or period, as if a collector had gathered them simply because they were old, not caring whether they belonged together in the same decor.

Had it always seemed like twilight in this house before?

Danal mentally slapped himself to drive away the buzzing voice in his mind. The flashbacks emerged like the memories of a stranger, someone he had never known, someone vastly different from Danal himself. But he fought against an even greater fear of asking questions.

Van Ryman padded around a corner, and they emerged into the firelit study. Van Ryman turned again, looking at him with a hopeful and desperate expression.

"I'd like to have a long talk with you, Danal. I need some answers."

7

The thrumming background noises in Rodney Quick's apartment barely penetrated his concentration. He didn't hear the heat exchanger working against the damp night air, or the tickings from the pipes, the clock, the appliances. The soundproof walls kept the city noises out and trapped the silence in.

Rodney stared at the dead surface of his Net terminal. Behind the thin glass, behind the phosphors ready to merge and regroup to spell out messages from the terminal, lay the gateway to The Net, the maw of the greatest source of information in the world.

Everything was on The Net—if you knew where to look.

Rodney cracked his knuckles and tentatively reached toward the terminal keyboard, but he abruptly got up instead and went about the apartment, switching off the lights one by one until he had blanketed the entire living area in protective, comforting shadow. In the dimness he made his way back to the terminal, moving carefully around the sometimes cushioned, sometimes hard corners of furniture. It was his own apartment, but often he felt like it turned into a stranger when all the lights were out.

It was irrational to think that anyone would see him now. But what he was about to do seemed better done in secret, in the darkness.

The terminal remained powered on always, and now the faint glow of amber phosphors seeped through the murky black background, waiting for the touch of the cathode rays. In the upper left-hand corner of the screen the rectangular cursor throbbed slowly, hypnotically. Rodney reached forward again and found the keys. His fingertips instinctively went to their familiar positions. In the darkness Rodney could barely see the ghosts of the main Net menu burned into the screen from many previous logons.

Upon returning home, he had procrastinated for a long

time. He flicked glances over his shoulder at the terminal. Wanting to logon, to begin the search, to get it over with.

But first Rodney moved toward the shower chamber as he pulled off his clothes, dropping them on the floor wherever they fell. He wanted to stand under the hot needles of water blasting away the cold sweat and the musty stink of fear, purging the day from his system.

And after the shower Rodney walked back into the main living area, naked. He looked at the terminal again and impulsively decided to wear one of his old robes made from Sri Lankan vat-grown silk fibers. He had not worn the robe in so long, he wasn't sure he could find it at first. Rodney wasted time looking for it. Eventually he pulled the limp wad of glistening fabric—sleek and black with a garish dragon etched onto the back—out of his low-priority storage bins, watching as all the wrinkles slithered into nothingness as he shook out the robe. He slipped it over his shoulders, feeling the slick, cool touch against his still wet skin. Rodney tied the sash tight across his waist, then went to the terminal.

Before he could begin to think again, he let his fingers race over the keyboard, logging on. Rodney had never learned how to type, but countless hours of practice had taught him to use four fingers and a thumb with lightning speed.

He pushed the Return key, waited for the system to acknowledge.

"WELCOME TO THE BAY AREA METROPLEX NETWORK.

"USERNAME:"

Rodney typed in his name with spontaneous flicks of his fingertips.

"PASSWORD:"

He hammered in his password. A few beads of sweat appeared of their own accord on his forehead. Rodney had a sixth-level Net password, two steps above the fourth-level passwords most adults had. He had worked his way up, sharpening his computer finesse and using it to advance himself. Net passwords were one of the only things in the world that were still truly earned. You had to earn each upgrade yourself, through your own merit skill.

"WELCOME TO THE NETWORK, RODNEY QUICK. HOW MAY WE HELP YOU TODAY?

?"

At the prompt, four other major menus appeared, asking him to choose between Communications, Entertainment, Calculations, or Information Services. Rodney chose the latter, then cracked his knuckles as he lifted his hands away from the keyboard. Steepling his fingers, he blew on them and half-closed his eyes, trying to think of the best way to attack the problem, to ask his question.

A sudden shudder whipped up and down his spine. His eyes flew open again.

Supervisor was an Interface. She could tap into what he was doing—even in his own home—if she wanted to. . . .

He had come home that evening in a sweat, trembling, barely seeing anything around him. Supervisor had renewed her attacks with a greater vigor, finding subtle ways to stretch Rodney's nerves, snapping them one by one.

This morning, before starting the workday routine, Rodney had inspected the roster and the banks of frozen pre-Servants. Other Servants milled around, monitoring temperatures in the vats, cleaning up, keying in data as they stared at the display panels in front of each tank. Rodney logged on to The Net, using his work account and password, and skimmed down the day's schedule.

He found his own name on the list of bodies scheduled to be resurrected.

Too astonished even to consider the coincidence of someone else having his name, Rodney called up the file. It contained only one line of text.

"WE ARE ALMOST ON SCHEDULE WITH YOU MR. QUICK."

His skin felt cold and white enough with fearful anger that he almost looked like a corpse already. Rodney tried to delete the file, but found that it had been password-protected.

The feelings of persecution and rage grew strong enough for a moment to drive down his terror, and he stormed about the room, shouting at the Servants, who obediently moved out of his way. One male seemed so intent on his tasks that he almost walked into the raging tech. "Go

55

screw yourself!" Rodney snapped, and the Servant looked down at his crotch in total bewilderment.

On one of the vats Supervisor had mounted a plaque with his name on it. "FOR RODNEY QUICK." Rodney's anger drained away like spilled milk. All that day Supervisor never showed herself.

Rodney couldn't run away. They held him in a web of dependence that had damned him. No matter where he went, he would have to use The Net and his password for money, for transportation tickets, for food, for identification. And every time he logged on, he would pinpoint his location, screaming out "Here I am!" to anyone who bothered to look. Supervisor was an Interface—she could find him herself, and she could come to get him if he ran away. Supervisor would do it quietly, at her own speed—but she would do it.

Now, though, if he could find the Cremators, perhaps he could win a small victory.

The Information Services menu spilled out across the screen. He selected "SEARCH DATABASE." Another menu came up, listing the broad divisions of the database, and Rodney wound his way deeper into the mind of The Net, tunneling through menu after menu after menu.

"SEARCH FOR WHAT?" the terminal finally asked.

"CREMATORS," Rodney typed, then sat back to wait. A "SYSTEM BUSY" message instantly appeared in the system line at the bottom of the screen. A second later Rodney scanned the summary paragraph, but it made no mention whatsoever of the group he sought.

Not terribly surprised, Rodney then looked for other ways to approach the problem. His peripheral vision vanished, and the rest of the world faded away as he rose to the challenge and devoted himself entirely to finding what he needed to know.

He tried anagrams of the word; he accessed the foreign-language dictionary databases and asked the computer to search for the key word in nineteen different languages. He followed every possible line of cross-referencing in an electronic wild-goose chase that led him through the labyrinths of The Net. He rose through the menus again and plunged in along an alternate route, asking different but related questions. Sometimes he received answers, but nothing helped much.

Rodney had honed and developed his own Net finesse during his teenage years, while his friends had discovered the Net simulation/adventure games and spent their time blasting graphic aliens or guiding their cursors through childish pixel mazes. But Rodney had learned how to run the tightrope of the computer network, skipping through directories and opening files no one else had even thought to look for.

Some of his age group smugly went into professions that would always be honored and safe: banking, politics, administration, engineering. All fine and good if you happened to be particularly bright, but Rodney knew he didn't have the brainpower to break into any of those fields. He didn't really care, though, so long as he found something other than the walking death of the wandering blues.

Rodney knew that he might have hope, if he worked hard enough—the good old work ethic from times gone by. The Net itself was the biggest employer in the Bay Area Metroplex, requiring such a vast number of operators, technicians, programmers, debuggers, hacker-security officers, database assistants, maintenance specialists, hardware engineers, systems administrators, not to mention the hordes of accountants, secretaries, administrators, and other electronic paper pushers.

Right now, though, the supposedly infinite resources of The Net seemed not to be able to find a scrap of information about the Cremators.

Feeling a growing desperation and helplessness, Rodney pounded his fist on the side of the console.

He shuddered to think how Francois Nathans would react if he knew what his own technician was trying to do. For a moment a twinge of guilt made Rodney stop another search for cross-references to Viking funerals. Nathans *had* been good to him—but Nathans had declared war on the mysterious Cremators. And if a man like Nathans could not unearth a single detail about the group, what chance did Rodney have in finding them?

After the Servant Danal had been released and escorted off to his destination, Rodney had not expected to see any more of Nathans. Nathans was too important a man to bother with a mere technician, and Rodney had suspected with some chagrin that Nathans's first visit was just to emphasize how important the Servant was, not necessarily to commend any special work Rodney Quick had performed.

But Nathans did come once more, when Supervisor

wasn't around. "Rodney, I've checked into your background, and I am indeed impressed at what you have made of yourself." Nathans folded his hands and smiled. "Nothing angers me more than to see a man waste himself on useless, monotonous work, letting his brain turn to jelly. By caring about your future, by working to *learn*, you've made yourself an important part of what I firmly believe to be the most crucial corporation in the evolution of mankind."

Dazed and somewhat baffled, Rodney nodded and mumbled something that expressed his deep gratitude. He sincerely hoped that Supervisor was eavesdropping.

"If you ever have any problems, don't hesitate to come see me directly. Keep up the good work, Rodney." Nathans shook his hand. The other man's grip was dry but firm, not a mere token gesture.

Rodney had not dared to take him up on the offer, not even after the most serious of Supervisor's threats. Maybe this was an even bigger trap, a net within a net. And Supervisor had specifically warned him—forcing him back against one of the warm, bubbling resurrection vats and holding him there without even moving a finger—that if he ever went to tell Nathans about anything, she would destroy him before he could say a word.

His imagination churned away, surrounding him with horrifying possibilities: as an Interface, she could probably use The Net to make an elevator crash, a control panel overload, to turn any of the numerous appliances in his own living quarters into a weapon. . . .

He had to find the Cremators. He didn't want to come back as a Servant. Even then, Supervisor would probably keep him as her private toy. He had to find the Cremators. Even if he alienated Francois Nathans in the process. His situation had gotten too serious to leave any other alternatives.

"STRING NOT FOUND," The Net answered.

In disgust and frustration almost to the point of tears, Rodney gave up. He logged off, and the screen went blank, leaving him in darkness.

The wake-up alarm brought him out of the murky depths of nightmares. The sound drove an icy nail of fear into him as he realized that morning had come. His eyes opened wide, and he knew they would probably be bloodshot when he went to look in the mirror. It was almost time to go to work again, to confront another day.

Before even bothering to shower, Rodney went slowly into the kitchen area and powered up the coffee dispenser, letting the synthesizers and heaters begin to manufacture the one and a half cups he drank every morning.

Out of the corner of his eye, he saw the message light on his Net terminal blinking on and off.

Suddenly awake now, Rodney went carefully over to the screen, moving with a tension that made him seem to be stalking the terminal.

"YOU HAVE ELECTRONIC MAIL ITEM(S) NOT READ."

Probably just an updated Net entertainment schedule.

Rodney logged on and chose the Communications option from the first-level menu.

It could be an advertisement. Mass electronic mailings sent out to all Net users. Rodney had developed a program in his own Net account that would scan all such messages to see if they were electronically generated and sent to large user groups. Then he could toggle his system to ignore all of them, or throw them into a file for low-priority reading. But he hadn't had a chance to debug the routine yet. Yes, it was probably just an advertisement message.

He chose Electronic Mail from the Communications menu.

"YOU HAVE ONE MESSAGE."

Or maybe it was a survey. "Rodney Quick, we have selected you at random . . ."

He selected the message and displayed it on the screen.

"A REPRESENTATIVE WILL MEET YOU AT EXACTLY 11:33 A.M. WE THINK YOU WILL BE EXTREMELY INTERESTED IN OUR FINE MAPS AND DEMOGRAPHIC PROJECTIONS—MERCATOR, LIMITED."

To his amazement, the words vanished as he read them, as if the sensors on the Net terminal could scan his eye movements. The screen suddenly drew a map of the vicinity around Resurrection, Inc., highlighting one area. Then the screen went blank.

Frantically he tried to read the message again, but it had been purged. He dug deeper and found that The Net had no record of the message at all. No electronic address had appeared on the header to the message, no source-computer slugline.

Wide-awake now, Rodney chewed his lip, smelling the

freshly processed coffee from the kitchen area. Maps? A Mercator projection was a type of map that made the world look squashed flat on a piece of paper.

But "mercator" was also one of the anagrams he had used the night before.

8

Looking satisfied and possessive, Vincent Van Ryman shuffled into the expansive study. His slippers scuffed the carpet into dark contours as he walked. Danal paced smoothly just behind him, moving without a sound.

Van Ryman stopped, placing his hand on the top of an overstuffed chair. Danal instantly noticed the details, the front of the cushion where the maroon-crushed velvet had worn away, the heavily lacquered wood trim sporting a row of decorative brass studs.

Curtains had been drawn across the French windows, though the neighboring condominium buildings blocked out most of the sunlight anyway. Crowded bookcases surrounded the room, mounted on top of half-walls covered with clonewood paneling. Next to the bookcases, a Net terminal displayed a simulation/adventure game interrupted in progress.

The maw of a large fireplace was filled with jagged quartz crystals bathed by scattered laser light. Mirrored tiles covered the hearth and the inside of the fireplace, reflecting and shattering the light into a million glittering fragments. A large white-light hologram of an ocean scene hovered above the mantel, framed in garishly ornate bronze.

Danal stopped just inside the room, absorbing details and waiting as Van Ryman moved about. The dark-haired man occupied himself compulsively, seeming insecure, as if he didn't know what to do in the presence of his Servant.

"Why don't you sit with me, Danal? I was just relaxing by the fireplace." Van Ryman gestured again toward the Servant. "Sit, please."

Danal automatically went to the side of the overstuffed chair, stopped, turned to the front of the chair, stopped, placed himself in front of the cushion, stopped, and finally sat down with exaggerated care. He sat stiffly in the soft chair, refusing to relax into the cushion.

Van Ryman shrugged and walked over to a small table

beside the bulky black frame of a Grande piano. Danal could see that a touchpad synthesizer keyboard had replaced the ivory keys, and microspeakers had been installed in the otherwise empty shell of the antique piano. Van Ryman picked up a cut-crystal decanter partially filled with a honey-colored liquid; he neutralized the cork with a switch on the side of the decanter and poured himself a small amount into a snifter. From the other side of the room Van Ryman studied Danal for a moment and then poured a second snifter. He strode over, extending it to the Servant.

Danal accepted the glass automatically, but held onto it and made no move to bring it to his lips, though Van Ryman sipped his own with obvious pleasure.

"Go on, drink. It's Glenlivet—you'll like it."

Danal hesitated. "Master Van Ryman, I am required to remind you that I am only your Servant. I am not a human and I am not a guest. It is not necessary to treat me with such courtesy."

"Thank you, Danal. I consider myself reminded, and I choose to disregard your advice. Taste your scotch. We need to have a talk, a real talk, and I feel more comfortable if I think I'm talking to some*one*, rather than just tapping into a database."

"Yes, Master Van Ryman." Danal raised the snifter to his face, automatically inhaling and drawing in the strong aroma of the old scotch. The scent set his olfactory nerves tingling, rushing back to his brain for advice, setting off bells and lights, awakening other neurons that had until then been stubbornly asleep. He wet his lips with the Glenlivet and stepped up the workings of the microprocessor so he could analyze and concentrate on the initial touch of the alcohol before he drew in a mouthful.

The scotch burned his lips, but he let a small amount pour over his teeth and across his tongue, feeling its slow progression. His tongue awakened, and the insides of his cheeks felt pleasantly seared. He swallowed and concentrated on the sensation as the Glenlivet flowed down his esophagus, seeming to warm and tingle his chest from the inside out. His mind recognized the taste, the experience, and stretched a little further toward awakening.

Then he returned to real time, where Van Ryman had barely had time to blink, still watching him.

"Thank you, Master Van Ryman."

Satisfied, the man turned and went over to the black-lacquered piano bench and sat down, straddling it so he could face the Servant. He regarded Danal in silence and took a deep swallow of his scotch before he spoke again. He wouldn't look at Danal as he talked.

"I suppose you've already been given a superficial gleaning of my personal file. My father Stromgaard"—he allowed himself a faint, pleased-looking smile—"was one of the founders of Resurrection, Inc. He and Francois Nathans put it together and made it fly. Nathans had the charisma, but eventually he pushed Stromgaard out of the business. I guess he forgot it was Van Ryman money that financed the corporation in the first place. No matter, my father found something much more important to devote himself to."

Van Ryman let the words hang as he looked up at the drab and passive Servant. Danal sat motionless, listening with simulated rapt attention.

The man rubbed his palms briskly together again, "Danal, I want you to think of me as your friend as well as your Master. Talk to me if you want, and be sure to answer the questions I ask. Servants are bound by their programming to do exactly what their Masters require, and I require you to trust me, to be as candid and as honest as you can. Understood?"

The Servant answered automatically, immediately, though his mind balked at the thought of implicitly trusting this man with the alien eyes and the face with a fun-house-mirror familiarity.

"Now then, Danal, before I show you the house, do you think you're up to some conversation? Or would you like to rest?"

Danal paused a moment, listening to the tone of the man's voice, the nuances of his expression. He could not decide if Van Ryman wanted to talk, or if he was rationalizing an excuse to be rid of the Servant for the time being.

"Whichever you prefer, Master Van Ryman. I am here to Serve you."

The man pursed his lips, then rubbed his hands briskly together. "Well then, I'll ask a few questions, and you answer as best you can." He paused for one uncomfortable moment. The lasers in the fireplace scattered purple light, distracting him. Van Ryman rested his elbow against the touchpad synthesizer keys; one prolonged note of cello tone filled the room until Van Ryman straightened again, too wrapped up in his own thoughts even to notice. "Tell me, Danal, what's it like?"

"I don't understand, Master Van Ryman."

"What does it *feel* like?" He seemed to gather up his nerve, and asked with more vehemence, "To be a Servant, I mean? What do you see, what do you think about, what do you *remember*? About death? You experienced it all and came back to us. What did you see there beyond the border?" His eyes looked glazed and distant. "Did you bring anything back with you?"

Guided by his inherent programming, Danal answered the questions in the order they had been asked, without thinking. "I see everything around me with great fascination. I want to learn it all again as fast as I can. I am intrigued by everything, and I want to examine. But I can't—I am a Servant. Servants have no curiosity."

"Nonsense." Van Ryman smiled, apparently satisfied with Danal's candor. "Here, to show you my goodwill, I'll let you inspect anything you see, if you wish. I'm a very congenial Master, and I'll let you do many things." His eyes narrowed almost imperceptibly, but Danal noticed. The line of tiny red pinpricks along his chin became visible again. "But you have to answer my questions in as much detail as you can."

"I will, Master Van Ryman."

"Good, good."

Danal walked slowly around the study, delighted, inspecting the dusty leather-bound books. He tried to show restraint, but he suddenly felt as if he had been freed, to inspect and touch and observe and analyze everything he could find. On the books he saw unusual symbols and strange languages.

Van Ryman broke his train of thought. "And about my other question, Danal? What about death itself? Do you remember anything?"

The Servant stood in front of the glowing laser fireplace, feeling the pleasant warmth from the thermal crystals. Purple light dappled his gray uniform. "Nothing clearly."

Van Ryman clutched at the ambiguity. His out-of-place eyes lit up and he sat straight on the piano bench. "But you do remember something? A picture, a thought maybe? Danal, this is very important. You have to tell me everything!"

Danal hesitated the briefest of moments as he analyzed the wisdom of confessing his flashbacks to this man. His Master. He wanted to Serve, to do his duty, and nothing else. His programming threatened him, clamping down with iron fingers on his free will. He had no choice.

"Yes, I do recall things. Strange things. I can't explain or interpret them. They aren't memories . . . more like flashes of something bigger buried deep inside."

"Yes! Tell me." Van Ryman's eyes seemed to be ignited with the fires of Hell, and he looked as if he enjoyed it.

With his back to Van Ryman, Danal stared at the white-light hologram in its frame above the fireplace, feeling more comfortable when he could avoid his Master's gaze. He touched one of the digital squares below the frame, and the angle of the hologram scene changed, panning down the beach and focusing on the rocks on the shore. The sun slanted toward afternoon, washing over the grass-tufted sandstone cliffs that formed a wall to the beach.

"It happened three times, four times. I can't make sense of the flashes," Danal answered, puzzled. "I can feel the information there, just waiting to be triggered by . . . something. And when it does, it comes in a burst, unconnected, like a line of text lifted at random out of a file."

Danal found a trail of footprints in the sand on the holographic beach, eroding as the tide washed in. The waves were tipped with gentle but dramatic whitecaps as they curled in toward shore, trapped motionless in three dimensions by the hologram. Absently Danal changed the view again, following the footprints.

"And what do these flashes show?" Van Ryman got up to pour himself a second snifter of scotch. Danal could tell by his Master's careful movements that he remained intent on Danal's answer. "Anything you see here, perhaps? In this house?"

"Yes," the Servant said slowly. "Yes, I feel a sense of familiarity about some things. And you, Master Van Ryman—it was very strong when I first saw you in the hall. Does any of this make sense?"

The man stood up with bright eyes, grinning. "More than you can know, Danal." Van Ryman seemed barely able to contain his excitement. "And these flashbacks, do you think they're messages? Messages from beyond death,

65

communications from Satan Himself? Pointing out that there's something special about this house, about *me*?"

Danal paused, then answered carefully. "I'm not sure, Master Van Ryman. That's a possible interpretation." It wasn't the right one, Danal thought, but Van Ryman already knew what he wanted to hear.

The dark-haired man nearly shouted with excitement and rubbed his hands together. His voice carried a whispered awe that Danal found frightening.

"It means we are expected!"

In the hologram two people lay naked and laughing by a rock outcropping on the wet sand: a man who appeared to be Van Ryman himself, smiling and at peace, with calm eyes; the other, a thin and supple woman, whose clean blond hair had been darkened by sea water and sand.

Julia!

The young woman—Julia?—stared out of the hologram at Danal, taunting his memory with her crystal-blue eyes. Her narrow features were dimpled and elfin, almost wraithlike. A gull hung up in the sky, and tide pools were scattered in the pockmarked black rock stretching out into the water, waiting for the waves. Julia had just tossed a stone into one of the larger pools, and the ripples echoed outward in perfect circles. The Van Ryman in the picture was watching her, though—not the stone, not the waves, not the gull. It seemed so different.

Alarmed, Danal folded the picture completely into his memory with all the speed the microprocessor would allow him. In the study, the real Van Ryman was too excited to notice the people in the picture for an instant, and Danal's fingers flew to the "Reset" button on the hologram, returning it to the default view of a serene and desolate oceanscape.

For some reason Danal didn't want Van Ryman to see the quiet, intimate picture. Irrational. Van Ryman was *in* the picture. But it was a different Van Ryman, one who had . . . who had discarded the fallacy of the neo-Satanists . . . under Julia's urging, all under Julia's urging. . . . A Van Ryman who would never have restored the gargoyles to the eaves of the mansion . . . one who would never look for messages from Satan in the disjointed flashbacks of a Servant.

Everything tumbled around in his head, letting the spurts of memory ricochet off themselves. Nothing resolved itself. Nothing made sense. But his Servant programming threatened to override—Danal had no right to question his Master, nor would he dare to.

He turned to face Van Ryman before anything else could happen, before he could lose his calm and passive Servant facade. "I am very tired now, Master Van Ryman. May I go to my room to rest?"

The man was too delighted to pay much attention to the Servant. "Yes, yes, of course! Thank you very much, Danal. I'll have to call Nathans right away."

Pressure built up in Danal's memory, and he reeled as he wandered out of the study. Too many impressions were striking his underloaded brain, and his mind would soon be a tangled mass of contradictions. Now truly weary, he went toward his room. He wanted to sleep . . . and to forget.

He left the study and walked down a hall, past a central sitting area and a wide, blue-carpeted staircase leading upstairs; above, a carved railing set off the walkway from where it overlooked the first level. The kitchen and dining areas, as well as the terrarium room, were through the sitting room and in another wing, but Danal walked blindly past the stairs and past the small sauna to a large room, a bedroom.

"Danal! Command: Stop! Where are you going?"

On Command phrase the Servant's muscles locked up and refused to function. Van Ryman bustled up in his green robe, looking suddenly uneasy again. Danal stood motionless and saw that he had almost entered the master bedroom of the Van Ryman mansion.

"I was trying to find my room, Master Van Ryman."

The man paused for a moment in indecision. The silence was magnified by Danal's distorted perception of time. "Well it certainly isn't *there!* It's upstairs, the second room. You'll see it—I've got it set up for you. Go! Why didn't you ask?"

"Servants are not supposed to ask questions, Master Van Ryman."

Leaving Van Ryman trapped by the truth of the statement, Danal brushed past him and went back to the stairs.

9

Francois Nathans paused alone in the doorway of an apartment building across from Resurrection, Inc. Carefully adjusting his disguise, he let his eyes grow accustomed to the sunshine before he emerged onto the crowded street. The wind had picked up, ruffling the pedestrians' hair as they moved back and forth. A lost piece of paper curled along the ground, brushing up against many legs that paid it no heed.

Nathans stood, waiting for the subtle transition to happen, for him to become an anonymous pedestrian. As far as anyone else could see, he was just another employee of a local business park, living in an island of apartment buildings surrounded by office complexes. Nathans breathed the outside air and set out, confident.

More and more often Nathans found himself using the passage from his private offices in the deep lower levels of Resurrection, Inc. to Apartment 117 in the complex across the street. It felt good to be alone, away from the pressures, and he had found no greater isolation than when he was surrounded by a thousand strangers.

Nathans wore a stiff denim jacket and black pants with silver stitching. Before leaving his office, he had changed his hairpiece to a longish spiky-blond style, since it felt like a "blond" day to him. As always, a fresh hairpiece felt good against his cleanly shaven scalp. Nathans selected a woven straw hat that cast his eyes into shadow, letting him stare with secret interest and curiosity at the other people on the street.

In no hurry, he watched the activity around him, pondering where to go for his walk. People always fascinated him, sometimes infuriated him, but never bored him. He stood under the hum of the smog scrubbers, contemplating, as an Enforcer hovercar moved slowly over the heads of the pedestrian traffic on the street; its black shadow looked like a shark swimming through the crowd.

Nathans stared proudly for a long moment at the massive Resurrection building across the street. *First the dis-*

covery of fire. Then the Industrial Revolution. Then Resurrection, Incorporated.

He couldn't remember if he had thought of that one, or if it was Stromgaard. Probably not Stromgaard—the elder Van Ryman had adequate business sense, and plenty of money to back the formation of Resurrection, Inc., but he just had no . . . charisma, or the relentless enthusiasm to carry the corporation to its true potential. After seven successful years Nathans had more or less usurped Stromgaard Van Ryman's position, pacifying the other man by letting him take charge of the new religion they were then forming, the neo-Satanists.

Nathans smiled a little, remembering his glory days, when he had tried to cajole start-up money for the Servant corporation from Stromgaard's pockets. Nathans had his own fortune, of course, but nobody knew about *that*, and he had to find a more obvious backer.

He had seen that the technology for reanimating the dead was nearly at hand—biomechanics, bioelectronics, and bio-organics had all developed extensively, but no one had integrated the separate subfields into a direct application. While others spent halfhearted attempts at creating human-style androids, and gave up in despair at the complexity and the cost, Nathans conceived of Servants as a cost-effective alternative.

Medical science had been unable to breach the barrier of death, to bring people back to life. The brain itself proved to be as large a puzzle for the neuro-engineers as the rest of the body had been to the biomechanics. But Nathans never even attempted to bring the mind back to life; he didn't want to resurrect people—he needed only the strong arms and legs to do work.

Nathans had gathered up the most brilliant researchers, the mavericks who wanted free reign in the lab and who wanted to be judged by their results and not by tedious paperwork. He brought the researchers together, gave them a combined focus and a challenge—if they could figure out how to do the resurrection process, each one of them could literally have anything he or she wanted.

The team admirably did as they were asked and also came up with a few extra useful items, such as the technique of surface-cloning, which had in itself proven useful on a number of occasions. A few members of the first team were now perfectly wealthy and perfectly happy off on islands someplace, Tierce in Fiji, Bombador and Smythe still living together in Samoa. Swensen now had her own genuine nineteenth-century farm deep in the isolated rural sections of Minnesota, working her fingers to the bone for the sheer joy of it. And poor Ferdinand, the maladjusted one, who had worked a different shift just to avoid the other members of the team—as his reward he had begged to become an Interface, and now spent his entire time catheterized, fed by IVs but linked to The Net and swimming in ecstasy in mankind's greatest collection of knowledge.

They had served him well, all of them, and Nathans sincerely hoped that each had gotten something to make him or her happy.

Nathans started to walk aimlessly, traveling in whatever direction the crowd's currents decided to take him. As he looked around, he remembered how horrified the common people had been by the first Servants. But after a year or two, the initial superstitious horror became a more rational fear: for a few months' salary of one blue-collar Union employee, a corporate owner could purchase a lifetime Servant instead—and Servants worked harder, worked longer hours, did not take breaks, never called in sick, never goofed off, and never dreamed of going on strike. As an even greater economic incentive, Servant laborers required less-strict safety standards, and never complained of poor factory conditions.

But the blues themselves had proven even more stubbornly ignorant than Nathans had expected. Looking at the forlorn, aimless people scattered in the crowd—in greater numbers every day—made him feel depressed and enraged. He wanted to shout at them, force them to see how they were wasting themselves. Why hadn't they seen what was coming? If they had so much as tried to train themselves, they could have moved into some other job—anything that required the smallest amount of thinking could not be done by a Servant. Rodney Quick had done it; after looking into Rodney's confidential datafile, Nathans was impressed at how the tech had worked his way up from a blue-collar background, using his own head and nothing more. Not at all like the other apathetic clods.

For the time being, the blue allotment paid for their existence, but the next generation would have to fend for themselves, find a way to survive by using their brains rather than just being assembly-line oxen, or they would perish.

The point of freeing mankind from manual labor was so people could spend their time thinking, philosophizing, educating themselves through the vast databases available through The Net. But the idea had backfired on him, and the people who had been freed from their workhorse lives refused to consider the infinite possibilities before them. With life so full, with so many things to do, with all the information in The Net for the taking if only they made the effort, the blues whined about being bored, with nothing to do.

It should have worked. it all seemed so simple and clear-cut. Because of their additional free time, the blues should have been demanding more art and music and entertainment, thereby creating the need for more artists and more musicians, all of whom could come from their own ranks. But the pornographic or slapstick drivel they demanded as entertainment was a long way from his expectations.

He had insisted on giving the blues the benefit of the doubt, naïvely believing that they did want the finer things in life but had been denied them because of social inequalities or economic pressures. But their dismal response appalled and offended him. He had spent a lot of time poring over The Net's databases, but he could find no justification for the voluntary ignorance of the general public—they simply didn't want to better themselves.

And that had forced him to make an important transition in his own philosophy: perhaps these people *were* the lower end of the human spectrum, atavisms from the Middle Ages, members of the species adapted for a different time in the human clock—and now their time was up. Survival of the fittest, applied to human society.

Nathans stopped at a display of groomed rosebushes nearly exploding with roses. An Enforcer guarded the hedge and watched closely as Nathans bent to smell one of the blooms. The plants had been boosted to produce dozens more flowers than they normally would; the roots would burn out, exhausted, in only a few years, yet it would be a spectacular flash of glory. But someone always had to pull out the weeds to let the flowers grow.

Nathans fervently considered this to be the next step in the evolution of mankind, a societal evolution to hone mental capabilities and to selectively breed out those who had no imagination, no personal drive, no powers of reason. Nathans thought it was a grand and subtle plan, for the ultimate benefit of *Homo sapiens*. Perhaps it seemed harsh, but he believed a more humane solution would have far more destructive consequences.

Subversive groups like the Cremators undermined his power, threw obstacles in the path of this social plan. Involuntarily his fingers clenched, and Nathans almost grasped one of the thorny stems of the boosted rosebush. Carefully he stood up again, smiled at the Enforcer, and made himself walk casually away. Nathans managed to control his frustrated anger, fighting down the urge to stretch out his foot and trip someone.

The Cremators baffled him. He had the greatest resources available in the entire Metroplex, probably in the world, and still there had never been a successful attempt by the Enforcers, or Resurrection, Inc., to locate a single member of the group. Nathans could not understand how anyone could manage to elude his intensive demands for information, but the Cremators had done their cover-up work better than anyone could have conceived.

He could not deny that certain pre-Servants had vanished without a trace, or that the public rumors about the Cremators had not been generated by the rumor division of the Enforcers Guild. But not only did the Cremators steal his potential Servants away—even worse, they increased the public fear and paranoia about Servants in general. Nathans was helpless, and furious that he was helpless.

He strolled along, passive, so in tune with the organism of the crowd that he rarely even bumped elbows with another person. Nathans pushed through a knot of congestion where five street vendors had set up their rickety tables. He stopped to look, perhaps to chat. It always pleased him to see that some of the blues used their spare time to make and create things.

He paused pensively in front of a jeweler's stall. In several trays were various rings, pendants, earrings, studs, buckles, all made from polished and skillfully modified debris: scrap metal, acrylic-coated paper, wood splinters suspended in colored resins. One of the pendants in the glittering, unarranged chaos caught his eye—a neo-Satanist star-in-pentagram made from twisted copper wire and epoxied onto a wafer-thin disk of porcelain.

Nathans reached forward to pick it up, carefully inspecting the work with a bemused expression on his face. While keeping an eye on everything else that happened at her table, the craftswoman dickered heatedly with another customer about an inexpensive clip-on nose stud. Nathans studied her carefully as he appeared to consider the pendant, still keeping his face in the shadow of his hat brim.

The jewelry vendor had long brown hair braided with a rainbow of different-colored ribbons, like the striking plumage of an extinct bird. She had strung herself with a tangled mass of jewelry, most of which seemed to be her own creations. The woman's face was wide, not very attractive; she had a few pimples, a few freckles, a few moles. But she had a pretty smile, and she actually wore a tie-dyed T-shirt, harking back to the wave of hippie nostalgia that had swept the Metroplex a few years before.

Giving up on the other sale, she plucked the nose stud from the dissatisfied customer's fingers and abruptly turned away from him to face Nathans. "Like that one?"

"Yes I do. It's very interesting," he said, sounding complimentary but uncertain. It was all a game; they both knew it.

"Are you a neo-Satanist, then?"

"Are you?" Nathans answered quickly, taking her off guard.

"No. I don't go for that sort of stuff," she said without vehemence, careful not to scare off a prospective customer. "But it's okay, I mean. We're all different, right?"

"Then why do you make a pendant like this, if you're not part of the religion?"

She shrugged, flipping one of her braids back. "I try to do lots of different things. And I have to make what the market demands, or else why bother sitting out here quibbling prices all day long? There's a lot of interest in this stuff. That'll be my third one sold today—if, of course, you decide to buy it."

Nathans appreciated her frankness. He and Stromgaard and Vincent had formed neo-Satanism with a consciously mischievous intent, as a simple joke at first and then an appallingly real joke as the stupid blues ate it up. If someone was foolish enough to be taken in by such a ridiculous and absurd religion, if someone would freely give money and fanatical energy to something that was such an apparent sham, then didn't that person deserve to be defrauded, a disgrace to the human race?

"Of course I'll take it," he answered the jeweler. "But you'll have to wrap it up for me, please." Before she could quote him a price, Nathans removed his Net card and swept it through her reader, transferring money from one of his fictitious sources into the woman's home account. The jeweler handed him the pendant in a white paper bag taken from a fast-food center. She nodded at the fair, but not overly generous, price he had credited her.

"Good enough. Thanks for not haggling!" she said. "It's such a pain in the ass."

Nathans tucked the bag inside the denim jacket. "Have a nice day."

He walked off again past the line of vendors, paying little attention to the flower sellers, the caricature artists, the middle-aged man selling cookies. Looking, smelling, experiencing, sensing the instincts of the mass mind of the public, he could almost feel his mental batteries charging.

Nathans particularly liked the singers, especially those who had written their own songs. A new style of mournful street spontaneity had grown popular, called the "blues' blues." A man and his sister sat together on a blanket, loudly singing improvised words to the music from a Tchaikovsky tape. Nathans stood listening while the others paused and then moved in. He quickly slid his Net card through the singers' reader, giving them a small donation. They didn't break their refrain to thank him, and that pleased him even more.

He walked again, looping around slowly, not anxious to return to Resurrection, Inc. Today he didn't really feel up to going past Soapbox Derby, though he never tired of listening to the people ranting there. Sure, most of the invective predictably attacked Resurrection, but Nathans felt gratified to see the people *thinking* at least, planning ways to change the world order. If they kept it up, they might actually succeed in raising their own social consciousness. Otherwise, they would be doing nothing more than assembling furniture, cleaning rooms, lifting boxes, and washing dishes, not thinking of anything beyond their own paycheck.

Out of curiosity, with a faint predatory smile on his face, Nathans slowly came up behind one of the wandering blues. The man's sluggish movements and dead lack of expression clearly tagged him for what he was. Feeling the game build slowly, Nathans shadowed him, not trying to hide his movements but somewhat appalled (yet not really surprised) when the blue didn't even realize he was being followed.

As they moved on, Nathans began to grow almost nauseated by the man's aimless course, his dejected stance. Nathans wanted to shout, to shake the man and insist that his life didn't have to be like this—was he a machine that without a mechanical job he was lost? Didn't humanity have the power to think, letting a man occupy himself with great things instead of trivial "busy" jobs?

Nathans narrowed his eyes, fixing his stare at the back of the man's head. It was going to be difficult for his own subtle revolution to come about, his own important alteration of society, his vision of the bright and optimistic future. Nothing could happen until most of these pathetic people went away.

A rush of excitement filled him as he reached into his pocket, pushing aside the white sack containing the neo-Satanist pendant and fingering a small tube the size of a penlight. A hisser, an aerosol weapon, a high-pressure subdermal sprayer that could paint a broad layer of toxin onto the skin, unnoticed. The poison would take hours to permeate the stratum corneum to the basal cell layer; once into the bloodstream, the toxin would begin to neutralize the serotonin in the man's brain, paralyzing all his muscles—including the diaphragm and the heart.

Nathans would be long gone by that time. It didn't pay to be blatant about murder. After all, he didn't have anything personal against this particular man, only against his medieval "life is a vale of tears" attitude.

He pulled out the hisser, carefully laying it against his wrist and hiding its tip with his curled fingertips. As Nathans came up behind the blue, he could feel his own blood pounding, his cells tingling with the anticipation. He always felt a sense of triumph when he could do something to bring about the great social change, rather than just sitting back and letting the cumbersome grinding wheels of evolution take their own course.

He saw the hairs on the man's neck, a few glints of sweat, the naked skin waiting. . . . The toxin was warm and gentle; he wouldn't even feel it sprayed on his skin. Nathans raised the hisser, exposing its tip.

But then he stopped himself, realizing that this wasn't what he should be doing. If his theory of inexorable social change was really true—and he knew it was—then *it had to run by itself.* It should not require overt action from him, any direct assistance. If the world truly worked according to the "survival of the fittest" paradigm, then it would have to take care of itself. One man killed would not make a difference one way or another.

Nathans hesitated, torn, wishing he could do something active for once. He admitted to himself that he would have enjoyed killing the man, but in the end he backed off, bleeding the compressed air out of the hisser as he let the other man move along with the crowd, continuing his ponderous trek.

The walk left Nathans feeling oddly refreshed, exhilarated in spite of the non-confrontation with the blue. He drew in another deep breath of the sweat-mingled air. The breeze picked up, and he had to hold onto his straw hat before it sailed off above all the other heads.

He felt he could go back to his office suite now, ready to play the part of the corporate executive again. Back in front of the great building of Resurrection, Inc., he read the placard from a distance before he ducked inside the apartment complex, finding his special key to #117.

"Servants for Mankind—Freeing Us from Tedium to Pursue Our True Destiny."

Nathans took the words to heart. The world, the universe was predictable. Everything would work out all right. But he was deathly afraid he wouldn't see the results in his own lifetime. He had to use all his resources to make sure that it did happen.

10

Danal left the lights on in his room as he lay awake on the narrow bed, motionless, slowly recharging his energy reserves. The house remained silent. It was long after dark.

Danal's austere room was sparsely furnished with a bed, a plastic chair and, looking out-of-place, an old, non-functional Net terminal on a small table in the corner. After all, Servants needed few comforts of existence.

Danal lay back, pondering, all alone in the mansion. To pass the night in peace, the Servant realized he could step down the workings of his microprocessor, so that time would seem to pass more quickly. But he was not anxious for his new life to flash by any faster. He didn't need to sleep, and he wasn't certain he'd be able to even if he tried. And Danal wasn't particularly sure he wanted to find out what kind of dreams he would have.

On an impulse he shut off the light and lay alone in darkness. His Master Van Ryman had gone away at dusk, departing for one of the neo-Satanist Sabbats as the population in the streets trickled away to do their evening's work before the Enforcers' midnight curfew. As he departed, Van Ryman left Danal with the provocative comment that he had free run of the house to do as he wished.

For the first time, unobserved by needle-sharp eyes, Danal felt able to let his wall down, to drop the Servant facade. It felt so stifling, so unnatural, to respond with mechanical efficiency and passive complacency. At the back of his mind he began to wonder if he was wearing the clever disguise of a Servant, if the flashbacks somehow signified that Danal had brought more back with him from death . . . or if all Servants were like this, all wearing a false disguise to fool the humans.

Danal stood up and left his room. Hesitantly he began to explore the big house, trying not to abuse the privilege. He wandered through the rooms, touching things with gentle awe, looking at hallways, at knickknacks, at a universe of tiny details.

Danal picked up a small vase that held a porcelain rose. He touched a kiln-fired ashtray, crudely made but with an air that suggested the piece was expensive. Danal looked at the elaborate furniture, one piece at a time.

He went into the different parts of the house, moving slowly in the silence. Off the master bedroom he saw a sauna room with faded old boards weathered from too much steam and hot water. He hesitated at the doorway, not venturing inside. The place seemed to exude a steam of memories as well, like psychic impressions swirling out of the cracked floor.

Just to the right of the front door was the cramped control room for the Intruder Defense Systems. The crowded and intricate panels blinked like city lights, but the ominous machinery frightened him, and Danal stood outside looking in, afraid to enter in case he might touch something.

In the open sitting room at the end of the main hall, the Servant found a low door half-hidden under the staircase that led up to the loft and the other two rooms. He felt drawn to the door, but when he reached the handle, he found it locked. Danal tried to pull at the knob, but it remained fastened. A sudden fear ran up his spine, and he turned to leave the door alone, trying not to think about it.

Danal walked slowly into the study, the room where Van Ryman had first interrogated him. In the following days, the Servant had been cleaning the house, or taking care of the plants and flowers in the terrarium room. He had also been attempting to cook, using fresh ingredients and unpackaged vegetables and meats, but even though he carefully and methodically followed the proper steps, he didn't seem to have any real finesse for cooking.

In the study he looked at the rugs on the floor, at the lacquered black Grande piano. Experimentally he ran his fingers over the synthesizer keypad, but the unit had been powered down, and no music emerged. He walked along the row of books, studying the neo-Satanist texts. Gingerly he opened one that sounded particularly sinister, the *Malleus Maleficarum,* and scanned across a few pages, but it all seemed like a gibberish of plastic Latin— words that were supposed to sound mysterious and arcane but had no actual meaning. Brownish-red ink sketched various shapes and symbols and things that looked like spells.

With growing enthusiasm Danal put the book back and stepped over to the white-light hologram on the mantel. The fireplace sat dead and cold, with a grayish crystal inside it. He worked the hologram's position coordinates again, maneuvering the beach scene until he found the image of Van Ryman and Julia on the beach. He stared at the picture, haunted, drinking in the details for a long moment. His heart felt heavy inside him, but he didn't know why.

Danal stood motionless and uneasy. Thinking, pondering, waiting. He heard his Master's words echo over and over in his head, *You may inspect anything you wish*.

He listened to the silence, knowing Van Ryman wasn't there, and stepped in front of the Net terminal. He looked at the vacant screen of glass, behind which words could come, evoking mysteries from The Net itself. He stared at it, nearly hypnotized.

Danal reached forward, almost touched the keyboard, drew back, stopped, thought for a brief moment, realized how ridiculous he was being, then reached forward again. He touched his fingers to the panel, and hit the Return key. Real, mechanical keys moved up and down as he touched his fingers to them, making knife-switch contacts. The screen came alive, responding:

"WELCOME TO THE BAY AREA METROPLEX NETWORK.
"USERNAME:"

Danal sat in the chair next to the terminal, resting his elbows on his knees, then typed some letters. With few other names in his nearly vacant memory, the Servant tapped out "VINCENT VAN RYMAN." The Net returned and prompted him for his access code. Danal felt dizzy for an instant, and hammered a complex, seemingly random pattern of thirteen characters.

The green pixels on the screen vanished briefly, and Danal channeled his thoughts through his own microprocessor, scaling his time sense up to the same speed as The Net itself. For almost a year, it seemed, random pixels ignited and flashed on the screen before the characters returned.

"WELCOME TO THE NETWORK, VINCENT VAN RYMAN. HOW MAY WE HELP YOU TODAY?
?"

Danal suddenly realized what he had done, that he had somehow keyed in Van Ryman's supposedly unbreakable personal Net password, a *tenth-level* access code. He stared down at the tips of his fingers in awe.

Danal logged off immediately and took two steps away from the terminal as if it would bite him, attack him, swallow him up. He turned and hurried back to his room, leaving all the lights on.

11

Rodney didn't like the faces all around him on the streets. He was supposed to feel safer among numbers, but somehow the people made him even more uneasy as he darted through the crowd—bumping elbows, almost tripping himself—to the meeting place.

The air, the surroundings felt extremely oppressive around all the uncaring pedestrians. He sensed too many *things* here, too many chances for a mass-trans vehicle to suddenly come careening at him, too many chances for Supervisor to cause a power surge and make a Net booth explode as he passed it, or send an underground repair-rat running amok to burst the seams of a power conduit just as Rodney Quick walked above.

Supervisor would take special care to leave Rodney's body intact—so he could return as a Servant.

He hadn't made his bargain with the Cremators yet.

But would Supervisor kill him here? Out in the streets? Or would she do it where she could watch in person?

Supervisor had not shown up at Resurrection, Inc. all day, and her unexplained absence seemed more sinister than her presence. What was she doing?

This morning his coffee from the vending panel on Lower Level Six had tasted odd, so odd that he quickly discarded it after touching no more than a drop on the tip of his tongue. And in his own shower Rodney had been suddenly blasted by a scalding spray, with all the cold water mysteriously gone—and nothing wrong with the controls. What if . . . ? He hurried along.

At the Cremators' specified meeting place, he paced nervously around the base of an auto-statue of some long-forgotten military hero. The auto-statue shifted its position several times a day to reenact different grandiose poses. Looking incongruously colorful, carefully trimmed geraniums rose around the feet of the great general like the gloriously spilled blood of many enemies.

Rodney chewed his lip and tapped his two silicon fingernails on the rim of the statue. He didn't have the slightest idea who the Cremators were or how to recognize them. He didn't know what to do. Two Enforcers stood nearby, motionless. They seemed to be looking at him.

He glanced at the chronometer on his wrist, saw that he had arrived two minutes early. No one else seemed distinct from the rest of the crowd; no one else seemed to be waiting for anyone.

Claiming he had an appointment with a dentist, Rodney had left Resurrection, Inc. for a few hours. Suddenly fearing that Supervisor might check, he made a last-minute appointment with a real, but inexpensive, dentist, an appointment he had no intention of keeping. But then as time slowly dragged by, closer and closer to 11:33 A.M., he began to fear that Supervisor might check further, to see if he had actually shown up for his appointment. Just before departing, Rodney sent electronic mail to the dentist's appointment address, telling him he would be a little late. . . . Rodney hoped he could afford to pay for both the Cremators and the dentist.

Suddenly Rodney realized that a short, thin woman had come up to him on one side, and before he could turn, a man approached on the other side. The tech almost jumped, flinching and ready to run, but the strange man spoke to him in a calm and soothing voice.

"We're glad you could get here, Mr. Quick. We are the representatives you wanted to meet."

Rodney felt a terrified relief, but then he cringed. "How do I know you're—"

The woman snapped at him, "What do you expect us to do, carry ID cards? Name tags? Shit!"

Avoiding her glance, Rodney could barely stutter an inane reply.

The male Cremator was a largely built man, dressed unusually but comfortable enough in his unusual appearance that he didn't seem strikingly noticeable. He stood tall and wore a beard looping around his chin, framing it in Abraham Lincoln fashion but leaving his lip clean-shaven. His skin was all the same tone, somewhat textureless, even pasty-looking, and Rodney wondered if perhaps the man was black and trying to hide the fact. But then he realized his own inability to see the obvious— the Cremators, incognito, of course. Covering themselves.

"You can call me Rossum Capek," the man said. "You can call her Monica. If you must have names."

The man was dressed in a khaki overcoat and wore a black top hat that made him look like something out of a classic Charles Dickens presentation. Yet when the Cremator spoke, his voice had a rich timbre, a confident and knowledgeable tone but not condescending. The slightest touch of condescension would have immediately put Rodney on his guard.

The accompanying woman, Monica, was thin and stern-looking with dark hair cut in a jagged page boy—she looked familiar to him in the vaguest of ways. She was dressed in a nondescript wrap decorated with hexagonal blotches of earth tones. Her eyes were alert, flicking back and forth—darker than dark eyes, opaque eyes, and Rodney suspected that she wore contact lenses augmented with extra micro-sensors. The woman said nothing and only watched Rodney, *watched* Rodney, making him feel uneasy.

Capek put a hand lightly on the tech's shoulder, and with an unyielding force, directed Rodney to walk with them. "Let's go to more pleasant surroundings. We have some very important matters to discuss, and I'd like to make things a little more congenial."

The two Cremators quickly guided him to a street corner where they could board a mass-trans vehicle. After only five stops Rossum Capek motioned for him to disembark. Air pressure hissed as the mass-trans vehicle spewed open its doors in front of a large shopping-plex. The man and woman rapidly escorted Rodney out onto the pavement again, flanking him right and left.

The propped-open mall doors had been smeared with fingerprints too high for any child to reach. Rodney didn't have time to discover the name of the particular mall as they ushered him inside—all shopping-plexes looked basically the same, anyway.

Capek knew exactly where he was going and moved ahead, confident that Rodney and the woman would follow. The various specialized shops blurred past, and Rodney caught glimpses of them with wide eyes, but most passed in an indistinct collage. Capek halted once to allow them to catch up.

"I know a delightful little café at the heart of the mall. It's rather exclusive, but we can talk there."

The café was indeed very exclusive. Almost empty, it was hushed and waiting impatiently for a luncheon crowd. Capek smiled and, without a word, the café host nodded and led the three of them to a small table deep in the back.

Rodney forgot his anxiety for a moment and savored the surroundings. The air smelled fresh from dozens of hanging ferns and potted plants, from moist terrariums on every table. Mingling with the smell of earthy greenery was also the complex aroma of fresh-baked bread.

Huge skylights of plate glass let the hazy sunshine pour through, dappling the interior cobblestone walkways. A colorful patio umbrella shielded each table from the bright sunlight streaming down. The sound of running water made the atmosphere seem even more peaceful, and Rodney realized that a tiny moat surrounded each exclusive table, more for appearance than for an actual barrier. The tech noticed as he stepped over the two flat stones to their table that the bottom of the shallow stream had been strewn with old pennies and dimes, apparently for decoration, artifacts from the days of tangible currency.

Capek held a wicker chair for Monica, and she sat down without taking her opaque eyes from Rodney. The Cremator sat down himself as Rodney awkwardly took his own seat. The tech looked at the two Cremators, first the man and then the woman, waiting in silence, but neither of them seemed ready to speak.

Momentarily a waiter appeared, walking lightly over the stepping-stones to stand expectantly beside their small table. Rodney saw with slight distress that he carried no menus. "I'm ready to take your order."

The waiter placed his hands behind his back and smiled with a vacuous stare. Rodney wondered if the waiter would be filing away their selections in his memory, or if he had a transmitter hidden somewhere on his uniform to send their order directly to the kitchen.

Capek folded his hands on the table and answered confidently. "I'll have an espresso, and she will have tea— Lapsang souchong, I believe?" The woman nodded.

The waiter turned to Rodney, who hesitated uncomfortably for a moment. The waiter immediately spoke into the silence, "If you're not in the mood for coffees or teas, sir, may I offer you something else? Some wine perhaps, or a beer?"

The Cremator interjected, "They do have a very good beer, Mr. Quick. They brew it themselves, in large oak casks."

Rodney grasped at the suggestion and nodded. After

the waiter had vanished, Rossum Capek made brief attempts at small talk, to which Rodney mechanically responded. Monica sat in silence, scowling, suspicious, until the waiter returned with their order.

The Cremator picked up the tiny white china cup in his large hands and took a sip of the steaming liquid. He closed his eyes in obvious satisfaction. Monica ignored her tea, but Rodney could smell a smoky, tarlike aroma drifting toward his nostrils. He took a swallow of his reddish-amber beer; he would have liked it colder.

"Now then, Mr. Quick," Capek spoke, finally getting down to business. Reflexively Rodney took another deep drink of his beer, looking around the castle-like terrarium in the center of their table. "You obviously know what services we offer, or else you wouldn't have been so persistent in trying to find us. However, you are the first from your, er, organization to express anything other than hostility toward our operations."

"I'm in a better position to be afraid than most people," Rodney answered. "I know what goes on there. That's why I've been trying so hard to find the Cre—"

"Careful!" The woman suddenly sat up straight. Her tea sloshed near the rim of her cup, spilling a drop onto the saucer.

"Yes, Mr. Quick. Please be vague if at all possible." Capek smiled patiently and made Rodney feel comfortable again. The tech understood their paranoia, though, and spoke in a hushed voice.

"Yes, I know what you promise. But death is such an unpredictable thing—how can you guarantee that you'll be able to . . . you know, carry out our agreement?"

"We haven't made any agreement yet," Monica interrupted. Her companion waved her to be patient.

"We can't make any guarantees, since death *is* such an unpredictable thing. But we do promise that we'll attempt everything in our power to see you safely removed from the resurrection loop. Since we don't make our contracts public, you can't know how many times we fail . . . but so far we've been successful in more than eighty percent of our attempts. We have greater powers than you might suspect."

Rodney tried to calculate how many contracts that meant, but then he realized that on Lower Level Six he saw only the suitable pre-Servants; others too old or too badly damaged would never have shown up on his roster at all. Many of those cadavers must disappear as well, not to mention the ones that vanished before an Enforcer could even log the death onto The Net.

Rodney tapped his two fingernails on the thick side of the beer mug and took another drink. Only a mouthful of foam remained on the bottom of the mug, and uncannily the waiter appeared, standing unobtrusively on the other side of the moat and not interrupting their conversation. In the lull he spoke over the trickling water, asking if Rodney wanted another beer.

"Yes," he said, feeling somewhat daring now, not quite noticing the effects of the alcohol but badly wanting to.

The waiter disappeared, and the tech dropped his eyes a little, speaking before the nervousness could build and before the other man could return with his second beer. "And what about payment? How much will all this cost me?"

Rossum Capek's face seemed distorted by the curved glass of the terrarium, and Rodney shifted his seat to see him more clearly. The Cremator finally removed his top hat and set it delicately on the tablecloth. "We'll determine what you can afford. We serve all concerned people, not only the rich or the poor. Our group operates on the archaic system of barter, so you won't have to directly transfer funds from your account."

"Barter?" Rodney frowned. "But—"

"We can't get payment through The Net," Monica finally spoke up. "The Guardian Angels are constantly sweeping all transactions to see if they can identify something they can trace to us."

Capek nodded. "We're in a precarious position, as I'm sure you can appreciate."

The Cremator sipped his espresso again, leaving Rodney to ponder for a moment. The Guardian Angels were a cadre of Interfaces who constantly monitored all financial transactions on The Net, searching for electronic fraud or embezzlement, tracing any transfer of funds for questionable dealings. Punishment for abuse, fraud, or embezzlement was severe, and Rodney knew the corporate moguls were more frightened of a reduced popular faith in The Net than they were worried about the actual crime itself. Superhackers had built a great many safeguards and fraud traps, and the Guardian Angels kept a detailed watch over the entire system.

The waiter unobtrusively placed a second mug of beer

on the table, hooking his finger around the handle of the empty glass and snatching it away. The Cremator fell silent until the waiter had left again. "For instance," Capek continued, "that's why you'll have to pay for this meeting today. We can't leave anything of ourselves behind. Your Mr. Nathans would be on us in a moment. He is very intelligent, and very angry. Our group's existence is too important to all people—we offer a crucial option to mankind. We can't risk being caught. Too much is at stake here."

Rodney fidgeted in the wicker chair, feeling the rough cushion prick the seat of his pants. He tried to steer the conversation back, growing nervous again, doubting that he'd get to the dentist in time after all. "What kind of barter are you talking about, exactly?"

The Cremator fingered the brim of his hat. "Occasionally we find ourselves in need of certain things, equipment, documents—I myself have a fondness for printed books. But most important, we need a pool of people as resources to buy things when we do need them." Capek swallowed the last of his espresso and placed the tiny cup upside-down on the saucer as he stood up.

"My companion will tell you some of the things you need to get for us. I've got other business right now, and it's best that we three leave at different times, in different directions." He straightened his khaki coat and replaced the black top hat on his head, tipping the brim at Rodney. "It was a pleasure meeting you, Mr. Quick. I hope we can work something out."

Rodney said "thank you" as Rossum Capek strode across the stepping-stones. Off in the café's jungled shadows filled with potted ferns, he saw the waiter pointedly not watching the Cremator leave.

Monica spoke quickly and firmly, expecting Rodney to listen. Her opaque eyes bored into him, and he took a reflexive swallow of the second beer.

"The most important thing you can get us, as soon as possible, is a liter of solution from the final resurrection bath. Preferably one of the mutated batches."

Rodney's unshaven eyebrow rose up. "How am I supposed to get that? Hey, and how do you know about the mutations?"

Monica looked sourly at him. "Don't ever be surprised by what we know or don't know. You work down in the resurrection levels. Find a way to smuggle out some solution before it all drains down the grates. Nobody will notice."

"But where should I take it?" He narrowed his eyes nervously. "How often is this sort of thing going to happen?"

"It'll happen as often as necessary." Her expression emphasized each word. "We'll send you transient messages by electronic mail, with portions of instructions. It's your body and soul we're talking about here, Mr. Quick. You don't expect it to come cheap."

Rodney hung his head sheepishly, staring into the disappearing foam on top of the beer. "No, I guess not."

The woman stood up, her tea untouched and cold, and shook her jagged page-boy hair. "Before you start complaining to yourself, think of your alternative. Do you want to be a Servant?"

Rodney felt a small glimmer of anger reawaken in him. "At least they're not worried about anything."

She whirled and glared at him with such a piercing gaze that he quickly averted his eyes and consciously drank the last of his beer. "How do you know Servants aren't worried? How do you know they don't remember anything but just can't show it?"

He couldn't respond before she splashed through the moat, ignoring the stepping-stones and getting the tops of her white boots wet. She walked off, trickling water as it beaded on the polymer surface of the boots. Rodney looked up at the skylight overhead, pulling his chair out to avoid the shadow from the patio umbrella.

"Could I get you another beer, sir?"

Rodney almost jumped as the waiter appeared at his shoulder. The taste inside his cheeks seemed to cry for another mug, and he wanted to sit and sulk. But before he could order, he suddenly remembered the cost, cringing at the café's lush—expensive—surroundings. He quickly changed his mind and waved the waiter away, sitting alone for a few moments, not eager to face the bill.

12

The tall, cylindrical headquarters of the Enforcers Guild stood like a pillar of one-way mirrors through which the Guild could see in all directions and watch over the entire world. A gray soup of clouds typical of mid-spring reflected from the Guild building, making its polished walls look like a smeared black-and-white photograph.

Jones stood out of uniform in the brisk morning air, wearing a tight black skin-shirt that made his dark flesh look the color of wood. Beside him Julia stood motionless, unaffected by the cold breeze that sent goose pimples down Jones's arm, seemingly unaware of his distraught and uncertain mood. Her loose gray jumpsuit billowed around her body; she looked like just another Servant for sale.

As they kept walking toward the mirrored building, the crowds thinned out quickly, as if pedestrians were afraid to approach the Guild headquarters. The weekend crowd was always a different sort from the everyday traffic on the streets. People wandered about shopping, frantic to get errands finished. Businessmen wore casual clothes, but remained near their own office complexes in a holding pattern, almost uncomfortable not to be at work. As always, scattered here and there, were a few of the wandering jobless blues, who probably never noticed what day of the week it was.

Jones noticed that the people on the street seemed to be avoiding him, shying away. He was used to that, the invisible prestige of the Guild that made him feel like a pariah. It saddened him to think that becoming an Enforcer had required him to sacrifice something so basic, so essential to a normal life. But then he remembered with a slight shock that today he was not wearing his armor. After a moment he understood that the people were avoiding *Julia*. This angered him, and he tentatively reached out to hold onto her wrist, as if daring someone to make an unkind comment. Couldn't they see that she was . . . she was a Servant.

Servants—just property, buying and selling, mix and match. If you don't need them anymore, just get rid of them. Jones winced, trying to swallow his guilt. That wasn't it at all. Julia would understand, if she understood anything. She gave no sign. She never did.

He entered the Guild building, with Julia tagging obediently behind. Off-hours and empty, the lobby smelled dank with disinfectant and the decontaminated residue of cigarette smoke from the smokers' lounge on Floor 2. The air carried several levels of subliminal noise, humming and hissing, static from the white-noise generator that supposedly created a more peaceful work environment. The air conditioner kept the air pumped to a just-below-comfortable temperature. He had not come to the headquarters off-hours since . . . since just after Fitzgerald Helms had died.

Now that the lobby was without other people milling about, Jones could see where too many feet had begun to crush the nap of the red dura-carpet. Overhead in the ceiling panels he could hear a repair-rat scurrying about its pre-programmed path, checking wiring, replenishing fluorescent cylinders, dissolving dust and grit. The building's directory screen had been shut off, leaving a blank gray rectangle on the wall above the two vacant desks where receptionists normally sat.

"This way, Julia." He moved quickly to the dead escalator that led to the mezzanine. He walked up the rubber-jacketed stairs that seemed frozen halfway out of sync. Julia followed.

The mezzanine level was also empty. He knew the entire building could not be deserted, and he was finally relieved to notice two other men standing together down one of the corridors, too far away to see clearly, and down another hall he noticed a Servant janitor patiently waxing a floor. Darkened cafeterias were lined up in the main lounge area of the mezzanine, even a couple of Guild-members-only bars that served drinks and sandwiches at lunchtime. A barber shop sat empty beside the rest rooms and showers; three public Net booths stood beside various potted plants in the open areas.

The one functional upper-floor lift waited at the far side of the open mezzanine area. Even though he and Julia were almost the only ones in the entire building, the lift still took almost a full minute to get back down to the mezzanine. He ushered Julia into the clonewood-paneled interior of the lift and then joined her, requesting floor 14 from the panel.

"SPECIAL ACCESS PERMISSION REQUIRED FOR UPPER-MANAGERIAL LEVELS."

Jones bent over to speak into the cloth-covered microphone patch. "I'm here to see Guildsman Drex. I have an appointment—my name is Jones, Enforcer, Class 2."

The lift door closed, sealing them in the narrow chamber; annoying easy-listening music wafted through the air as the computer electronically searched Drex's appointment calendar. The lift started to move upward, apparently satisfied that all was in order.

Jones took Julia's hand and patted it; but the hand was limp and the flesh felt cold.

He stood apart from her. Might as well begin the separation now. Jones let out a long, low breath, discouraged. He had never quite realized how strong his self-defense mechanisms of conscience and guilt had grown. He realized now—or at least he had been trying to convince himself—that he never should have purchased Julia in the first place.

Working at Resurrection, Inc., watching the way they processed the human bodies, the way they treated Servants as products—it had all made him pay attention to things he had not thought about before. Escorting Servants for hours and returning home to find Julia unmoved and silent still caused his stomach to tie in knots, raised an ugly head of guilt in front of him. He could speak to Julia and she would respond, but she would give only answers, never questions, never comments, never expressing an interest. She sat in a trance all day long; when he slept at night, she rested primly in the shadows, motionless, waiting for the daylight. No matter how hard he tried, Julia was not a friend, not a companion. It had an eeriness, an offensiveness, that Jones couldn't reconcile with himself.

He never should have gotten Julia in the first place.

Jones had placed a classified ad in the Guild's message and information transfer network. All such ads were immediately routed first to the upper-management levels, and then slowly worked their way down one level at a time as the higher echelons declined the items for sale or exchange. Rank did have its privileges.

Jones didn't know what happened to used Servants. Since a Servant's tiny battery pellet would continue to power the microprocessor for a century or so, a Servant must certainly be expected to outlive its owner. Jones couldn't believe that Servants would be destroyed (no, Resurrection, Inc. would say "deactivated" or "decommissioned") when they were no longer needed. When someone returned a Servant to the corporation, the Servant was probably reprogrammed and sent out again— who was ever to know?

But he couldn't bear the thought, even the slim possibility, of Julia—blank, mannequinlike Julia—being destroyed because he had cashed her in for a refund. Jones had no intention of making a profit. He wasn't doing this for the debt, not for the money. In fact, even after only a short month of owning her, he had decided to ask a fairly low price, less than he had paid for her.

His ad had trickled down the Guild hierarchy, finally being snapped up by a fourth-level Guildsman, Mr. Drex, still in upper management, a good owner for Julia. Drex had asked Jones to come and show him his female Servant.

Jones did not know Drex, nor had he even heard of him. But the administrative system of the Guild was so intricate and complex that few people bothered to learn of anyone in authority other than their own immediate supervisors. Jones didn't think he even knew the name, offhand, of the ultimate boss of the Guild itself, nor did he particularly care.

The lift doors slid open, and Jones quickly moved out into the black-and-white tiled upper-management levels. Everything in the Enforcers Guild was supposed to be black-and-white, he thought ironically. The managerial levels were not ornate but efficient. A few other lights supplemented the fluorescent panels set into the ceiling. The air conditioning here felt even cooler than in the lobby.

Jones stared for an instant, and then the doors of the lift slid shut behind him. Julia wasn't with him. He whirled and quickly punched the button again, opening the lift. "Come on! Don't just stand there!" He tried, and succeeded, to build up some frustrated and impatient anger to direct at her. He didn't really want to be angry at her. She couldn't help it. Would she always remember him like this?

Julia moved out and followed him dutifully. Far down

the hall a silhouette of a man waved at him. "Mr. Jones! Down here."

Jones signaled that he had heard and quickly strode off. "Julia—Command: Follow!"

He flicked glances back and forth as he passed other darkened offices; in the off-hour shadows he could see the individual offices decorated to each manager's preferences. Jones felt suddenly self-conscious, wishing he had chosen to dress in a more formal fashion. Too late now. This would be just a simple business transaction anyway.

One entire wall of the Guildsman's office was a giant, polarized plate-glass window, from which he could look out on the dizzying panorama of the city many stories below. Sunlight poured in, bright but filtered of the damaging intensity that would have caused the top of his expansive oak desk to blister and peel.

Drex stood as Jones and Julia went through the door, keeping his gaze mostly on the Servant. The Guildsman had thick salt-and-pepper hair cut squarely about his shoulders and with a geometrically precise straight cut to his bangs. The wrinkles about his eyes had been accentuated with indigo dye so that his crow's-feet looked like a blue web spreading out from where his eyelids met.

Drex wasted no time and spoke with slippery words in a cultivated, professional-manager voice. "So, Enforcer, this is your personal Servant? Julie, you said her name was?"

Testing, Jones could tell, testing. "No sir. Julia. That was her name in life, according to Resurrection, Incorporated."

"Yes, yes, I see." Jones could tell that the Guildsman was paying little attention to him.

Drex stepped from around his desk, and Jones saw that he was really quite short, standing only as high as Julia's nose and barely up to the Enforcer's shoulders. Drex looked at the Servant with probing eyes, waiting, and then turned to Jones with a slight hint of impatience in his voice.

"Well? Undress her for me, please."

Jones made no move for at least two seconds. A crease rippled the dark skin of his forehead. "Undress her? What for?"

The Guildsman scowled, and then suddenly smiled with feigned patience and understanding. He folded his hands together in front of him. "I don't mean any offense, or to make any implications about your character, Mr. Jones, but I naturally need to see that she hasn't been beaten or bruised, or is deformed in any manner."

Jones told himself that this made quite adequate sense, although the gleam in Drex's eyes made him uneasy. The Guildsman leaned back against the wooden desk, brushing aside one of his piles of hardcopy as he watched.

Feeling uncomfortable and filled with distaste, Jones quickly undid the front of Julia's gray jumpsuit. He blinked and his eyes went blurry with shame. He didn't want to know if they were tears. Julia didn't move until Jones muttered under his breath, "Help me, please." With the slightest of motions the Servant shrugged out of the jumpsuit and Jones tugged it down her body, letting it drop to the floor.

Drex stood up, smoothed the back of his trousers with a brush of his palm, and took one step forward to stare at Julia. Even though the light streaming through the plate-glass window left no shadows in the room, he squinted his eyes, making the indigo-dyed crow's-feet clench together.

The Enforcer swallowed awkwardly and stepped back, trying to hide as Drex slowly paced around Julia.

Her skin was pallid but smooth; her eyes had a great, blank, innocent look to them. The Guildsman bent closer to look at her fist-sized breasts tipped with pale bloodless nipples, the naked and hairless folds between her legs, the curves of her buttocks.

He made a little humming noise of satisfaction, but Jones was taken by surprise when the Guildsman suddenly turned and addressed him. "All right then, Enforcer, why are you trying to get rid of her?"

Jones felt cornered, trapped, and out of self-defense he spoke plainly, "I guess I don't need a Servant after all. I've had her only for a few weeks and I, I just . . . it was different than I thought. I work at Resurrection, Incorporated, you know, escorting the other Servants and . . . if I may speak openly, sir, I just didn't want her anymore."

Drex nodded and absently ran his spread fingers through the thick black/gray strands of hair, but the resilient and perfectly straight bangs immediately fell back into place.

"Very well, Enforcer. I'll take her. At the price you ask." He looked up and motioned to the console at the side of his desk. "Please logon, enter your password, and I'll transfer into your account. Do you mind if I have the Guardian Angels check your title to this Servant?"

"No, of course not. It's clear."

As they transferred the money, Jones felt a heaviness sink deeper and deeper into his chest, but the momentum of the transaction pushed him along and he tried not to think, following only the instructions second by second as they happened. Finally he swallowed and was surprised to find how dry his throat was.

He stood before the Servant and said, "Julia, Guildsman Drex is now your master. You have to obey him just like you would obey me."

"Thank you, Enforcer. That was nice." Drex smiled, sincerely this time. "It's been a pleasure doing business with you." His tone had a certain dismissal to it.

Jones hesitated a moment, looked searchingly at Julia's eyes, but again he saw nothing. "Good-bye, Julia," he said, finding his voice hoarse. She made no response.

"Thank you, Enforcer," Drex repeated, punctuating his words with an impatient finger tapping on the desktop. Jones had no choice but to leave.

Julia didn't turn as he walked out the door.

13

"Danal!"

The Servant looked up as Van Ryman's voice reverberated through the intercom system. Danal stopped his vigorous polishing of the stair railing and quickly ran down the carpeted stairs with precise control of his feet, making almost no sound.

He paused as the locked door under the stairs called out to him again, yanking at his puppet strings of dreaded curiosity. But he pushed past it and into the study, where his Master Van Ryman was waiting.

Van Ryman's face changed immediately upon seeing Danal. He looked up from the scattered books and papers on the rolltop desk against one wall of the study. The French windows were open, letting a cool breeze in; Danal could hear the faint hum of the Intruder Defense field surrounding the house. The fireplace had been shut off, and only the overhead lights illuminated the room.

Van Ryman carelessly rolled and folded several ancient-looking scrolls, charts with planetary signs, constellations, and other symbols. His eyes were bright but bloodshot, and he had not shaved, giving the impression that he had slept little.

Sometimes Van Ryman looked at Danal in awe or in worshipful expectation; at other times his eyes seemed to have a wistful look, a loving expression; and yet in contradictory moments, he looked at Danal with scorn and distaste. It was as if Van Ryman were seeing three totally different people.

"Ah, Danal," he said and wiped both of his hands on his shirt, sitting back. "Please make me some tea. Red hibiscus, I think—I'm in the mood for something . . . bitter. And hurry—when you come back I'm going to have a *very* important mission for you."

He paused and looked up at Danal for emphasis, "This will probably be the most important thing that either one of us has ever done." Van Ryman quickly bent back to his documents.

Danal acknowledged the orders and went into the kitchen area. The white tile and stainless steel glistened from his thorough cleaning the day before. Sometimes he suspected that Van Ryman saddled him with tedious and trivial cleaning jobs just to keep him occupied, making a good show of needing a Servant.

Danal dispensed a small Pyrex beaker of water and slipped it into the insulated heating chamber; a moment later he used the beaker's handle pads to lift the boiling water out. Turning to the small tea cabinet, he selected the drawer filled with hibiscus blend and removed a small amount by hand. As the strainer slowly sank to the bottom of the beaker, Danal watched as the hibiscus petals caused a bright scarlet color to seep into the water, red like foaming arterial blood.

Blood.
Bright red.
Steaming under the light of black-wax candles and torches.
Echoing chants like thunder.

The flicker built in his mind, thrumming. Sparks of fragmented visions came and went in front of his eyes, each like a miniature nova.

He paused, cradling the fragile webwork of the oncoming memories, terrified of the revelation and too frightened to hold it back. He suddenly jerked his head upward, gritting his teeth, trying to keep control of his identity. He forced himself to pick up the beaker and pour the bright red tea into a thin porcelain cup.

But a different force grabbed hold of his mind, relentlessly cracking open his buried thoughts like a cruel stepfather throwing skeletons out of the closet. Danal moved like an automaton as he reached forward to the knife rack embedded into the wall. He seemed to be straining against a rubbery nightmare, reaching forward, groping to run away from his past.

He removed one of the wide kitchen knives from its whet-slot and held it out gingerly, staring at it in blank-eyed horror as visions caught themselves on the glint of the blade and exploded in a panorama of dark ritual in front of his mind's eye.

The kitchen knife became a sacrificial knife held in his hands. Runes and symbols had been electrostatically etched on the stainless-steel blade. He saw robes—white, scarlet, black. He heard the chants, synchronous, nonsensical, augmented by the microspeakers hidden in the ceiling of the yawning sacrificial grotto.

Rah hyuun!
Rah hyuun!
Rah hyuun!

But it was like he was on both sides of the mirror, both priest and victim. Holding the knife and wearing the black robes of a High Priest, he stared down at the naked and bound form on the altar stone.

And also, but what seemed to be a different time: He looked up, straining against the bonds, the sacrificial victim, feeling the cold from the engraved concrete of the altar biting into his back. The wide blade of a rune-carved knife rose up, catching torchlight on its tip.

But then a switch again, from the point of view of the High Priest: The hilt, made of simulated human bone, felt dry against his uncallused fingertips. He brought the knife down. He watched the victim as bright, foamy arterial blood sprayed upward, scarlet, like thick hibiscus tea.

Rah hyuun!
Rah hyuun!

Victim: He didn't feel the tip of the sacrificial knife pierce his chest. The chant filled his head, filled all the heavens. A brilliant blackness exploded outward simultaneously from his heart and brain. . . .

And Danal found himself fallen on the kitchen floor, like a survivor cast free from the wreckage of a ship. The thin teacup still wobbled on the counter where he had abruptly released it, but it hadn't spilled.

The colors, the vibrant pain, the growing confusion and uneasiness about his former life, all made Danal reel. The thick scar in the center of his chest throbbed in remembered pain.

The Servant stepped up the workings of his microprocessor until subjective time had almost stopped; in his own time frame he spent the equivalent of half an hour composing himself, calming his responses, searching for answers—or at least to hide from them. . . .

Returning to the surrounding world, Danal balanced the

smooth cup on a saucer. Walking with a methodical gait in his slow-time that allowed him to keep careful poise, the Servant left the kitchen, returning to the study. Van Ryman had rolled the top down on his desk, locking it. He sat in the overstuffed chair, watching Danal come in with the tea. The dark-haired man rubbed his hands together.

"Your tea, Master Van Ryman." The Servant extended the cup forward; in an offhanded way Van Ryman gestured for him to set it on a small end table instead. The man did not seem to have noticed any additional delay caused by Danal's flashback.

"Please turn on the fireplace, Danal. But leave the heat off."

"Yes, Master Van Ryman." The Servant felt under the mantel of the fireplace until he found a pair of switches. He flicked the outer switch, and purple light flashed down, scattered from the quartz crystals and the mirrored panels of the hearth, and sent a scintillating violet glow about the room.

Danal hesitated under the oceanscape hologram, but he forced himself to look away, terrified that he might have yet another explosion of visions.

Van Ryman took one sip of his tea, grimaced at its tartness, and then smiled in satisfaction. "Now then, Danal, for the errand I mentioned. I want you to return to Resurrection, Incorporated. You have an appointment to meet with Francois Nathans, in person. He's very interested in your well-being." He allowed himself a slight smile. "And in our success. He's eagerly expecting you." Van Ryman rubbed the palms of his hands together vigorously, and once again Danal felt that something was terribly out of place, even deeper than the Master's out-of-place eyes.

"Will I be escorted, Master Van Ryman?"

"No!" Van Ryman responded. "You have to do this alone. Your own actions are very important. You won't understand now, but if everything works out as it should . . . well, we'll see."

Van Ryman stood up, leaving his tea almost untouched, and went over to the rolltop desk. He produced a key from a leather thong around his neck and twisted open the desk's catch, sliding up the oak slats and revealing the scrolls and books crammed into the desk cavity. He rustled through the papers until he yanked one out of the stack.

"I'll let you in on a secret, Danal. Listen to this, from The Writings." He ran his finger down the handwritten pages, ticking off several items.

"You are Danal. Danal, the Messenger. You are the Prophet. You are the Bringer of Change and the Fulfiller of Promises. You are the Stranger whom everyone knows. You are the Awakener and the Awakened. You are the Destroyer. Our hope rests in your future."

Van Ryman closed his eyes for a moment, then quickly came back to himself, pushing the paper inside the desk and slamming down the desktop again so that it locked by itself.

"Come with me, Danal. We need to prepare you."

Uneasy and baffled by what Van Ryman had said, the Servant followed him into the foyer. Destroyer? Bringer of Change? Neo-Satanist ritualistic babble—it meant nothing to him. He wished now that he had taken some time alone in the house to look at the documents, to familiarize himself with the theology that his Master Van Ryman took so seriously.

But the last flashback gnawed at him: the sacrifice, the pain, the excitement—and he found himself afraid to unearth any more.

Van Ryman opened the doors of a narrow coffinlike closet in the front hallway. He withdrew a beige trenchcoat with slate-colored lining and shook it out before extending it to Danal.

"Here, you'll have to wear this. A Servant walking alone in the streets will look too . . . vulnerable."

Danal passively took the jacket and slipped it over his jumpsuit. The cloth felt stiff and alien, encasing him in something which, as a Servant, he felt he should not wear. Unconsciously he slipped his hands into the deep pockets.

Van Ryman took two small objects from a shelf in the closet. "By disguising you, Danal, we should be able to throw any suspicious people completely off the track. You'll be much safer this way."

He placed a thin stencil template of an inverted star-in-pentagram on Danal's forehead and sprayed red grease-paint with an airbrush. The mark stood out brightly on his skin.

The Servant felt uncomfortable and frightened, but he

could not refuse his Master's direct wishes. This seemed to be too carefully planned, too well rehearsed.

"There, much better! Now you're marked as a neo-Satanist—you should be all right. They can still tell you're a Servant by your skin, but only if they look." Van Ryman glanced at the stenciled star-in-pentagram. "You'll need to wear a hat, too."

From the depths of the closet the dark-haired man produced a fuzzy black stocking cap that slid neatly over Danal's smooth scalp but left the red pentagram showing clearly against his forehead.

Danal felt like a mannequin, a toy that was about to be wound up and set on a course he had no choice but to follow. Van Ryman moved with an intensity, captivated and involved in the game, filled with eagerness overlying an anxious dread.

Danal waited passively as Van Ryman opened the door of his Intruder Defense control room. Switches and panels and surveillance video screens glittered and glowed.

"Danal, you know how to get to Resurrection from here, don't you?"

"Yes," he replied. A detailed map of the entire Metroplex had been burned into his microprocessor.

Van Ryman seemed to be only half listening. "Good." He quickly punched some keys on one of the already logged-on terminals, establishing a direct communications link with Francois Nathans. Danal tried not to listen.

"He's coming. You'd better get ready," he said to the screen. The voice receptor picked up his words, encoded them, and transmitted the message directly to Nathans's electronic address. "This is the trigger moment we've all been waiting for."

Van Ryman turned to Danal. "Open the front door."

The Servant did. Mid-morning sunlight entered the foyer, illuminating the dark shadows inside. He could see the black textured concrete of Van Ryman's walkway extending to the public sidewalk, and from there to the streets and the people and the entire city—people who hated Servants and, he recalled uneasily, who disliked neo-Satanists as well.

Danal could barely see the hazy hemisphere of ionized air indicating the Intruder Defense field near the boundaries of Van Ryman's property. Van Ryman fiddled with the controls and without looking up announced, "Go now, Danal. I've opened the door field. I'll be watching and ready when you come back."

"Yes, Master Van Ryman." Indeed he did see a portion of the blurred air become fully transparent again as the deadly field was reshaped in a small area, enough to let him pass through.

"Danal." Van Ryman came to the porch to see him. He hung onto his words breathlessly. In the slanted sunlight the Servant could see the line of faint pinprick scars on his Master's face and jawline. "Good luck."

Danal stepped out, began to walk, and kept walking, feeling paradoxically naked in his neo-Satanist disguise, uneasily vulnerable and trapped.

Alone, he tried to sidestep the psychological battlefield of the streets. As he walked, the mansion fell behind him, with all its gables and towers and its too polished gargoyles. He felt like a walking time bomb, the jagged tip of an iceberg thrusting itself upward from his past.

You are Danal. Danal, the Messenger. You are the Prophet.

He walked purposefully, knowing Van Ryman would be watching through his monitors until he was out of range. He let the streets swallow him up. Conflicting emotions and confusion made his heart heavy. As a Servant, he had already felt the latent antagonism of the people, but now, marked with the sign of the neo-Satanists, he could feel even more clearly the angry, disgusted stares of the crowd.

You are the Bringer of Change and the Fulfiller of Promises.

Danal wondered if the protection supposedly offered by the pentagram mark on his forehead was worth the wrenching, disconnected feelings in his stomach. He felt no wonder and awe at the streets' varied impressions. The pedestrians' quick glances and muttered obscenities were also laced with fear. He was *not* one of the Satan worshippers

not any more!

Near Resurrection, Inc. he stood as if hypnotized, staring into the feathered surface of the pool surrounding a splashing fountain. Warm salt water gushed from ornate, abstractly phallic orifices. Overhead, a pair of out-of-place seagulls floated on thermal currents, searching for garbage that someone might drop into the fountain. Prominently painted on the concrete lip around the pool were the words, "DO NOT DRINK."

You are the Stranger whom everyone knows.

Danal stood as fine droplets of mist from the fountain splattered against his polymer trenchcoat. He shouldn't be hesitating. He shouldn't be stopping. But then, he shouldn't be uneasy either—as a Servant, he had been given clear-cut instructions; he should have been concerned only with following them.

You are the Awakener and the Awakened.

In truth, Van Ryman had not told him to keep the pentagram, had not Commanded him to continue wearing the disguise at all. Danal understood what the Master had implied, but without the binding Command phrase, a Servant was free to interpret orders as he wished. Danal continued to rationalize to himself, thinking rapidly, trying not to wait too long by the fountain before someone might become suspicious.

You are the Destroyer.

On impulse he splashed water on his forehead and scrubbed with the corner of his trenchcoat, staining the cloth a greasy red. He tossed the sopping black stocking cap into the water and it slowly sank to the bottom. He leaned over the fountain to see his reflection. The mark was gone.

He felt as if he had cast one of the leering gargoyles off his back.

14

Supervisor began by playing the second movement of Beethoven's Symphony No. 7, selecting it from the Net library of music and setting the piece on auto-repeat. The slow, quiet beginning drifted out from the thin band of microspeakers at waist level around the room. She used the keypad tattooed on her palm to activate the implanted speakers in her head, hooking her mind up to the direct electronic translation of the music.

She closed her thick eyelids, reveling in the pure digitized tones, receiving the *real* music from the inside in an ecstatic experience that few other people could ever have. She allowed herself to savor music in private, where no one else could see her. The somber andante tempo set the mood for her search.

In further preparation, Supervisor removed her sleeveless purple tunic and neatly placed it on the meditating chair. Standing naked, she undid her three equal braids, brushing the bluish-blond hair out into a fine web that sent stray strands drifting with leftover static electricity. She would never admit the apartment was too empty, too lonely; with all The Net for company, no Interface should ever get lonely.

Supervisor took the wand, laying an impedance path from the wall's power plate along the floor to the center of the room, where she would be sitting. She lit incense, then switched off all the lights, leaving only darkness except for a dim red glow from the photo-receptive mood specks painted on the wall.

Supervisor arranged her stocky body in a lotus position on the floor, sitting in the center of the impedance path. She could feel the pleasant pressure of the neutral-textured carpet against her buttocks. The temperature in the room was perfect. She controlled her breathing and listened to the music for a few minutes, closing her eyes, washing away all barriers. Then she brushed her fingertips against the keyboard on her palm, logging onto the computer network.

In the back of her mind Supervisor had already begun to formulate a strategy for her search. The Cremators. The information must exist somewhere on The Net. She decided to find them, expose them. The problem would occupy her entire mind, her entire body, and she would be taken away from this . . . triviality. Supervisor would once again prove her incredible worth to Resurrection, Inc.

Of course, she chose to seek out the Cremators for the sheer challenge rather than out of any sense of duty to the corporation. Life presented so few challenges. She savored the tingle of excitement that skittered along her spine.

Personally, Supervisor didn't care about what the Cremators did; moral qualms were for weaker people who had no interest in seeing the greater universe. Resurrection, Inc., with its power and visibility, balked at the resistance of anyone opposing their operations; the Cremators fought for another way of existence, with a philosophy perpendicular to that of the corporation. And, regardless of any objective assessment of their motives, Supervisor had a deep admiration for the Cremators' ability to elude all the intense searches for so long.

Francois Nathans had used his best hackers and database jockeys, but no matter how talented they were, they still suffered under the handicap of being only human. An Interface was really the only appropriate person to conduct such a search.

Supervisor generally regarded normal humans with a semi-tolerant distaste. She recognized that though they might strain themselves to the limit, they were still bound by the vulnerabilities and unpredictabilities of a biological organism; they could not possibly have the speed, the reliability, the framework of logic, or the breadth of experience of an Interface.

Since her rigidly conditioned childhood, Supervisor had given up all fleshly pleasures—not just sex but also mundane personal contact, the visual stimulation of sightseeing around the Metroplex, and the joys of eating. She saw the latter as only a means of taking in energy, although occasionally in private she did allow herself the detachment necessary to enjoy the art of well-prepared foods and carefully blended liqueurs. She found it infinitely more pleasurable to be floating in the Network, tunneling down different avenues of data, sorting through bright information that she didn't even have to remember because she could access it again anytime she wanted.

Some humans did have the right idea, though it was far too late for them to ever become a true Interface like herself. Rodney Quick, for instance, was a capable human; he knew how to use The Net. She didn't dislike him—in fact, he flattered her with his ridiculous fear of her authority. Almost unconsciously, she had responded to his fear by making herself dictatorial and intimidating. As another challenge, she had decided to push her powers to the limit, to do what Rodney seemed to expect of her, to destroy him as efficiently and as intricately as she could.

Supervisor had no active malice in mind, because malice was a human thing. But Rodney's occasional "Quickening" of the female Servants late in his shift showed that he was still too closely concerned with physical stimuli.

Supervisor had run three other people into the ground, setting her nets and slowly drawing them tighter. A game, intricate and challenging, and ultimately satisfying. Normal humans would consider this to be cruel and malicious, but she recognized her need as perhaps a misguided backlash from her own exotic childhood; other humans had normal aggression-dampening routines, beating on people, picking on things, pulling the wings off of flies.

By causing Rodney Quick's death and resurrecting him as a Servant, she would in a way be bringing him one step closer to the ideal. If only the resurrection process weren't so flawed. If planting the microprocessor in Rodney's brain would order his thoughts and physical actions, make them more easily controlled by the person himself, then this could only be a step in the right direction. However, after seeing some of the Servants walk out like mannequins, she thought the process had overshot the mark and developed something more machine than human. Unlike the perfect amalgam that she herself was.

The Net accepted her logon, and she felt her consciousness link up with the stream of information. The various directories stood like vast gateways in front of her, each leading down an infinite hallway of mirrored doors. Every directory was like a separate museum of knowledge, with more facts than any single mind could hold.

Supervisor had left her tangible body behind, and she

knew that if she could bend back and look at her Net-self, she would see only a blurred locus of incandescent light that moved down different datapaths. This was home. This was peace.

She had experienced The Net many times before and needed only a moment to reorient herself to her new physical state. With all the energy of The Net to draw on, with the secondary power pouring into her body through the impedance path from the power plates on the wall, she had no risk of becoming tired.

She began her search.

As an Interface, Supervisor had the ability to move down any path without the hindrance of passwords, able to go up and down, in and out, digging into any file she required.

She started by assimilating all the pre-Servants known to be missing—the known Cremator successes—and then she used a complex routine to unearth all past records about them. The previous data activity of a deceased person remained accessible only for a certain time before it was erased or stored on a separate omnidisk. Dumping the data into an open-ended file, she activated another routine to correlate all the information, searching for parallels.

Supervisor spun down other paths as the sifting routine churned away behind her. She moved into the Enforcer log files of corpses found during routine duty, and then cross-checked those names to make certain every cadaver had actually been delivered to Resurrection, Inc.; some names had likewise disappeared in between lists, and she dumped them into the growing file behind her. Third, she checked The Net's master death record, scanning the obituary files and collating them with the first two lists, looking for other names that had disappeared along the way.

The growing number of sub-files churned through cross-checking routines that spit out the coincidental occurrences, leaving only the genuine anomalies. Supervisor began to grow alarmed—she doubted if even Francois Nathans suspected the scope of the Cremators' involvement.

She folded herself back to the output end of her processing file, searching the missing persons' outgoing electronic-mail files. The computer started storing and assimilating and correlating all the information, looking for common pathways, common messages sent.

Every one of the names had been searching through The Net for the Cremators, some with real skill and imagination, others with almost pathetic clumsiness. But somehow they had all found their target. In less than a second Supervisor scanned the paths of all the outgoing messages, frustrated to find that none of them led anywhere. They were all blind attempts to contact someone, anyone: vigorous database searches, or just short letters doggedly sent out to "The Cremators" over and over again.

Then, changing her plan of attack, she began a backlash routine to go over the files again, this time searching for common messages received. With a large enough control sample taken from other random people on The Net, she was quickly able to eliminate the spurious messages, the mass mailings that everyone received.

After several iterations she found one thing, one message they had all received and all deleted; it came from the same electronic address. She used a grave-digger routine to unearth the original message, but was able to gather only selected pieces of the text. It seemed innocuous enough, a simple business advertisement about a mapmaking and demographic-studies consulting firm. She flashed down another data corridor, trying to reference the firm's control number, and found that the company did not exist.

Mercator.

Cremator.

She tunneled down the return path of the deleted messages, elated with the challenge, the possibility of success. Along the way she encountered several dead ends, false cross-links, booby-traps that would have been successful against even the best superhacker. But she was an Interface. She made it through to the home directory.

And she found the Cremators.

All of the information had been hidden from her before, and in awe Supervisor scanned the deepest secrets of the Cremators. In growing horror she found information that amazed her, made her feel like an idiot for not suspecting—

Supervisor turned to flee in triumph, but found suddenly that the electronic gateways, the datapaths ahead of her, began shutting down one by one. She could feel the influence of other Interfaces, different from any she had ever encountered before, nearly unreal minds that almost never left The Net. They had hidden themselves in the forest of files and directories, like predators waiting for her. As they moved forward, she could see their electronic identities, blurred formless things of bright colors, moving in ambush around her.

The gateways closed on all sides, closer and closer. United, the other Interfaces were infinitely stronger, and Supervisor could not break through. She could see the knowledge of the Cremators all around her and was trapped by it. Although she battered her consciousness against the barriers, they became stronger and stronger, as her fear and helplessness grew.

More and more interlocks were placed around her as the other Interfaces rerouted the datapaths. For the first time in her memory, Supervisor was severed from The Net, trapped inside, completely isolated on a data island. Her incorporeal form had no voice with which to shout for help. And there was no possible way for her to get out, ever. . . .

Back in the apartment, Beethoven's Symphony No. 7 automatically stopped, rewound, then repeated itself again and again and again.

15

The mammoth headquarters of Resurrection, Inc. rose like an incredible barrier in front of Danal. Still hiding his Servant identity with the beige trenchcoat, he looked at the building in brooding awe.

Other people milled about, but most of them moved hurriedly toward the enclosed plazas as an early spring rain started to fall. The Servant stood oblivious, but conscious of every droplet of water striking his skin.

". . . return to Resurrection, Incorporated . . . meet with Francois Nathans . . ."

Danal walked toward the nearest transplastic revolving door, the entrance for workers and visitors.

"He's eagerly expecting you."

Danal pushed his way through the door, grasping the long brass handle as if he were a pallbearer. He had been here before. This place had given him a second birth, but he remembered nothing else about it. He had been brought in at night, through a different door, probably with a shipment of other corpses, processed and turned into what he was now. But the techs had not been thorough enough. Too many stains of his past life remained, coming back to haunt him in incomprehensible flashes and painful knives of memory.

Danal wondered if the techs could purge his brain again, start him over fresh and clean and untainted. But for some reason he found that prospect more frightening than just learning to live with his past, to live with the shadow of a person he had once been.

As he entered the carpeted lobby Danal saw the main receptionist sitting behind a glossy black landscape of her acrylic desktop, tapping with impossibly long fingernails on a keyboard. Her eyes were a cool purplish color from her mood-responsive contact lenses.

He shrugged off his trenchcoat and stood exposed as a Servant in his gray uniform. The receptionist looked up, mildly surprised at the audacity of his disguise, but then she seemed to recognize that no Servant could have done such a thing by himself.

Danal's voice sounded dry and lifeless to his own ears. "My Master Van Ryman instructed me to come here. I am to see Mr. Francois Nathans."

This is the trigger moment we've all been waiting for.

The receptionist turned away, ignoring him completely as she spoke into an intercom port. "He's here, Mr. Nathans."

Danal heard no response, but the receptionist seemed to acknowledge something. She looked coolly at him again, but this time her eyes were brown. "Take the fourth lift on the right. That's a direct line down to Mr. Nathans' main office. Command: Go."

Before Danal could say anything, his Servant programming took control and sent his feet moving toward the indicated lift. In the back of his mind Danal resented her use of the Command phrase, which locked him out of any discretion whatsoever. He had obviously shown himself to be reasonably independent just by coming here alone; the shackling phrase relegated him to the status of a puppet, and she could have seen that she didn't need to use it.

As Danal moved away, the receptionist stretched out her arm to take the dripping polymer trenchcoat from him. He had no choice but to let her have it. He didn't know if she was keeping it for him, or just making certain that he couldn't drip rainwater in Nathans's office . . . or maybe she was stripping him of something that could hide his identity as a Servant.

The dampness on Danal's pale scalp and face dried quickly, and his gray jumpsuit had already volatilized most of the moisture in the fabric. Danal hoped his Master Van Ryman would not notice he had lost the black stocking cap. He didn't want to explain what he had done.

The special lift doors opened automatically for him as he approached. The doors waited like an open mouth with the fangs cleverly hidden.

The doors hissed shut, and the lift obeyed his voice command, suddenly plunging downward, deep below ground level to the main offices of Francois Nathans. The lift didn't seem to distinguish between the words of Servants and those of humans. After a moment Danal stepped out, dizzy but reorienting himself quickly.

The corridors felt dim and cold from the heavy air conditioning; a high humidity level and a faint musty smell made the place seem dank. Ahead of him a wide double door of walnut-attribute clonewood stood partly open, inviting. He took one step out of the elevator and the doors closed behind him. Listening, he could hear the whirring machinery as the lift chamber reset itself back to the main lobby level.

The Servant moved to the door of the office, stepping silently on the thick maroon carpet, though he knew that Nathans must have heard the arrival of the lift. He placed one hand on the brass handle of the heavy door, pulling it open wide enough to admit himself. Some instinct warned him not to knock. He could feel shadows around him, an oppressiveness, as if he were deep below the Earth's crust.

His nerve ends tingled with a handful of invisible needles. His mouth felt dry and tasted like metal. Warning bells sounded in his mind, but he took a quick, cold breath and steeled himself, tensing his muscles to keep the mental turmoil trapped within.

Something was going to happen.

He felt like a rubber band stretched to the breaking point.

Danal stepped into the chamber. "I'm here, Mr. Nathans."

In an eye blink he saw all the baroque furniture, the tapestries, the faint illumination from thick black candles on the desk, the bookshelves, the reception table. A thick plate-glass window showed murky water on the other side, with large and small fish swimming in shadowy shapes out to the limits of visibility; Danal didn't know if Nathans had had a large aquarium installed, or if they were indeed under the water of the Bay.

His eyes locked on Nathans, who was off in a corner hastily donning an embroidered white robe. Though Nathans's back was turned, Danal could see he was short and bald, with real rubies implanted decoratively on his naked scalp. Nathans turned to show his face and smiled thinly at Danal, but the smile seemed directed inward.

"Welcome, Sacrificial Lamb," Nathans gloated.

He made the neo-Satanist sign of the broken cross.

The juggernaut of memories buried beneath Danal's

thin Servant facade exploded, suddenly becoming a raging black monster lunging to the end of its chain . . . and the chain snapped. Using the blurred reflexes from his microprocessor-enhanced brain, Danal leaped forward, unable to control his reflexive fury.

Nathans!
Satanist!
Schemer, murderer!

He hated this man, loathed him with a passion strong enough to transcend death. Danal's Servant identity scrabbled to regain control, but his former self was too strong, too murderous. The Servant's arms shot out with his hands rigid and his fingers extended together like wooden stakes.

His resurrected mind, the other Danal, meant to strangle Francois Nathans, but his hands moved in such a blur of speed that they plunged through the skin of the bald man's neck as if it were cheese and snapped his spinal column, wrenching the exposed vertebrae out of place. He withdrew almost before the blood began to gush out.

Even viewed through the microprocessor's slow-time, the universe seemed to stop for an instant, poised on the tip of the blade before plunging down into disaster.

Immediately Danal realized what he had done.

Nathans did not seem to comprehend that his life was ended, and continued to smile for a brief instant before an expression of shock dropped onto his face.

Danal stared in horror, and finally blood spurted on his uniform. Then the bald man lurched forward, as if trying to grapple with Danal, caught his shoulder but could not hold on, and slid down the Servant's chest to the floor. A long scarlet smear emblazoned the gray jumpsuit.

Danal's throat was as dry as paper, and he stumbled back, gaping at Nathans as he fell. Shadows across the aquarium window seemd to grow larger, pounding to get in; then Danal realized the pounding was in his temples.

He had broken the most fundamental Servant programming.

His chest throbbed with fire, as if from a cold sacrificial knife. He could feel the long scar on his breastbone writhing like a dangerous worm.

Nathans lay on his face in a puddle of blood that was

already disappearing as the dirt- and lint-destroying enzymes in the carpet fought to clean up the mess. Danal saw the intricate stars, pentagrams, and astrological symbols embroidered on the white robe.

"Sacrificial Lamb."

Just who was the victim after all?

Lulled by a false sense of privacy as the lift doors enclosed him, Rodney caught himself whistling an aimless tune. He stopped, then smiled, then grinned, as he realized that he had been almost happy for the last couple of days. He kept warning himself not to get his hopes up, yet another part kept reminding him that this was the first hope he'd had in a long time.

Supervisor had not shown herself for three days.

By the end of the second day Rodney had been jumpy, edgy, fearing some trick, some trap. But now, after several shifts all alone, at peace, unharassed, able to do his job in Lower Level Six, he began to fantasize that perhaps Supervisor had been reassigned.

The tech began to remember, and unconsciously embellish, everything that Francois Nathans had told him: the commendations, the praise for work well done. Rodney hoped that, since he had confessed his fear of Supervisor, perhaps Nathans had done something about it.

On Lower Level Six the pre-Servants floated in their vats, the operations continued, and Rodney felt himself starting to open his eyes again. He looked for details in things instead of only shadows. He began to smile and even whistle. He took delight and amazement in everyday objects he had not noticed for years.

Rodney wondered if this was sort of a reverse love, feeling so incredibly happy when someone else was *not* around.

Now he had decided to take Francois Nathans up on his standing invitation to "drop in whenever you like," to find out for himself exactly what had happened with Supervisor, to learn if his happiness should indeed be genuine or if it was only a fluke, a brief pause before the nightmare began again.

After the lift doors closed, and before the inane music could begin, Rodney spoke into the input speaker, "Lower main administrative offices. Francois Nathans, please."

The lift requested his identity, and he spoke his name and entered his Net password. The terminal made no response until the elevator chamber obediently plunged downward.

If Supervisor was indeed gone, by some miracle, and if his life continued with the giddy lightheartedness that he was experiencing now, Rodney began to think seriously of perhaps rescinding his contract with the Cremators.

Within two days he had already purchased for them some ropewire, some spotlight bulbs, and a piece for an antique generator that burned hydrocarbon fuel. He had had to ransack the lists of technocollectors in order to find someone willing to sell him, even at an exorbitant price, the old flywheel.

Overall, the cost of the items had not amounted to much, and certainly not as much as he had expected to pay the Cremators. But he didn't know how much longer it would last, how often they would request that he make these "little" purchases.

The worst one had been smuggling out a liter jar of the lukewarm, pinkish amniotic solution from a mutated batch. In a carefully rinsed soft-drink container he had caught some of the draining solution, then sealed it in a vacuum-flask. Nervous all the time, convinced that Supervisor was watching, that she would catch him at his theft. What if Supervisor was in some way connected with the Cremators, and she knew what he was doing all along? How did he even know that Rossum Capek represented the real Cremators?

But if he let himself believe that, he had no hope left in the world.

Rodney received his messages by electronic mail, and they were deleted as soon as he read them. He had to pay attention, or else he might not be able to remember the details of what he was supposed to do. And if he screwed up, he didn't know how many chances the Cremators would give him.

He had never again seen Rossum Capek, or Monica, or even the same representative twice. He always delivered his purchases to a different place, but everything always went smoothly.

"If I need to get in touch with you," he had once demanded, "how will I be able to find you?"

"We'll know if you need us," answered the Cremator, a freckle-faced twelve-year-old boy. "And if we don't know, you don't really need us."

Somehow it all seemed a little spooky.

As the lift doors split open and he almost stumbled out onto the private offices of Francois Nathans, Rodney Quick swallowed, looking for some saliva in his dry throat. He puffed up his determination again, knowing that he was going to find out what was going on, one way or another. Who the hell did Supervisor think she was?

And then he had no time for anything else as a Servant exploded toward him. He saw a splash of blood on the uniform; he saw a crumpled, white-robed body—Nathans!—lying on the floor in a liquid pool of deeper maroon on the carpet.

As his jaw slowly dropped in awe, Rodney saw the door burst open. In one infinite moment he saw finger-wide indentations of crushed and splintered wood from the Servant's grasp as the gray-clad figure pushed the door open and came lunging toward the lift.

Rodney was in the way.

A Servant? A Servant!

Rodney realized too late that he should move, that he should run. The Servant was somehow out of control.

Almost distractedly the Servant tossed him aside with unheeded strength, heaving him back against the far wall. But everything was so incredibly fast—no one could move that fast.

Rodney slammed into the wall with the force of an avalanche. His nerves surrendered before he could feel the explosions of pain, but he heard a multitude of bones crack and shatter like popcorn in a furnace.

Rodney suddenly saw that he had fallen on the floor, pooled up like torn rags in the corner of the lift. His eyes seemed to be filling with blood from the inside. He was able to catch a frozen snapshot of the Servant's face looking down at him with an expression of total disbelief and horror.

Rodney realized, without a doubt, that he was a dead man. He had been prepared for death for a long enough time, but then an almost limitless despair opened up below him—of all places, he was going to die in the tightest administration levels of Resurrection, Inc. Before he lost complete nerve control of his facial muscles, they formed themselves into a last mask of sorrow.

There was no way in the universe that the Cremators would ever get hold of his body now.

As the technician fell, sliding to the ground with his neck and the back of his head crushed against the wall, Danal finally wrenched the wild horses of his old self to a halt, quelling further rampage. Tears seeped into his eyes even before the tech had come to a rest on the floor.

' He hadn't meant to do it. It was an accident. He wasn't able to stop himself. He had lost control and the demons had escaped.

Francois Nathans was slaughtered, but Nathans had intentionally unleashed something buried within Danal, recklessly playing with a deadly weapon. But the tech had simply stood in the way at the wrong moment, before Danal could get a grip on his accelerated reflexes, on the juggernaut within him. Danal had only meant to brush him aside, just to knock him out of the way.

What good were apologies now?

Before the tears could blur his vision, Danal picked up Rodney Quick's broken body and carried it like a doll into Nathans's office. Gently he lay the tech on the sofa and straightened his arms. Blood seeped from the back of his head into the red crushed velvet of the arm rest.

Danal recognized him as the technician who had been present at his awakening down on Lower Level Six, and felt a deeper sadness. Rodney Quick.

"I'm sorry I can't do anything else for you," he said in a whisper. "I'm sorry."

The Servant lurched blindly into the lift without looking back and mumbled for the elevator to take him back to the lobby. He stared at his sticky hands, and his face went slack. Even with stepped-up thinking, he couldn't resolve his questions, his contradictions, his suspicions.

Who was he, really?

His ingrained Servant conditioning almost shorted itself out in an utter failure to comprehend. The dark personality submerged beneath Danal's outer skin had broken through his Servant identity, leaving him helpless, overriding his real wishes. The most terrifying part was that it had been so easy—Danal had been helpless to stop it from happening.

Was this what he had wanted to know? Did he want to remember who the original Danal had been? What type of person could be capable of such abominable, unprovoked actions?

As the lift pulled him upward, he felt the scar on his chest from the sacrificial knife, and he once again allowed the flashback of the neo-Satanist ritual to flood into his mind, making his temples pound.

What had he done to deserve a death as violent and as terrible as that? With the heart cut from his chest by a dull blade?

Danal no longer wanted to discover the origin of his flashbacks. He wanted to start all over again. He wanted to be a simple Servant, following orders, without the slightest inkling of his past. He wanted forgiveness for his awful crime.

But he would get none—they would terminate him. He would die again.

The lobby spread out in front of him as the lift doors parted, but now the microprocessor seemed to be driving his brain at a snail's pace. Events whirled around him like a maelstrom of razor blades. He stepped out of the elevator, holding his blood-covered hands dumbly before him.

Several people noticed him at once. The receptionist looked up, cocked her head, and calmly screamed in the exact pitch that activated the droning alarms.

One of the Enforcer escorts had just entered the lobby and stood contemplating the large Metroplex map on the wall, searching for the location of his next delivery. Danal noted instantly that the Enforcer was tall and thin, and his hands and wrists showed black skin that was normally covered by armored gloves. The same Enforcer who had escorted him to the Van Ryman mansion, seemingly a lifetime before.

As the alarms throbbed through the intercom, the Enforcer whirled and fumbled at his armor. Behind the black visor he seemed to be trying to grasp the situation and to choose the proper weapon for combat.

In a daze Danal turned away and stumbled toward the transplastic door. It was too late now. He saw no way out, and he still had no answers.

"Servant! Halt!" the Enforcer shouted, finally sliding a wide-barreled pocket bazooka from its holster.

Danal hesitated a moment. The Enforcer, in his alarm, had not used the Command phrase. Danal knew he would be terminated if he stopped. He had murdered Francois Nathans and Rodney Quick.

He did not want to die a second time.

Danal had no other decision to make. Without a thought he burst toward the door, pumping his legs faster than any normal human could. The Enforcer blinked in amazement and confusion. The receptionist screamed again.

The Enforcer pointed his weapon and launched a projectile.

Danal plowed through the revolving doors as a blast shattered the transplastic and blew shrapnel outward. The Servant let out a cry of pain as something ripped through his shoulder, but he swallowed his fear and rushed into the milling streets.

"Rebel!" the Enforcer cried, and his voice cracked. He fired again, blasting away the debris of the door, and climbed rapidly through the jagged opening.

Danal floundered among the gawking pedestrians, trying to swim through the crowd, but somehow he could not cloak himself in anonymity. The crowd hated him, hated Servants. They stared at him with mocking expressions. But they would not help; they hated Enforcers, too.

The Enforcer danced through the churning bodies and fired a third time.

A woman beside Danal screamed and fell to the pavement with blood dribbling out the back of her head. The Servant felt ice begin to form in his stomach as he ran, waiting for a projectile to pierce his body and detonate, leaving nothing for anyone to resurrect. He dodged, running much faster than his pursuer but much slower than any exploding bullet that might be launched after him.

The Enforcer stopped, looking down helplessly at his weapon, perhaps in horror or confusion, but the visor hid all expressions.

Danal's chest ached where his original heart had once been, but that heart had been torn from him by a murderer's hand, and had been replaced with a biomechanical pump. Danal clutched his torn shoulder and saw the clear synBlood oozing between his fingers.

The Enforcer moved again, shoving a man out of his way. Someone else screamed next to the fallen woman. The Enforcer took out his riot club, swinging it but hitting no one.

"You can't treat citizens like that!" someone shouted. The crowd's anger began to ignite like a match.

In the wake of Danal's flight, a man fell into an old woman; he regained his balance and angrily swung at her. The Enforcer fired twice, but into the air this time.

Several screams echoed in the crowd as Danal fled farther. A man struck the Enforcer from behind, but he turned and convulsively struck him full in the face with the riot club. Some of the people were hitting each other in a senseless release of their anger.

And Danal ran to escape from the mob that was drawing in like a noose around the hapless Enforcer. The black monster of his imprisoned memory battered his Servant identity, and Danal fought against releasing it.

He was a murderer. Unprovoked, he had slaughtered two men. He had resisted direct orders from an Enforcer, and he had fled from justice.

He was terrified by his own capabilities, by what was locked in the mausoleum of his dead memory. He did not want to know what his flashbacks signified. He wanted only to forget.

He looked ahead of himself with tunnel vision, seeing only the path of least resistance, the confused route that let him avoid as many people as possible yet left enough of them in the way to baffle the Enforcer's line of fire.

Just ahead of him, Danal fixed his gaze on a thin man with salt-and-pepper hair, grinning and strutting proudly down the street with a female Servant. Details flooded into his mind—he saw the insignia of a Guildsman on the man's lapel; he saw indigo lines tattooed into the wrinkles around his eyes; he saw one of the Guildsman's knobby hands massaging the female Servant's buttocks. She seemed not to notice at all.

The other Servant wore the usual unattractive gray jumpsuit, but Danal could see that the old man had placed a long blond wig on her head and flowers in the artificial hair. He had draped jewelry on her neck and wrists. She walked like a piece of livestock.

The Guildsman turned, startled, as Danal nearly ran into him, and then gaped as he noticed the long smear of Nathans's blood on his jumpsuit and the wound on Danal's shoulder bleeding clear synBlood. In reflex to her Master's actions, the female Servant turned to look at Danal as well.

Her crystal-blue eyes were empty. The resurrection process had washed the sea spray from her face, and her artificial hair had been combed by someone else. Her elfin, dimpled features were waxy and lifeless.

But it was still the face on the beach, from the hologram on Van Ryman's mantel.

JULIA!

Suddenly his real memory burst open, all of it. Thousands upon thousands of thoughts stumbled hungrily into the light of day. His old self, his true self emerged.
And Danal *knew.*
He screamed as the agony struck him, almost making his knees buckle, making the pain in his torn shoulder feel like a mere annoyance. The world vanished in the resurgent flood of his flashback as his life and his violent death on the sacrificial altar rose up to stare him in the face.

Van Ryman
Van Ryman!
I AM VINCENT VAN RYMAN!

He saw that the old Guildsman had already hurried Julia away, frightened by the rampaging Servant. Danal watched her in anguish for only a moment, fixing the scene in his mind, then ducked blindly down a crossway, then another, until he had run far enough ahead of the mob to feel relatively safe. But he could no longer hide from his returning memories.

The man I Served is an imposter,
usurper!

He tried to sort out his thoughts. And everything fell back into place, just where it had always belonged.

PART II

Flashback

16

Danal kept running by instinct, from a need to continue fleeing from something.

He could see several Enforcer hovercars soaring overhead, skimming the tops of the buildings, converging near Resurrection, Inc. If he concentrated, Danal thought he could still hear the sounds of the angry mob even above the normal background noises of the city.

Danal wondered when the Enforcers would send out their special tracker teams to locate him. Or would they even bother? Would they assume he was dead? Had they even discovered that Danal had been the cause of the uprising?

The Servant stumbled into a residential area of towering condominium buildings. The streets—all of which had been named after extinct wildflowers—were curved in a conscious attempt to break the illusion of a geometrically ordered city.

Danal almost wished he could see through the buildings, look straight down some of the convoluted streets. Julia remained out there somewhere. He had seen her—a Servant like himself. But was she *Julia*? Or was the true Julia gone, leaving only a walking body behind? He could remember the last time he had seen her—the real Julia. The memory had returned now, if he could find it, if he was able to dig through the pain. . . .

She had been sitting across from him in the formal dining room of the Van Ryman mansion, resting both elbows on the tablecloth. They were laughing. It had started out as an argument, but they had consciously steered the conversation to more lighthearted things.

They talked and drank cheap pink champagne—Julia liked cheap pink champagne. Their two new Servants, a male and a female, stood attentively outside the door of the formal dining room. Danal—the real Vincent Van Ryman—had purchased the Servants to allow him more time alone with Julia, now that he had given up all his neo-Satanist activities. Danal/Van Ryman hadn't noticed that the Servants' eyes looked too attentive, that their thoughts seemed too alert.

Julia giggled, but then stopped laughing abruptly. Van Ryman looked up and saw that the room had gone blurry, and the champagne suddenly had an awful aftertaste of chemicals. The world went out of focus, and then faded to black. . . .

He awoke in the artificially dank stone Sabbat chamber underneath the mansion. Manacled to the walls—it all seemed weirdly Gothic and melodramatic. Francois Nathans was there, and Julia was not.

"Julia? What happened to Julia?"

Nathans made a wry scowl. "Oh how noble of you to think of the poor lady first, Vincent. She's already dead—dumped on the street and deleted from The Net. But you're a much bigger PR item. Our first 'Traitor to the Faith.' I couldn't have dreamed up a better unifying force if I tried. We'll have a special Sabbat in your honor, Vincent, and no one will know the difference . . . because you aren't *you* anymore." Nathans laughed. "Oh boy, we're going to milk this for all it's worth!"

Vincent Van Ryman pulled against his chains, and felt cold as he slowly reached forward to touch his face—

Danal slammed the door on the clamoring memories, holding them at bay for later, making them wait. Until it was safe.

The Servant found himself stumbling down one of the winding streets where the backs of the condominium buildings butted up against each other. He could see the worn fences of the lucky first-level dwellers who had their own tiny yardlets fenced into little honeycombs. The denizens of the upper stories had to remain content with small terraces above, looking down at the ground.

Unseen behind one open patio window came the shouts of two men and one woman arguing in a language Danal could not identify. On another patio an older couple lay on stained chaise longues, stretched out, motionless next to each other.

Danal felt exhausted, with the world pounding around him, too much happening all at once. His head buzzed with the reality that had just struck him, from the events that in such a short time had changed him from a normal, obedient Servant to a renegade.

He leaned up against the fence, sheltered by a large

garbage receptacle and the shadow of the twin condominium buildings. Resting for a moment . . .

Danal took a deep breath and let the nightmares come to him. He was afraid at first, but he opened the door quickly and snapped it shut again, allowing only the first memory—the last memory—to come out.

"Rah hyuun!

"Rah hyuun!"

The chanting filled the air with a drone like a locomotive, augmented by the chain of speakers around the grotto ceiling.

Vincent Van Ryman was drugged, and he stumbled. The inside of his head felt fuzzy and his vision had narrowed to the width of a pencil shaft. Around him he saw robes—white, red, black—signifying the ranks of Acolyte, Acolyte Supervisor, and Coven Manager, with various markings to indicate the different sublevels of authority and mastery of neo-Satanism.

The grotto was lit by candles and red strobe lights that provided a shadowy, hypnotic atmosphere for the ritual, possibly enhanced by odorless hallucinogenic drugs wafting through the enclosed air.

Danal/Van Ryman knew he was doomed, about to be sacrificed. He was not bound or restrained in any way, but he had no will to make his arms or legs move. It took all his concentration merely to remain standing or to stumble forward when someone directed him.

Nathans wasn't there; Nathans never took part in the actual rituals. He kept his hands clean. He remained out of sight. But with Vincent Van Ryman—the former High Priest of the neo-Satanists—turned against him, Francois Nathans had yanked invisible strings, setting his own wheels in motion, proving to be a formidable enemy.

The ritual moved forward, but Vincent's brain seemed to have slipped a gear, plodding ahead at a greatly reduced pace. He had conducted it himself a dozen times before, but now he could not remember the words, the details of the High Sabbat. Except he knew that at the culmination of the High Sabbat, someone always died.

And as he recalled this, he felt hands grasping the numb skin of his arms, roughly yet gently. Red-robed men urged him toward the poured-stone altar into which had been molded various signs and symbols. In a corner of his mind he remembered designing many of those symbols himself.

Van Ryman could not resist. His arms slowly moved up to fend them off, but he felt a stinging in his neck. One of the Coven Managers herding him toward the altar withdrew his finger; he saw a glint from the silver thimble-needle that had been dipped in curare. Vincent knew it would take only a moment, and he felt the vestiges of his muscle control dissolving into mist.

He lay back, barely able to feel the rough stone of the altar against his naked back. He stared up at the ceiling, originally hewn from the end of a deep subway tunnel but now embellished with papier mâché stalactites.

"*Rah hyuun!*

"*Rah hyuun!*"

Van Ryman felt the vertigo engulfing him as the chanting reached its climax. He could not move or even turn his head now. It was a major mental effort simply to blink his eyes.

Then the chanting stopped abruptly. The tape-recorded choir cut off, and the neo-Satanist attendees stopped their own voices a moment afterward. He felt the hushed silence pounding at him.

Into his field of view he saw, like a mirror moving up in front of him, his own face, his stolen face, fixed with a fanatical, confident expression, looking triumphant. The real Van Ryman could see a line of faint red pinpricks along the imposter's jaw. Then he caught the glint of orange candlelight on the edge of the wide, rune-marked sacrificial dagger, the arthame.

The imposter spoke the last words, the benediction of the High Sabbat, as he brought the arthame down. "Ashes to ashes, blood to blood; fly to Hell for all our good!"

Van Ryman was not able to blink; the curare denied him even an instinctive flinch. Blackness and pain exploded outward from the center of his chest as the blade drove in. . . .

Danal came up out of the memory gasping, sucking cold air into his lungs like a drowning man clawing his way to the surface. Servants did not sweat—their body temperature was too closely regulated to make perspiration necessary—but he felt drenched with an emotional backwash.

The memory of the High Sabbat scorched the backs of his eyes, yet the pain slowly grew more endurable. The mental ache did not fade, but he learned how to tolerate it, how to face his own past. He stepped into the middle of the winding street, leaving behind the fixation with his memories. Danal had more practical considerations for the moment.

What was he going to do now?

He couldn't go back. He couldn't ask for help. The imposter remained at Danal's own home, playing the part of Vincent Van Ryman. Danal had no place there. The imposter had planned something, lured Danal into the exact actions he had unwittingly performed like a pre-programmed machine.

But Francois Nathans was indeed dead at the Servant's hands. Some of the self-directed horror faded as Danal remembered what Nathans had done to him in life, but Nathans had never been stupid. The killing had been too carefully set up, as if Nathans had specifically planned to trigger Danal's murderous rage. As if he had a death wish, or something else in mind. Had he been trying to commit suicide? Not Nathans. Was there something more, something that Danal still could not see even with the return of his memories?

The Servant finally began to heed the screaming pain in his shoulder. He cocked his head and looked down at the torn gray material of his jumpsuit, at the cut-meat remains of his shoulder where the shrapnel had struck him. Clear, saplike synBlood oozed from the wound.

Doctor. Medical attention. He would have to be repaired. Servants had difficulty healing themselves. The synthetic blood did carry micro-platelets to dissolve and coagulate, sealing leaks upon exposure to air, much like some antifreeze solutions sealed mechanical leaks. But the wound sealants in synBlood were not very efficient, good mostly for minor injuries. After all, if a Servant was too badly damaged, you just got a new one, right? The slow healing could be Danal's greatest danger, letting him bleed to death before he could have someone adequately seal off the injury. Even in that case, the synHeart would dutifully keep beating, and the microprocessor would continue to drive his brain while the bloodless body rapidly burned itself out.

Danal searched his mind, accessing all the general information stored in the microprocessor until he found the implanted map of the Metroplex. Inside his head Danal located the nearest medical center.

The red swath of Nathans's blood stood out like a

banner on the front of his jumpsuit. Danal would have to explain the blood and his own injury. He wasn't certain if the center would treat him at all. He set off, trudging down the street, mentally slowing his synHeart to retard the bleeding. He would worry about explanations later.

17

By the time Danal arrived at the medical center, he had climbed to the middle stages of dizzy euphoria, feeling light as air and drained of blood. The world seemed to be moving slower.

The transplastic doors glided open in front of him, smooth and silent on their chrome tracks. He plodded inside, peripheral vision suddenly gone fuzzy. Black spots danced in front of his eyes, like holes in the universe that winked in and out of existence.

Several Servants worked behind the expansive front counter, keying information, moving boxes, delivering papers and supplies. Other patients waited in separate privacy cubicles surrounded by bright plastic plant-things, but the reception area seemed relatively empty. The casualties from the street riot had apparently not yet overflowed the other medical centers closer to Resurrection, Inc.

Danal stumbled up to the counter, trying to speak, but his throat was too dry. A female Servant stood with her back to him, paying no attention to his arrival. One of the fluorescent light panels overhead flickered spasmodically, as if struggling to throw out just a few more photons before the repair-rats replaced it.

An overweight nurse/tech strolled out from another corridor to meet the wounded Servant. Her hair had been dyed black and looked like plastic; her face was weighted down with so much makeup that Danal doubted he could see a square centimeter of her real skin. Thin surgical gloves covered her hands.

The nurse/tech looked at him with a puzzled, somewhat astonished expression. Dried blood from Francois Nathans stained the front of Danal's jumpsuit, and the Servant's own colorless synBlood darkened the fabric around his ragged wound. She spoke with a thin voice he would not have expected from her matronly body. "What do you want here, Servant? Has there been an accident?"

Danal placed a blank mask on his face and calmly answered her. "I was told to come here to be healed." He used the last of his mental strength to wrench him back to awareness of his surroundings.

Still not sure what to do, the nurse/tech refused to move. Then she clutched at her usual routine and stepped back behind the counter to reach a Net terminal. After hitting a few burst keys, she called up an input screen and looked at him with detached professionalism.

"Okay, how were you injured?"

Danal responded automatically with the self-programmed answer he had pounded into the front of his brain. "A riot in the streets. A stray projectile struck me. The Enforcer told me to come here." His Servant programming rebelled, trying to deny the lie and state the bald facts, but Danal was able to control the other self.

"What's your ID number? And who is your Master?" she asked in a flat voice, routine questions to her.

Danal balked and covered his momentary hesitation with a sigh of pain. Vincent Van Ryman was not his Master. Vincent Van Ryman was not even real, not anymore. An imposter now had the name and the physical appearance, but the real Van Ryman was dead, living again only as a simulacrum of disguised flesh, resurrected memories. Danal couldn't give out his ID number. That would be like a beacon for anyone trying to track him down, a signal for the Enforcers and the Guardian Angels to locate him, to terminate him once and for all.

But the black dizziness swam in front of him, like shark fins cutting the water of his consciousness. His synHeart labored, almost ready to burn out. His blood vessels seemed to be running dry. Danal couldn't worry about the future if he didn't survive the present.

"Vincent Van Ryman. My Master is Vincent Van Ryman," he said weakly. He stated his ID number a few digits at a time until the nurse/tech had all the information. Danal felt his joints begin to go haywire on him. For some reason his knees wobbled in and out, and he slumped against the countertop. He was oddly reminded of the moment of his rebirth, as he had emerged dripping from the vat and unable to control his own reflexes, and Rodney Quick standing there taunting him.

But Rodney Quick is dead. I killed him.

An accident.

Danal became partially aware again as the nurse/tech

bellowed for one of the human orderlies. He felt a man's ungentle grip on his waist and his uninjured arm. Their words drifted around his ears, and he was only vaguely able to comprehend them.

"Help me get him to one of the sterile rooms. Then go to the trauma chamber and find some of the extra bottles of synBlood." (Nurse/tech.)

"Can't he go to a repair center or something? I thought we didn't fix Servants here." (Orderly.)

"Consider it good practice, then." (Nurse/tech: with cold sarcasm.)

But when Danal tried to move his legs, tried to help carry his own weight, the blackness in the air suddenly reached out to swallow him up. He reeled, and lost control of the door in his mind.

Unchecked, all the dead memories swooped after him as he fled undefended down into the unconsciousness. . . .

"I'd like to start a religion. That's where the money is," Francois Nathans had said.

It was just the start of a conversation, an exchange of ideas. But it altered the lives of Vincent Van Ryman, his father Stromgaard Van Ryman, and Nathans himself.

Young Vincent had been eighteen years old at the time. He went himself to answer the door signal, but he knew it was Nathans even before he opened the door. Outside, the muscular and ever-watchful Servant body-guards kept their strategic positions around the Van Ryman mansion. The bodyguards would have excluded almost anyone except Nathans.

With the growing blue-collar opposition to Servants and Resurrection, Inc., several terrorist attacks had been directed at the mansion itself. Perhaps the single private dwelling stated too blatantly how much wealth and success Stromgaard had achieved by putting blues out of work. Nathans, on the other hand, kept several dwellings, none of them elaborate and all of them very secret.

Vincent's mother had been killed five years before, assassinated while she walked with her son on the streets. She fell next to him, still trying to walk but with a half dozen projectile holes in her body. The thirteen-year-old boy thought immediately how lucky he was to survive, and wondered if he'd be a target as well. Anger and shock maybe, but it was hard to feel deep sorrow for her.

His mother had always treated Vincent as a burden, much as Stromgaard now did.

Vincent let Francois Nathans into the well-lit front hallway of the mansion, smiling as the tall man clapped him on the shoulder. "Hello, Vincent."

Though it was dusk, they had several hours yet before Nathans would have to worry about the Enforcers' curfew. Silhouetted in the dampening stillness of sunset, the Servant bodyguards stood motionless and threatening around the house.

Vincent saw that Nathans had chosen to wear a silvery hairpiece this time; the older man wore silvery hairpieces only when he had something important on his mind.

"Where's your father?" Nathans asked him, as if he didn't know.

"In the study, playing Net games." Vincent tried to keep some of his unconscious sneer in check. He hated how Stromgaard wasted his time, and wasted the capabilities of The Net, by using the entertainment directories and nothing else.

Vincent had watched his father slowly drift further and further into the background of running Resurrection, Inc. As the work grew more complex, it required a special kind of mind to manage it all, more than just a competent resource organizer (which, Vincent believed, was all his father could really be).

Nathans had shouldered more of the burden. While the elder Van Ryman sulked and grumbled mostly to himself about how Nathans was taking over what was rightfully Stromgaard's, he basically ignored his son.

Vincent had grown used to it over the years and trained himself to find his own means of entertainment. The younger Van Ryman learned to occupy himself with The Net. He had grown quite proficient in searching the databases and in doing programming. He became more and more impressed with The Net itself, finding little he could not do once he set his mind to it. He created several false identities on the electronic-mail network—not a difficult task, since some members of special-interest groups operated under pseudonyms, keeping their private lives anonymous. Vincent then carried on five different fictitious lives, all of which allowed him to look at society from different angles.

Nathans shrugged off his jacket and threw it over one arm as he strode down the hall to Stromgaard's study. In the background, Vincent could hear some of the electronic sound effects as Stromgaard played his idiotic games. He heard a rapid succession of *bleeps*, then a *whoosh*, and then a quiet curse from his father.

Nathans waited outside the study door with a half-smile on his face. He flashed Vincent a conspiratorial grimace, then entered the room.

Stromgaard did not condescend to acknowledge the other man's presence. The elder Van Ryman always seemed to be searching for a way to annoy Nathans, but Nathans blithely ignored it, which perturbed Stromgaard even more. Sometimes his father's childish attitude embarrassed even Vincent.

Vincent made ready to go back upstairs, where he spent most of his time. He never took part in their discussions, but this time Vincent paused on a whim and moved closer to the study as he heard Nathans's opening gambit.

"I'd like to start a religion. That's where the money is."

Stromgaard greeted the proposal with silence, but Vincent could sense that Nathans had captured his father's attention. The elder Van Ryman waited for him to continue.

"As the saying goes, the first priest was the first charlatan who met the first fool. We could cash in on that."

"Why?" Stromgaard asked. "You don't have enough money? You don't have enough to do lording over Resurrection all by yourself?"

Nathans smiled, sidestepping the implied accusation. "It's not actually the money, Stromgaard. I was thinking more along the lines of something for *you* to do. You're . . . phasing out of your duties at the corporation. You obviously need something else to occupy your time." He pointed to the Net screen on which Stromgaard's game score still flashed. "Annihilating alien invaders? You're more talented than that."

"I'm not interested in religion," the elder Van Ryman said. "And I'm not feeling much like a messiah lately."

"No," Nathans countered, pacing the room, thinking out loud. "Messiahs are . . . boring. They've been *done* so many times, you know. I had something more in mind like . . . well, something new."

Stromgaard let out an incredulous laugh. "Something

new? In a religion? Have fun trying to come up with an idea."

Nathans sat down in the overstuffed chair and poured himself a glass of the Glenlivet Stromgaard always drank. Vincent occasionally sipped a small snifter of the scotch himself, mainly when trying to be part of someone else's conversation, but he personally disliked its pungent taste and the way it lingered for hours in the back of his mouth.

"Well," Nathans continued, "that's what I was hoping to discuss with you tonight. A brainstorming session, like we used to have when you weren't moping around all the time."

"I'm fresh out of ideas. Come back some other day." Stromgaard punched a few keys on the Net keyboard, initiating another game.

Vincent stepped into the study, and spoke up before the two older men could see him. "You could run a computer model on The Net. Have the system design the most viable new religion, given an up-to-date analysis of current events and social trends."

His father turned away from the screen and scowled at him. "Vincent, go to your room."

"No," Nathans interrupted, "I'm in the mood for ideas."

Feeling a little bit giddy at what he was doing, Vincent continued. "I was listening, sorry. But The Net could analyze all the world's religions, correlate the main theses that seem to have the most impact, the greatest chance of hooking new followers, and then we can put it into the context of modern-day society—create something new, but with all the good parts of the old."

Nathans grinned at him with bright eyes. Vincent felt a warm flush, but kept his pride in check. Stromgaard turned away from the Net screen and let the video spaceships play by themselves for a moment before they all annihilated each other.

"You can't do that," his father said. "It's much too complicated. We'd need an army of superhackers and programmers."

"Give me ten minutes," Vincent said and took his place at the keyboard. He canceled the game and quickly stepped his way down through the menus. He paused and couldn't resist turning to his father. "The Net is good for more than just games. You'd see that if you spent more time exploring it."

He began to set a few datastrings in motion, building a broader relational file. "I'm going to run a lot of the tenets through a logic routine, and have it discard anything that really makes no sense at all."

"Ah no, Vincent, you're missing the point," Nathans said. "I don't want it to be believable, not believable in the least. There's a larger plan at work here. I want to make our religion ridiculous, because I don't want to mislead any intelligent people, the ones with even a modicum of potential in their cranial chambers. I want to lay a selective trap, something that only the terminally stupid will fall into. Intelligence is the only thing we've got that sets us apart from other animals, you know."

Vincent blinked and nodded, but Nathans seemed to have launched into a well rehearsed speech. "The popular religions are at the root of the problem, teaching people *not* to think for themselves on pain of losing their Eternal Salvation. 'The world holds two classes of men—intelligent men without religion, and religious men without intelligence.' A tenth-century Syrian poet wrote that."

"Nobody will believe you," Stromgaard said in a confident voice.

"Mankind's track record says otherwise. Think of all the people who, despite utter and overwhelming proof to the contrary, still believe in magic apples and talking snakes to explain the creation of the world?"

"Oh, don't even start, Francois," Stromgaard sighed. "You're going to give me a headache. And we're not interested."

"Let me make my case! I've done my homework because I intend to do something about this. If you're going to help me, you have to understand my rationale."

"Who says we're going to help you?"

"Doesn't it bother you that, just because the Bible the Sun goes around the Earth, the religious fanatics go out and burn an astronomer or two at the stake for proving otherwise? It's been done. Would you swallow a story about a fish swallowing a man, then spitting him out safe and sound three days later, never mind that the hydrochloric acid in gastric juices would eat through a tabletop in a few seconds?"

Vincent paused at the keyboard to listen, but then continued with his work, eager to show his skill with The Net.

"It goes on and on, but let's not just pick on Judeo-

Christians," Nathans continued. "What about Islam? One God omniscient and omnipresent, yet He seems to have a fine-tuning problem—He can't hear your prayers unless your head points toward a particular latitude and longitude? How could anybody believe such things?"

"Like believing a man could rise from the dead?" Stromgaard retorted, with a glint of triumph in his eye.

"Without due process! Besides, it takes us a little longer than three days.

"Religion is like a wet blanket to the thinking man. In Seventeenth-Century Russia, the Eastern Orthodox Church went to war with itself over whether the faithful should make the sign of the cross using two fingers symbolizing God and Man, or three fingers for the Holy Trinity— thousands and thousands of people died in the struggle! It's pathetically funny in a way."

Stromgaard sighed. "That was centuries ago, Francois. It doesn't matter anymore."

"But it hasn't changed! The Vatican just released an announcement that people no longer need to be actually present at the Pope's Christmas Mass to receive his blessing, because 'improvements in technology now allow us to transmit God's forgiveness electronically.' And the Moslems are all excited because they've developed a new selective disintegrator 'for Allah' that'll let them remove the fingers and hands of thieves according to Islamic law, keeping the pain but doing away with all the mess."

Nathans shook his head wearily, as if in despair. "Progress doesn't enlighten people—it just makes them stupid in new ways."

Stromgaard snorted, narrowing his eyes. "You're going off on another one of your crusades, Francois. Years and years ago you were trying to solve the world's crime problem, and what ever became of that? Now it's religion. Next you'll be working on the world food shortage or something. You storm ahead and argue a lot and leave us all in the dust. Why not just give it a rest?"

Nathans looked at him with a sour expression. "You must have something against grandiose ideas, Stromgaard. I'm giving you something to think about. Mull it over. Expand your mind. It looks like you're getting out of practice." He glanced around the study. "Do you have something to eat?"

"No," Stromgaard answered flatly.

Vincent turned while The Net continued to labor. "But if you want people to expand their minds, then what's wrong with having them ponder metaphysical things, like religion?"

"Ah, Vincent, thinking about such questions is fine, but when philosophy becomes a *religion*, then people stop considering the ideas and pay more attention to just following ritual. Once you're convinced that you have The Word Of God, you stop bothering to think about the details. How could a Supreme Being ever be wrong? Then your brain begins to atrophy."

Nathans ran a fingertip along his lip, thinking. "Maybe the Eastern religions . . . they're not quite so preoccupied with their own importance. Hmmmm. No, take a look at Taoism—they happily worship gods of robbery and drunkenness, and take their pick from eighty-one different heavens, while the Buddhists, being much more conservative, limit themselves to a mere thirty-one heavens. No wonder they believe in reincarnation—a poor wandering spirit can't figure out where else to go!

"Consider some, like Orthodox Judaism, that have stagnated in their rituals and symbols. They may as well just videotape their services and play them back year after year, generation after generation. Nothing ever changes. It's always just the same mechanical gestures, the same memorized phrases. Nothing has been brought into the context of the modern world—do they think we're all still shepherds in the Middle East? Are we still supposed to placate the old things that used to go bump in the night?" Nathans sat down, exasperated.

" 'Religion is comparable to a childhood neurosis,' Sigmund Freud said. And he was right."

"Got it!" Vincent interrupted, turning away from the Net terminal. Nathans looked up at him, and Stromgaard regarded him skeptically. Vincent happily continued, "It's a little bit unexpected, though. It looks something like Satanism, in an updated form."

He pointed to the screen and listed out the results of the relational search. "You want something that the people will find exciting, something that seems slightly forbidden, which I take to mean something *dark*. You'll want it to be titillating, so throw in a little racy symbolism, some suggestive rituals, maybe even sex during the high ceremonies. And you want your deity to be bigger than life, very powerful but within reach—not some ethereal, all-pervading god spirit that never interferes in the affairs of mortals. We want an Old Testament-ish dictatorial entity that rewards the faithful but does all sorts of unpleasant things to unbelievers. Try the popular conception of Satan—it all fits."

"Satanism . . ." Nathans pursed his lips, considering. "But placed in a modern context, a new Satanism. Neo-Satanism! I like the sound of that."

Stromgaard looked as if he had been left out of the decision entirely, and was about to speak up when Vincent's enthusiasm stopped him. "Let's do it!"

18

Later. Much later.

As if from a great distance, Vincent looked down at the victim on the altar. The young woman—formerly a student, then turned activist, and then, for some unknown reason, suddenly a fanatic neo-Satanist—lay back in anticipation, naked except for the flimsy white robe, most assuredly not a virgin. She thrust her small, not quite rounded breasts up toward him as he stood in his black High Priest robes.

They hadn't needed any drugs at all with her, no tranquilizing or disorienting substances to keep her quiet through the ceremony. She lay back, grinning a self-satisfied smile, without the slightest doubt on her face, absolutely confident in her beliefs.

Vincent could hardly keep the scorn from his face. Nathans was right—how could these people be so gullible?

The candles flickered; the incense made the underground room seem too stuffy, too perfumed. Sounds echoed in the large vault, making it seem like a vast, unpleasant womb. Not quite familiar with the High Sabbat ritual, some of the white-robed Acolytes continued the meaningless chant, following along in their printed program leaflets. Vincent ignored them.

Behind the altar, the "sacred relics" of neo-Satanism sat on display in separate transparent showcases. A black (plastic) claw torn from Satan's finger when He turned his back on Heaven in disgust, deciding instead to come and look after mortals. Another relic: a blackened hoofprint burned into the linoleum when Satan had appeared in Wittenburg to make his famous bargain with Dr. Faustus in the sixteenth century (it didn't seem to bother any of the converts that linoleum hadn't been created until more than three centuries later). And a small vial of semen from when Satan had impregnated a twentieth-century woman named Rosemary.

Vincent dragged his gaze over the chanting crowd and prepared to strike. He raised the blade of the arthame over the naked woman's chest. She cocked her head back, anticipating, distantly awed by what she expected to see.

"If you believe all that," he couldn't resist mumbling under his breath, not sure if she could hear or if she was even listening, "then you're brain dead already."

He brought the blade down. It was always the same, and by now he had lost his revulsion, his guilt, and felt no sympathy at all for the victims, for people who would allow themselves to be so easily manipulated.

Vincent had considered it an elaborate joke at first, a game, a trick to play on the masses—but they were supposed to catch on, and everyone would laugh sheepishly and admit they'd been fooled. Yet to his horror, the people turned the tables on him—they had embraced neo-Satanism with all the fervor that The Net had predicted. It amazed him at first, and then appalled him.

Back at the beginning. Nathans tilted the chair, locking his fingers together behind his neck. He smiled to himself, and spoke aloud to Vincent, who was busily concocting "holy writings," scribbling complex and nonsensical poetry on some artificially aged parchment.

" 'Man is insane. He wouldn't know how to create a bacterium, and creates gods by the dozen.' The French philosopher Montaigne wrote that."

Vincent looked up from his writing. "You sure read a lot."

"No. I just memorize a good many quotes. That way it seems like I read a lot, when I don't really have the time."

Vincent rolled up part of the parchment, careful not to smear the ink. They planned on claiming that this particular scripture came from ancient Arabia, and he wondered how anyone would explain the existence of felt-tip pens in that far-flung land. Sadly, he doubted anyone would question it at all.

"I've been using The Net to do a lot of my researching for me," Vincent said distractedly. "It's funny some of the things that turned up. Did you know that Satan means 'adversary' in Hebrew? Yet Lucifer means 'light bearer.' That's an odd contradiction, don't you think?"

"Fit those details in. The more mysterious names and ancient-sounding words, the better."

"I've even come up with a rationale for worshiping

Satan," he offered. "For instance, why should you waste your time worshiping a good god? If he's truly good, then he'll never do anything bad to you. You're better off trying to keep the evil Satan happy, appease him with a few rituals and sacrifices, so he won't harm you. You're covered on both bases."

"No, no, no—" Nathans stood up and went over to close the French windows against the gray fog outside. On his way back to the chair, he switched on the fireplace. "You don't argue using concepts. You have to claim dogma and leave no room for rational thought. If someone challenges you with irrefutable logical arguments, you need only say 'the Lord works in mysterious ways,' or 'all things are clear to those who have Faith.' "

They heard Stromgaard moving down the hall, going up the stairs, and then returning again to exit the front door without speaking to them. The elder Van Ryman kept himself busy with the business details of forming the new religion, and left the philosophical discussions to Vincent and Nathans, who seemed to enjoy them more.

Earlier, as they had all sat in front of the mirrored hearth, Nathans stressed the importance of ritual, how the proper gestures and repetitions were pivotal to a successful religion. The ritual had to be simple enough to be remembered easily, yet complex enough that one had to *learn* it, rather than mindlessly following along. And it also had to have an air of mystique, a dark power behind it to lure the converts.

The elder Van Ryman had been in charge of contacting a professional choreographer, who helped them to design the elaborate rituals. The choreographer, a bitter woman who could no longer dance because a nerve disease had taken from her the precise use of her arms and legs, immediately took up the challenge and derived remarkable rituals based on, but not obviously evolved from, common religious ceremonies. The Black Mass, or the Sabbat, became a parody, an inverse of the Catholic mass, with the worshipers reverently making the sign of the broken cross.

Although Nathans had specifically intended neo-Satanism to be Stromgaard's bailiwick, the elder Van Ryman again proved his inadequacy. Vincent and Nathans had forged far ahead philosophically, but kept Stromgaard busy and distracted with a great deal of the nuts-and-bolts work. Confidentially Nathans had told Vincent how he hoped they could occupy Stromgaard long enough to get the religion formulated. After the major groundwork was properly completed, neo-Satanism could function by itself, even with someone like Stromgaard at the helm.

One thing Stromgaard had indeed helped them with was designing a hierarchical structure in the new priesthood. Stromgaard himself had devised the management levels of Acolytes, Acolyte Supervisors, and Coven Managers, with the various numerical ranks in between. A hierarchy kept the converts feeling like they had their own place, he said, giving them something to work toward, some ladder to climb up.

"I think we should also engage a professional graphic designer to come up with a logo for neo-Satanism," Vincent suggested.

Nathans's eyes lit up. "Yes! Symbols—we're going to need plenty of those. Crosses, stars, rosaries, mandalas, communion wafers—it's all just to keep you thinking about the abstractions and not the contradictions."

Vincent brought out a small stack of printouts, handing them to Nathans and then somewhat offhandedly spreading the sheets so Stromgaard could look on as well.

"I've come up with a list of special demons according to mythology." He pointed to the list. "Abaddon. Asmodeus. Eurynome, the eater of carrion, Satan's own prince of death. Oh, and I also found that in order to summon a demon, your circle is supposed to be drawn exactly nine feet in diameter—that's a little over 2.7 meters."

He pointed to the second sheet of hardcopy. "I've also found several people to put in our Hall of Fame, if you want to call it that. Theophilus, a sixth-century cleric who sold his soul to the devil in order to obtain Church office." He scratched his head. "There's something inherently paradoxical about that. Anyway, Roger Bacon is another. And Sjømunder the Wise of Iceland, who was without a shadow because Satan had extracted it as payment for services rendered. Friar Bungay, who was slain along with the sorcerer Vandermast when they dueled each other, using demons as their weapons. And of course Dr. Faustus of Wittenburg. Charles Dexter Ward. The Arab, Abdul Alhazred. I'm open to suggestions for any others.

"And finally," he said, gathering up the papers and looking smug, "I think a nice finishing touch would be for us to come up with a few holy relics of our own, some tangible objects, solid things to point to as proof in case any of our new converts are a little bit skeptical."

"Proof?" Nathans cocked an eyebrow. "We can just say the angel Moroni popped down and conveniently did away with all the evidence. It's been done before."

Vincent frowned, but then decided that the other man's sarcasm had not been directed at him. Nathans muttered an apology and waved for him to continue. "I was thinking that we might want to try and find an untranslated original copy of the *Malleus Maleficarum*, the 'Hammer of Witches.' It was a book actually used to justify the burning of witches in the Middle Ages. It's sort of exactly the opposite of what we're looking for, but the name sounds so sinister, no one would doubt its authenticity."

Nathans looked at Vincent, then shifted his gaze to the elder Van Ryman. "Good idea. Stromgaard, you could probably track down that book better than either of us, am I right?"

Then came the advertising blitz, subtly secretive, but staged by some of the best publicists Stromgaard could hire. Through it all, Vincent remained isolated in the mansion, looking at the neo-Satanist scheme from a detached and partially amused stance. But he felt a growing amazement as the inverted star-in-pentagram logo began to appear in prominent places, placed there by zealous new converts. One evening he saw a dancer on a Net entertainment channel wearing a pentagram pendant in her ear.

To keep up the charade, the appearance of the Van Ryman mansion changed, undergoing a metamorphosis to make it look more like the abode of a High Priest. What had once been a white-painted, black-roofed facsimile of an old Midwestern farmhouse had been turned into a dark and sinister-looking haunted house. Vincent watched from behind his upstairs window as a crane came in and uprooted the picket fence surrounding the house, replacing it with a barricade of black iron spikes. The rooster weathervane on the rooftop became a cavorting demon pointing in random directions. Pipes connected dry-ice pumps to the sprinkler network under the lawn, releasing eerie mist each dusk. Under the eaves of the roof and around the gables now stood a line of hideous gargoyles, one to represent each of the special demons in the neo-Satanist Writings.

And Nathans had been right. With remarkably little effort the religion of neo-Satanism was becoming a business success rapidly approaching the success of Resurrection, Inc.

"Vincent, there's something you have to help me with," Stromgaard said. His voice was dull and somber. Nathans sat unobtrusively at the far end of the long dining-room table, watching but saying nothing.

Vincent had seen his father rarely during the past few weeks. Now, though, Vincent could see that Stromgaard had grown precariously thin, haggard and gaunt. His eyes were stained with bloodshot lines, and the shadowed hollows around them looked almost dark enough to be attributed to makeup.

Stromgaard removed a packet and spread the contents on the wood surface of long table, moving the decanter of Glenlivet and setting it distractedly on the floor. Vincent bent forward to see various NMR images and two x-ray plates showing the intimate inner detail of some human being—he presumed it to be his father. Trails of dark smudges showed up in an alarming number of places where they shouldn't have been.

"It's all over inside of me. My entire lymph system. There's no place it hasn't touched," he said slowly, as if each word were a stone he choked out of his throat. "Right now I can feel it, like a parasite, hiding inside me and trying to peek out." Stromgaard started to tremble and then, very uncharacteristically, he put his face in his hands. Vincent stood frozen, not knowing what to do.

For the past year and a half neo-Satanism had been running smoothly, with Stromgaard Van Ryman as its High Priest. Vincent assisted in some of the ceremonies, as did some of the other highly placed converts, but the others were fanatics who actually believed in the religion. Nathans helped neo-Satanism as well, but for the most part remained invisible in the background—he had once compared himself to the Wizard of Oz, running the show from behind his curtain. Stromgaard was the figurehead, the visible power, the focal point in the public eye.

Nathans stood up and patted Stromgaard on the shoulder, then he turned to Vincent. "He's probably got a month left, maybe two."

Vincent stared in silence, absorbing the information. He waited, and finally Nathans spoke again.

"He needs you to take his place as the High Priest of the neo-Satanists. You're the heir apparent."

The younger Van Ryman snapped out of his trance and looked at Nathans, wide-eyed. "Me? Isn't it enough now? Haven't we brainwashed enough people?"

"No," Nathans answered firmly. "These are people who have to find themselves a religion—it's like theological masturbation. If they don't join neo-Satanism, then they'll become Fundamentalist Christians, or Scientologists, or something else. At least we're honest with ourselves about our motivations."

"And I'm supposed to take his place, carry on those sacrifices, attend the rituals, and pretend I believe in all that stuff?"

"It's for a good cause." Nathans shrugged. "The betterment of humanity—we're keeping the marching morons occupied while the rest of us continue what mankind was destined to do."

"You're sounding very high and mighty, Mr. Nathans," Vincent responded.

"I have every right to. Nobody else is thinking about our future." He rubbed his hands together, as if dismissing the subject.

"Now then, we have to discuss the transition. I'm afraid poor Stromgaard is not going to be able to perform his duties much longer, and already he is keeping himself pumped up on enough drugs that he's not always as clearheaded as he used to be. We want the transition from father to son to be spectacular and dramatic, and I'm afraid you're not going to like it much, Vincent. But it has to be done."

Stromgaard Van Ryman lay on the altar, still garbed in his red-trimmed black High Priest's robe, while Vincent stood beside him, wearing his own black-and-red robe. Vincent shifted the razor-sharp arthame from hand to hand, fidgeting.

The ceremony progressed as it always had, and Vincent found himself mechanically offering the expected gestures. But his mind was elsewhere.

"I won't feel a thing, Vincent. I will be drugged and

floating high in the sky long before you even begin the Sabbat," Stromgaard had said. *"The pain is already so bad I can hardly stand it. It's eating me away and I can feel every bite it takes."* He clutched Vincent with a desperate clawlike hand.

"Don't force me to shrivel away until there's nothing left," he pleaded, "It'll only get worse. Much worse.

"I'll keep myself drugged to euphoria until you finish the High Sabbat. Give me at least that much dignity. Let my own choice enter into it. Besides, it's the best thing for neo-Satanism." Stromgaard said the last comment as if he meant it fervently.

The younger Van Ryman looked down between the folds of the old High Priest robe and saw the gaunt, almost skeletal remains of his father. The ribs protruded; the skin had a grayish cast to it. And Vincent even noticed a wide birthmark on the right side of Stromgaard's chest that he had never seen before.

Stromgaard Van Ryman's eyes were strange and glassy, unfocused and staring deep into infinity. His chin was covered with stubble, and the knuckles on his hands stood out like knobs on an old tree.

I won't feel a thing. This is what I want.

The crescendo of the ritual rose, then fell, then rose again to an even higher peak before it stopped abruptly. Vincent turned to look at the faces of the gathered neo-Satanists, searching. They stared back at him, some curious, some expectant, some wearing no expression at all, just a blank, confident acceptance.

He turned back to his father and shifted the arthame to his left hand so that he could deliver a hard and swift final blow.

"Ashes to ashes, blood to blood; fly to Hell for all our good!" he intoned, and then, mostly to himself, "Goodbye, Father."

19

Deep in the lower managerial levels of Resurrection, Inc., Francois Nathans stared at the bloody corpse of the man who looked exactly like him. The dead man lay facedown on the carpet, still dressed in the white symbol-embroidered neo-Satanist robe. Nathans knelt and rolled the man over, looking down into his face.

It gave him an eerie sensation, like looking at a snapshot of his own death. Nathans had watched the whole thing from a hidden monitor, astonished by Danal's explosive speed and violence, but he didn't feel a great deal of pity for the dead look-alike—the other man had been fully aware of the risks, and he'd agreed to accept them.

"A man has amnesia. We're trying to awaken his memories, trigger them to return," Nathans had explained it to the volunteer. "We don't know how he'll react, and there could be some risk. There'll *probably* be some risk. The man is a Servant."

But after seeing the large sum waiting to be transferred into his Net account, the volunteer had motioned for them to begin the surface-cloning that would give him the face of Francois Nathans.

Now Nathans looked down at the murdered man again, saw the line of faint red pinpricks where the clone-infection had spread, and saw where Danal's blinding speed had neatly split the double's throat like a spoiled fruit.

Nathans felt a warm thrill trickling down his spine. Something had snapped, some part of Danal had come back, some part of the original Vincent Van Ryman had broken through the wall of death and reawakened his old anger.

Pondering, he moved slowly over to Rodney Quick's body on the sofa. That was something Nathans had not counted on. A shame, too. He had been somewhat touched to watch the regret and dismay on Danal's face as he placed the dead technician on the couch. But things were moving too fast right now. Nathans could mentally collate the events later.

He picked up the young tech's body and stumbled with it outside his office, back to the elevator. He positioned Rodney's body against the wall, to look as if he had been attacked and then discarded. Then Nathans went back to seal the door of his own office. He had other things to take care of before he could sound the alarm down in the lower levels.

The door to the secret alcove opened and an Enforcer came in, moving rapidly from the passage to the street above. The Enforcer was outfitted in glossy dark-blue armor with crimson ringlets on each arm-piece. He quickly came up to Nathans, moving with a fluid assurance in his dark armor.

"The riot out there is getting worse. We've got Special Forces coming in now. Should be under control fairly soon."

"What are you doing here in that Elite Guard uniform?" Nathans demanded. "This is Resurrection, remember? I'm supposed to hate the Enforcers. Get changed immediately!"

The blue-clad Enforcer nodded stiffly. Nathans then indicated the dead look-alike on the floor. "I want you to get rid of this. And completely destroy the body—make sure no one sees you."

The Enforcer mumbled his reply and wasted no time getting to work.

Nathans placed his hands behind his back and went over to the thick underwater window, staring out at the murky shapes behind the glass. He flicked a switch and sent spotlights into the water. Sharply defined yellowish beams plunged out into the murk where they occasionally struck the shapes of large grayish fish.

Danal had responded. Now they were past the first major hurdle. The experiment might work after all.

Nathans jumped out of his reverie and went to the direct network-link terminal. Making sure the Elite Guard was not in view, he punched a few buttons and came face-to-face with an image of the captain of Resurrection's specially assigned team of regular Enforcers.

"We're busy right now, Mr. Nathans," the captain said impatiently. "We'll give you a report as soon as we can compile one." The other Enforcer reached forward to blank the screen.

"The Servant must not be harmed," Nathans interrupted. "All other priorities are secondary. You have to get him, rescue him from the mob."

"I understand that, Mr. Nathans. It's too bad he got away in the first place, isn't it?" the white-armored Enforcer said. "We've informed all our men except one Enforcer. We're not able to contact him. His suit radio must be out of service."

"Who? Which one?"

"Jones—the man who first went after your rebel Servant at the scene. His weapons fire could have sparked the disturbance outside. Your receptionist believes the Servant was struck in the shoulder by one of his shots. Jones was in the lobby at the time and acted exactly the way he should have. Commendable, under any other circumstances."

"I'm not interested in any other circumstances! I want you to make damn sure my Servant is not harmed. You don't understand how valuable he is."

"That may not be possible by now, sir." The guard captain had a maddening hint of disrespect and scorn in his voice. "As I said, we've lost contact with Enforcer Jones, and the disturbance is getting pretty bad. A mob would probably focus around a Servant, especially one running from an Enforcer. He may not have had a chance."

Yes, Nathans thought, *but you don't know how fast that Servant can move!* With his knuckles Nathans rapped the key that blanked the screen. He clenched his teeth together and stared out the murky window again.

Damn! Now that he really needed the skills of a good Interface to organize all the different things taking place at the same time, Supervisor had blanked out, failed him right when he needed her.

Interfaces could apparently become lost in The Net, leaving their bodies behind and unable to find the way back to their own minds. It happened sometimes. And no one could determine whether these Net burnouts were accidents or suicides.

In such a case, one could do nothing except put the comatose bodies in tanks and force feed them for the next few decades. Nathans recalled the introverted scientist, Ferdinand, one of the original team who had developed the resurrection process: for his chosen reward Ferdinand had asked to become an Interface and spend the rest of his natural life swimming free in The Net.

Nathans shook his head at the waste, but Ferdinand had been happy.

Supervisor had no such excuse—she had simply failed to appear at work for several days, until Nathans sent two reluctant Enforcers into her darkened den. Surrounded by unpleasantly warm, stale air and burned-out incense, they found her emaciated, uninhabited body.

Not relishing his next communication, Nathans drummed his fingertips on the side of the keyboard before finally entering the proper sequence. In a moment the face of the false Vincent Van Ryman appeared. The imposter had his dark square-cut hair in disarray, and he looked agitated and very old, but with a young man's face.

Nathans placed a reassuring smile on his lips and spoke. "It worked."

The imposter's expression became saturated with relief. "And? What's our next step? What happened?"

Nathans hesitated a moment. "But he got away."

"What!"

"The trigger was more dramatic than we had anticipated. He broke loose and moved with such blinding speed it was amazing! He killed my double, and then fled. On his way out, he also killed one of my technicians. An Enforcer shot him, but he escaped into the streets, where he seems to have started a sizable riot."

The false Van Ryman tugged at his hair, squeezing his eyes shut in a painful wince. "How could you let him get away!"

"I didn't have much choice in the matter. Now be quiet and listen."

But the imposter frantically continued. "What if he comes back here? If he remembers things, then he'll know what we're trying to do! What if he tries to kill me?" The imposter suddenly looked over his shoulder. "I'm turning the Intruder Defense Systems on and they're staying on, so don't try to come and see me."

"Calm down!" Nathans barked. "I don't think he remembers anything specific—he hasn't got it all back yet. He's seen only me, and there's nothing else from his past that he could blunder into."

"Well, what about all the details around here? What about all this time he's been in his old house? Looking at me? All that must have been sparking something—I could tell."

"Yes, yes. But that was a gradual pressure, building

152

up, preparing him. When he saw my double, he got a severe mental jolt. He has to get another jolt like that to regain everything. All he's got now are some of his emotions, vague responses. We'll be safe for the moment."

"*Once* you find him," the imposter muttered.

"We'll find him. Don't worry."

Looking angry and very distressed, the false Van Ryman signed off without acknowledging. Nathans let out a lungful of air, whistling between his teeth, and sat back down to concentrate. He flung off his tousled light-brown hairpiece and used his fingertips to massage his scalp where the thin surgical scars still itched.

20

As Danal plodded back to consciousness, he saw the concerned face of the matronly nurse/tech staring down at him. Reality returned with the force of a released bowstring.

Danal realized how much stronger he felt, renewed. He turned his head to see that the wound on his shoulder had been covered with flesh-colored plaskin; after an hour or so, the synthetic melanin in the plaskin would adjust itself to the exact color of the skin it was supposed to match.

The nurse/tech regarded him with a hardened and calculating gaze that looked alien on her heavily made-up face.

"You were muttering while you were unconscious. Like you were having a nightmare." She watched him closely as she spoke. "Servants aren't supposed to have nightmares."

He looked around the room quickly and saw that he and the nurse/tech were alone. Her brow creased as if contemplating a difficult decision. "Should I go notify your Master? Maybe he can explain why you were having nightmares."

"No!" Danal burst out. He hoped he could restrain his own power this time, that he could merely knock her unconscious and out of the way. He would have to flee again. The thoughts and the decision charged through him instantly as the Servant leaped to his feet. He reached out with his arm, intending to strike her on the back of the neck, to knock her aside.

But the heavyset nurse/tech moved with equally blinding speed and impossible strength as she blocked his blow and grabbed his arm in an unbreakable grip like a steel hinge. Her rubber-gloved hand shook slightly as he strained against it with all his might, but then she turned him and forced him to sit back down on the padded table. Danal's eyes grew wide, and he stopped resisting.

"Now," the nurse/tech said firmly as she peeled off

one of her gloves to reveal the pallid, bloodless skin of her hand. "Tell me. Truthfully. Do you *remember* anything of your first life?"

He had met Julia under one of his pseudonyms.

Even after taking the High Priest's mantle of the neo-Satanists, Vincent had continued to pursue his alternative lives on The Net, the identities under which he carried on business and correspondence.

Using the name of Randolph Carter, Vincent kept up a long running dialog through the electronic mail with a woman named Julia. For weeks they exchanged rhetoric back and forth, with Randolph Carter arguing for one basis of religion, basically repeating the earlier discussions between Francois Nathans and himself, and Julia responded with the same logic, but interpreted through a different point of view, reaching very different conclusions.

Vincent quickly grew to respect the mind behind those discussions and proposed to meet her in person.

They sat down together in a worn plastic booth at a bustling cafeteria. The clatter of an automatic dishwasher came from the end of a conveyor belt; listless cafeteria patrons piled their dirty dishes and trays on the belt and didn't stop to watch as the dishes slowly traveled around into the back rooms filled with hissing water and chaotic sounds. Multicolored section barriers broke up the large room; forced-air currents made an invisible corral around the small smoking area. The buzz of conversation rose and fell in the air.

Julia leaned across the nicked and stained tabletop and smiled at him. "We can be more alone in a place like this. And we can discuss anything we want."

Julia was thin, of medium height, and wore her long blond hair simply, parted in the middle and hanging down behind her shoulders. Her eyes were bright, and Vincent thought he could see dozens of thoughts behind them, waiting to be brought to the surface. Her high cheekbones and delicate face made her seem fragile, but she argued vehemently and intelligently, in a no-nonsense way that quickly dispelled any impression of helplessness.

They both had coffee, which Vincent found to be a rather bitter, recycled-tasting restaurant blend; Julia had insisted on paying for hers. Almost impulsively, Vincent kept stirring his cup as they talked; she slurped her coffee and more than once sloshed over the edge of her cup as she gestured animatedly.

"But suppose, just suppose," Vincent said, "that the neo-Satanist movement isn't supposed to be true, or even believable. What if it's more like a net to capture some people with their own silliness? To show them how gullible they can be? What if it's like a trick, a practical joke that has, well, backfired?"

Julia considered this for only a moment. "Then whoever planned it was wrong from the start. If you have such power and influence, then you shouldn't purposely mislead the public. Why not take them down the right path from the start?"

He sat in silence for a long moment. She seemed puzzled, but waited. "I'm Vincent Van Ryman," he said in a soft voice.

And then, of course, he told her everything.

Vincent rented a hovercopter, and the two of them went alone up the coast to the Point Reyes seashore. Julia had read a great deal and filled her conversation with interesting and exotic trivia, but she had never before left the boundaries of the Metroplex, nor had she ever been inside a hovercopter.

Vincent awkwardly worked the unfamiliar controls that lifted the vehicle up from the rooftop pad and swung around to the side of the building. He enjoyed watching Julia's rapt attention as she splayed her fingers on the curved windowshield glass and peered out, wide-eyed and looking at the chesspiece buildings of the Metroplex from far above.

The copter shot northward, and the boundaries of the Metroplex faded rapidly into wooded hills and crowded, tourist-filled seaside communities. The old road below wound precariously along the side of a cliff that plunged far down to the ocean. A few breakers against the rocks looked like tiny flecks of foam in a gigantic basin.

Vincent felt somewhat daring as he swooped the hovercopter down to skim barely above the surface of the choppy water, paralleling the cliff face. Spray bounced up and misted the windshield. Julia clapped her hands and laughed—nervously, it seemed.

Far ahead, partly surrounded by wads of fog rising in the morning heat, Vincent could make out the lighthouse on its tiny promontory jutting out into Drake's Bay. The ocean rolled beneath the craft, and the sheer cliff beside them rapidly gave way to a wide expanse of beach next to a black honeycombed cluster of tide pools. Vincent flew ahead, then circled back; under the clear water the beach gradually sloped beneath the depths.

The hovercopter settled onto the sand, blowing up pebbles and debris. From what he could see, they were completely cut off in an area accessible only by air.

Julia jumped out of the craft and gleefully ran to the breakers. She kicked off her shoes and splashed up to her knees in the water, heedless of the rocks on the beach. Vincent laughed at her wide-eyed expression of shock.

"It's cold! It's freezing cold!"

"Of course it is. It's the ocean."

She splashed out and tried to brush droplets of water from her calves. "But the ocean is supposed to be warm."

"Not Point Reyes." He turned back to the hovercopter and opened up the storage compartment. "Come on. Let's have a picnic."

Vincent had gathered a lunch for them, even purchased a wicker picnic basket so that it would seem more like the real thing. Handing Julia the basket, he took the blanket out of the bottom shelf and went to spread it on the sand.

As they ate, Julia kept breathing deeply, looking around, staring at the tall beach grass and the sheer cliffs towering above them. Seagulls flew in the air.

After lunch, they went exploring up and down the beach. Julia seemed fascinated with the tide pools, squatting on the rocks and looking down into the orphaned puddles, poking her fingers at the small sea anemones, tipping over snails, and watching the thumb-sized hermit crabs crawl over the palm of her hand.

"I found you some seashells," Vincent said. She accepted them reverently from his hand and put them into the pocket of her blouse.

Back at the copter, Vincent withdrew some equipment and began setting up on a tripod.

"What are you doing?" she asked.

"I want to capture this. So I can remember every wonderful detail of this day." He carefully paced off a distance and erected the beam-splitter on a second tripod, then returned to focus the holocamera's laser on the splitter. Satisfied, he set the splitter on an automatic slow-scan, panning down the long beach and the ocean, following their footprints in the sand. Later, Vincent would pack up the camera and treasure the disk. Already he intended to project the hologram as a grand mural on the study wall.

"I'm very happy. Did you know that?" Vincent said with an alien tone of amazement in his voice.

She smiled and flipped her long blond hair behind her shoulders. "Yes. I gathered that."

They made love on the blanket on top of the soft yielding sand. The seagulls flew overhead and cried righteous indignation at the humans' brazenness. The waves pounded with a sensual power, a whispering, rushing sound that made everything seem perfect.

And everything *was* perfect. They didn't even notice their stinging sunburn until that evening.

If he had pressed the point, Julia probably would have moved in with him anyway, but first she insisted that he publicly denounce the neo-Satanists and expose the sham.

Julia had put another dimension into his life, showing him a world that didn't always have to be dark, uncaring, self-centered. She gave him tenderness, she made him malleable again, she smoothed out the jagged edges of his personality.

Next High Sabbat, Vincent commanded all the neo-Satanists to listen, and he confessed everything. "All of this"—he indicated the grotto, the robes, the relics, the symbols—"is the biggest practical joke in history. All of neo-Satanism is make-believe, fabricated—we concocted it one night when we were bored. We brainstormed all the Writings. We choreographed the rituals. We graphic-designed the symbols."

He cracked open the display cases that held the relics. "The hoofprint in the linoleum—didn't anybody realize there's a three-century gap between the time when Faustus lived and when linoleum was invented? And this, the black claw of Satan . . . plastic. Plain old plastic." He pulled off his High Priest's robe and tossed it on the floor in disgust.

"Go home. Spend your time in something worthwhile. Try to better the world, or better yourselves. We were just pulling your leg." He turned his back and walked toward the exit alcove. "I'm a little disappointed how easily you fell for it."

Vincent left the sacrificial chamber, slipping into the

dark and hidden catacombs that would take him to a mass-trans station, where he could catch a skipper back to the mansion before curfew. He had no desire to see any part of the tumult he had left behind. . . .

Like a careening pendulum, once set in motion he rapidly turned against the neo-Satanists and became their most outspoken opponent. In a press release Julia had written, Vincent told the cult's dark secrets and the sham. Normally reclusive, Vincent Van Ryman appeared on several news services and found himself quoted liberally in the current-events databases.

He sent a copy of the press release to Nathans with a note that said, "Sorry, Francois. But this has gone on long enough."

Vincent had not spoken to the other man since meeting Julia, and he wanted to let Nathans settle down before trying to get in touch again. Now that Vincent spent his days with Julia, he seemed to have little time for anything else.

Sweating and precariously balanced on the eaves of his home, Vincent dismantled the gargoyles from the roof gables; Julia stood on the ground next to the sharp wrought-iron fence, apparently ready to catch him if he fell. Later, armed with paintbrush and scrubbing tools, she went about defacing all the pentacles from the mansion.

Afterwards, as dusk settled on a very different Van Ryman mansion, they sat in the sauna next to the master bedroom, drinking iced tea. A full pitcher rested on one of the floorboards, water beading down its sides from the heat and the steam.

"I think I'm going to purchase a Servant, maybe two," Vincent suggested. "That way we can have more time with each other."

She closed her eyes and nodded wearily. "Mmmm." She ran the cold, wet surface of her iced tea glass along her chin and jaw, relishing the coolness. Vincent thought she looked content.

He felt satisfied himself. He had been afraid that challenging the neo-Satanists would be much more difficult, with far greater repercussions. But it had been so easy. And it was all over now.

21

Jones ran blindly through the streets, waving his hands in front of him though the crowd had long since thinned out. He breathed heavily; the damp air whistled through his nostrils unfiltered.

The Enforcer wore only his armored boots and his black skin-pants; everything else was gone. He had discarded the rest of his armor in scattered pieces during his dazed flight. The suit radio had gone with it, smashed violently under someone's feet. His skin crawled with the memory of hundreds of hands grasping, groping, tearing, trying to kill him by sheer force of numbers. His ears roared, but Jones kept himself from screaming, from releasing the pressure still building within him. What had he done? How had he deserved this? The Enforcer continued to run, trying to flee farther, hide deeper into anonymity.

Enforcers didn't run. But right now his Guild status didn't concern him. Most of all he wanted to forget the nightmarish memories, sharpened by his own fear. . . .

As the rebel Servant had vanished down the streets, moving faster than seemed humanly possible, Jones found himself trapped by the swelling, murderous mob. He had killed someone. Maybe more than one. The people surrounded him like the web of a voracious spider. Chaotic anger filled the air, making it difficult to breathe with the sweat and shouts and liquid hatred. Hands, bodies, people pushed at him. Some of the pedestrians began to throw things. Jones felt his armor battered and pummeled—and he struck back. He fired his weapons, hoping to awe and frighten the mob, to drive them away, to give him some breathing room.

He was an Enforcer. Fitzgerald Helms had died for Jones to get into the Guild. He wasn't after the pedestrians—he wanted the Servant. He had to stop the Servant, because he didn't want to think where the Guild would demote him if he screwed up one more time. Jones had no more amnesty units left to his name.

But the Servant had escaped—wounded but gone, and the mob remained. The mob wanted only blood anyway, and they hated Enforcers almost as much as they hated Servants.

A suicidal old man managed to snatch one of Jones's weapons and cradled it gleefully in his gnarled hands, but the Enforcer shot him. The weapon spun away into the crowd, and moments later someone else picked it up and began shooting indiscriminately. Jones realized with horror that several people in the crowd were laughing.

Two more people reached for the other weapons bristling from his armor. Training and blind reflexes took over now; panic smothered all thoughts from the rational part of his brain. Moving jerkily, Jones shot in all directions until the pocket bazooka was empty. But still the people didn't fall back. Someone yanked the heater-knife from its socket at his side, and the seal broke with a thin *pop*. The hot blade glanced off the Enforcer's white armor. Grasping hands tore the other two projectile weapons from their sockets, and Jones knew that even the dura-plated armor couldn't withstand such an attack.

The people continued to press forward. Frantic, unable to escape, Jones fled deep inside himself, letting the body fend for itself. Uninhibited, his hands instinctively chose the last alternative open to him.

Someone was trying to break his arm, but the Enforcer managed to wrench it free, silently blessing the slickness of the polished armor. His finger found a depression in his chest plate and pushed a release button.

Dense clouds of stinging black smoke poured from the joints of his armor, pushing the mob back with its foul smell. Hidden by the smokescreen, Jones pulled off his helmet and threw it far into the unseen crowd. He held his breath and ran through the blinded and choking people, trying to remain unobtrusive, shedding pieces of his armor and hoping to become invisible, normal, just another face on the street. The armor was his protection, a part of him insisted; it made him an Enforcer, someone to be feared and respected, and he shed it with a growing horror at himself. But he had to get rid of the armor, had to get away from the clutching, murderous crowd. . . .

Still moving mechanically, dazed, Jones came to an enclosure between two tall blank-faced buildings. A chain-link fence surrounded the enclosure, topped with glis-

161

tening barbed wire. Inside the fence a mushroom forest of satellite dishes stood skewed at various angles, looking like a haphazard array pointing toward invisible targets high in orbit. Some of the dishes were solid, some made of wire mesh.

The shadows of the struts and the dishes beckoned him, and some irrational impulse told him he had to get inside. Jones glanced along the ground, found a crumpled aluminum can, and tossed it at the chain-link fence, watching carefully for sparks.

The Enforcer felt a rush of adrenaline again as he visualized the hands reaching toward him . . . his own weapons stolen, playfully turned against him . . . the mob's anger pouring down on him like boiling oil, knowing that in an instant he would be torn limb from limb. . . .

Jones grabbed the chain-link and scrambled up. He paused at the barbed wires, wondering if they might be coated with some deadly substance or a paralytic drug. Even though he had no armor protecting him this time, his Enforcer training had taught him how to avoid barbed wire. He swung his slim dark body over and let himself drop to the ground. The armored boots absorbed much of the impact, and he crouched, looking around, then quickly sought the safety of the tangled shadows.

His chest heaved as he lowered himself under one of the deepest shadows, sheltered from sight. Jones let the last adrenaline course through his bloodstream, making lap after lap of his circulatory system. And then he drowned in a numbing grayness of exhausted sleep.

He awoke long after nightfall. Cool darkness around him made the satellite dishes seem like alien sentinels. He could look through the wire mesh of one of the dishes to see scattered stars far above, most of them washed out by the ambient glow of the Metroplex.

Jones sat up with a jolt and looked at his wrist chronometer. After midnight—past curfew. And he was an Enforcer, out of uniform, with no ID.

He shuddered. He had left his armor behind. Was he even an Enforcer anymore? He had deserted his duty. He had let another rebel Servant escape. He had killed pedestrians. He had been the cause of a bloody riot.

How would the Guild look at it? Would they punish him, demote him to some even worse job? Would they dismiss him, make it impossible for him to find other work—force him to become one of the jobless blues? Or would they quietly kill him?

Jones crouched, unmoving, debating with himself whether he should try to avoid the Enforcer curfew patrols, try to make it back to his own dwelling without being caught; or, if he should just stay put where he was, shivering in the wet coldness of the night, and hope nobody found him before morning?

Hiding under the skeletal support beams of the satellite dishes, he felt lost and cold and confused. He was a disgrace. He didn't want to confront his peers. Only the familiar surroundings of his apartment would help. He wanted to go home. He wanted to clutch at the things around him like a security blanket.

Jones grasped the chain-link fence and started to climb. He froze, motionless, when the fence rattled in the after-midnight silence. He waited, then scrambled the rest of the way up. From this direction the barbed wire slanted outward, much easier to crawl over.

He dropped to the ground and tried to remain in the shadows of the buildings, slipping from one street to the next, looking for familiar landmarks, trying to get his bearings. Off in the distance and in the after-curfew silence, Jones could hear the sounds of one of the mock street battles staged by the Guild. But this one was far away. He was safe.

The lights from the silent hovercar stabbed down at him as he tried to cross an unlit intersection. Jones stopped dead in his tracks and then slumped his shoulders in defeat.

While he and Frampton had been on their curfew patrols, most people caught out after midnight tried to escape and hide, making the Enforcers use the hovercar's scatter-stuns, but Jones knew flight was useless. He surrendered without resistance.

The Enforcers emerged from their vehicle and strode toward him. Jones waited, feeling fear grow, but he dismissed it—he had had enough of fear for one day.

The shorter of the two Enforcers gruffly began to quote the specific sections of the Guild code Jones had broken. The black man raised his hand and began to quote the same words in unison until the other patrolman stopped speaking.

"I know," Jones said. "I'm an Enforcer, too. Used to be on curfew patrol." He gave his name and ID number, and told his story, knowing exactly what the two curfew patrolmen thought of it; he himself had encountered enough different excuses while on patrol. "Maybe you have an A.P.B. out on me?" They had to, of course. He was an Enforcer missing in the line of duty. Someone had to be looking for him. He could explain.

The taller of the two Enforcers, who had not yet spoken a word, entered Jones's ID number and description into a portable Net terminal. Jones waited for it all to be verified, but then the silent Enforcer keyed everything in again, as if he were deeply puzzled. He called the other Enforcer over and keyed in the information a third time.

Jones began to feel a dread growing in the pit of his stomach. What had the Guild done to him now? All this was getting to be too much, and he didn't think he had anymore panic left inside him. "Look, I can take you back to my apartment. You're going to have to escort me there anyway. The Net will let me in, and I can prove my identity to you."

He waited, exasperated. The two Enforcers looked at him, then looked at each other as if considering.

"I can prove it! Come on."

"I think you'd better do that, Mr. Jones," the shorter Enforcer finally said. His voice came out hollow behind the face mask.

Jones followed the two Enforcers to the large armored hovercar. He almost clambered in front with the two patrolmen, but then stopped himself and complacently went into the segregation chamber.

The chamber had no windows, and Jones sat sulking, drawing his knees up against his bare chest. Shivering a little bit, he wondered what he was going to do. He felt the hovercar lift off and rise up into the air. He waited; it seemed like forever.

But at last the hovercar drifted back to the ground again, and he heard a muffled thump as it came to rest. Jones blinked and stepped out into the darkness as the pressurized hatch hissed open. The two Enforcers flanked him on either side. He recognized the tall complex of Guild dormitories, and he glanced at the repetitive rows of windows stacked up several stories—each window looked the same, and Jones couldn't begin to guess which one belonged to his own quarters.

Watching Jones somewhat skeptically, the two curfew patrolmen escorted him to the terminal mounted beside the sealed door. Showing a confidence that he did not feel, Jones entered his logon name, ID number, and access code. His knees felt weak with relief as the screen flashed "ACCESS GRANTED" and the door opened.

"We'd better accompany you to your room," the shorter Enforcer said.

"Certainly," Jones said, feeling more confident now. The three entered, taking a lift up to the sixth floor.

He reached his door and said, trying to hide the relief in his voice, "This is it. I'm sorry for the trouble, and I'll be facing a few reprimands tomorrow."

Jones opened the door and took a step inside. He saw motion in the dimness of his own room, and he let out an audible gasp of surprise as two blue-armored members of the Guild's Elite Guard stood up simultaneously from where they had been waiting for him.

The two white-armored curfew patrolmen stiffened in shock and seemed not to know what to do. Jones wanted to say something, but the words crumbled in his mouth. He had seen the Elite Guard only once or twice, escorting very important people or in extremely dangerous high-visibility missions. He could not imagine what he had done to attract their attention.

The two Elite Guards stepped closer to Jones. "We'll take him now," one of them addressed the curfew patrolmen. "I suggest you don't report your pickup. We'll handle all the details. Now go back to your patrol."

The white-clad Enforcers saluted mechanically and turned to leave, almost as if they were running away.

Jones stood motionless, terrified. One of the Elite Guards closed the hall door, sealing the room and leaving the three of them alone together.

22

"Tell me about it," the nurse/tech said.

Still frightened and confused, Danal reached into the open trapdoor of his mind, hauling out the last captive memories like strongboxes from a musty cellar.

Vincent Van Ryman's carefree, euphoric attitude had lasted only a few days after he had denounced neo-Satanism. At first he felt victorious, childishly proud of himself and happy to have made a difference. Several times Vincent tried to contact Nathans, but the other man refused to speak to him, not acknowledging or even reading Vincent's messages. Vincent brooded over his mentor's cold treatment, sad and somewhat disappointed. Julia convinced him that Nathans would calm down, given time.

Then he received the first death threat from a disgruntled neo-Satanist cult member, someone whose focus in life had been stripped away because of Vincent's cynical revelations. Other, different threats came in rapid succession. Particularly vicious were the jobless blues, so long dejected and hopeless, the ones who had fastened upon neo-Satanism as a new light at the end of their tunnel. Now they felt cheated once more.

Vincent received anonymous messages dropped into his electronic mail files, one of them even addressed to Randolph Carter, his carefully guarded secret identity. Someone tied a handwritten threat to a rock and threw it at the shatterproof transplastic windows of the Van Ryman mansion. The rock thumped harmlessly off the glass, disturbing Vincent and Julia from a game of cribbage in the study.

The vehement anger behind the threats bothered Vincent. Julia had convinced him that the truth was always best, but now he began to feel a growing horror, wondering if perhaps these people didn't want the truth, but preferred something exotic to believe in.

Vincent went outside, picking up the rock from the

thorny shrubs around the house. Whoever had thrown it was gone, fled into the thinning crowds as dusk began to settle over the Metroplex.

Some of the threats were crudely veiled, and some were blatant and explicit. He knew that simple Servant bodyguards—such as his father had owned years before—could not offer sufficient protection, especially if one of the disgruntled fanatics decided to blow up the entire mansion. He glanced at the scrawled threat, then destroyed the note before Julia could see it.

It gave him an odd, warm feeling to realize that he was actually more afraid for Julia's sake than for his own.

With his father's share of the neo-Satanist profits, Vincent Van Ryman set about compiling the most effective, most sophisticated Intruder Defense System ever designed. He supervised its installation himself and spent hours studying its complexity, poring over blueprints as he sat on the hard floor of the study, legs crossed, soaking up the warm purple glow of the crystal fireplace.

A deadly force-field shell surrounded the boundaries of his property, making a protective dome over the mansion; intricate computer-monitored surveillance systems detected external motion, activating additional alarms when objects moved too close to the perimeter; a pack of repair-rats labored in the conduits beneath the ground, mechanically inspecting and maintaining the network of power cabling.

Three times within the first week Vincent found blackened corpses slumped against the invisible force field, people who had tried to creep up to the mansion from the back.

Isolated in their little island of protection, Vincent and Julia sat back, absorbed in each other for the time being, content with each other's company and needing no one else. Together they decided to get a pair of Servants for the cooking and cleaning and housework, leaving them more time with each other. They ordered one male and one female Servant, Joey and Zia.

The Servants filled their roles, did their jobs, remained unobtrusive and patient in the mansion. Waiting. Vincent did not notice until too late that Joey's physical build was oddly familiar, identical to his own. Vincent had been too naive, too trusting; he of all people should never have underestimated Francois Nathans.

On their last evening together, the night of Julia's

murder and the beginning of Vincent Van Ryman's long nightmare that transcended even death, Julia sat across from him in the formal dining room, resting both elbows on the tablecloth. It had started out as an argument, when both of them slowly let down their careful barriers of close confinement. Their mutually obsessive companionship began to wear on the nerves after a while. But for the time being they steered the conversation to more lighthearted things.

They talked with their mouths full, savoring the meal the two new Servants had cooked for them. "I'm glad we decided to give them both gourmet programming," Julia said as she slurped a mouthful of fettuccine. Joey and Zia stood just outside the door of the formal dining room, watching with oddly alert eyes.

Vincent picked up the bottle of cheap pink champagne to refill both of their glasses. The bottle seemed slippery and unwieldy; he knocked it over, spilling half the contents on the tablecloth. Vincent couldn't reach forward fast enough to catch it. The champagne foamed as it spread across the table. It all began to look blurry to him. . . .

Julia giggled at his clumsiness, but then stopped laughing abruptly—

He awoke in the artificially dank chamber underneath the mansion, manacled to the walls. He recognized it as the cellar room where they used to have secret Inner Circle meetings with some of the highest-ranked neo-Satanist fanatics. But he and Julia had sealed the door, plastered over the opening. Who had torn it open again?

As his eyes came into focus, he noticed that Francois Nathans waited there. He couldn't see Julia.

"Good. You're finally awake," Nathans said, taking a step toward him. Vincent gaped at the other man, confused, not quite ready to believe that Nathans would actually do anything to harm him. He looked at his wrists and ankles chained to the wall.

"Manacles, Francois? You've got to be kidding."

Nathans smiled to himself. "It appealed to me."

Vincent felt dizzy again, and a rush of confusion swirled around his head. Nathans? What was he doing in the mansion? Why hadn't Nathans answered any of his messages before?

"Julia. What happened to Julia?"

Nathans made a wry scowl. "Oh how noble of you to think of the poor lady first, Vincent. She's already dead—dumped on the street and deleted from The Net." Nathans seemed to take a wry pleasure in watching Vincent's response.

"I don't believe it."

"When have I ever lied to you, Vincent?" The man's cool expression gave only faint hints of the anger that seemed to boil inside.

Vincent wanted to imagine that he had hurled himself against the chains, wanted to think that he had vengefully tried to strangle Nathans where he stood. But instead Vincent felt as if someone had struck him in the stomach with a sledgehammer, knocking the wind from his lungs and destroying the will to live. He slumped against the stone wall like a beaten pet. Nathans drew a deep breath, as if not pleased with his own decision.

"You, on the other hand, are a much bigger PR item. Our first 'Traitor to the Faith.' I couldn't have dreamed up a better unifying force if I tried." Nathans laughed, "Oh boy, we're going to milk this for all it's worth."

Vincent's mind spun in circles, trying to find something to hold onto. Julia couldn't be dead. They had just been talking and laughing together . . . Nathans would never turn against him—he had taught Vincent so much, discussed so many things with him, hung so many dreams on his head. Nathans was too great a man, too sharp a thinker to stoop to childish and petty revenge games.

Vincent saw movement out of the corner of his eye as a doctor stepped forward. Vincent noticed that a star-in-pentagram logo had been embroidered on his white jacket.

The doctor spoke to Nathans, completely ignoring the captive. "Now that he's awake, the drug must be out of his bloodstream. We should be ready to begin."

"We need to take some blood samples, Vincent," Nathans said flippantly. "I hope you don't mind."

Vincent found the strength to struggle, but the manacles held him, and both men managed to grip his arm, holding it motionless. Vincent rolled his eyes downward to watch as his dark and syrupy blood bubbled up from the vein into a small sterilized vial. He breathed heavily as the doctor smeared his arm with coagulant. The medical man carefully packed the vial of Vincent Van Ryman's blood in a padded case, which he then snapped shut.

But Nathans wasn't a murderer—he wouldn't just kill Julia in cold blood.

"He'll have to hold absolutely still for the next part," the doctor mumbled to Nathans as he fitted another hypodermic syringe with a capsule of yellowish liquid. He turned toward Vincent, and as Vincent cringed backward, the medical man injected him in the neck.

"Sorry," Nathans said.

Vincent gasped and then felt his muscles turn cold, swallowed up in a blanket of frozen jelly. The rest of his body felt like a deadweight dangling from his brain stem.

"A nerve paralyzer, Vincent. It'll wear off, sooner or later. For now, we have to see about giving you a new image."

Vincent's tongue thickened in his throat, but with the greatest effort of will, feeling as if he were commanding every nerve one at a time, he managed to croak out a single word before his mouth froze half open.

"Why?"

Nathans's eyebrows shot up, and his left fist clenched convulsively. He seemed to have been waiting for Vincent to ask his question. "Why? Because you told—that's why! Don't you realize how much damage you caused? You may have snatched away mankind's last best hope for the future! You idiot, I trusted you! I saw promise in you, but you turned into a romantic sap instead!"

Nathans hung his head. His eyes glistened, and his face flushed red. "By introducing Servants, I offered common people the greatest gift—an opportunity to become part of the intelligentsia, the elite, free of charge. No strings attached. All they had to do was take the trouble to learn, to better themselves, use their free time to benefit us all. But they snubbed the offer and held tight to their ignorance instead. So with neo-Satanism I shoved their own stupidity right back in their faces—and they ate it up!"

The man's rage continued to pour out, and he looked ready to pound Vincent's face even as he hung paralyzed, suspended like a marionette on the manacles.

"Can't you see? Of course neo-Satanism is a sham, but the people have to realize it for themselves! You've cheated them out of their own realization. Prophets have been giving the public an endless string of different truths since the beginning of civilization. Now, by your confession to them, by giving away our secret, you became just another debunker, just another man at a podium with another story to believe in. You've stolen the opportunity of self-enlightenment away from thousands of them. So many, so many!"

The doctor lifted Vincent's chin upward, holding his slack jaw in position. Another needle, another syringe—only this time the doctor left a thin line of pricks, one after another, along his jawline, up behind his ear. The medical man hummed to himself as he moved with the careful precision of a tattooist, jabbing with the needle, squirting a tiny amount of the milky gray substance under Vincent's skin, and then moving half a centimeter over to repeat the process.

Nathans seemed to have calmed himself again. "You probably never heard us speak of surface-cloning, Vincent. That was something we kept under lock and key at Resurrection, Inc. While my special hotshot team worked on developing the resurrection process, one of the bioengineers stumbled upon a spinoff process, a special type of permanent biological disguise. Your father knew about it, but he didn't quite see its potential.

"You see, after taking a blood or skin sample from one person, we can use the genetic information to 'grow' an identical face on someone else, to clone someone's appearance. We strip the nuclei from the cells and then piggyback the genetic information on a special virus. After we've cultured the virus, we can inject it into many sites on the imposter's face, beginning a 'clone infection.' The virus spreads, carrying with it someone else's genetic information." He smiled, but kept anger burning behind his expression. "A new face is going to 'grow' on you, Vincent, spreading slowly. You'll be someone not so recognizable. We can even do your hands, if we want to change the fingerprints."

Paralyzed, Vincent could not blink, could not cringe, could not respond—he sagged against gravity, humiliated. Preoccupied, the doctor injected a string of clone-infection nodes around his hairline, pricking the scalp.

"The whole process will take about a week. I'm told that the itching and burning sensations are almost unbearable while you're growing a new face. But don't worry, we can keep you pleasantly sedated until all that's over with. Now that we have a clean blood sample from you, your own double can begin the same process of his own."

The doctor finished and put away his equipment. Without a word to Nathans, he packed up the case containing Vincent's blood sample and carried it reverently up the stairs.

"Maybe you've done irreparable damage to my plan, Vincent. But there might be a way to fix things, sort of a last-ditch effort. We have someone who matches your physical build and genetic type. We'll give him your face, your fingerprints, and when he's completely ready, he will *become* Vincent Van Ryman. It won't be perfect, because he'll only look like you, but he's studied your mannerisms, and his fingerprints will be identical. Only a retinal scan, voice print, or maybe a chromosomal match will tell the difference. Besides, we used drugs to get your Net password while you were unconscious, and that's really all he needs.

"I have already written the publicity speech for when 'you' make a sensational return to neo-Satanism, born again, denouncing your previous heretical babble. Then everything might be back on track again. We could survive this after all—no thanks to you."

Behind his unblinking eyes Vincent thought he saw a reflection of his own shock, horror, and bafflement. Francois Nathans was his idol, his friend, his teacher . . . and now his condemner, his torturer. At the same time, Nathans looked furious with Vincent, choking on righteous indignation.

"In a few weeks, after your new face has grown and you look just like any other neo-Satanist convert—and when your replacement has fully taken his role as High Priest Van Ryman—we'll have another High Sabbat, with you as the guest of honor at the sacrificial altar.

"And no one will know the difference . . . because you aren't *you* anymore."

23

An hour after all evidence had been cleaned from his lower office chambers, Francois Nathans received reports that the disturbance in the streets was completely quelled. He felt strangely relieved and overjoyed that the Enforcers had found only one destroyed Servant among the casualties, a female Servant—definitely not Danal.

He had somehow gotten away. Now all that remained was for Nathans to find him.

Nathans felt sleepy, mentally exhausted, with his stamina and his nerves stretched and frayed. He dimmed his office and lit a scented candle, letting the warm, flickering illumination soothe him. Turned down so low that he could barely hear it, a scratchy tape of Fats Waller sent strains of jazz through the dimness.

The message light sprang to life on the communications screen in front of him, and Nathans required a great effort of will to lift his finger and respond.

A white-armored Enforcer appeared on the screen, fidgeting. Nathans opened his eyes, trying to stare the man down, but he could see no response behind the black polarized faceplate.

"Mister Nathans?" the Enforcer asked.

"Yes? What is it?"

"I—I have been instructed to inform you that there has been another . . . that the body of the technician Rodney Quick has disappeared. We suspect it might be the Cremators, sir."

It struck him like a knife in the back, an unexpected blow from a forgotten adversary. Nathans surged fully awake. At another time he would have found this exhilarating, but too much had already gone wrong for one day. He clenched his fists, whitening the knuckles as he struck the side of his desk. For a moment he could find no words, and then they all seemed to burst out of his mouth at once.

"But how could he have been taken? He was right in our own building! Who was watching him? Where was he

173

taken for storage? How could someone have gotten to him?"

The Enforcer looked ready to break down. "We took him to the resurrection levels, sir. With Rodney Quick killed, there was no other alternate tech designated for that section. We had the riot to attend to, sir, and trying to find your Servant. But we didn't think there would be a problem. There shouldn't have been. And now he's gone, without a trace. As far as we can tell, no one entered or left the resurrection levels."

"Then your information is wrong!" Nathans snapped.

"There's another thing, too—" the Enforcer began, hesitant and uncertain.

"What?" Nathans stared furiously for a moment, then dropped his gaze. No use frightening the man so much he couldn't speak.

"One of the Servant assistants in Lower Level Six seemed extremely agitated when we tried to question her. We had to use the Command phrase to get her to respond at all, but she dropped to the floor before she could answer. Rolled up her eyes and fell over. Apparently dead. I swear we didn't do anything to her. It seems that she nullified her own microprocessor."

Nathans sat back heavily in his chair, frowning deeply. "But how? How can that be?" he mumbled, mostly to himself.

"Sir?" the Enforcer asked in a filtered voice coming out from the communications screen.

With a backhanded gesture Nathans muted the screen and continued to mutter to himself. Servants committing electronic suicide? Rodney Quick taken from Nathans's own doorstep at Resurrection, Inc.? Danal lost in a mob?

He tried to think of a suitable curse to spit out of his mouth, but could come up with none.

All evidence suggested that the Cremators did not take their subjects at random, only those who entered into a special contract. Did Nathans have a traitor in his own midst? It was a particularly sharp blow to think that Rodney Quick could have been involved with the Cremators. He felt infuriated and blindingly impotent.

He gritted his teeth and switched on the screen again. The Enforcer almost jumped. "I don't care what you have to do. Or how you go about it. But I want you to *find* Rodney Quick's body."

With a gesture of finality Nathans blanked the screen,

watching the nervous Enforcer vanish into a dark screen. He paced the room, talking to himself, thinking through possibility after possibility. Some of them worked out in his favor, some of them didn't.

Like a whispered voice in the background, Fats Waller continued to sing the blues.

He had not quite managed to walk the perimeter of the room twice before the message light signaled again. Nathans scowled impatiently at the interruption, but then he realized the communication came from a different channel, one of the more highly secured outlets.

A blue-armored Elite Guard stared back at him as the screen came into focus. "We've found him."

Nathans felt a surge of excitement. "Who? Rodney Quick?"

"Who?" the Elite Guard asked.

"Never mind. Who did you find?"

"Your Servant, sir."

Nathans gripped the edge of the desk, feeling his heart pound. "Where is he? Is he injured?"

"We think he's holed up in a medical center in another district. One of the Guild Interfaces spotted his name and ID code entered into The Net. A nurse/tech apparently processed him for some physical repairs. As your receptionist implied, Enforcer Jones seems to have injured him during his escape. He's been recuperating there most of the afternoon."

"Can we get him? What's the situation?"

"Probably. We'll have to be careful."

"Damned right you will! I don't want him damaged. He's too valuable. I've got a lot riding on that particular Servant. Do you understand?"

"Ours is not to reason why." The dry tone from the faceless Elite Guard almost startled Nathans. "We'll capture your Servant."

Nathans rubbed his hands briskly together, but then realized it was an old habit he had picked up from Stromgaard. "I'll wait for you to bring him to me."

24

And then the ritual of the High Sabbat, viewed through a drug-fogged haze. He saw the crowded people, the altar, the symbols—

Rah hyunn!

Rah hyuun!

—the imposter wearing the face of Vincent Van Ryman, holding up the sharp-bladed arthame as the real Vincent lay back, paralyzed, unable to move, unable to cringe. But perfectly able to feel the biting steel maul its way into his chest.

"Ashes to ashes, blood to blood; fly to Hell for all our good!"

"I remember the pain of the knife, like an explosion. And then . . . everything turned black, a *hard* black, like a polished rock. I can't describe it," Danal said, focusing his gaze deep into the distance. "Then I was blinking my eyes and looking out of the vat on the resurrection levels. Amniotic fluid was draining down into grates in the floor—I could hear it. All of that's very vivid. A tech stood in front of me." He hung his head. "I killed him later on."

The nurse/tech didn't seem concerned. "Nothing in between? Just the knife thrust and then waking up in Resurrection, Inc.?"

Danal paused, wrinkling his forehead as he considered. "Nothing. It's almost like a cassette tape that's been spliced together. First my death, and then a gap, and then . . . coming back."

The nurse/tech did not seem surprised, as if she had heard it all before.

Suddenly Danal's own mind doubled back on him, and other questions—previously held at bay by his recurring memories—began to push forward. "But who are you? You're a Servant! You *were* a Servant . . . you're alive!"

She smiled placidly. "Just like you."

Her words came back at him like a splash of cold water on his face. "Are there . . . others?"

"Yes, others who have *awakened*—through some traumatic experience—and now they can access the memories of their previous lives. After you meet Gregor, he'll explain it a lot better than I can."

Danal sat with his eyes wide and his mouth slightly open in wonder. Possibilities echoed inside his head, and he had to hammer them back, forcing them to come one at a time so that his consciousness would not be overwhelmed by awe. "What do we do now?"

The nurse/tech grasped at his practical question, as if the more esoteric explanations made her uneasy. "First of all, we have to get you out of here. And soon. I entered your ID and your Master's name into The Net—anybody with sense enough to look will be able to track you down, sooner or later. We'll have to get you out unobtrusively, to a safe place."

Then her eyes grew hard. "But one thing I absolutely must impress upon you, something you have to keep at the front of your mind above all else. Something you can't forget."

"What?" he asked.

Like someone sharing a secret initiation, the nurse/tech lowered her voice. "We must not be discovered. If the public knew that Servants can awaken, maybe return as lost loved ones, or lost enemies—well, I don't want to consider the consequences. People are already uneasy enough about us.

"We've got to keep it secret—that's our greatest advantage. We Wakers can do things, support ourselves, and plan for our future. It's delicate stuff, with such far-reaching consequences as the future of all Servants, so we've got to proceed with the utmost care. We don't want massacres of Servants, and we don't want an upheaval of all society, you know."

She seemed to run out of patience with herself. "Gregor will explain it all to you. He's a lot more eloquent. For now, I'm more concerned with getting you to him. Stay here a minute."

The nurse/tech left the bright room, sliding the door shut behind her. She hurried out to the front lobby with a firm, businesslike stride, but stopped abruptly upon looking out the transplastic entry doors.

Outside, the black hulking shape of an Enforcers Guild hovertransport hung in the air with its tonguelike ramp extending to the ground. A second transport lowered itself into position. White-armored Enforcers filed out of the first craft, taking positions near the door. An Elite Guard, accompanied by one regular Enforcer, strode to the sliding transplastic doors; his midnight-blue armor made him look much larger than he actually was.

Several of the techs and waiting patients pushed excitedly to the window, watching and whispering to each other; some patients seemed completely apathetic, scanning Net periodicals or staring at the artificial plant-things in the lobby.

As the doors slid open for the Elite Guard and the first Enforcer, the nurse/tech moved quickly to meet him before anyone else could speak. The Elite Guard seemed startled by her abrupt presence, and she used it to push her advantage.

"Yes, Guildsman, how may we be of assistance? I can see this is serious. Please be careful. The safety of our patients is paramount."

The blue-armored Guard turned his opaque visor toward her. "You have a Servant here. He was injured, and someone healed him."

"That *is* our business after all," she said, smothering her own sarcasm.

"My orders are to apprehend him."

The troops of Enforcers outside had surrounded the center. Other men in the second hovertransport stood waiting.

"Are we in danger from this Servant?" She placed a worried tone in her voice. "May I ask what he's done?"

"No, you may not. Please direct me to him." The accompanying Enforcer tensed, letting his hand stray toward a weapon.

"Yes, yes. One moment." The nurse/tech bustled behind the counter, bumping her hip. She rattled her fingers over a keyboard, ostensibly calling up information on Danal, stalling for time, trying to think.

"Ah, yes. He was injured in the shoulder, but he's recuperating now. Claims his name is Danal—well, of course his name is Danal, since Servants can't lie." She let out a little laugh. "Says here that the attending physician suspected your Servant might be violent or something. Here, follow me."

She bustled off down one of the corridors with the two armored men marching closely on her heels. "He's in this one—it's one of our high-security chambers, designed to restrain the more violent patients and to ensure that they can't escape."

"Good." The Elite Guard pulled out his scatter-stun, and the other Enforcer did the same. They both tensed. "Now let us in."

The nurse/tech activated the door, and both men leaped into the empty chamber. Just as quickly she reversed the switch and slammed the door back into its closed position, affixing the edges with magnetic seals. Smiling to herself, she illuminated the "CAUTION—VIOLENT PATIENT" designator and turned rapidly to walk away as the two trapped Enforcers began to pound on the door.

For lack of a better idea, the nurse/tech activated the emergency fire alarms as she hurried back to Danal's room. An urgent ratcheting sound filled the halls; the other people in the medical center milled about, confused.

The nurse/tech slid open the door to Danal's room and threw him an apron like those worn by the orderly Servants. "Put this on. And come out in just a minute. Trouble. I think this is going to be tough."

The nurse/tech popped out into the hall again, ushering the people toward the front door. "We all have to evacuate! We've got a situation here. The Elite Guard wants us out—come on, let the Enforcers do their job! Everybody out!"

Without their Elite Guard leader the massed Enforcers outside seemed completely at a loss when the patients and medical personnel began to crowd out the doors. The Enforcer troops could not retain control, short of stunning the front lines of the people, and they did not want another mob disturbance so soon after the riot outside Resurrection, Inc. The uncertain chaos outside even exceeded the nurse/tech's expectations.

As she returned to get Danal, she noticed that the door of the confinement chamber had buckled outward slightly, glowing a dull red as the two trapped Enforcers used their own weapons in an attempt to blast out.

Danal emerged from his room, uneasily wearing the orderly smock. The stain-killing enzymes in his own gray jumpsuit had by now managed to dissolve much of the stain from Nathans's blood, and the apron made him look more unobtrusive.

The grating evacuation alarm continued to pound through the air, adding to the confusion. The nurse/tech grabbed his arm and propelled him toward the front.

"Everybody *out!*" she shouted, then lowered her voice to Danal. "Remember what I said. No one can find out about us, especially not the Guild. We'll take advantage of the confusion and try to get away, but they've got two transports of Enforcers out there. Somebody must want you very badly."

"Nathans is dead. I'm surprised the imposter has that much influence."

As they reached the lobby, the nurse/tech put on a harried commanding voice. "Servant! Take that box and follow me. Quickly!"

The nurse/tech pointed to a box filled with small vacuum-sealed bottles; a label, "BIOLOGICAL SAMPLES—IN STRICT CONFIDENCE," stood out prominently on the outside of the box. Danal picked up the package, made sure to keep a blank, mechanical expression on his face, and followed her outside. He tried to hide his face behind the box, though Danal doubted any of the Enforcers had a good description of his facial characteristics anyway.

Some of the Enforcers stood rigid, as if at attention; others ran around, chasing people, trying to look authoritative.

The nurse/tech hopped from one person to another in the crowd, seeming to tend the displaced patients. One man squatted on the ground, crying, staring at his knees. The nurse/tech went by, patted him on the back, and went to a woman who was adjusting her own bandages on a burned hand. "You all right? Good."

She moved on. Danal followed her obediently, like a good Servant. She spoke to him quietly out of the corner of her mouth. "Over there—see it? If we're careful, I think we might be able to just walk out of here."

Danal looked where she indicated. A block and a half away, one of the broad KEEP OFF THE GRASS patches glowed threateningly with its lush, vibrant green lawn, fenced off with a knee-high barricade. One Enforcer stood stationed beside it, presumably to make sure no one slipped and fell into the deadly disintegrator patch. The single Enforcer seemed to be watching the chaos around the medical center, but made no move to help out.

When the two nearest Enforcers moved aside to break up a fight between a medical center tech and a patient, the nurse/tech stepped up her pace and bustled down the street, trying to get away from the crowd.

Behind them, the trapped Elite Guard and his accompanying Enforcer burst out of the medical center entrance, finally successful in blasting their way through the door of the confinement chamber. Both of them had weapons in each hand. They began shouting, causing a large commotion.

The nurse/tech did not look back, but moved more quickly instead. Danal saw the lone Enforcer ahead of them by the disintegrator patch and prayed that he wouldn't pay any particular attention to them.

"Hey! Wait! You—" one of the Enforcers behind them bellowed.

The nurse/tech broke into a run. "Follow me! Now!"

Danal dropped the box of samples with a crash at his feet and leaped over it as it fell. Someone else shouted, and a *ping!* exploded at Danal's feet.

"No, you idiot! Not projectile weapons!" someone screeched behind them. "We've got to take him *alive*! Scatter-stuns, everyone!"

Danal ran. The Enforcer in front of them stood with his legs spread, intimidating, but not moving from his position. He held one gloved hand out, waggling it slightly in a strange gesture. The nurse/tech almost seemed to nod and ran directly toward him.

"Danal! Command: Follow!"

Unable to resist and suddenly feeling betrayed by the Command phrase, Danal leaped after her. He heard the buzzing hum behind him as scatter-stun fields radiated outward.

He and the nurse/tech had almost reached the lone Enforcer. The gaping deadly maw of the KEEP OFF THE GRASS patch shone a beautiful green, beckoning.

Then suddenly Danal's left leg went completely numb and useless as a scatter-stun field struck it. His own momentum carried him forward, but he tripped and fell directly into the arms of the waiting Enforcer.

The white-armored man grappled with him, wrestling the Servant in a bear hug. Danal tried to struggle, but the Enforcer began to tip backward, stumbling into the low fence surrounding the disintegrator patch.

The nurse/tech let out a wild howl and also leaped to

tackle the Enforcer. All three of them toppled over the low barricade toward the deadly shimmering grass.

With the speed of his microprocessor Danal felt himself falling with agonizing slowness, unable to escape. The last thing he saw was the sharp and distinct green blades of grass. As he reached out his arm to try to stop their fall, Danal saw his own hand disappear into nothingness as a brief rush of ozone filled his nostrils. Then the rest of his body fell through, engulfed completely.

PART III

Awakening

25

Danal dropped through the disembodied blackness, flailing his arms. He could see nothing, but he sensed the tumble of the other two bodies as they fell together.

With a jolting abruptness, strands of nylon rope knocked the breath out of Danal's lungs, and he lurched wildly up and down until he finally came to rest on a wide net strung from above. He struggled and turned around, looking in the direction his mind remembered as "up." About fifteen feet above, he could see a blurry green square of prismatic light, like watching an illusion from behind. As Danal's eyes adjusted to the shadows, he could discern the supporting ropes stretching upward from the net, fastened to three overhanging girders.

Nothing made sense. He found himself intact, not a cloud of atoms scattered apart by the disintegrator field. He drew a deep breath, tasted a rich salty and musty tang in the air. He heard a faint rushing noise down below . . . and could even make out occasional snatches of conversation somewhere out in the darkness.

Beside him, the Enforcer managed to get to his knees on the wobbly net, apparently nonplussed. Danal tensed, ready to fight back if the Enforcer drew one of his weapons, but the armored man pulled off his helmet instead.

Stunned, Danal saw that his head was pale and bald—a Servant.

The nurse/tech shook herself, then let out a long sigh. "Well, we're in for it now."

In the grip of confused astonishment, Danal could not respond.

The Enforcer/Servant ignored him for the moment as he crawled to the edge of the swaying net, hindered by his stiff armor. He reached a rope ladder with which he hoisted himself onto a narrow wooden platform above. "You were a good plant, Laina. But it had to end sometime." He turned to Danal and smiled with a calm expression and an almost tangible personal warmth. "I'm Rolf. Welcome."

The nurse/tech—Laina—reached for the rope ladder herself as the Enforcer/Servant disappeared into the darkness. The white skirt rode up on her thick legs, exposing darkened panty hose that made cadaverous skin look like normal flesh. Danal remained motionless, squatting on the gently swinging net, looking in bafflement at the square of greenish light high above.

"But . . . we're still here! We fell through the disintegrator—"

"Maintenance opening."

"It was one of the KEEP OFF THE GRASS patches! I watched us fall through."

"Maintenance opening."

"What's going on—please?"

Laina seemed to hear the plaintive desperation in his voice and paused to give him an explanation. As he listened, Danal began to chink some of the gaping holes in the mysteries, though questions continued to pour around the edges.

"This is the Bay Area Metroplex, remember?" Laina began, "When have you ever seen the *Bay* in all your life? All you find is Metroplex, buildings and roadways and office plazas. Years and years ago our dear sprawling city butted up against the ocean and spread out over the water, where the builders could still sink their pilings to hit bedrock." She spread her arms to indicate the shadowy forest of pilings. "This was all oceanfront property!

"In the beginning, they left maintenance openings so workers could go down to check the conditions of the pilings, to inspect the support beams, but that's all been forgotten now that we've got Net-programmed repair-rats to do all the routine maintenance. However, that still leaves the maintenance openings up on top. Some crazy city planner covered them with patches of holographic grass. Maybe they thought it would look pretty or something."

She smiled and raised her painted eyebrows; her thick lipstick looked wet in the dusty light. "Holographic grass. Oh, people must have seen some clod fall right through the illusion—hence, a 'deadly disintegrator blanket.' But it's been a long time now, and *we* make sure The Net doesn't give out any real information about the maintenance openings. I doubt even the human bigwigs know the truth."

She stood on the narrow platform and placed her hands on her hips. The wig covering Laina's smooth scalp sat cockeyed in front of her eyes, knocked loose by the long fall. "Well, are you just going to gawk at me or do you want me to show you around? Gregor probably wants to know what's going on."

Danal worked his way over to the rope ladder, twice losing his balance on the lurching net. He could see only darkness below like a bottomless open mouth. Somewhere beneath him, he heard the soft rush of waves curling around countless pilings and girders.

"So who's this Gregor you keep talking about?"

The nurse/tech offered her hand to help him up. The grip felt cool but strong. "He's our fearless leader."

With a Servant's precise control Laina led him along a narrow walkway, a wooden board barely ten centimeters wide. Danal recognized similar walkways extending from place to place, level to level, and interconnected by rope or metal ladders and occasional platforms.

"After curfew sometimes we use the KEEP OFF THE GRASS patches to get up there. But most of the time we choose less dramatic means—we found several openings and passages into the lower levels of buildings, once we knew where to look."

"After curfew?" Danal sounded surprised.

"Sure, why not?"

"Not worried about the Enforcers?"

She made a wry expression. "It's not difficult to be smarter than a bunch of bored Enforcers."

Intermittent bright lights hung from various supports and girders; cords dangled like snakes in the rich shadows, tapping into the vast and intricate power conduits of the Metroplex. The dangling lights ahead looked like a pattern of stars over the dark Bay water. Large crates forming a stockpile of food and hardware hung in nets suspended from crossbeams and looming over the walkways.

Laina quickly worked her way down two rope ladders, bringing him closer to where he could hear the rippling ocean. Then Danal began to see people, other Servants dressed in a hodgepodge of clothing, some in gray jumpsuits, but mostly they wore bright and vibrant colors. All of them moved with a purposeful semblance of normal life, without the mechanical apathy of ordinary Servants.

"Are those all . . . Wakers?" Danal asked.

"You bet." Many of the others stirred, watching his arrival. Some smiled; some looked worried.

The Wakers' network of hammocks, platforms, suspended lights and ropes made a virtual world of its own. Some of the Wakers lay back under the harsh lights, sunning themselves, apparently working on their melanin to regain some skin color, though the clear synBlood would never let them have the ruddy appearance of life.

Near his ear Danal heard a clicking and scuttling noise. He looked up to see a pair of articulated mechanical repair-rats making their painstaking rounds—tediously maintaining things, checking conduits and wires, fixing structural damage. Tiny scanner lights endlessly swept over their field of view, correlating the picture with a master plan fed to them by a remote Net link. The repair-rats each carried a bevy of tiny tools and synthesizing equipment to repair any deviations they detected.

Laina noticed the repair-rat and swore under her breath. Danal realized the mechanical drones had been dismantling one of the hanging sunlamp fixtures. She reached up to deactivate both repair-rats and switched them back on after moving them to a different crossbeam. "There, it'll take them *days* to get reoriented." She clucked her tongue. "We basically ignore the damned things, except they always try to undo the intentional changes we've made down here. It's a constant battle."

Danal found the problem to be delightfully normal.

Gregor waited for them in a semi-private area. Low to the uneasy water, where several pilings clumped together and blocked him off from sight, the leader of the Wakers reclined on a wide hammock. A sturdy plank platform had been attached to the pilings and supported by ropes from above, forming a firm floor. Several sunlamps beat down with a harsh yellow glow. Stripped to the waist, Gregor lay back, sunning himself and reading a thin hardcover book, *Frankenstein*.

The nurse/tech led Danal along the narrow, creaking walkways and climbed down into the leader's area. Gregor placed a bookmark on his page and snapped the volume shut as he sat up. The hammock swayed as Gregor gripped its edges.

"You'd better tell me what happened, Laina," Gregor

said before she could speak. Danal saw that the leader of the Wakers was a large man with high cheekbones, a heavy jaw, and distant brown eyes. Dark circles around his eyes made him look deeply concerned—not angry, but heavily burdened.

Laina kept her control and beamed at the leader, though her voice had a petulant tone. "It's your orders, Gregor, to assist other awakened Servants at all costs. But wait until you hear who this *is*—"

She introduced Danal. He responded uneasily, still not completely at peace with all he had learned, too much too fast. Between the nurse/tech and Danal, they managed to tell his story. He had hoped the pain would die away with another retelling—the wounds still ran as deep, but they did seem a little more bearable now.

When they had finished, Gregor looked impressed. He pursed his lips. "Vincent Van Ryman? And an imposter. Knowledge is a powerful thing, Danal, and you've just greatly increased our power." He stroked his chin and regarded the three support pilings with a distant gaze.

Danal felt baffled, and honored in a strange way, but before he could ask Gregor to explain himself, he heard someone else approaching, running recklessly down the narrow boards.

With a thump another Waker landed on Gregor's platform, panting. Danal saw him to be a young boy with grayish freckled skin that looked splotched and diseased with his Servant pallor. The boy seemed agitated, gave Laina and Danal only a cursory glance, and then spoke to Gregor. He wore part of a disguise, some flesh-colored makeup that had been smeared, and a reddish wig tucked under his arm.

"We've lost Monica!" he burst out. With time-slowed clarity Danal saw Gregor stiffen and sit like a statue, afraid. The boy continued. "At Resurrection, Incorporated! After we managed to get Rodney Quick's body free, some Enforcers came around and interrogated the Servants." The boy swallowed, then continued. "She— she terminated herself so she couldn't answer them."

Gregor hung his head. "Not Monica . . ." he mumbled. The boy Waker stood waiting, looking at the leader, then at Danal and the nurse/tech. But Danal had focused on a different comment.

"Rodney Quick?" He could hardly believe what he

had heard. "That—that's the technician, the one I killed! What were you doing with his body?"

"We had business with him." Gregor scowled, but seemed to use the question as a crutch to lift himself up from his grief. The leader looked at him with a hard, cold stare.

"We are the Cremators."

26

After curfew, at high tide, all of the Wakers gathered down by the water level. Danal sat in awe, counting forty-five Wakers, forty-five other Servants who had regained their memories.

Smoky torches hung in metal racks on the sides of the pilings; a black feathering of old soot streamed up the concrete. Danal could smell smoke from the creosote and burning wood, mingling with the sour odor of the sluggish sea. The reflected torchlight looked like fireworks cast upon the water.

"Come on, this is something you have to see," Gregor had told him. "It's our most sacred gathering."

Danal hesitated, uneasy. "Are you sure I should?"

Gregor's fixed gaze seemed filled with understanding. "You're one of us now. Everything we do is open to you."

Danal squatted on the platform nearest the water, withdrawn from the other Wakers, still confused, numb. Laina sat near him, wearing a bulky Servant jumpsuit instead of her nurse/tech outfit. The other Wakers seemed to respect Danal's wish for privacy.

Three Wakers swam in the water, naked, exuberant in the cold sea. The water would clutch at them when the tide turned and began to march back out to the unseen sea, but for now they enjoyed the freedom. Danal saw their carefree attitude, but he recalled too clearly—like pounding heartbeats in his head—the death of Julia, the betrayal by Nathans, his own murder at the High Sabbat. . . .

"Cremators?" he had asked Gregor, astonished. "But . . . why?" He sat for a moment, then shook his head. "I don't understand."

"To keep others from coming back. Returning from death, as we did. We can't destroy Resurrection, Inc., and I would not, in good conscience, try to. But someone has to offer the living this crucial choice, whether to risk becoming Servants, whether to risk remembering."

Danal was unable to choose among the many things he

did not understand. "But how? How did I awaken? How did *you* get your memories back?"

Gregor shrugged. "It's in the resurrection process. The bacteria in the final purging stage have a habit of mutating. We're doing some of our own analyses, but we're restricted by our limited manpower, you know, and because we have to be so damned careful when using other facilities. Apparently, a more potent strain of the purging bacteria can loosen some of the roadblocks to your old memories. The ones that are mercifully sealed away by death. Through one mechanism or another, all of us Wakers have regained our pasts, and our own thoughts and personalities.

"From your story, Danal, I suspect that Francois Nathans intentionally set you up, created the conditions for you to get your memory back. You should be able to figure out his reasons better than I can. But you claim Nathans is dead anyway, so the why of it all doesn't really matter."

"Are you saying that Nathans knew how to awaken Servants all along? Does he know about you?"

"No, you're jumping to conclusions. Other batches of the purging solution have mutated, and other Servants have indeed awakened, but anyone—including Nathans—would think these were just isolated instances. Any Servant would be disoriented and confused after getting the memories back—you remember it yourself. The first thing a newly awakened Servant does is to seek help in the obvious way, from humans. Most of these spontaneous Wakers are spotted, and summarily deactivated at Resurrection, Inc.

"But does anyone suspect our presence? Not at all. We wouldn't survive an hour if anyone did, especially Nathans. You know how he hated the Cremators."

Danal pondered this, and Gregor continued, "Have you ever heard of a story called *R.U.R.*? Rossum's Universal Robots?" Danal shook his head. "Well, it's a rather obscure play, but important when it first appeared in the year 1921. It was written by a Czechoslovakian named Karel Capek, and he first introduced the world to the term 'robot.' Derived from a Czech word meaning 'involuntary service.' Now, Rossum's robots weren't ratcheting mechanical monstrosities with blinking lights and buzzing voices, but organic, humanlike servants to do all forms of tedious and unpleasant manual labor.

Sound familiar? Rossum's robots eventually awakened to their condition and took over the world, destroying all mankind."

Gregor let out a long sigh. "I certainly have no intention to parallel that, although I do use the false name of Rossum Capek when I put on my disguise and go out to meet prospective clients for the Cremators."

"Like Rodney Quick," Danal muttered.

"Yes, like him."

Down by water level, the Wakers were quiet, expecting something. Gregor sat among them, merely one of the group—Danal could not tell from appearances that he was their leader.

One of the Wakers, the burly man who had previously posed as an Enforcer, came up to Gregor. "All the repair-rats are out of the vicinity. They won't set off any fire alarms."

Gregor nodded. He looked at his own chronometer and consulted the hardcopy of a tide table. He carefully folded the table and thrust it into his pocket, then nodded to the swimmers. They dove under the water and swam together between the clustered pilings into a deep blanket of shadows.

Danal watched and waited with a kind of dread as he saw something emerge, floating on the water, pushed and pulled by the three Waker swimmers. It was a raft of some kind, scattered with wood shavings, kindling, paper, and broken logs. The sweet chemical smell of a volatile hydrocarbon drifted to his nostrils.

As the raft came into the full light, Danal saw laid out upon the piled wood debris was the body of Rodney Quick. He cringed and felt the nurse/tech's hand on his shoulder. He tried to leave, but Laina held him back.

"I shouldn't be here," he said.

"You, of all people, should see this," Laina countered.

The technician's body had been washed carefully and clothed in a clean white robe. Surrounding the unlit pyre lay flower petals and brightly-colored ornaments. The Wakers swam harder, bringing the bier close to the gathered crowd. Gregor stood up and swept his gaze over the Wakers, speaking formal words in a baritone voice:

"This man bore the name of Rodney Quick. That cannot be taken from him, though he is gone now."

"He's gone now," the Wakers echoed.

"He will remain wherever he is now, the World of Light, and nothing will ever bring him back."

The other Wakers muttered appreciatively.

"We are the Cremators. We preserve the soul by destroying the flesh."

"Preserve the soul by destroying the flesh."

Other people took torches from their holders and tossed them to the three swimmers. Treading water, the Wakers caught the torches and then simultaneously set alight the bier containing Rodney Quick's body. As the flames caught on the naphtha-soaked kindling, the three swimmers went to the side of the raft and pushed, swimming furiously, until the pyre began to drift away. Gregor had timed it perfectly, for the outgoing tide drew the raft with it.

The other Wakers began to moan a somber yet somehow joyous chant. Gregor stood tall and took a deep breath, and then quoted poetry in a kind of eulogy.

"This man bore the name of William Shakespeare. He was a great and literate man, and is remembered long after his death. He wrote,

'To die, to sleep;
To sleep: perchance to dream: ay, there's the rub;
For in that sleep of death what dreams may come
When we have shuffled off this mortal coil?' "

Gregor recited the lines from memory, in a rich and serious voice. The other Wakers sat enthralled, listening. The leader paused and then intoned again:

"In another place, another play, William Shakespeare said,

'Life's but a walking shadow, a poor player,
That struts and frets his hour upon the stage,
And then is heard no more; it is a tale
Told by an idiot, full of sound and fury,
Signifying nothing.' "

Danal felt a deep, stabbing sadness and guilt, but also a faint wonder at the proceedings.

Gregor drew a long breath, as if exhausted, and then spoke a final time as the gathered Cremators waited, watching Rodney's pyre drift away, burning bright.

"This man bore the name of Percy Bysshe Shelley. He was a poet and a revolutionary. He wrote a poem of a traveler coming upon a ruined statue alone in an empty and deserted wasteland:

'And on the pedestal these words appear:
"My name is Ozymandias, king of kings:
Look on my works, ye Mighty, and despair!"
Nothing beside remains. Round the decay
Of that colossal wreck, boundless and bare
The lone and level sands stretch far away.' "

Gregor closed his eyes. "After Percy Bysshe Shelley drowned during a storm, his friend Lord Byron built a pyre for him on the beach. While the villagers watched, Byron swam back out to his own yacht, turning to gaze at the flickering beacon as the growing fire freed the soul of Percy Bysshe Shelley and turned his body to ash."

Above, the Cremators had set filters and traps to capture any smoke before it could waft upward and be seen rising through the KEEP OFF THE GRASS patches, though so late after curfew no one should have noticed anyway. The dripping Waker swimmers pulled themselves back up onto one of the platforms. The receding tide carried the still-burning pyre along with it, and Danal could see the flickering light drifting farther and farther from him. By morning the ashes of Rodney Quick would be dispersed far out to sea.

Danal wished he could get rid of his memories, his guilt so easily.

Gregor made a motion of dismissal, and the gathered Wakers stood up, beginning to move away. "Thank you all," Gregor said.

Danal came up to the leader as the other Wakers began to leave. As if anticipating his question, Gregor said quietly, "All this ritual and ceremony means nothing. But it makes us feel honored, and content with ourselves."

Danal frowned, puzzled, and noticed a thin woman approaching Gregor, looking frightened. The leader smiled warmly at her. "Yes, Shannah. Come and meet our new companion. His Servant name is Danal."

She looked distractedly at Danal and then back to Gregor. She was extremely gaunt, almost skeletal, and dark rings of sleepless anxiety encircled her eyes. Unlike all the other Wakers in their world below, Shannah still wore a long fluffy blond wig to cover her Servant baldness.

"I've decided, Gregor . . . I'm going back," she whispered.

"Ah, no, Shannah." He shook his head slowly. "Please don't."

"I've thought about it so much, Gregor. I've made up my mind."

"You know I don't approve," he pleaded with her. "We have to survive until we *know* more. I don't want to lose you."

Shannah's eyes glistened. "But I keep remembering the tunnel, the bright light, the chimes. The peace. It's calling me, Gregor. I have to go back to whatever's there."

The leader sat regarding her in silence for a long moment and then finally seemed to come to a personal acceptance of her reasons. Danal watched carefully, trying to understand.

"When?" Gregor asked.

Shannah swallowed. "It better be now. I'm ready."

Gregor put fingers to his lips and gave a shrill, birdlike whistle. The departing Wakers stopped to listen.

"I wish you'd reconsider this, Shannah."

She didn't answer him.

Gregor spoke aloud to the gathered Wakers once more. "Shannah has chosen to make her return journey now. We must all bear witness."

The other Wakers seemed surprised and saddened. The skeletal woman stretched out on her back, listening to the whisper of the sea. Danal could still smell the acrid smoke from Rodney Quick's disappearing pyre. Shannah brushed her palms across her slick gray jumpsuit.

"Candles?" she whispered. "I like candles. Can you light some?"

"Of course, Shannah." Gregor smiled at her, trying to deface his grief. The freckle-faced boy Waker rapidly climbed up a rope ladder and returned a few moments later with a handful of thin yellow candles. Shannah sat up and watched wonderingly as they surrounded her with the candles.

One by one Gregor lit them. Shannah stared fixedly at the flame nearest to her shoulder. Her breathing grew faster and faster and at last she lay back, closing her eyes and letting a peaceful sigh pass through her lips.

"Say my epitaph, Gregor. I want to hear it."

Gregor closed his eyes as if searching for something appropriate. Shannah whispered impatiently, "Hurry."

The leader looked up. "This man bore the name of

Edgar Allan Poe. He was a troubled soul who died young, grieving for lost love, but he left behind many true and somber words, such as these:

'And all my days are trances,
And all my nightly dreams
Are where thy grey eye glances,
And where thy footstep gleams—
In what ethereal dances,
By what eternal streams.'

And, perhaps best of all:

'Is all that we see or seem
But a dream within a dream?' "

Shannah rested the back of her head on the water-marked, worn plank. Her lips drifted into a smile of ecstasy. "Thank you, Gregor." She straightened her fluffy blond wig, and then let out a long, low breath. Her face suddenly fell slack as she stopped her synHeart and shut down the microprocessor in her head.

Gregor and the other Wakers let out a keening hum and looked up. With rapidly shifting glances they searched the air, gazing higher and higher to the invisible girders and pilings above, as if watching for Shannah's departing soul.

27

Fear made Jones stumble like a drunken man. The two Elite Guard flanked him and briskly ushered him to a lift shaft. He followed mechanically, dazed. He wanted to hide, or apologize to someone, or demand answers, but the two Guards marched in silence as if daring him to speak. *What did I do?* he wanted to shout, but the halls were empty, silent, and none of the other Enforcers would do more than put eyes to the spyholes in their rooms.

The lift doors closed like a guillotine as the three men began to rise upward. Jones immediately felt claustrophobic. Still only half dressed, he felt his sweat turn cold in the air.

They emerged at the roof-level parking bay. In the black early hours of morning an eerie silence clung to the Metroplex. Without a word the two Elite Guards nudged him and began to walk across the poured-stone of the parking bay. Jones felt the implacable hardness of their armor and saw the determined way in which their shoulders were set.

He thought of Fitzgerald Helms for a moment and felt a bottomless sadness. Helms had to die before Jones could get into the Guild—and now his career would end like this. What would Helms have thought?

The Guards had let him throw a robe over his shoulders, but Jones still carried his white Enforcer boots in his hands. They marched with muffled footsteps across the parking bay to a private hovercar that had been painted a dark flat blue to be invisible against the night sky.

For a moment Jones thought they were going to lock him in a segregation chamber in back, but instead they made him sit close between them in the main cabin. As the craft rose up into the air and banked sideways, Jones looked down at the Enforcers' dormitory he had called home for two years, thinking it might be the last time he'd ever see it. Probably, if the Elite Guard were involved, something terrible was going to happen to him.

Jones swallowed, feeling his Adam's apple plunge down and up again in his throat. He had no chance. Nothing would help. Maybe he could reason with them. "I still don't understand." His voice had a thin, whining quality to it. "Why can't you tell me—"

"No," one of the Elite Guard said brusquely. The other Guard continued to pilot the hovercar, paying no attention. As they soared on, Jones looked down at the lights of the intricate but deserted arteries of the Metroplex. For a moment he was struck by the fact that of all those people cowering down there, no one would miss him. He had made no real friends—Jones festered with the death of Helms even after two years, and it was his own damned fault. That's right—wasn't one supposed to wax philosophical while being led to an execution? He was out of uniform—would they just jettison him here, high above the Metroplex? Or would they dress him up as a gang member, someone supposedly killed in the violent afterdark street battles?

The hovercar homed in on the mirrored monolith of the Enforcers Guild main headquarters. Jones's stomach tightened and his breath came in shallower snatches as they neared the tower.

The hovercar cruised in to the private landing dock reserved for the Guild's highest management personnel. Jones felt his uneasiness grow, and his brain churned over and over, trying to comprehend what he had done that was so terrible to warrant such special punishment. He had lost the Servant. He had started a riot, but that wasn't his fault. He had discarded his armor—he had made major mistakes, certainly, but by the book, by his Enforcer training, hadn't he done what he was supposed to do? What was he supposed to do now?

The pilot powered down the hovercar's engines and disengaged the door. At the top of the tower the wind whistled around the walls of the headquarters, smelling damp with an oncoming spring storm. During the flight Jones had had an opportunity to slip on his white armored boots; now they stood out garishly against his dark skin, his black skin-pants. He cautiously emerged from the hovercar and then nearly tripped down a set of access stairs as the second Elite Guard hurried him along.

His legs were shaking. Other stairwells on the roof apparently led to other offices or lift shafts.

At the bottom of the stairs they reached a sealed doorway into the headquarters. The first Guard typed in a long and complex access code; a silent moment passed, then answering flickers of light came from the screen by the door. The Guard entered a responding password, and with an ominous, cobralike hissing, the door slid open into the highest levels of Guild headquarters.

"In you go." Blindly, without thinking, Jones stumbled forward. Darkness clung everywhere, and he blinked his wide eyes, trying to see. He realized after he had gone several steps that the two blue-armored Elite guard remained motionless outside the door on the steps. Would they kill him here? Why had they even brought him this far?

Jones looked around himself in a vast open space, a penthouse office covering perhaps an entire quadrant of the building's top floor. The air seemed to stick in his throat; gooseflesh crawled up his arms. From the towering vantage of the headquarters he could see the lights of the Metroplex strung out.

Warm light glowed from an aquarium covered with a wooden tabletop, as if it were some odd sort of furniture. He could hear the bubbling of the tank and see the moving colorful forms of the fish. They were trapped inside their glass cage, pointlessly going back and forth, bumping up against the unseen walls. . . .

Behind a huge semicircular clonewood desk, Jones finally saw a darkened figure waiting for him.

"Former Enforcer Jones," a biting voice spoke from the shadows, "you've caused me a great deal of trouble today."

Jones cringed and froze. He didn't dare turn around, but he thought sure he could sense the two Guards each drawing a projectile weapon, aiming at him—

With a melodramatic twist the figure behind the desk brought up the lights from rosy banks around the rim of the room. Jones concentrated on the man at the desk, puzzled; the man had black and oily hair that looked oddly out-of-place slicked back behind his ears, but then Jones recognized the man's face after all.

Francois Nathans.

"I planned everything so carefully. So intricate. Too

200

complex, I guess. Plenty of spots where a stupid mistake could drastically alter the outcome.

"I didn't count on *you* acting like you did."

Nathans shook his head and made a distasteful noise. "Hell, I can't do anything about it now. I can grill you, reprimand you, shout my lungs out at you—it might make me feel good for the moment, but Danal is still dead. My only chance to see if it would work—thank you, Jones, for making me feel so helpless!"

Jones swallowed again at the man's bitterness and finally found his voice. Would it help to be submissive? Would anything help him now? "What are you going to—" He paused, then suddenly bridled at the audacity of this man. "Hey, wait a minute! I'm a Guild member. You have no right to threaten me like that. You might run Resurrection, Inc. but you have no right to be here, at Guild headquarters!"

Part of him felt appalled at the outburst, but he realized nothing he said or did would change things. Jones had never felt a particular pride in or allegiance to the Guild, but it did have its own sort of honor. As questions began piling up one after another in his mind, he turned to the two Elite Guard for support. But his voice simply did not carry the confidence or tone of authority to make them even pay attention. One of the Guards held an electronic sweeping device, scanning the outer stairway. The second Guard stood at attention as the first stepped outside, still scanning, and closed the door. The second sealed it tightly from the inside. "All clear, sir."

Nathans folded his hands behind the large desk and smiled petulantly. "And who do you think runs the Guild, Mr. Jones?"

Jones stopped, feeling a lump of ice snowballing in his stomach. "I . . . have no idea."

Nathans smiled. "Well, now I think you do."

Jones consciously closed his mouth. "May I please sit down?"

"By all means." Nathans turned up the lights another notch. His smile held many different undertones, and it looked almost artificial.

Jones suddenly wondered if Nathans might be taking his revenge. Maybe it made Nathans feel satisfied if he could rub Jones's face in a secret he would have no opportunity to divulge.

"Oh, I was behind the Guild when it started, years before I conceived of Resurrection, Incorporated. I hope you like stories, Mr. Jones? Good.

"You see, I decided that private security forces might be more effective and more motivated for maintaining law and order than any state-run, unionized police system. I won't bother you with the details, but it turned out I was absolutely right.

"Working behind the scenes, I slowly managed to consolidate all the private conglomerations of security systems and conformance-assurance personnel into the Enforcers Guild. Collectively, the Guild edged out the cumbersome state-run police departments."

Nathans's voice seemed to carry an almost nostalgic tone. Restlessly he stood up from his desk and walked over to stare out the darkened windows. He pressed his face close to the glass; the lights from the room stretched his reflection into odd forms.

"It was all so easy that, frankly, I was a bit suspicious at the time. So I decided to push a little harder, to see just how much we could get away with. But if it didn't work, you see, if it backfired—I knew heads would roll. That's why I kept my own involvement secret, at first. Fame and notoriety is one of the most useless forms of success mankind has yet invented."

Nathans interlocked his fingers behind his slick black hairpiece and turned to face Jones again. "We put Enforcers all over the place. Their presence was unmistakeable. Escorting people to make them feel important. We even had them guarding things like statues and fountains and KEEP OFF THE GRASS patches—" He cringed for a moment, and then continued.

"But the crime rate dropped. Incredibly. We had to make up new laws just to give all the Enforcers something to do. We started street tension of our own, simulated gang wars after curfew so the people would keep thinking they needed us. We even made up the bloody curfew!" Nathans shook his head. "And the poor bastards bought it—hook, line, and sinker!"

Jones sat stiffly in the chair, sweating. Everything he had followed, all the training, the patrols—the ethics for which Helms had been killed—all because Nathans wanted to play power games. He kept his mouth shut, but Nathans must have been able to interpret the sickening distaste on his face.

The man slapped both palms on the mahogany-attribute desk. "Don't you see! I didn't do it! You think this is a police state? No! Because the people allowed it to happen. They didn't do a damn thing to stop it, because they convinced themselves it was a Good Idea! There's simply no excuse for that. I hoped that by pushing and pushing, it would finally spark their social consciousness, get someone involved. Our society has to change by itself, of its own choice, not have change forced upon it."

He let out a long and heavy sigh. "Sometimes I'd like nothing more than to be caught at my own tricks. Even if they threw me out, at least that would prove people are paying attention out there! I thought this would be like an electric shock to stimulate our stagnant culture. Teach them a lesson, so that they never get caught sleeping again."

He cracked his knuckles and looked at Jones.

"So far, though, I'm deeply disappointed. All they're interested in is the path of least resistance, letting me do whatever I want, no matter how much damage it causes." Nathans spoke through gritted teeth and pounded his fists on the table for emphasis, then stopped and lowered his voice. "Sorry for the outburst. I'm having a particularly unpleasant day."

Jones sat rubbing his temples and asked haltingly, with his eyes closed, "But if you're Francois Nathans, the Resurrection man, I don't . . . how can you possibly be running Guild headquarters? Resurrection, Inc. *hates* the Guild."

"Ah." Nathans briskly rubbed his palms together and then stopped himself, almost embarrassed. "That's a perfect example of creating a perceived need for the Enforcers Guild. You see, if I set it up that Resurrection hates Enforcers, but it still needs Enforcers for protection, then that gives the Guild an incredible legitimacy, doesn't it? Then other corporations won't hesitate to engage the services of Enforcers, if even Resurrection, Inc. has to."

Jones let the convoluted logic sink in until it finally made an appalling kind of sense. And when it all made sense, he began to grasp just how much Nathans had told him—far too much. The terror came yammering at his ears again.

Should he try to run? While Nathans had his attention elsewhere? Could he somehow get past the two Elite

Guards, take the hovercar, and fly off—go somewhere? Someplace outside the Metroplex? He'd never been outside before.

He felt his heart pounding from just considering the idea. He could sense sweat on his forehead, knowing it was going to trickle into his eyes at any moment. Jones tensed, felt his muscles tightening up, knotting.

The sweat dropped into the corner of his eye like a tear, and he felt everything drain out of him in an instant. No. He'd never make it past the two Elite Guards. After all the incredible Enforcer training Jones had endured, honing his body, his reflexes, these two blue-armored Guards had been through ten times more, and would be that much faster, better.

Jones swallowed. It was a waste of time to put it off any longer. "You're going to kill me, aren't you? For telling me all this."

Nathans looked shocked and stared back at the black man. "Let me tell you one very important thing, Mr. Jones. I value my life very much, and I certainly don't look forward to dying. Life is what allows me to accomplish things—life is our one chance at everything. Consequently, I respect life, yours or anyone else's. I don't believe any crap about a fate worse than death because, as the cliché says, while there's life there's hope. I do not kill, except in the most extraordinary circumstances. And I do not plan to kill you."

"Then what are you telling me all this for? I didn't want to know it."

Nathans's response came back at him like an electric shock. "Because you are the newest member of the Elite Guard, Mr. Jones. Welcome to the Club."

Jones blinked in astonishment. He felt yanked in a completely different direction, leaving him disoriented. "But what if I don't—"

"You have nothing to lose, Jones. Come log on, see for yourself."

Haltingly Jones went to the large semicircular desk and bent closely over the Net terminal. He punched in his logon name and his password and got to the first-level menu. "Now what?"

"Check your user status. It'll take the Net accounting people a month or so to delete your old password."

Baffled, Jones requested a biographical update. His

fingers shook, and he made several errors before finally entering the right command. He stared as the pixels formed themselves into his own obituary.

ENFORCER, CLASS 2.
KILLED IN MOB UPRISING WHILE PURSUING
REBEL SERVANT
OUTSIDE RESURRECTION, INC.
SECONDARY NOTATION FOR DISTINGUISHED
SPECIAL SERVICE TO THE GUILD
ABOVE AND BEYOND THE CALL OF DUTY.

Jones saw the date and continued to stare, unable to move. Nathans blanked the screen. "It's a trick," Jones whispered.

"Yes, and a very good one. But you can try it on any terminal in the Metroplex. Once The Net's been fooled, you may as well be dead anyway. Welcome to the Elite Guard."

His head spinning, Jones walked dazedly back to the chair and sat down, almost missing the cushion. He didn't have the capacity for anger in him—he still didn't quite grasp what had happened.

"Mind you, Jones, this is a singular honor. Very few people are chosen for this. Congratulations."

Jones found himself confused again, wondering if he should indeed feel proud of himself. He had never dreamed of becoming an Elite Guard. A slow, tentative feeling of wonder began to replace his sick terror. An Elite Guard? Had he done a good job after all?

"Does that mean you captured the rebel Servant, then? The one who caused all this? The one I was trying to chase?"

Nathans soured and turned his back angrily, looking out the wide windows. Jones saw the man's back stiffen as he kept clenching his hands. "No. He escaped. He is dead."

"I thought you wanted him alive."

"I did! But he somehow got the help of a nurse/tech—they both killed themselves by jumping into a KEEP OFF THE GRASS patch. They even took another Enforcer with them! In full view of dozens of people! Now there aren't even any damned *atoms* of him left!"

Nathans abruptly stopped shouting. "I had a lot at stake with that Servant, and now it's all gone."

But Jones frowned and pursed his lips as he sat back in the chair. The Servant had jumped into a KEEP OFF THE GRASS patch? Distracted, he realized that this bothered him, nagged him even after everything else that had happened.

Nathans saw the expression and stopped abruptly. "What is it, Jones?"

The black man looked up, afraid again. "Nothing," he mumbled.

Nathans rose to his feet and strode closer. His eyes looked at Jones intensely. "You look like you just thought of something." His voice became warm and smooth. "I'm your superior now, Jones. I'm interested in any fresh ideas you have. Show me I didn't choose wrong to pick you for the Elite Guard."

Jones's head spun, and he reluctantly answered in a low voice. "You probably don't remember the reason I was sent to be an escort at Resurrection, Inc., Mr. Nathans. In my previous assignment I was trying to stop another rebel Servant"—he looked carefully at Nathans—"and she escaped by jumping into a KEEP OFF THE GRASS patch, too. Like she knew something about it the rest of us don't know."

He heard Nathans's sharp intake of breath. The other man turned toward him, and Jones could see his eyes glistening with surprise and fascination. "That's . . . very . . . interesting."

28

Danal jumped down from the thin crosswalk, perfectly coordinated, and landed with barely a sound on Gregor's enclosed platform. In the harsh light of the sunlamps the leader looked up, absently rubbing his fingers on the pages of his book. He slid a yarn bookmark in place and snapped the cover shut.

Gregor waited in silence, holding his squarish chin between the thumb and forefinger of one hand. Danal finally spoke in an abrupt burst of words. "I spent the last day with your Wakers—"

"Your Wakers, too," Gregor interrupted smoothly.

"The Wakers." Danal paused, considering a tactful way to proceed. He saw a pile of neatly folded clothing near the corner, as well as an assortment of hats, wigs, false facial hair, and various flesh-colored creams and pigments. "I'm impressed with the organization, the brotherhood, you've put together. The Wakers seem to be a very close-knit group."

"They are."

"But—" He paused, troubled. Waiting, Gregor drifted back and forth on the hammock and motioned for his guest to sit. Danal squatted down on his heels. "But what are you . . . *doing*? You're all living from day to day down here, but it's just hiding. You have the power to take some action. Why don't you flex your muscles?" Danal focused his gaze on the leader's face. "You strike me as too conscientious a man to sit back and not do anything."

Gregor let out a long sigh, and Danal watched him. "I'm glad you think that way. We *should* be doing more than just sitting around and patting ourselves on the back. But we just don't know enough. I'm wrestling with ambivalence—that's the main snag."

"Ambivalence? How can you possibly be ambivalent?"

"Think about it. We are Servants who have regained our memories. Now, do all Servants have the same potential to awaken, like we did? Or are they really just mindless machines, just another use for a discarded body, like Resurrection, Inc. would have us believe? Are Wakers a fluke in the resurrection process?"

Danal gave no indication of whether he agreed or disagreed. Off in the shadowy distance someone was singing a low melody in a foreign-sounding language.

"That's not what I believe," Gregor continued. "And mind you, this is only my intuition. We're too small a group to be a valid statistical sample. But I suspect all Servants do have the potential for reawakening those old memories. If they want to."

Gregor folded his hands and bent closer to Danal. "What do you remember *in between*? Between life and death and life again?"

"Nothing," Danal said, wondering why Gregor had changed the subject. He sifted through his memories, but the answer remained the same. "It's just a blank. I told Laina, like a smooth, hard barrier."

Gregor smiled. "Then let me show you how to penetrate it."

From a wooden crate underneath his hammock he removed three candles and set them on the floor of the platform. He lit each one, then dropped the still burning match over the side. It fell down into the dark water far below.

"I believe the resurrection process snatched me away from a world of light, from a greater place—Heaven, for lack of a better word." Gregor spoke in a quiet voice, tinged with a respectful awe. "I can't remember exact details, though I do occasionally get glimpses—like my first flashbacks, only more maddening because these are visions of a higher reality, not just a past that fits into the world I can see around me."

Gregor reached up, switching off the sunlamp with his fingertips. "Now then, sit in a comfortable position."

Danal hunkered down and adjusted his feet. He ignored the rough boards against his legs.

"It's impossible to describe. Language simply has no analogies for what you experienced. It goes beyond explaining. But you'll know what I mean—you've already lived through it, and died through it."

Gregor took him through the motions, telling him to speed up his microprocessor, to shut out all outside influences, to concentrate on the hard boundary between his two lives.

"It'll take time, because you've got to convince your subconscious that you're really willing to face what you remember. But you have to keep pounding on the door without a rest, until it opens."

Danal closed his eyes.

Inhale.

Exhale.

The microprocessor sped up his mind, slowed down the universe. He focused everything inward, centering on the moment of his death. The last memory. The protective shell that cut him off from anything beyond, making his thoughts slip off its hard surface.

Danal went through the stages of forced relaxation, meditation. Without concern he realized he had begun to feel numb all over, but he refused to relent his pressure on the barrier.

Death had hidden something more from him, something much more significant even than all his other flashbacks. He had so far uncovered only the tip of the iceberg. He hoped he could cope with the rest of it, if he could manage to dredge it to the surface.

Inhale.

Exhale.

Then he began to experience a pleasant rising sensation, a detachment, and ever so slowly a separation that led to an otherworldly ambience. It was definitely unlike a dream.

And finally the black wall began to dissolve in front of him.

The pain—that came first. The blade of the arthame dagger bursting through his skin, sliding across his sternum, then stabbing sideways deep into his chest cavity; he felt a *rip* as the tip broke through the pericardium and then cut deeply into the muscle of his heart. Vincent Van Ryman's every nerve seemed to have been dipped in hot oil, sending excruciatingly detailed information to his failing brain, but now he viewed it all through a distorted lens.

Then silence, a fresh, clean silence. Danal let himself experience the wonder and the awe of the impressions, unable to put even shadows of words to them. The absolute quiet felt brilliant, clean and sharp. And then slowly swelling from the background he noticed a muffled tonal mixture, a noise like a musical buzzing, bells and chimes.

No sense of touch, warmth or cold . . . he began to

detect motion, though he could not pinpoint exactly what was moving—without sensory organs, all movement seemed dizzying and distorted. He was pulled along a dark tunnel, spinning upward, dragged by a force he could not understand into a pitch-black catacomb.

Then, with an inaudible *pop*, he suddenly emerged outside his body, seeming to float up near the ceiling of the sacrificial grotto, stopped by the papier mâché stalactites. He looked down at the bloodbath, at himself slain on the altar. Danal felt an uncanny displacement, but the dead man no longer even looked like him because of the surface-cloning.

On the heels of that thought came a rapid-fire burst of Vincent Van Ryman's life, all his memories exploding outward at once. The visual images were vivid and nearly instantaneous, with no definite sequence, but it all made sense to him.

The memory images blurred together, smeared out into a glow that grew brighter and brighter. Around him, Danal began to perceive other spirits, bright colored lights—his escorts.

His thoughts floated in a euphoric, untroubled sea of utter contentment. Ushered by the other spirits, tantalized by the beckoning light ahead, he moved toward a borderland which may or may not have had a physical substance. Danal somehow thought he had almost reached a destination, an arrival.

Then suddenly the black barrier of forbidden memory clamped down on him again. Everything stopped abruptly. Danal tried, *needed* to break through, but the wall remained firm, impenetrable no matter how much he pounded on it. . . .

"That was deeper than most Wakers are willing to look their first time," Gregor said after Danal had described his experience. The leader had not moved, or even seemed to blink an eye. "But they always hit a wall somewhere."

Danal placed both hands flat against the platform, trying to steady himself. In the past few seconds his entire perception of reality had been skewed. In an undefinable way Danal began to wonder if his other concerns were somehow less significant. "But what's beyond that last barrier?"

"No one's ever been able to breach it," Gregor said, sounding defeated. "And that leads me to my biggest question—*is* there anything more? Or have we seen all there is?"

Danal frowned silently and said nothing. Gregor seemed impatient. "You don't see the problem, do you? What were all those memories? Were they just buried in my dead brain somewhere, or were they carried back with my . . . soul, if you want to call it that? Is there really a difference between the body and the soul? We have to find the answer to that question—it has such staggering implications!"

Feeling more confused than ever, Danal shook his head. "What do you mean?"

"Look, if they are just stale memories buried in my resurrected mind and nothing more, then . . . who am I? Am *I*—with a capital letter—just some leftover impressions embedded in this old temporal lobe"—he tapped his forehead—"that didn't come out in the wash? Is my own soul really back in this body now, or am I just a better machine, one that can access a few old memories from the real Gregor, who is now dead and gone? And how the hell can I tell the difference?"

Gregor seemed deeply upset, and answered his own question. "Of course there's a way. If I can indeed remember my death, my out-of-body experiences, actually getting into the world of light—if I can remember the whole thing without a gap, from death all the way through to the sudden moment of resurrection again, then it obviously can't be just some buried memories, can it? The real Gregor wouldn't have left such visions in his dead brain, because Gregor's body never experienced those things."

Danal frowned. "But isn't what—what I saw close enough? The tunnel, the light, the life flashbacks, the other spirits? How could all that be left in my physical brain if I was dead already?"

"No. Put yourself in the role of a pure skeptic, Danal. And I am, at heart, a skeptic." Gregor sighed, as if he had been through all this before. "The tunnel, the light, the out-of-body sensations, the chimes and bells—you were dying. Your brain was literally giving up the ghost. Who knows what kind of distorted perceptions you might have experienced? Your dying nerves giving spasmodic impulses, firing at random, making you think you saw lights, heard sounds, sensed presences. And the flashbacks of your life—couldn't that have been a colossal memory dump of your brain at the last second? Flinging open all those mental doorways that kept your thoughts neatly organized?"

Gregor shook his head, still deep in thought. "Oh, sure it seems farfetched, but it is a possible rational explanation. Occam's Razor isn't sharp enough for me—I have to be absolutely sure. I need to have a *continuous memory*."

The leader closed his eyes. "I spend hours and hours alone, meditating, trying to reach the center of my experience. We Wakers don't really know what to do. Which stand should we take? Should we stop Resurrection, Incorporated? Or should we help them to make certain the resurrection process never produces another Waker?

"Should we voluntarily kill ourselves to go back—like Shannah—if these Heaven flashbacks are indeed the real thing? Or should we instead try to awaken all other Servants?

"No, after my own mental anguish—and the other Wakers seem to be of the same opinion—I can't condone trying to awaken other Servants on purpose. They're at peace now, and their souls are . . . are where they should be, wherever that is."

Danal seemed cowed by his death visions, trapped by a new perspective. "Then, maybe the Wakers can't do anything right now."

"But we have! Don't forget, Danal, we're the Cremators. It's the least we could do, the most conscionable alternative that would still let us make a difference. I conceived of the Cremators to eliminate the possibility of people returning as Servants against their wishes. If, after death, we do go on to something else, don't you think it's a terrible crime to take someone away from that? As the Cremators, we give them all the option of their own choosing."

Danal frowned, puzzled. "If you think that other world is a better, brighter place, or if you think we have some sort of destiny there, then why *don't* you just tell all the Wakers just to shut themselves down? Like Shannah? It doesn't make sense that you tried to stop her."

Gregor looked uneasy and did not answer for a long time. "I won't ask anyone to return to death, not until I'm positive of the outcome. Just a minute ago, I raised the possibility that I might not be the real Gregor. So, if I kill myself, what will happen to *me*?" He vehemently tapped his chest. "What about this unique person, The-Waker-Who-Thinks-He-Is-Gregor? I don't want to destroy my individual identity forever, even if it is just a recycled life."

One of the candles sputtered and blew out from a stray draft. Gregor stood up and stretched. Danal felt his feet cramping and got up from his cross-legged position on the hard wood.

"It's food for thought. But remember, Danal, I don't lead these people. They generally look to me for advice, and they generally listen to what I say, but I'm no leader. I don't want to be. We Wakers have been down here for four years now, and I suspect we'll be discovered sooner or later, no matter how careful we are. I can only hope I solve my own moral dilemma by then. Otherwise I won't be able to advise the rest of them what to do."

He spread his hands, looking helpless. "For now, the only thing we can do is . . . just survive."

29

The doors closed in the simulation chamber, and Jones turned around, staring at the smooth, colorless walls. Once the projector started, he could almost imagine that he was surrounded by reality. Jones shook himself, loosening up. He felt his muscles, sensed his reactions coiled up and waiting to spring. If he didn't think about it too much, the Elite Guard training was exhilarating. He already knew that the ordeals ahead of him would be a dozen times tougher than his original Enforcer training.

He ran a gloved finger down his blue armor, stiff and new, with a half-circle scarlet arm-ring that signified the lowest rank of the Elite Guard. The armor had been polished, but it remained dark and neutral, invisible in the night, impressive by day. Ominous-looking spines stuck up from his shoulder plates, and other gadgets implanted on his helmet made him appear alien, frightening, powerful.

As always, Jones accepted his situation, his place, but in the Elite Guard he forced himself to use a little more optimism. Fitzgerald Helms would have been proud of him, so proud he would not have needed to say anything—Helms and Jones had had enough rapport to dispense with all that. They had once looked on the Enforcers with a kind of superstitious awe, and the confidence of the Elite Guard made them seem like walking gods.

He didn't feel overly sad to leave his life behind. Nathans had seen to it that all of Jones's possessions were smuggled away and returned to him. And Jones did not resent the opportunity for a fresh start, a new beginning, with all the prestige the Guild could hammer into him. It seemed for the best. Nathans had explained it all to him.

"Tell me, Jones, have you ever seen an old Enforcer?" Francois Nathans had asked him. "Think about it—anyone who's been on patrol for more than, say, five years?"

Jones shook his head, but listened carefully. Just by

the way he moved and talked, Nathans demanded complete attention. But Jones didn't mind.

"That's right, there aren't any." Nathans smiled; his eyes sparkled. "It's another part of our philosophy. You see, if Enforcers were to survive a long time, grow old, and comfortably retire, what would the public think? That Enforcers have a safe, padded job? Tsk, tsk.

"No, after you've been an Enforcer a few years, we look for ways to transfer you out. Some really do die, of course. The less competent ones go into management. But others, the talented ones whose deep psychological profiles show them to be completely trustworthy—they're allowed into the Elite Guard. You're one of the special few, Jones."

Special. Jones felt a strange sensation, a confidence, a feeling of importance—he had never been treated this way before. Nathans had taken a special liking to him, observing some of his training, even chatting with him on a friendly level. An Elite Guard—he had never dreamed of it.

He heard a clicking sound as the invisible projectors behind the wall screens began the simulation. Off in a control room someone was watching how he prepared himself, how well he reacted to the imaginary situation. He had to beat his last score. Jones took a deep breath and felt his body tense, shoving all his cluttered thoughts aside and focusing only on the simulation. Nothing else mattered, did it?

Holographic images jumped out at him from all sides of the simulator chamber. The neutral, rounded walls vanished into a normal street scene with all the details, making Jones almost convinced that he stood outside again, patrolling the area around Resurrection, Inc. Up near the ceiling he saw a null score glowing in thin green numbers. But it wouldn't stay zero for long— he'd see to that, all right.

Jones tensed, made ready to reach for his weapons—all deactivated for the exercise—but then forced himself to relax a bit. Too much tension would reduce his accuracy and could drop his score. He looked about him at the illusory scene, trying to identify the target, the place from which the trouble would come. This always seemed to be the hardest part of the challenge.

Two children, laughing and yelling, ran past him from out of nowhere. Jones jumped and nearly fired at them, and then caught himself as they disappeared into the crowd. He felt sweat break out on his forehead. False alarm. If he had been really on patrol, might he have just fired? Worse, had the observers noticed his reaction?

Up near the ceiling he saw the glowing green score drop by ten points, and he momentarily resented that fact more than the possibility of slaughtering the children. Would Nathans be disappointed in him? He didn't want to let the head of the Guild down.

Nathans had assigned Jones to watch over the first investigation team for the KEEP OFF THE GRASS patches. The man arranged for him to engage the services of a Net database jockey, or, if he got desperate enough, perhaps even one of the Guild's precious Interfaces. With his own Net access suddenly boosted from fourth to seventh level, Jones could search through the more detailed databases previously denied him, but he had never been terribly proficient with The Net. He took it as a challenge, to prove his worth as an Elite Guard. He wanted to come up with a rational answer for the existence of the patches, and Nathans wanted to find out what had happened to Danal.

Jones cursed himself for letting such thoughts distract him, especially now. A disturbance began to grow in the holographic crowd, but though he turned right and left, Jones could not identify its source. Then in the distance he saw a Servant running. Other people in the crowd turned, focused on the Servant, and drew toward him, blocking him off.

Jones froze for an instant, wondering if this could be a recurring nightmare. Nathans had probably chosen the simulation with a specific reason in mind. But Jones would not let the man down.

Purposefully Jones drew his weapons, a scatter-stun in one hand and a rapid-fire projectile gun in the other. He knew the scatter-stun would be no good unless the Servant came closer, but Jones hoped to dispatch him before then.

He raised his projectile weapon, pointed it at the running gray-clad figure. The Servant looked up at him, gaped for a moment—then Jones fired without hesitation. If he did not delay, his score would correspondingly increase. As he pulled the trigger, though, he noticed the holographic palm trees fluttering like tattered brooms.

The computer would throw in factors such as simulated wind and the distortion of the walls.

The projectile missed, striking instead one of the pedestrians reaching out to grab the Servant. Jones heard his score change, and he raised to fire again before he looked up.

To his surprise, the score had increased by twenty points, even after accidentally hitting the pedestrian. He shot again, and this time he struck the Servant in the shoulder. The Servant spun, injured, trying to reorient himself. Jones released another projectile and began to move his feet as if running toward the Servant.

The computer automatically adjusted the illusory view. The victim fell twitching on the sidewalk as the other people pressed close.

A second Servant appeared, running from the opposite side of the simulator. The crowd suddenly turned, but half of them began clustering around Jones, perhaps angry because of the slaughtered pedestrian.

Jones turned his scatter-stun on the approaching mob and mowed down anyone blocking his shot at the second Servant. He watched his score increase again. With a clear shot, he fired once more, paralyzing the renegade Servant's arm. The Servant dropped the metallic equipment she carried and continued to run frantically.

A third shot, and this time the Servant pitched forward, still trying to move, but with her hips paralyzed. Jones let fly with three exploding projectiles.

His score had soared up to a new high point. He had beaten his previous mark! The computer lingered on the images of all the dead, innocent pedestrians who had gotten in his way. Innocent? Jones suddenly relived his own nightmare visions of groping, clawing, tearing hands of the mob trying to destroy him as Danal fled into the distance. Innocents? Any of these pedestrians could be murderous, a potential instigator of a mob.

Jones swept the scatter-stun around him in an entire arc, levelling the approaching crowds until the weapon's charge sputtered to a halt. The other pedestrians stopped, their mob mentality quelled by his show of force.

Jones breathed out a long and heavy sigh and surveyed the people, wondering if the simulation was over. The timer crept around almost to the finish. But then he noticed that six other Servants had shambled out of the alleys, out of the doorways; they stood looking at him mindlessly.

Experimentally Jones raised his pocket bazooka and shot one of them. They were just simulations, after all. A great burst of points appeared on his score. Puzzled, Jones fired again. Two more of the Servants fell, broken into large pieces of torn flesh that oozed clear synthetic blood. Again Jones received a significant bonus of points.

Is that what they wanted him to do? Were they trying to train him to fire at Servants? Jones lowered the weapon, resisting the obvious ploy. What sense did that make? What purpose did it serve?

He looked at the fallen Servants. Two more had come to take their places, and the other three Servants began to shuffle away, going about their jobs. Did Nathans want him to shoot all those Servants? Jones's score beckoned, begging him to add more points.

Actually, Servants had been at the core of Jones's troubles all along. The more he considered the possibility, the more valid the conclusion became.

Jones had almost lost his life in the riot after the rebel Servant Danal escaped, and because of that Jones was officially dead (although he had been promoted after all, so that didn't count). Danal. A Servant.

And Julia? He had gambled at happiness when he bought her, but she met his kindness, his love, his devotion, with utter and complete apathy, without a spark of humanity. Julia was a Servant, but surely with the care he had taken she could have shown something? Hadn't Danal worn that wild human look in his eyes? Why couldn't Julia have had that? Why couldn't she have returned his attentions? Julia. A Servant.

And back in his curfew-patrol days, what about the other Servant, the female who had stolen equipment and tried to escape? Because of her, Jones had been taken from tolerable patrol duties and reassigned, reprimanded. Servants.

And the hatred and unrest from the jobless blues, out of work because of Servants—wasn't that what had caused the death of his friend, Fitzgerald Helms?

That wound struck him deeply. Servants.

He retaliated, lifting his pocket bazooka again and firing at the holographic crowd with an accuracy born of anger and misguided revenge. All five remaining Servants fell in rapid succession. Shaking, Jones slammed the empty weapon into its armor socket as the time ran out.

The scene froze on the walls, but still he saw the images of blasted Servants lying scattered about on the streets. He relaxed. He doubted he'd ever beat this score. A blinking light appeared in front of his eyes.

"GAME OVER."

30

Apply the flesh tone liberally to face and neck—don't forget the ears. Cover the arms up to the elbow. Reddish-pink stain to add color to the lips. Bite down on the dye bubble to flood the inside of the mouth with red color, and then rinse thoroughly to keep the teeth clean. Eyelashes, eyebrows. Touch up with blush and darker tones to add realism, to add human flaws. Hairpiece or some other covering for the head.

Incognito. Almost like a living, breathing person again.

Danal waited, sitting on a park bench and looking up at the tall buildings around him. The hard metal slats of the bench felt cool against his leather jacket and patched pants. Discreetly he kept his hands buried in his pockets. A leather skullcap hugged his head with flaps over his ears, making him look like an old aeroplane flyer.

Danal knew exactly what the Cremator client would look like; he was confident the man would be on time.

The client appeared out of a side street, looking lost and uncertain—a middle-aged man dressed in a perfect business suit, a thin stylish tie studded with reflecting sequins. His hair was carefully cut at just the right length; instead of contacts, he wore decorative spectacles with a tiny chronometer implanted in one lens. Under his arm he carried a large, colorfully wrapped box topped with a pink bow.

"Is that for me?" Danal stood up and intercepted him.

The man stopped abruptly and stared at him, sizing him up. "No," he mumbled, trying to remember the right phrase, "it's for John."

"Okay. I'll give it to his wife, then," Danal answered easily.

The client looked relieved and handed the box to the disguised Servant, then fled down the street without looking back. He tried to hide himself in the crowd, but there weren't enough people on the sidewalk to do so. Danal watched him for a moment, calmly amused, and then sat back down on the bench.

He didn't need to inspect the box to know that it contained some packaged chemical supplies, two books for Gregor, analytical tools, and some rope-wire—all things the Wakers needed.

Danal considered the box and the client with a somewhat detached apathy. After Gregor had shown him how to access his death memories, Danal's perception of reality had shifted radically. Over the past week he had come to accept his situation with an easy passivity. His other concerns, his leftover anger—no, Vincent Van Ryman's anger—at his betrayal and at the death of Julia, all of that seemed distant now and inconsequential.

Below in the dark, listening to the ghostly whispers of the ocean and the creaking timbers around him, Danal had spent much of his time meditating. Legs crossed, he sometimes sat with Gregor, sometimes alone, journeying deep within himself, confronting the wall, the Heaven flashbacks. It all came back to him with never ending wonder and awe—the pain, the tunnel, the chimes, the lights, the spirits . . . over and over again.

But still he could not breach the last barrier.

The universe had stopped being clear-cut and understandable for him, and everything held its own facet of the cosmic mystery. For the benefit of the Wakers in general, he helped with the Cremators' activities. As Laina and Gregor had both predicted, Danal now considered himself fully one of the Wakers. But none of it really mattered to him. He lived from day to day, in no particular hurry to make any major decisions.

He spent many hours reviewing his old memories, dwelling—not morbidly, but with a different kind of fascination—on Death, the events leading up to his own death; how he had sacrificed his dying father; how he had killed Nathans in the lower levels of Resurrection, Inc; how Nathans had killed Julia—and that, in turn, brought him back to thinking about his own death again.

He viewed his former life as Vincent Van Ryman with greater and greater detachment, as if it were someone else—and indeed it was someone else, since that person had been on the other side of death. Vincent's problems were no longer Danal's problems. . . .

The Servant picked up the gift-wrapped box and started to stroll casually down the pedestrian walk. He would wander around aimlessly for an hour or two just to make sure no one was watching. Besides, he felt like taking a long walk. He had used extra care to apply his disguise, and he enjoyed the freedom a normal appearance gave him. When he grew tired, Danal would find one of the other access openings to down below.

He didn't mind killing time. He enjoyed every moment of everything now that all existence seemed basically the same.

As he passed an unoccupied public Net booth, Danal suddenly felt an amused fascination for his old identity as Vincent Van Ryman, a wave of nostalgia. Earlier, he had stared at the looming Van Ryman mansion for long moments before moving on. The Intruder Defense Systems had effectively kept him away, even if he had wanted to approach it.

Now, as he stared at the empty Net booth, Danal realized that The Net still thought Vincent Van Ryman was alive, since the imposter had stolen his entire identity. And Danal still remembered his old password.

Curiosity tugged at him, and he stepped inside the booth, propping the gift-wrapped box up against the wall and closing the privacy screen. He entered "VINCENT VAN RYMAN" at the prompt and punched in his tenth-level password. The Net willingly accepted the logon and waited.

He stared at the upper menu and, after a slight pause, went into his own electronic mail for a glimpse at the imposter's activities. Still only mildly interested, Danal ignored most of the mundane business messages and neo-Satanist concerns.

But then he saw one message that made him stop cold. It was passworded, but Danal easily remembered his own receive-mail passwords. According to the status line, the message had been sent by Francois Nathans only two days before. . . .

Nathans turned to show his face and smiled thinly at Danal. "Welcome, Sacrificial Lamb." He made the neo-Satanist sign of the broken cross.

Danal entered his mail password and read the message.

Nathans lay on his face in a puddle of blood—

Francois Nathans must be dead. Danal had killed him.

A long scarlet smear emblazoned the gray Servant jumpsuit.

Just who was the victim after all?

222

Danal scanned the message as his eyes widened. One of the false eyelashes flaked off.

"We have disposed of my surrogate. Danal killed him cleanly, and we're leaving no other ties to this whole mess. But now that Danal is GONE, we should decide whether to find another test subject or drop the idea altogether. Without Vincent himself COMING BACK, the effect won't be as dramatic."

Danal gaped at the message and read it over again. Nathans's surrogate? Who had Danal murdered? Surrogate?

Remembering his old Net skill, Danal quickly checked the Net periodicals and the news databases for the day he had supposedly committed the murder. The death of someone like Francois Nathans would certainly have appeared in all the current-events listings.

But he searched and found mention of Nathans only in reference to Resurrection, Inc., where the riot had taken place. In growing amazement and disbelief Danal checked Nathans's Net activity, and found that the man had used the system every day for the past two weeks.

Nathans was not dead.

Danal had been tricked. Once again.

As it all came crashing down upon him, he fell abruptly back into his own existence. Like nails being hammered into a coffin: trusting Nathans as a philosophical brother, having grand schemes for bettering the world; Julia, who had tempered his zealous obsession with love and perspective; losing it all when the trapdoor of treachery made everything drop out from under his feet.

It woke him up like a slap in the face, and he gripped the gift-wrapped box tightly enough to wrinkle the colored paper. He felt his jaws ache from clenched teeth. Part of his determination for revenge returned, but it clashed with his newfound empathy of life and death. Wasn't all this behind him now? But what Nathans had done— The conflicting emotions forced his goal sideways and changed it.

Danal thought of his ordeal, his death, his life, his love, and with a bright fire of determination he reached a firm decision.

He would find Julia again.

31

Net conduits, like twisted metal straws, stretched upward into the main city above. Using stolen alloy-chewers, the Wakers had breached the conduit coverings and tapped their own wires in, sending jury-rigged connections down to a row of mismatched terminals, some taken from decommissioned public Net booths, others from standard home units. The glow from the screens penetrated the shadows: amber, green, and gray.

Two Wakers sat at the keyboards. Rolf, the Waker who had masqueraded as an Enforcer, stared glassy-eyed and motionless, gripping the sides of the terminal as if wrestling with something. The other was the young freckle-faced Waker whose pale, translucent skin now looked splotched with darker marks of discoloration.

As Danal came up to them, the boy Waker stared at him with something like impressed awe. Danal regarded the boy for a moment, then smiled. "I'm Danal," he said, leaving the end of his sentence hanging, like a question.

"I know," the freckle-faced Waker said, and then remembered to add, "My name's Rikki."

Rikki looked to have been about twelve or thirteen at his death, but lines of concentration around his eyes made him look much older. He had been through death and back and would never be a boy again, no matter how many of his memories returned.

"Gregor said I could come here. To see what you're doing," Danal offered. He actually had something more important in mind, but he would approach that delicately.

Rikki seemed to snap out of his amazement and blinked. "Of course! Well, here are . . . our terminals, and Rolf is in the guardian mode right now. My shift is about to begin. The other terminals are for doing the usual Net stuff, if you need to."

Rolf didn't flinch, not even as Rikki said his name. "Guardian mode?" Danal asked.

"He's linked up to The Net, watching all the input and

output channels. See, we have to divert queries, keep track of anyone who seems too interested in the Cremators or the KEEP OFF THE GRASS patches, anything that might get us into trouble." Rikki stopped himself and seemed flustered. "I'm not telling this all in the right order.

"See, with our microprocessors we can tap directly into The Net, almost like an Interface. Rolf and I, and other Waker volunteers, are like Guardian Angels for the Wakers. When we . . . link up, we can restring databases, divert informational queries, things like that. No one suspects. Not even the real Guardian Angels, and we have to be very careful about that. The people have an incredible blind spot about The Net—they trust it too much. They don't even think about the information they find there. And since The Net tells them the grass patches are really deadly disintegrators, they just plain don't look for contrary evidence, though there's plenty of it if they'd open their eyes." He shrugged. "It doesn't take much to think faster than they do."

Danal indicated the jury-rigged terminals. "But how do you tap into The Net? With a stolen password?"

Rikki looked at him, puzzled and surprised. "Well, a lot of us still have our own passwords from before. See, it takes so long for Net Accounting to reassign out-of-date passwords, many of us still use ours. We can use chromosomal match, retina scans, or other ways to prove our identity, even if the records say we're dead. Once a password works, we share it among ourselves."

"Enforcers can kill you for sharing passwords!" Danal said automatically.

"We've done plenty of other things the Enforcers wouldn't like. Besides, we're all in this together. 'Bound by a common tie that runs deeper than simple human trust.' Gregor says that." Rikki hesitated; he seemed eager and expectant, looking at Danal out of the corner of his eye. He found his voice again.

"What are you going to do for all of us, Danal? We're really anxious to know."

"What do you mean?"

"Well, you're . . ." Rikki looked around, then spoke more bravely, "Gregor sits around thinking all the time. I mean, he really *is* worried, but I bet you're willing to do something, instead of just sitting here. Now, nobody's ready to be a better leader than Gregor, but some of us are getting tired of just waiting.

"See, we were all nobodies—even Gregor, he was just a librarian, a historian, and no one missed him when he died. But you're so famous. Vincent Van Ryman! Now we've finally got someone who might make a difference!"

Danal pursed his lips. "It doesn't matter if I'm famous or not. Why don't you all just come forward? You'd get enough publicity to make your point, tell your story. Anybody coming back from death is enough to make people pay attention."

Rikki shook his head vigorously. "We can't just come forward. Watch this." A slight grin crossed the boyish face, then he spoke in a sharp tone.

"Danal, Command: Slap your face!"

Involuntarily Danal's left arm jerked up and he struck himself flat across the cheek. His eyes flew open in shock, but he could not stop his reaction.

"Sorry," Rikki said, "but anyone can do that to us. Any time. With just a simple word or two, they could shut us all up forever. If we go public now, we would have to roll over and do whatever anyone Commands us. Those aren't very good terms for rejoining society, do you think? We're still Servants, Danal, no matter what all we remember. We've been trying to deprogram ourselves, to get rid of the Command phrase, but it doesn't do any good. It's tangled up too deep with the microprocessor that keeps us alive."

Danal's face stung from the slap, and he frowned. "Have you told anybody? I mean, real people?"

"No," Rikki answered.

"How about your own family? Did you have a family? Have you gotten in touch with them?"

"No!" Rikki cut him off. "Yes, I had a family. I had a younger sister, and a mom, and a dad. Both of my parents worked. When I died, I think it was some kind of . . . accident. Out in the streets people were throwing bottles, stones, cans. We were trying to run, to get inside a . . . a café, I think, and something hit me in the throat. It hurt, and I blacked out." He rubbed his neck, where a twisted scar showed what had apparently been his death wound. "And then I was a Servant. Boy, was I surprised."

Rikki made a sarcastic little grin, but then his eyes looked wistful and distant. "My dad had just taught me how to play chess. I wasn't very good, but I understood it, and it was an adult game. It was interesting because we used a real board, and pieces you moved one at a time with your hand. The game seemed so much more real than the computer versions of chess. I think this is probably the way they used to play it a long time ago."

But then suddenly he bit his lip and looked back at Danal. "No, I haven't told them I've awakened. It would be like killing myself all over again."

Danal looked at him helplessly. "But what do you expect me to do?"

Rikki seemed shocked that he would even ask the question. "You're important enough—with your scandal, with Francois Nathans and the imposter, we can get the public interest long enough to tell our stories. It'll distract them before someone, say, from Resurrection, can use the Command phrase and shut us all up."

"Nathans is still alive," Danal said, clipping his words short.

"Yeah, we found that out yesterday. We were going to let you know."

Danal saw his chance and did not hesitate. "I need you to do something for me. And then maybe I can help you."

Rolf sat up suddenly from his terminal and blinked, somewhat dazed. Upon seeing the other two Wakers, Rolf snapped himself back to his surroundings. He nodded, and Danal returned his greeting.

"I'm going in. It'll be just a second," Rikki said.

"Don't wait too long." Rolf seemed cursorily confident in Rikki's abilities. "No queries this time."

"There usually aren't," the boy Waker mumbled.

As if in a conspiracy between themselves, neither Danal nor Rikki spoke again until the other Waker had walked briskly away along the narrow wooden catwalks.

"Shouldn't you go in? Watch The Net?" Danal asked.

Rikki brushed the question aside as if it didn't matter and whispered to Danal in eager fascination, "What are you going to do? How can I help?"

"I need to find someone."

"Who is it? Is this part of a plan? I knew you'd do something to help us!"

Danal frowned slightly, but considered the question. "Well, I think it'll solve some of the questions Gregor's worried about. Then maybe he'll do something. But at the moment, this is really for me alone." Danal swallowed, uneasy, but forcing himself to push ahead. "Her name is—was Julia. I . . . loved her."

Rikki's eyes lit up. "You mean *the* Julia?"

"You know?"

"Yes, we all know the story. This is Julia, the one—the one Nathans killed."

Danal stared at the terminals, wishing that he could do everything himself without having to open up to someone else's questions.

"Yes. He said he wiped her from The Net, and then he brought her back. As a Servant. I saw her on the streets—that was what finally brought all my memories back." Danal fell silent for a moment, and Rikki waited for him to continue. "But of course she couldn't recognize me, not with the surface-cloning of my face. I don't look like me anymore. But I know she's out there, and I have to find her."

Danal found that he was almost afraid to have Julia back, but he had no choice but to find her. "I don't know if you'll be able to track her down, if Nathans has deleted everything about her from The Net."

With a glint in his eye Rikki said, "Nothing is ever really gone."

"Can you do it?"

The young Waker shrugged and drew a deep breath, considering. "It'll take a lot of time, and I'm on assignment here as a guardian. See, we don't really have the manpower to watch The Net more carefully, so I can't let everyone down. If I track down Julia for you, I'd have to put aside those duties." He looked uncertain but anxious to help.

"Well, how often do you really need to divert a database search? How many queries do you get when you sit there in a trance for hours and hours?"

Rikki absently scratched the side of the keyboard. "Not very many. I could—yes, I *will* try to find Julia for you." He seemed to be taking it as a personal challenge.

"Should I get someone else? Or you can do it when you're not on guardian duty."

"No. I want to do this." He lowered his eyes, then spoke more quietly. "But don't let Gregor know about this. He won't approve, I'm sure of it."

"What's there to approve?"

"Reliving your past."

Trying to avoid Rikki's gaze, Danal glanced up at one of the fuzzy green patches of holographic grass far above. Actual sunlight filtered through the image. Before he could look back to Rikki again, a transparent plastic beverage bottle, nearly empty, fell through the hologram, bouncing and pinging on the girders.

"Listen, and I'll tell you everything about her."

Then Danal began to spill the story, everything he could remember, every facet of Julia's personality, every eccentricity, every unusual detail. And Rikki sat back, transfixed, absorbing it all, not needing to write anything down. Danal told how he had once communicated with her under the identity of Randolph Carter through the electronic mail; he described where she had lived, what she had done. He tried to tunnel backward to find every offshoot of information that Rikki might be able to use.

Danal described her physically in intimate detail. He described her business dealings, described all the things they had done together. Nathans had probably set up a cumulative Delete program, a virus function to track down and destroy all interconnected paths of the person Julia. But Danal hoped feverishly that some line of information had not connected with the others.

Taking a different tack, he described when she would have been killed, which implied the time frame for her resurrection. He carefully described everything he could recall of the Guildsman who had been escorting her down the street—the indigo-dyed lines of crow's-feet around his eyes, the square-cut graying hair.

Rikki's eyes looked bright but distant, already contemplating ways to attack the problem. "I'll do what I can. I might have to give up a couple days of guardian duty. But I'll find her."

"Don't jeopardize the Wakers for me," Danal cautioned and continued, to himself, "I need to see her again, either to bring her back or to say good-bye."

Danal sat alone down by the edge of the water while the structures holding up the Metroplex loomed above him like a vast cosmic cathedral. Listlessly he ate a handful of vegetables grown in a hydroponic garden the Wakers tended under a long bank of sunlamps. Three days he had sat in an agitated patience, avoiding Rikki, letting the young Waker work in peace.

Now someone slipped up to him quietly, startling Danal

in his distraction. He turned and saw Rikki clad in a tight-fitting Servant jumpsuit; the boy Waker would never grow, and his twelve-year-old Servant body would remain locked in its appearance of youth.

Danal swallowed his mouthful so quickly that he nearly choked. "Shouldn't you be on guardian duty?"

Danal knew, before the freckle-faced Waker said anything, but still the response sent his synHeart pounding.

"I found her!"

A whirlwind of rose-tinted images flooded past his mind's eye—the first meeting in the cafeteria, the hovercopter trip to Point Reyes, making love on the beach, tearing down the stone gargoyles, drinking iced tea in the sauna.

Julia.

"Now what are you going to do?" Rikki said.

Danal stood up and grasped the rope ladder leading upward, more to steady himself than to go anywhere.

"I'm going to go take her back."

32

"Are you *commanding* me not to do this?" Danal challenged Gregor. They had not called an actual gathering, but Rikki had made certain that a good many Wakers—mostly the impatient ones—came forward to watch.

Taken by surprise, Gregor looked uncomfortable and awkward, but Danal pressed him before he could respond.

"Remember when you said you weren't really a leader here, that we can follow your advice as we see fit? Were you just kidding, or what? All the time you wrestle with your morals and your questions, but your questions aren't any more valid than mine!"

"That's not what I said, Danal. I want you to think about what you're going to do. Is it wise? Answer that yourself." His eyes looked wide and dark. Gregor folded his hands clumsily together, as if he didn't know what to do with them.

Danal tried to be more compassionate. He didn't like acting a showman in front of a crowd, but he needed to clear the air between Gregor and himself before he could do anything else. "I have to know, Gregor. If she's there, or if she's gone forever. I have to find her again."

The leader mumbled under his breath. "It's no secret what you intend to do afterwards."

Rikki interrupted, and the other Wakers stood by the boy, eager, expectant. "Gregor, we've got to start answering all those questions about . . . us. No one's going to give away the answers. We don't get a prize for just waiting around."

In the pause that followed, Danal bent closer to Gregor. From above, the sounds of creaking and settling emanated from the girders and pilings. "Francois Nathans murdered her, Gregor," he said, feeling pain. "I may have changed a great deal because of you, but I still need to know whether to hate him or not."

Gregor looked defeated for a moment, and Danal was the only one who saw his slight nod. "Just remember Danal, we're not the same anymore. She won't be the same, not after what we've experienced. Even if she remembers her past, things can never be as they were."

"That doesn't mean I have to be satisfied with the way they *are*," he whispered in reply.

"I'm Guildsman Drex, you blasted thing!" he shouted at the doorway voice-receiver. "Drex! I live here. Do a voiceprint check. How the hell was I supposed to know a glitch would change my own password?"

Reluctantly, it seemed, The Net allowed him to enter, and as he scramble-sealed the entrance, Drex felt himself safe and protected in his own rooms, mercifully away from the pressures of the Guild for another day. Tension headaches and gastric disorders—fringe benefits of a management-level salary.

It all ran over and over again in his mind, muddled together in columns of names and numbers. Instant statistics, keeping track of the locations and assignments of over a hundred Enforcers, making sure that his assigned section of the Metroplex was given its quota of protection. Drex would not last as Guildsman very long if his sector showed either a particularly bad crime month or a notably clean tally. Deviate from the norm? Never!

Meetings that went on and on with plenty of rhetoric, 'setting goals,' 'initiating studies,' 'interfacing' with all his counterparts. It devoured his time and kept him from answering the long queue of electronic-mail memos waiting for him. Though he remained endlessly busy, Drex never seemed to get anything accomplished—always so many little things that made him scurry back and forth, talking to people, keeping this person happy, meeting that person's demands.

But in the comforting womb of his suite, Drex was on his own time now. He wished he could lift the job from his shoulders and store it away in a closet someplace.

He increased the wall illumination slowly; he liked the warm dimness, and he didn't think he'd be doing any reading anyway.

The Servant sat where he had left her in the morning. "Julia! Aren't you going to welcome me home?"

"Yes, Master Drex," she answered in a flat voice and stood up stiffly. "Welcome home."

Julia rarely wore any clothing at all when he was home alone with her. He preferred it that way. But he realized that sometime during the day she had independently donned her gray Servant jumpsuit, as if with some last vestige of instinct. It seemed odd and it bothered him, but he couldn't figure out why.

Sighing, Drex went into his sleeping area and activated the floor. The heaters began to work, and the crosslinked polymer strands altered their structure, slowly turning the hard, rubbery floor into a soft and pliant cushion on which he and Julia would sleep. Drex stepped out onto the sleepfloor, feeling his feet sink into the pleasantly warm floor substance. "Come here, Julia."

He had already eaten from a machine at the Guild headquarters, but now he wanted to relax, to loosen up, to burn off some of his restless energy. Drex began to unfasten his clothes. He didn't think he had the patience to give Julia detailed step-by-step instructions now. That had proved awkwardly funny in the past, but tonight he wanted just some quick sex and then a long sleep. Drex barked at the walls to dim the lights further, and his suite began to feel more homelike, more comfortable.

Julia shuffled over toward him and almost lost her balance as she stepped onto the soft sleepfloor. Drex sat down casually and propped himself up on one elbow. As he smiled at her, the indigo-dyed crow's-feet clenched together around his eyes.

A series of muffled melodious tones interrupted him as The Net spontaneously unscrambled his door code. The entrance to his suite whisked open by itself.

Drex sat up sharply, puzzlement outweighing his fear. Silhouetted in the reddish glow from his walls, four figures stood in the entryway and, in unison, they walked into his rooms.

"How did you get in here! Who are you?" Drex demanded, trying to struggle to his feet, but the soft floor did not cooperate with him. He shouted for the lights to come on fully; the illumination dazzled him, but didn't seem to bother the four intruders. He blinked and tried to wave the brightness away so he could see again.

"We've come for your Servant," one of them said.

Taken aback at the ridiculous idea, Drex scowled. "Well, you can't have her! What are you talking about?"

His eyes grew accustomed to the light, and immediately he noticed something odd about the intruders. Two of them marched purposefully forward toward Julia, then gently took her by the arm. "Come with us, Julia."

Outnumbered and beginning to grow afraid, Drex could do nothing but stand helplessly.

Then he recognized the pale dead skin of the intruders, their hairless faces, smears of makeup, their bald scalps imperfectly hidden by caps and hats, as if they had been in a rush to throw on disguises. A numbing horror started to grow in him. Servants? Impossible! But the more he stared at their eyes, their faces, their actions, the more certain he became. It couldn't be possible. Servants did not act as vigilantes to free their own kind. It was absurd.

"Command: Release her!" he shouted in an authoritative tone.

As if they had grasped a hot iron, the two Servants escorting Julia jerked back their hands and stood paralyzed. With some amount of self-satisfaction Drex watched their faces fall.

Then, before he could think of something else to say, before his lips could begin to shift themselves into a smile, one of the other Servants launched himself at Drex with dizzying speed. The Guildsman couldn't move his eyes fast enough as the intruder flew forward to clap his hand across Drex's mouth, stifling any further words. The force of the Servant's hand crushed his lips against his teeth, smashing his gums. A crunching pop and a nauseating pain told Drex that two front teeth had broken free of their sockets. He tasted a mouthful of blood. He tried not to whimper.

Drex collapsed weakly to his knees as the Servant released him. "Not another word from you," the Servant said coldly, "or I'll pluck out your vocal cords once and for all!"

Blood dribbled from between Drex's bruised lips. His skin crawled at the dry, cold touch of the Servant's dead flesh. His eyes were bright with infuriated and helpless tears; his body shook as he fought back sobs.

Without looking at Drex again, the leader of the Servants went hesitantly over to Julia and lovingly, it seemed, ran his pallid fingers along her cheek. The male Servant's face shone with childlike awe.

"Julia," the Servant whispered.

The four intruders hurried her out the door. She followed them without resisting. They even had the maddening courtesy to close his door and scramble-seal it behind them.

234

Now Drex's tears of rage burst forth, and he spat out blood and teeth. Squatting, he pounded on the floor, but its soft, warm texture absorbed the blows and tried to comfort him.

33

Blank slate.

Julia gazed at him, not moving, as if someone had awkwardly positioned a rag doll. Danal stared back, trying to lock eyes with her, until he finally looked away. His knuckles clenched white. Damn, it had to work! He shook his head, ignoring exhaustion, and stood up, realizing how sore and stiff his knees had become. He wanted a drink of water; his throat felt dry.

The other Wakers left them undisturbed down at water level. "Don't you remember anything?" he begged. With the harsh sunlamps shining down on Julia from far above, Danal almost pictured himself as an evil interrogator in a room. Turning his back, Danal avoided looking at this caricature of Julia—it hurt him too much. *Julia* had gone away and left only this puppet behind.

"Yes. I remember everything I have been told," she answered.

Danal jumped a little, then frowned at himself. "I mean about your first life, with Vincent Van Ryman?"

Her voice had a numb, prerecorded quality to it. "No. I don't remember anything."

Danal took a deep breath, closed his eyes for a moment, and continued.

Dangling cords swayed from above as he pulled a high-resolution terminal toward him—the kind intended for home use, much like the one his father Stromgaard had long ago used to play electronic games. Danal called up the protocol of images he had compiled.

"Look at these again, Julia. I want you to give it your full attention." It was the sixth time he had shown them to her, he knew, but he clenched his teeth and forced himself to keep trying, relentlessly. "I've already explained why I need you to remember. You're a real person named Julia who was killed and brought back to life. I want you to find those memories. *I* did it—I know you can."

The grayness of the screen dissolved into a long view

of the isolated oceanside of Point Reyes, not exactly the spot he and Julia had once visited, but the closest file image he could find. "We went there, you and me. It was your first time in a hovercopter." The vivid memories flooded into his own mind, so bright, so clear; his eyes took on a faraway look, and he smiled.

The scene changed to a full-detail image of Vincent Van Ryman's face, lifted from one of the Net periodicals. "That was me. This was you."

The next image showed a graphically massaged photo of Julia; Rikki had processed a new image of the Servant Julia, adding hair, expression, *life*, to make her look as she had once been, with high cheekbones and pointed chin, pretty features, bright eyes ready to disagree or to laugh, depending on her mood.

Next came the inverted star-in-pentagram logo. Summary files lifted from the current-events databases, describing how Vincent Van Ryman had challenged the neo-Satanists. "Do you remember these? The neo-Satanists? What we did together?"

"No."

With Rikki's sophisticated Net skills, they had been able to recreate on screen almost exactly the white-light hologram of the beach, the one that had rested above the mantel in the Van Ryman mansion. "Do you remember this picture?"

"No."

Danal searched for the slightest hesitation in her voice, the slightest hint of doubt or uncertainty, but found nothing.

"We made love on the beach."

He fell silent and swallowed. His throat felt thick, as if it contained a despairing sob waiting to be released. His synHeart felt heavy enough to have been molded out of lead. Danal reached out tentatively with his hand, extending his fingertips. He traced a line from her eye, brushing down her cheek, wiping away an imaginary tear. How he wished she would shed a tear! Her skin felt dry and cool, with her body temperature carefully regulated.

Danal reached out with his other hand, cupping her chin. He ran his fingers down her cheeks, over her lips. She lifted her head up slightly with his gentle pressure, but her eyes remained empty. Danal found himself breathing rapidly, deeply. A smear of tears covered his eyes.

"Oh, Julia . . ." he said softly. His lips moved, but no words came out. "I'm so sorry."

He raised her chin a fraction more, then bent forward to kiss her lightly on the lips. The kiss was cold, and Julia did not participate.

Danal turned away, hanging his head and trembling.

He heard a jingling, sloshing sound and looked up to see Laina making her way down the rope ladder. Ice cubes tinkled against the sides of a pitcher she carried.

"I brought you two something cold to drink," she said brightly, but then looked at Danal, lowering her voice. "Were you ready?"

He sighed. "Yes, let's try it." He turned to Julia. "Do you like iced tea?"

"Whatever you wish."

Danal restrained himself from making a frustrated outburst. Laina removed two tall glasses from pockets in her gray apron. He poured Julia a glass and handed it to her; she accepted it but did not drink.

"We used to drink iced tea. Especially in the sauna. On the day we tore down all the gargoyles."

He paused after each phrase, listening and watching. Laina observed the two of them for a few moments and then left without making a sound.

Nothing.

Danal stood out in the air, feeling the light rain against his thick layers of flesh-tone makeup. He had been impatient before, careless, when they went to recover Julia. It had been at night. Drex usually worked late, and Danal had not wanted to take the time for more than quick disguises. He'd been eager to go from Gregor after their argument, eager to get it over with, but even the clod Guildsman had seen through their disguises—it almost cost him, and all of the Wakers, everything.

Listlessly he held an umbrella, but paid little attention to whether it blocked the raindrops or not. Beside him Julia stood in her gray jumpsuit, soaking wet but uncaring. Danal drew his red-checked jacket closer around him.

Somehow the Gothic Van Ryman mansion looked *right* with black clouds looming behind it. The cockeyed weathervane spun one way and then the other, ignoring the direction of the breeze. Runnels of rain trickled off the wings and fangs of the gargoyles lurking in the eaves. The black wrought-iron fence looked like a line of spear points barring their way. Danal stared at the house himself, feeling helpless anger still gnawing at him. Someone claiming to be Vincent Van Ryman relaxed inside, enjoying a stolen life.

Tiny flashes of light blinked in a half-dome around the house as raindrops struck the deadly field of the Intruder Defense Systems—the protection systems he had installed primarily for Julia's safety . . . for all the good they had done. A strong ozone smell hung in the air.

"Just look at it a while longer," he said hoarsely.

Danal had taken her to the same cafeteria where they'd first met. They sat in the same red plastic booth; they drank their coffee, listened to the clatter of dishes on the conveyor belt. Danal even tried to start the same conversations. Julia lifted her cup and swallowed the hot coffee, staring ahead. People began to look sideways at him, and Danal realized that he shouldn't have brought a Servant into the cafeteria. He didn't want to call attention to himself. They left.

Other people walked blithely past the Van Ryman mansion in the rain. "April showers bring May flowers," Danal said to Julia; she did not respond.

They could not stay much more—the imposter could be watching him through the video monitors. Did the imposter even suspect Danal was still alive? Danal had fallen through a KEEP OFF THE GRASS patch—would the imposter be worried at all anymore? Would he think he had gotten off, successful and free? Or might he recognize a disguised Danal and a Servant Julia loitering in front of his mansion?

Danal reminded himself that the imposter was Joey—a man disguised as a Servant, along with his partner Zia—whom Vincent and Julia had welcomed into their home. Danal found it slightly ironic, now that he was a real Servant disguising himself as a man.

His last hope lay in showing her the looming mansion. Julia obediently stared at it in the rain, looking up at the gables and windows. Water ran down her bald scalp, beading on her pallid skin. She blinked rainwater out of her eyes and continued to look.

"Well?" Danal finally lost his patience. "Does this seem familiar to you? At all?"

"No," Julia answered with flat but brutal honesty.

"It's no use," Danal said quietly.

Laina looked at him, understanding, but with a slight scowl. "You're giving up hope, then?" She refilled his glass with the last of the iced tea, but now it tasted bitter.

"Her memories are dead and buried. They're completely gone, wiped clean." Danal hung his head. He could no longer even look at the walking husk of Julia. He had sent her with Gregor through the levels of the underground world to be occupied with menial tasks such as keeping the persistent repair-rats from undoing the constructions of the Wakers.

Laina reached up and patted him lightly on the shoulder. He looked at her and realized that she had dressed in part of her white nurse/tech uniform. She wore it for her own comfort, now that it no longer did her any good in the medical center, but she wore none of the excessive makeup, letting her bland Servant face stand on its own instead.

"You know, if it helps any, we've done quite a bit of research for ourselves. Rodney Quick got us a little more than a liter of a mutated batch of the final resurrection solution—that helped a lot.

"Apparently, the mutated solution weakens the barriers holding our memories back. But it takes something else, repeated shocks to our memories to break them open. You're giving Julia the shocks all right, but if the barriers were never loosened in the first place. . . . Well, there's nothing you can do about it. The mutated solution is really the key, and her resurrection was probably routine."

Danal's jaw muscles tightened, masking a sea of inner turmoil. He sat up to look Laina straight in the eye, and she seemed startled by the expression on his face. "I can't kid myself any longer." His voice came out sharp and cold. "And now I don't have any reason in the world to forgive Nathans."

Danal leaned back on his hammock and stared up into the swallowing darkness. Laina looked as if she wanted to say something to him, but maintained her silence. He didn't look at her. His burning anger seemed to feed on itself, leaving him motionless.

From below, Danal heard the gentle creaking of crossbeams as someone climbed up to where he and Laina sat together.

"Careful, now." Gregor's voice came from under them, then the leader hauled himself up to the main platform. The Servant Julia mechanically followed him up the ladder; as her hands appeared at the topmost rung, Gregor bent to help her up. Gregor dwarfed the silent Servant woman, but she seemed barely aware of his presence. Though Danal had begun to lose patience, Gregor still treated Julia with full courtesy and respect.

"Gregor, I've decided to stop trying," Danal sighed, as if confessing. "I've done everything I can think of, but still Julia's memories won't come back."

"For that, I think I'm glad," Gregor said carefully, watching Danal and not wanting to start an argument, respecting the other's decision. "I'm not sure it would be a kindness to give her memories back, to pull her away from . . . wherever she is."

Danal closed his eyes for a moment. He once again ran through the visions of his death experience, rapidly now—the chimes, the tunnel, the light, the familiar welcoming presences around him. He was suddenly struck by something he had not realized before. While he could no longer remember the identities of those other gathered spirits, his escorts, he was convinced that Julia—the real Julia—had not been there. This perplexed him, for surely she would have come to welcome him into death?

Breathless, young Rikki dropped to the platform from above with a loud thump, too agitated to use the ropes. His face lit up when he found Danal. "I've found her! Again! There's another Julia!"

Danal lurched off the hammock and landed on the balls of his feet. "What?!"

"It's hard to explain, but I've found another Julia!"

Gregor interrupted, keeping a serious expression on his face. "How could you have found someone else? You're supposed to be on guardian duty."

"Oh, I gave up some of my time for the searches," he answered curtly and turned his attention back to Danal. But Gregor raised his voice.

"And put us all in jeopardy? All Wakers?"

"It was only for a little while. Nothing happened."

Danal stopped any further argument with his own impatience. "What are you talking about, Rikki?" He looked at the Servant Julia standing motionless beside them.

The boy Waker shrugged. "My search routines kept churning away, deeper and deeper into The Net. See, after we had located *her*"—he indicated the Servant Julia—"I forgot about the routines. I didn't think they'd come up with anything different—that's for sure.

"But I found someone else, really hidden deep. She seems to have only the faintest hint of a correlation with this Julia, or your Julia. But it's real. I can't tell you anything more, but she is alive. Not a Servant."

"Where is she?" Danal whispered.

"Tough security. In a quarantined hospital complex, held in absolute isolation. It's almost as if they don't want anybody to see she's there, you know?"

Danal focused his eyes off in the distance, suddenly feeling hope again. With his double-think mentality, it would be just like Nathans to have created a decoy Julia, this Servant, made to look like the real Julia through surface-cloning, just as the imposter had taken Danal's own place as Vincent Van Ryman. What if the real Julia was still alive, locked away someplace, a final card for Nathans to play?

What if Julia was still alive?

His breath came in short bursts. "I have to know." He looked around at all the faces, almost pleading. "But how am I going to get in, if he's got tight security all around?"

After a moment of silence Laina chuckled a bit. "Piece of cake." She straightened the skirt of her white nurse/tech outfit. "After all, it's just another medical center."

PART IV

Confrontation

34

The polished visor hid Jones's impatient smile as he
hurried through the back passageways to the neo-Satanists'
sacrificial grotto. Some of the walls bore graffiti, most of
it influenced by the cult. Reddish mood-light poured
from fluorescent panels above, but the place stood empty
so early in the morning. He knew Nathans would be
there.

Jones couldn't wait to tell the other man. He'd never
imagined he could discover something so important, so
incredible all by himself—certainly not in the barracks,
certainly not on a community Net terminal. The knowledge made him feel proud with a happy self-confidence
he had never experienced before. He had done something, accomplished something, completed a meaningful
and important purpose.

Because of Nathans's insistence on absolute secrecy
regarding his connections to the Guild, Jones was forbidden to show his Elite Guard colors in any area fre-
quented by the neo-Satanists, though the man's public
involvement with the cult itself was murky at best. It
seemed a bit extreme to Jones, but he knew Nathans
must have his reasons.

Jones wore his old white uniform, a plain Enforcer
again, feeling strangely out of place. He seemed to be
lowering himself now that he had earned the right to
wear Elite Guard blue, but, on the other hand, it brought
back a spark of nostalgia. The white armor made him
seem comparatively unobtrusive, even at dawn, when he
had entered the mass-trans station. The outbound cars
were nearly empty, as most commuters traveled the opposite direction, streaming into the Metroplex for their
day's work. Sitting alone, Jones looked at the scratched
transplastic window, fidgeting in his armor and staring up
at the sky. As curfew finished for the night, one late
patrol hovercar rushed silently overhead, making for its
Guild hangar deep in the Metroplex.

At the destination-request terminal Jones entered the

confidential code used by the neo-Satanists, ensuring that a special transport would be waiting for him when he reached the last stop on the fringe line. He sat and waited, drumming his fingers on the seat as a stream of darkness and light passed the window.

When forming the cult, Nathans had diverted his own workers from their regular labor to the construction of a spectacular secret ceremonial chamber deep at an unknown end of the mass-trans system. Later, anyone initiated into the cult received the special destination code that allowed them to go down into the grotto.

As he disembarked, Jones felt his skin crawl in unconscious reaction to his own superstitions. The Guild served a purpose, and now that he knew more he could respect that; he could see the importance of the Enforcers, especially the Elite Guard—but neo-Satanism was something else altogether. He didn't know why Nathans would bother with it.

Breathless, Jones brought himself to the bottom of the stairs and stopped short in front of the doorway leading into the High Priest's private chambers. The chronometer on the lower right-hand corner of his visor said "6:13 am"; he was a few minutes late already.

A mere handful of people knew the password to enter the private chambers, and Jones hummed the mnemonic to himself, "Roy G. Biv Deserves Fudge." Nathans had trusted him with the password, though Jones was uneasy with his increased amount of assistance in neo-Satanist activities. In his stiff white gloves Jones punched the letters one at a time.

The iron-studded door crawled open, protesting. Clouds of grayish-brown smoke curled upward from the doorway, reeking of sulfur. Jones automatically switched on the mask filters behind his visor and stepped into the room, baffled. Had something caught on fire? He tensed— was Nathans all right? Low orange lights suddenly came on, and an impossibly heavy footstep thundered down as a huge figure came into view.

Jones took a step backward in utter disbelief. The figure was a nightmare, a demon nine feet tall with bulbous muscles and brick-red skin. Curved horns, like massive construction tools, rode on its forehead, and a purple glow stabbed from its eyes as the creature gazed at Jones. It opened its mouth in a snarl as it stomped forward, exposing white fangs like sharpened pencils.

Though it walked on cloven hooves and ungainly animal-like legs, it moved with frightening speed and fluidity. Blue arcs of electricity skirled up and down its swishing arrow-tipped tail.

Jones yelped, terrified, and in one liquid motion he drew a pocket bazooka in one hand and a projectile weapon in the other. He crouched and aimed—

"Stop!"

Both Jones and the monster froze. Nathans emerged from the shadows, laughing. He flicked on the fluorescent lights and opened air ducts to draw away the brimstone smoke.

"Relax Jones—meet Prototype." The man smiled with childish delight. "He's a completely autonomous, fully functional *android*."

Astonished, the Enforcer stuttered to himself, but could not find his voice. Nathans continued, talking like a proud father, "Maybe you thought androids were impossible? That's what Resurrection always implied, and gave us Servants instead." He dismissed that thought with a wave. "Never impossible, though—simply not cost-effective. It's a hell of a tedious process to duplicate every single nerve and muscle fiber in a biological body. 'Servants for Mankind—Freeing Us from Tedium to Pursue Our True Destiny' and all that rot. Prototype here is just to show it can be done, although I've taken the liberty of embellishing his body."

Nathans tapped one of the curving horns. "Okay, Prototype, you can go back to the chamber and continue your inventory." Obediently the android turned and shuffled with a strange grace out of the room and into the large neo-Satanist storage vaults. "He is, after all, still like a Servant, so I've put him to work back there." Nathans adjusted his orange-red hairpiece, long and kinky this time. "Please take off that helmet, Jones—no need to keep up a charade for me."

Jones slipped off the lightweight helmet and blinked in the open air. Nathans watched him closely, and the Enforcer suddenly realized that his facial expressions were now exposed as he talked.

The room around them was sparsely furnished, intended to give the High Priest Vincent Van Ryman space to pace and ponder. Neo-Satanist symbols decorated the walls, with the inverted star-in-pentagram logo prominent. Musty-looking books lined the shelves.

Jones noticed Nathans moving with a carefully hidden sense of anxiety. The Enforcer worried for a moment, but Nathans kept up a good mask. "Now then, did I want to see you for something? Oh, yes!" Before Jones could spill out his discovery, the man continued, "You know that all the Elite Guard have their own specialties, their own turf, you might say. You, on the other hand, are not yet attached, and I have decided that you're perfect to assist me in my less-than-official Guild duties."

"You mean helping with the neo-Satanists?" Jones swallowed, and tried to keep a whine out of his voice. He didn't want Nathans to be angry or disappointed with him. "But, I really—"

Nathans looked squarely at him. "Now, don't complain. I see you standing there sweating, just waiting for me to turn my head so you can fidget! Stop this knee-jerk nonsense of revulsion toward neo-Satanism. It's all a fairy tale. Anyone with a brain can see that. I know you understand my reasoning, Jones. You're certainly intelligent enough, and I've explained it to you carefully.

"We have to polish the human race. It's time to scrape off the scum floating on the human gene pool—" Nathans seemed to let his control slip, and his eyes grew too bright; his hands shook. "But this social evolution business takes so damned long! We don't live forever, you know. And since I'm doing all the work to set the wheels in motion, I want to be alive to reap some of the benefits."

He sighed, though, and some of the frenzy seemed to drain away. "Now that we have no way of knowing the results of the Danal experiment"—Nathans shot a sad and bitter glance at Jones; ashamed, the Enforcer hid motionless behind his armor—"I've had to find some other way to hurry us along.

"Tonight is Walpurgis Night, you realize, one of the most important ceremonies of the year. In fact, this could be one of the most important events in the history of mankind. The High Sabbat should be a catalyst of something much more.

"Now, Jones, I trust you completely. I'll need your assistance with some of the preparations. This is very important. I've got some cannisters of a chemical labelled Rhodamine 590 over against the wall. Take that and make sure it gets mixed into the vat of cheap red wine set up in the Sabbat grotto—but be careful not to get any on your hands. I also want you to check the pump systems and make sure all the new Sacred Fonts work properly. I just had them installed." Nathans's eyes twinkled beneath the carrot-colored wig.

Be careful not to get any on your hands? "What is this Rhodamine? What does it do?"

Nathans smiled brightly, but it made Jones uneasy. "Ah, I looked long and hard for something like it. It's a dye used with lasers, a brilliant orange red. But it's also a mitochondrial poison, extremely toxic and wonderfully fast-acting. Ranks right up there with cyanide. Cyanide's been done to death, of course, and I wanted something a little more exotic."

Jones stood motionless, wearing a puzzled and horrified grimace on his face. He wished he could put his helmet back on and hide behind it. "But . . . poison? What for?"

"For tonight's communion, of course." Nathans flicked his eyes at Jones. His gaze had an intensity that made the Enforcer want to cringe, afraid, then the man's expression changed to one of indirect scorn. He motioned placatingly. "Look, I'm not going to ask them to do anything against their wishes—it'll be their own choice completely, as it has to be. That's why I had to find a fast-acting poison. I do feel sorry for the first victim or two, the ones who really don't know." He sighed. "But after that, after they all see how deadly it is, surely no rational, intelligent person would drink? Would you? Of course not. But I'm betting that some of them will, and good riddance to them! Surely you don't feel sorry for people like that?"

Jones didn't answer. He could hardly even move—Nathans couldn't be serious! He suddenly looked at the man in a different light. No, not Nathans—it had to be some trick, a joke. A joke, right?

Nathans continued, unaware of Jones's thoughts. He spoke distractedly, as if preoccupied to the point of helplessness, "My problem for the moment is to make sure our High Priest is up to the task. He's been cringing for weeks, hiding behind his Intruder Defense Systems. A bit emotionally disturbed, as he always has been." Nathans mumbled to himself, and this alarmed Jones as well. Nathans had *never* talked to himself before.

The Enforcer interrupted. Maybe by announcing his discovery, he could focus Nathans's attention again. "I found out something very strange about the KEEP OFF THE GRASS patches last night. I bumped into it almost by accident."

Nathans regarded him, as if distracted and caught up with his own workings for the evening's High Sabbat. But his eyes widened in fascination and amazement as Jones described the maintenance openings, the raised city over the water.

"The funny thing is, I know the team of hackers has been trying for weeks to uncover any scrap of information, but they always came up empty-handed. I certainly didn't expect to find anything myself, but I thought I should at least try. So last night I sat down at the terminal and just punched in a routine query—and I got a direct answer. I read it—I know what I saw. But I tried again this morning, and The Net said it had no information."

Jones dropped his voice and raised his eyebrows, as if sharing a deep secret. "It's almost like someone was tampering with The Net. Diverting my queries and covering themselves so well that no one ever suspected. But I caught them off guard and got the information!"

Fascinated, Nathans stared off into space. "We alter The Net all the time for neo-Satanism: it's not that complicated, if you have the right access and you know what you're doing. But someone else is doing it, too! And without my knowing it! That's remarkable—I never even thought . . . what a blind spot!" He tapped his fingertips together, and his eyes glowed as connections started to form.

"There could be an entire underground world down there," Nathans mumbled to himself. "If these tamperers are so carefully hiding all information about the KEEP OFF THE GRASS patches, we can assume that they live in—or at least attach some extreme importance to—whatever is down there. How much else don't we know? Damn! That's frustrating."

He drew in a quick breath, exclaiming to Jones, "And that means Danal might be alive! If he and that nurse/tech deliberately jumped into the patch, she must have known something. Hmmm."

The Enforcer could imagine the mental wheels churning behind Nathans's forehead; the process fascinated him, but he offered no suggestions himself. The man finally sat up.

"I want you to keep this absolutely confidential. This could be vital information, depending on who these Net tamperers are . . . and if they have anything to do with Danal. What would they want with a Servant who regained his memory?" He scratched his hairpiece.

"I want you to go right away and—" He frowned. "No . . . damn! You'll have to wait until dark. But before curfew, it has to be before curfew! Find a deserted street with one of these 'maintenance openings.' Take one other Guard to help you, and verify what you've just told me—see what's under there.

"And you'd better go fully armed—people with an operation this sophisticated won't take kindly to being discovered."

Somewhat overwhelmed by Nathans's rush of words, Jones nodded and fitted his helmet back on.

"But most important of all, I must have a report from you before the High Sabbat tonight. I have to know what you find, and I'll need your help with some of the final preparations for the ceremony." He smiled beneath his red mop of artificial hair. Jones's uneasiness all rushed back to him.

"It's really going to be something to watch."

35

"Elite Guard!" Laina whispered. "What are they doing in here?" Two of the blue-armored Enforcers marched down the dim hall of the hospital complex's security wing, then vanished around the corner.

"Don't talk to me!" Danal hissed out of the corner of his mouth. "Don't even *look* like you're talking to me!" As he walked beside Laina in her nurse/tech uniform, Danal kept his face blank and lifeless, as any Servant should. Next to them marched burly Rolf in his own set of white Enforcer armor, their 'security escort.'

The checkpoint guard at the entrance to the high-security wing verified their story on his Net terminal. Rikki had come through again, planting the proper story, the proper authorizations.

"I'm supposed to escort them wherever they go," Rolf said ominously behind his polarized visor. "Orders." The similarly uniformed guard passed them on, then went back to playing his Net interactive games.

The halls of the vast hospital complex were quiet and drowsy in the early morning silence. Outside, a thick blanket of damp fog seeped into all the alleyways as the sun rose, muffling sounds.

"This is wing six. Down that hall—it should be Room 29-A." As Laina spoke, the heavy makeup made her face look artificial.

Another white-armored Enforcer stood at attention outside Room 29-A. Without hesitation the three imposters walked up to him. The guard tensed, but seemed reassured by Rolf's presence.

"We have to let them in," Rolf said gruffly. "The nurse/tech has special treatment for the patient. I'm supposed to escort her and the Servant, but . . . ah, because of the importance of this patient, I'd feel better if we both watched over them. Cover your ass—get me?"

The other Enforcer agreed appreciatively. "Good idea."

Confident, the other guard turned and punched in the

electronic combination for the door, stepping aside to let Laina and Danal enter first. Rolf and the guard stepped into the room side by side.

As soon as the door automatically closed behind them, Rolf wrapped his massive armored arm around the other Enforcer's helmet. With a twist he wrenched off the helmet to reveal the startled face of a pimply youth. Before the exposed Enforcer could speak a word, Laina jammed a hisser into his face and blasted him. Rolf stuffed the helmet back on the guard's head as he began to slither to the floor. He caught the unconscious Enforcer under the arms and eased him down to keep his armor from making too much of a clatter.

Danal paid no heed to this, but stood gawking at the sterile room's only inhabitant. The neatly made bed bore a quaint patchwork quilt; a lamp and small writing desk added homey but pathetically ineffective touches of comfort.

Sitting in an overstuffed chair and staring at them was the hideously disfigured remnant of a woman. Growths and tumors tangled her face as if with rivulets of melted wax. Most of the hair on her head had been swallowed up by crumpled ridges of insanely growing skin. But two hardened and intelligent eyes stared coldly at them from between twisted eyelids. When she breathed, air came through her distorted nose and mouth in a whistling, sucking sound.

Yet behind the havoc of her face, Danal could see the ghost of Julia's appearance, a hint of the woman to whom he had once opened his heart. But the eyes themselves spoke differently. Danal thought he recognized her gaze, but he had seen it only a few times before—eyes set on the face of a woman masquerading as a Servant. . . .

"Zia!" Danal gasped.

She turned her face disbelievingly toward Danal, the Servant, scrutinizing him with sudden interest. As she drew a labored breath to speak, she looked as if all of the questions suddenly canceled themselves out in her mind.

"Van Ryman—you were Vincent Van Ryman. I thought you'd come back to haunt us, one way or another." Zia paused and pulled another sucking breath through the opening of her mouth. She smirked in a hideous grimace. "I take it you're the welcoming committee for the Francois Nathans Fan Club?"

But Danal didn't hear her. All words caught in his

throat as the implications of Zia's presence hit him like a sledgehammer. She wasn't Julia. He staggered, taking half a step backward. Tears flooded his eyes again; his throat burned.

Julia was dead after all, leaving nothing but a walking mindless automaton, empty. Danal's hope shattered into sharp pieces. He hung his head and shuddered, trying to say her name out loud. He needed to sit down, to collapse, but he locked his knees instead. He barely felt Laina gripping his shoulder. It didn't matter anymore.

Danal spoke toward the floor. His voice carried a bleak, devastated undertone. "So what happened to you?"

Zia linked her fingers together and cracked her knuckles. Danal saw that her hands were also covered with tumors and malformed growths. "What the hell does it look like? Apparently the wonderful surface-cloning process doesn't always work like a charm." Her fingers jerked convulsively, as if she wanted to tear the fabric of the chair. "The bastard guaranteed it would work." But then her volatile expression changed, leaving only a dry bitterness.

"And what's Joey doing now? He must be all high and mighty alone in the mansion. He was a slimer, always acting more important than the rest of us. I was supposed to be with him—he took your place, and I was supposed to be Julia. Sure! Simple. Piece of cake. Just give us a few weeks of your time, Zia, and we'll touch up your face a bit. Make you look just like Julia. Surface-cloning, the magic of modern technology. Besides, it was all for the good of neo-Satanism."

Her bitterness oozed out of the words, making her seem pathetic. "Joey and I would pick up right where you two left off, and nobody'd know the difference . . . except for our radical change in philosophy." Zia shrugged. "But you did that already once before, so we weren't losing sleep over it.

"Joey's genotype was a perfect match to yours, a model case for the surface-cloning technique, and we couldn't hope for anything better. His disguise grew on his face like it belonged there.

"Me, on the other hand . . . well, I didn't get along quite so well with Julia's chromosomes. Something went wrong. The clone infection went rampant, and my new face grew in every which direction." She snorted, "Not something to write home about."

254

Laina's eyes widened as she listened, but she said nothing. Danal didn't know whether to resent the malformed imposter because she was not Julia, or if he should pity Zia as another one of Nathans's victims. "Why does he keep you here? Why bother? Why doesn't he just kill you"—Danal's voice cracked— "like he killed Julia?"

Zia made a rude noise with her mouth. "Francois Nathans is too genteel for that. He needs to keep me quiet about his botched plan, but I was one of his favorite tools, remember. Malleable, willing to make the greatest sacrifices for a good cause." She scowled. "Obviously, I can't go out anywhere. And even without my rather shocking appearance, I don't have an identity on The Net *anyway*, since I was supposed to take Julia's place. I need surgery every week or so, otherwise my nose and mouth grow together, and my eyelids seal shut. But Nathans takes care of me just dandy—what more could I want in the whole wide world?"

Before Danal could say anything, Zia rapped her fingers on the arm of her chair. "I haven't set off any alarms, you know, but I damn well could. What do you want coming here? This was a big risk . . . just to visit? Touching. How come you didn't bring any flowers or candy or get well cards?"

Danal mumbled his words through a gauze of grief. "I thought you might be the real Julia."

Zia shrugged bitterly. "I tried. But I ran into some unforeseen complications." She laughed again at him, a hooting sound from her misshapen mouth, then she stopped abruptly. "Don't you have anything better to do?"

Danal swallowed and clenched his fists, helplessly angry at her. But he would not let it bother him, he would not provoke her—it wasn't her fault. He said his words slowly through gritted teeth, coming to a decision as he spoke, "I'm going to stop Nathans. I have had quite enough of him."

"Ah, the brave hero, fighting for what's Right!" Zia taunted, "Then you'd better hurry up—tonight's Walpurgis Night."

Danal started as he realized she was right. "Walpurgis Night. I forgot."

Laina met his eyes. "What's that?"

"A long time ago, back in Eastern Europe, all the

witches gathered in the Hartz Mountains and had their greatest Sabbat of the year. May Day Eve—Walpurgis Night. It's usually a big deal for the neo-Satanists. Nathans will have a sacrifice or two, kill a few more people." Danal's voice began to shake. "My imposter will do the sacrifice, pour more blood on the hands of Vincent Van Ryman."

Zia smiled with her lumpy mouth. "Understatement rears its ugly head—oh, it's much more than that this time. You're a great hope for us all if I know more than you do, and I've been stuck here in this single room!

"This is going to be the *last* of the High Sabbats, and Nathans is going to wipe out all the followers of neo-Satanism. He's lost patience with them and wants to end everything with a bang. He'll poison them. He'll trick them, as he always has. Audience participation in a big way, and this time they'll all die."

Her voice began to quaver, and suddenly she looked pathetic, not defiant at all, with all traces of sarcasm replaced by defeat. "When Nathans comes to visit every once in a while, he tells me his upcoming plans. He likes to talk about his grandiose schemes, and there's no way I can shut him up. He thinks I'm interested."

She scratched absently at one of the waxy tumors on her cheek. "He told me—me!—that anyone who joined such a sham as neo-Satanism was incapable of rational thought. Anybody who couldn't think for himself didn't deserve the benefits of society. Do you think it means they're all incapable of rational thinking? I think it means they were misled by a charismatic leader and some sophisticated gimmicks. I was misled, too—*I* fell for it. Is that a crime worth dying for."

"Have you done anything to stop him?" Laina asked.

Zia laughed in a grating, burbling sound. "Me? You've got to be kidding! I'm cooped up here with a guard at the door every day. What the hell am I supposed to do? Look at Nathans and turn him to stone? I'm almost that ugly, but not quite."

Danal swallowed uncomfortably. "Tonight . . ." He looked at Laina, then at Rolf. The burly Waker had propped the unconscious Enforcer against the wall and stood listening in silence. "Nathans is forcing our hand."

He bit his bloodless lip and took a deep breath, assuming the role of leader. Anger rode behind his eyes, but he kept it under control. Galvanized, he fixed his gaze on

Zia. "Do you want to get out of here? Come with us? There might be something you could help with, when we confront Nathans."

The malformed imposter looked surprised and suspicious that he'd even ask. She spread her arms to indicate the hospital room. "And take me away from all this?" She stood up, and Danal saw that her slim figure resembled Julia's exactly. She could walk and move unhindered: the surface-cloning disarray had destroyed only her face and hands.

Zia set her jaw. "I'll come if I can help kill him."

36

Zia gazed at the underground world, swallowing details. With her distorted face and stretched eyelids, Danal could not quite interpret her expressions, but he could sense Zia's growing awe. She had remained silent as they smuggled her through a sublevel basement entrance, all of her sarcastic bitterness dissolved away. She seemed astonished to be free from the hospital complex; she looked intrigued by the very existence of the Wakers and the world they had built under the city; but most of all, she was delighted to know that Francois Nathans suspected nothing of the Wakers whatsoever.

She sat by herself, silent and daydreaming on a hammock as the other Wakers discussed the new turn of events. Without bothering to use gloves or a rag, Zia had removed the hot sunlamp bulb above her head, keeping herself in murky shadows, but she wore her deformities without cringing, brandishing them for all the Wakers to see.

Danal locked his fingers together behind his smooth head, stretching his elbows back until he could feel the joints creak. He let the silence hang for a moment, turning his gaze on the gathered Wakers.

Gregor sat back on his heels and watched Danal make his case, rubbing his big square jaw and waiting. Danal spoke carefully, gauging their reactions, then decided it was time to stop and let them judge for themselves. Before any of the Wakers could speak, Gregor stood up and faced Danal.

"Let me be your straw man for a minute. A devil's advocate, if you'll forgive the pun."

Danal watched him, trying to detect hostility or resentment in the Waker's eyes, but he saw only disturbed consideration.

"Why should we Wakers give up everything we've worked for? You want us to expose ourselves to Nathans and all the neo-Satanists—but that'll put us at their mercy. Your reasons aren't good enough. It sounds like a personal vendetta to me."

The other Wakers watched, tense. Rikki. Laina. Rolf. Forty others. Were they perceiving this as a showdown? Julia would be out there somewhere, silent and patient, probably sitting motionless as she had been told. Danal did not want to clash with Gregor, but he couldn't let himself hesitate.

"It's more than that. If I go by myself, I can't win—I'm sure of it. And half a victory in this game isn't worth anything at all. I need your support, all of you. Look at Zia, remember what Nathans intends to do tonight at the High Sabbat—you're a conscientious person, Gregor. Isn't stopping him the *right* thing to do?"

"You tell me, Danal—which is the lesser of the two evils? Saving the neo-Satanists or protecting the Wakers?"

The others began to murmur softly, and Danal knew he had to try a different tack. Water trickled below, and somewhere in the darkness a repair-rat clicked and scuttled. The entire world of girders and pilings seemed alive and waiting, coiled tight. He considered long, forming his argument, then his eyes lit up as he spoke.

"Gregor, if I can defeat Nathans completely and utterly, take away his power . . . then Resurrection, Incorporated will be mine. By right. I think we can do it—with the scandal that's sure to follow and with my story." He paused, measuring the dramatic effect. He felt tense and uneasy. So much depended on this, so much.

"Then the Wakers can perform all the above-board research they want, with the best equipment possible—maybe you can come answer all your questions, Gregor. And if we Wakers hold Resurrection, then we can implement whatever decisions we reach. Should we stop making Servants? We could do that if we wanted. Can we fix the resurrection process so Wakers never happen again, and the lost souls really do rest in peace?" He paused. "Can we find some other way to bring Julia's memories back?

"We can't do any of that unless we win against Nathans. Tonight. He's forcing our hand, I know. But we'll have to turn that to our advantage. And we can't win unless I get the help of all the Wakers."

Danal waited, feeling the regular beat of his synHeart, but Gregor made no further response.

"You have to admit he's got a damned good argument,

Gregor," Laina interrupted. Many of the other Wakers murmured in agreement.

Gregor looked at Zia's chaotic features again as she sat watching them, moving from lighter to deeper shadow as she swayed on the hammock. Danal watched the expressions on Gregor's face change, and he knew the other Waker had made up his mind.

Danal found a public Net booth and slipped inside. The timekeeper in his head told him that barely an hour had passed since the meeting of the Wakers, and already things had begun in earnest. He breathed deeply, feeling the tense excitement pounding through him. Soon it would all be over. He only wished it had never begun in the first place.

The air was damp and cold, with gray clouds sopping up the skies. Other pedestrians moved quickly along the sidewalks, heads down, and paying little attention to anything else. A mass-trans skipper churned past, stopping at corners, but no one got on or off. Several jobless blues sat next to each other in silence on the poured-stone lip of a dormant fountain. The cold streaked their cheeks with a pink flush.

Danal looked up between the tall buildings to where the jagged gables of the Van Ryman mansion jutted into the grayness. He had picked the particular booth for a specific purpose, so he could see the mansion. It would act like fuel for his anger, his determination.

"Nathans destroyed my life and my love," he said to Rikki beside him, "but the man in there stole my identity, my self. That's a more personal insult, and I'll confront him alone. This'll be our first blow."

Zia had also suggested they confront the imposter Van Ryman first. "Yeah, Nathans is the guiding force behind neo-Satanism and all their plans. But the imposter is the High Priest. Even if we get Nathans now, Joey'll still complete the massacre tonight. Why not take him out first, since he can cause the immediate damage? Besides, that'll make Nathans sweat a little bit."

Danal and the boy crowded into the booth, avoiding the cold and damp. They had gone out together, dressed as father and son, to begin the preparations. Rikki seemed to revel in his role and hung close to Danal, asking questions, pointing out things. Back at the Wakers' camp, Gregor and Laina worked on other plans. Danal wished he could be in both places at once, but he had chosen to be here, on the streets, where he could actively see the mansion, feed his enthusiasm.

In the Net booth Danal logged on as Vincent Van Ryman and then straightened up as the main Net menu showed on the screen. He rubbed the back of his head, trying to massage away the knot of tension there. He gracefully moved aside from the keypad. "All yours," he said and turned the terminal over to the freckle-faced Waker.

Rikki made a show of cracking his knuckles before he let his fingers fly over the keypad. Occasionally he paused and scrutinized the screen, then set off in another direction. With the speed and intensity of the boy's finger strokes, Danal quickly lost track of what he was doing.

"I didn't know there were so many repair-rats in the whole Metroplex!" Rikki cried as the display formed on the screen. "Look at them all!" Danal peered over the boy's shoulder. Numbers and coordinates scrolled up and off the screen in an almost endless stream.

"And those are just the ones in this section, too. They're self-replicating, remember?" Danal tapped on the images. "But we only need a couple of them."

Rikki found two repair-rats in the vicinity of the Van Ryman mansion, then erased all the others from the display.

"I'll take over from here," Danal said.

Rikki looked at him with a touch of condescension. "You sure you don't need any more help?"

Danal lightly punched the boy in the shoulder. "I'm not a complete idiot. I used to be pretty good on The Net—I think I can handle some simple controls now."

As he talked, he set the blips of the repair-rats to work on the wiring of Van Ryman's Intruder Defense Systems. Danal lost himself in trying to remember details, blueprints, electronic schematics. He opened another window on the screen, trying to connect with other libraries, but the details of Van Ryman's Intruder Defense Systems were, understandably, impossible to get. He let out a long breath and went back to work, forced to rely on his memory. He had designed the systems—his intuition would be right.

Rikki watched him in fascination, crowding in, but Danal paid no attention. Outside, a middle-aged man pressed his face against the Net booth for a moment, staring at them, but then he left. Rikki switched on the privacy screens.

"Are you going to disconnect the Intruder Defense Systems?" Rikki asked. "So you can get inside?"

"No. I don't want to do anything he'll notice. I'm not worried about getting in—I left an escape hatch for myself when I designed the systems. It's beating the imposter once I get inside—*that's* what I'm concerned about."

Sitting by the fireplace playing cribbage with Julia . . . relaxing in the sauna and drinking iced tea . . . feeling like an idiot as he balanced on the gables with a crowbar, trying to remove the gargoyles . . . flying the hovercopter, swooping down close to the ocean and watching Julia laugh in terrified delight. Those were *his* memories, from *his* life—no one could steal them from him. He remembered her image in the hologram over the mantel, and superimposed on that he saw the Servant Julia, mindless and unthinking. Some things are too sacred to steal. It made him actually look forward to confronting the imposter.

"The repair-rats will take a couple of hours to finish," he said to Rikki. "I need to stay here and direct them. Why don't you make sure Gregor isn't changing his mind about tonight?"

"I want to stay here and help—"

"You'll help me the most if you go make sure Gregor hasn't changed his mind. Besides, I need some time alone to . . . to set my mind, you know? I have to get ready for this."

Rikki nodded. "Good luck, then." Awkwardly he gave Danal a quick handshake before he slid open the Net booth and dashed off into the streets. Danal settled back to wait, running thoughts over and over in his mind until it was time. He watched the coordinates of the repair-rats on the screen as they worked out of sight underground.

37

A drizzle was coming down as Danal stalked toward the Van Ryman mansion. By now the sun had set, marking the beginning of Walpurgis Night, but he could barely tell any difference in the murky skies. The repair-rats had finished their work. He was about to begin.

Most of the pedestrians had been driven to shelter from the cold and the rain, leaving the streets hushed and empty. A wind stirred the dead fronds of a nearby palm tree, making it sound like a rattling witch's broom.

Danal wore a Servant jumpsuit defiantly, making no attempt to hide his identity. *Let the imposter be watching,* he thought, *Maybe he's got a guilty conscience.* He smiled grimly to himself. *I never thought I'd be my own avenging angel.*

The drizzle clearly outlined the hemispherical screen of the Intruder Defense field as droplets struck it and flashed into steam. Behind the field, visible as if he were looking through a slightly distorted fishbowl, Danal could see the ornate spires and reptilian shingles of the Van Ryman mansion. The new gargoyles grimaced down at him on the other side of the invisible wall.

The cold drizzle came down on him, beading on his smooth skin and trying to soak into the jumpsuit. His synHeart had begun to pound, but he stepped it down, calming himself, feeling adrenaline lift him into a clear-minded euphoria.

He edged around the house, around the Intruder Defense field. No one would stop him now. He wouldn't allow it. He had to focus his attention completely. Danal looked at the structure of the roof, followed the gables with his eyes, until he located the spot under one of the colorful enameled hexagram tiles. Then he crouched on his knees and edged up, ignoring puddles on the ground, until he almost touched the field itself.

The light drizzle would make finding the opening much easier.

He could smell a thick ozone stench from the ionized rain. Danal sat back, opened his perceptions, and stared at the glimmers as raindrops spangled against the field. Looking for the illusion, looking for the hologram projected across the opening. He stepped up his microprocessor, watching, until he finally saw the pattern mirrored. As one succession of droplets struck the invisible wall, an identical sequence—the illusion—was reflected exactly one meter away.

When installing the Systems a lifetime ago, it had taken a great deal of effort to design a distortion in the field for emergency access. But Vincent had insisted on being able to get into his own home regardless of who controlled the Intruder Defense Systems.

Danal stared a moment longer until he was sure, then pushed his head and shoulders through the unseen doorway, praying he had not misjudged the hologram. Vividly and mercilessly he recalled the blackened corpses of the first demonstrators who had tried to penetrate the field.

Danal froze and breathed an exhausted sigh of relief, then scrambled the rest of the way through. He stood up in the relative shelter and warmth under the field, brushing the mud from his jumpsuit. Up above, he could see the spangles of raindrops as they came down. Both he and the imposter were trapped here within the deadly field—it seemed like an arena.

Danal walked down the black poured-stone walkway and purposefully ascended the steps. He felt tall and powerful. He stared up at the eaves, watching the weathervane turning back and forth on its random motor. The gargoyles seemed to cringe from his presence now that he knew their secret. Danal smiled again, but brought his expression under control. The imposter would probably be watching by now.

He opened the front door of the house and stepped into the maw of shadows. The carpeting drowned his soft footsteps, but by the light of the dangling chandelier Danal could see the startled imposter coming to meet him. The Servant stared at the man's stolen face and felt disoriented, as if looking into a bent mirror.

Danal turned and closed the door, shutting them both inside.

The imposter came forward two more steps to face him, and stopped, nervous. His face was drawn and haggard, and he looked at Danal with a contradictory mixture of eagerness and dread. The Servant regarded him in cold silence, trying to choose from his handful of accusations.

The false Vincent Van Ryman spoke first, astonished. "Nathans said you might be alive after all." He drew a deep breath, and a vision-driven fire seemed to ignite the man's resolve. Danal couldn't answer, choked by his anticipation, his conflicting anger. It seemed like a long, long moment, but he knew his silence lasted only a second or two.

"Very well, alone then," the imposter muttered and rubbed his hands briskly together. "Follow me, Danal. This is perfect. We're about to embark on the most important event of the Technological Age."

The false Van Ryman shuffled down the corridor. Somewhat baffled but ready to jump at any trick, Danal followed him past the control room of the Intruder Defense Systems, past the study in which so many events had begun, to the open sitting area overlooked by the upstairs rooms. The locked door beneath the staircase had once haunted Danal's buried memories, but now it, and the underground chambers beyond, offered only healed nightmares, the private meeting place for the neo-Satanist Inner Circle, where he had been held prisoner as the imposter grew the face of Vincent Van Ryman. . . .

The imposter removed a key hanging from the leather thong around his neck and opened the door. A dank smell wafted upward, and the false Van Ryman drew a deep breath.

"I'm so glad you came back, Vincent—I really did want to see you again." He turned to lock his gaze with Danal's. "Will you join me for a little Sabbat of our own? It *is* Walpurgis Night, you know, and it's only fitting that things should end this way."

Without waiting for a response, the imposter turned and descended the stairs. Danal hesitated, confused; he had not expected this at all, and could not tell if the imposter was admitting defeat or if he had some deeper plan for luring Danal ahead. But the Servant realized it didn't make any difference—he would never consider turning back now. Danal ducked his head and entered the passageway.

Paint, carefully done to look like moss, lined the cracks of the shallow flagstone steps, and a cassette played the sounds of echoing drips of water in the musty air. Stone benches surrounded a chipped granite pedestal; pentagrams, runes, and demonic symbols had been engraved into the sides of the podium, with the registered star-in-pentagram logo of the neo-Satanists prominent. Flickering electric candles stood like pitchforks in three brass candelabra. A Net terminal was set into two massive stone blocks on the wall, and the white-painted squares on the keypad looked like rows of teeth from a grinning skull.

"Wait here," the false Van Ryman said confidently as he reached behind the curtains covering an alcove, withdrawing a billowy black High Priest's robe trimmed with red on the sleeves. He glanced at his chronometer.

"Tonight it's all coming to the end." He donned the robe, shrugging his shoulders and straightening the fabric, then took a step toward the Net terminal. "With your sacrifice, Danal, we can set the final wheels of the universe in motion."

The Servant cast aside the charade as he dropped into microprocessor speed again. Without a word he lunged forward, grabbing the folds of the imposter's black robe and throwing him up against the stone blocks of the wall. He was careful to check his hand so as not to kill the man, but his fingers still slipped through the fabric and gouged the false Van Ryman's chest. Friction from the cloth burned against Danal's fingers. The imposter struggled, but the Servant's reflexes countered every effort.

"You stole my identity, you bastard!"

"I gave it to you in the first place," the man spat back, almost amused. The imposter's eyes narrowed slightly. Too late, Danal realized that this was no mere look-alike—Nathans had selected him for his cunning, his intelligence and resourcefulness. The false Van Ryman barked an order.

"Command: Release me!"

To his horror Danal's hands automatically withdrew as if he had touched hot wax. The Servant's legs took two quick steps backward. He let out a helpless cry.

"Command: Stand still!" the imposter snapped.

Smug in his triumph, he collected his dignity, straightening the black robe, and looked at the helpless Servant. He briskly rubbed his hands together again, wiping away the nervous sweat from his palms. "You're still a Servant, Vincent. You have to obey my Commands." He

266

bent over Danal; his breath smelled of Glenlivet scotch. "Listen."

He turned with a swish of his robes and went over to the stone pedestal to snatch up a mammoth leather-bound tome, one of the neo-Satanist holy compendia thrown together by Vincent Van Ryman and Francois Nathans. The imposter flipped to a finger-smeared page and began to quote from memory. His eyes never left Danal's.

" 'And all have their missions, and all will Serve, though they may not know it. The greatest of these will be called Danal, and he is the Messenger. He is the Prophet. He is the Bringer of Change and the Fulfiller of Promises. He is the Stranger whom everyone knows. He is the Awaker and the Awakened. He is the Destroyer. The return of Satan rests in his deeds.' "

The imposter's eyes widened in his own fervor, and he spoke so vehemently that droplets of saliva sprayed from his mouth. "Danal. We chose that name while you were still in the vat, because of The Writings, to force fulfillment of the prophecy." He furiously flung the pages to another spot and quoted again, shoving the book in the Servant's face. "Look! It says, 'Sacrifice both the living and the dead,' Satan said. 'And I shall return to regain what is mine.' "

He snapped the book shut with finality, and carelessly let it drop to the floor with a thump. "It's all in The Writings—proof positive. The meaning is clear. You should be sacrificed again, and Walpurgis Night is a perfect time."

"I *wrote* most of the damned Writings!" Danal stood like a gargoyle himself, immobile but filled with hatred. He couldn't move. The Command phrase locked all his muscles.

"I know. I was with you."

A horrible suspicion began to creep upon Danal, and the imposter stopped himself, smiling in wonder. "Ah, you don't know, do you? Nathans wouldn't have told you."

Danal stared at the imposter, wide-eyed. The look in the man's gaze, the build of his body, his mannerisms as he moved—all somehow clicked together like the flash of a switchblade snapping open. Stromgaard.

The man chuckled. "You should see the look on your face, Vincent!"

"You're dead," Danal said in a low voice.

"So were you," the imposter countered, "but my death was only staged."

Danal recalled the night of the sacrifice, seeing his "terminally ill" father dying and wasting away on the altar stone. He could still feel the nauseating *packing* sensation, the crunch of bone, as the sacrificial dagger bit into his father's nearly skeletal chest. Blood sprayed upward. The heavy stubble on his jaw . . . *covering a faint line of pinpricks?*

Stromgaard was dead. He had to be. The muscles in Danal's neck stood out as he tried to shake his head, to deny it. But the Command phrase kept him motionless.

"I wanted out of your little games," the imposter continued. "And, frankly, I was getting sick of all the cold cynicism from you and Nathans about our religion. Don't you have any sense of wonder left in your lives? Can't you give supernatural events the benefit of the doubt?

"Through surface-cloning, Nathans gave me another face so I could walk unrecognized, and we used one of the neo-Satanist converts to take my place on the sacrificial altar—there were so many willing ones! A pathetic story and some heavy makeup convinced you to do just what we wanted. It was for the best, it was for the good of the religion, because it showed a dramatic change of power from one High Priest to his successor." Stromgaard Van Ryman scowled as if he had swallowed something bad.

"I was there at the Sabbat. Do you know what it's like to be in the audience while you watch your son kill his own father?"

"You seemed perfectly willing to murder me when the roles were reversed," Danal countered.

"No matter." Stromgaard shrugged. "I traveled, I went on pilgrimages to the original Salem, Massachusetts, to the Hartz Mountains of Eastern Europe, to the Balkans, to Budapest, to Transylvania. I studied The Writings, all of them, with an open mind, not with your rude sarcasm. It was all going so smoothly—I was perfectly content as an ascetic. Until you betrayed us! You and the whore!"

Danal strained until he thought his muscles would burst, but he still could not unlock the invisible binding of the Command phrase.

"That's why I came back, to save the religion. For the good of neo-Satanism. You deserved everything you got,

Vincent. For betraying the hopes of thousands of people, for mocking things you didn't even try to understand." He shook his head, sadly, it seemed. "But now we've brought you back, all the way back, and you can redeem yourself by unleashing the next Millennium."

Danal remembered swimming through death—the warm darkness, the comforting light, the chimes, and the final unbreakable wall of memory he could not penetrate. "You don't know how cruel that was. Bringing my memories back was the worst."

"It was necessary," Stromgaard said.

"Why? Why was it necessary?"

"Nathans had his own reasons. And I had mine." The imposter's face took on an expression of impatient scorn. "Nathans is afraid of death, even though he surrounds himself with it at Resurrection. He wants to be alive to enjoy the benefits of the perfect world he's working so hard to create. Hah! And if a resurrected person can regain all his memories, then Nathans himself can live on as long as he wishes. That's what he thinks. If he dies, he can just be resurrected, have his memories triggered, and live again. His own kind of immortality. Not realizing, of course, that after tonight when Satan and the New Age have come, all his efforts won't count for anything at all."

Van Ryman led the Servant over to the terminal on the wall, commanding him to follow. Danal moved woodenly. He had no choice. Sweat broke out on his forehead; he resisted with every grain of his free mind, but his body paid no attention, listening only to the Commands. Now, at least, he could move. He had a chance, so long as Stromgaard allowed him to keep his voice.

"And *your* reason for bringing back my memories?" Danal prodded.

"It's obvious, Vincent—" he snapped. "If you paid any attention to The Writings. 'Sacrifice both the living and the dead,' says the Word, 'And I shall return to regain what is mine.' "

"We sacrificed living victims and even some Servants, to no effect. But I figured it all out—it all fits. 'Both the living and the dead'—that's you, a Servant who was once dead and then reawakened to his old life. And you're Danal, just like The Writings say. We have to sacrifice the same victim, first as a living person, then a second

269

time as a resurrected Servant, a Servant with all his memories, with his own soul back. That's very important."

"I wrote that passage!" Danal exclaimed. "It doesn't mean anything. You know that—we did it right in front of your eyes!"

Van Ryman looked intently at Danal, then spoke in a low awed voice, "And how do you know your hand wasn't *guided*? By some greater power?"

Danal could hardly believe what he had heard. "Don't be absurd."

"If you have Faith, no answer is necessary. If you have none, no answer is possible."

Despite himself, Danal made a scornful noise. "That's exactly the type of invincible ignorance we lashed out at in the first place."

"But it does make sense. You wrote the truth without even knowing it. Think about it—Satan's been dormant, sleeping because His followers were too few for too many centuries. But now neo-Satanism has grown strong—and because of Resurrection, Inc., the dead are walking again, just like in a dozen prophecies.

"Now you, Vincent, were sacrificed to Him, and then we brought you back to life. We snatched your soul from Satan, ripping it like candy from His claws. How can He ignore that? He is awakening—I can feel it. He'll follow you *here* to reclaim what was given to Him."

Van Ryman removed a handful of glistening electrodes from the innards of the Net terminal, and turned to look at Danal with bright and distant eyes. "Hold still, now." Stromgaard positioned the electrodes in a clump at the back of Danal's head. The Servant tried to clench his fists, but his body refused him even that.

"I had plenty of time to think, to meditate, and I received a Great Revelation. It was wonderful, Vincent—it would make you breathless! You see, for centuries, Satan hasn't been able to possess anyone because cynical mankind has learned to resist. You know, by materialistic thinking, by skepticism, by forgetting how to fear the unknown. But mankind has created his own downfall—building with his own hands a mind that'll be Satan's greatest possession of all! One single mind to dominate the Earth and control everything. The Net!"

Before, Danal had always been too jaded to see the fervor in the eyes of someone who actually believed in the cult. But now Stromgaard's face showed a beatific, glazed look of anticipation that defied all rational thought. Danal found that frightening.

"The Net has no resistance, no inhibitions, no moral or religious qualms that can dim Satan's fires!" Stromgaard continued. "Once Satan has possessed The Net, He can control the entire world in a second. All machines, and all men, will have to bow to Him." He closed his eyes and took a deep, exalted breath.

"Meticulous reasoning, Vincent, carefully thought out. You should appreciate that. We sacrificed you in the traditional manner the first time. Then we stole your soul back from Satan, and now I'm going to offer Him a different type of sacrifice." The imposter attached the last of the electrodes to Danal's smooth scalp and straightened the wires leading to the terminal. "I'll deactivate the microprocessor that keeps you alive, and send the pulse into The Net. If Satan wants your soul back, He's going to have to follow . . . and discover the incredible world awaiting Him!"

Danal smirked, playing him along. "And I suppose you're doing it here, alone, to get all the glory for yourself? If it works, you'll be the most powerful man in the world, because you alone helped Satan to return?" He needed to manipulate the conversation around to where he could strike back.

"Why shouldn't I? Nathans stole Resurrection from me. *You* stole neo-Satanism from me, even when we were just developing it. Neo-Satanism was supposed to have been mine, Vincent. For me! Now I'm getting something for myself at last. I'm the only one who truly believes in what the three of us created. You and Nathans think neo-Satanism is just a game, a bunch of parlor tricks. But I know better. When Satan returns, He'll know me and what I've done, and He'll be grateful."

Danal laughed in delight. "I don't think so!" It was almost over. Van Ryman had not Commanded him to silence. He heard the invisible sound of the trap as it sprung.

"What do you mean?" Stromgaard's eyes narrowed.

He shrugged, almost coy. "Don't forget, when I regained my memory, I remembered all my Net access codes, too. And now I've got the last laugh!"

"What have you done!"

Danal allowed his lips to curl up in a smile, and remained silent for as long as he dared, letting his father's insecurity and uneasiness build. "I'm a Servant—I don't have any future in my old life. So I deleted my entire identity from The Net this afternoon. Vincent Van Ryman no longer exists. If Satan does possess The Net, he's not going to have a single burned-out chip that remembers you!" He laughed again, a full, self-satisfied sound, then turned bitter. "You did the same thing to Julia."

"No!"

Danal put a smug expression on his face. "Check it for yourself if you don't believe me. I'm in no hurry."

Van Ryman's face writhed in his utter fury and disbelief. He lunged at the white squares on the Net keypad, snarling at the screen. Danal yanked the electrodes from his head, and let them drop to the floor. "Stay where you are!" Stromgaard snapped.

Danal slipped into his stepped-up perception of time, watched Van Ryman's fingers go through the logon procedure, then hit the thirteen-digit password. The imposter stared at the pixels on the screen until they authorized his link with The Net . . . activating the trap.

On acceptance of the logon, the incredible power of the entire Intruder Defense Systems poured explosively into the single terminal—following one line of the circuitry rerouted by the repair-rats. The plastic coverplate shattered. A power surge leaped back through the keypad into the imposter's body. Silver arcs of electricity skittered over Van Ryman's fingers and hands like the talons of a demon, blasting him. His dark hair lifted with the static discharge, like the puff of a dead dandelion.

Danal dropped back to normal time. Stromgaard Van Ryman toppled rigidly backward with the smell of smoking flesh. Faint wisps of steam rose up from his black robes.

Danal didn't allow himself a moment's sadness for his father—Stromgaard had chosen his path long ago. "I would never delete my own identity," Danal spoke softly to the dead man on the floor. "Not when I expected to win."

He sat down on one of the stone benches as the events caught up with him. Danal felt numb, and his mind whirled. He had just killed Stromgaard, and that would be only the beginning. The momentum behind the wheels he had set in motion would come crashing through them all before the night was over. When he had buried all the memories in a safe mental place, the Servant went back up the dank stairs into the house, his house, and shut down all of the Intruder Defense Systems. He hoped it would be for the last time.

Then he sent out the signal of his victory that would bring all the Wakers to him.

38

Jones's dark armor melted into the shadows of the wet street. He and his Elite Guard companion waited. Off in the distance he could hear faint bustling noises as the Metroplex began to wind down into a coma for the night, but here, in a senior citizen's area, all was quiet already. As Jones had requested, the two nearby streetlights flickered and went dead, leaving the area in deeper blackness. At the far end of each street, white-clad Enforcers turned the occasional pedestrians back.

With the streetlights out of the way, Jones moved forward and crouched down on one knee, afraid to come too close to the KEEP OFF THE GRASS patch. The other Elite guard stayed back, seeming aloof and annoyed, but tense. Jones edged closer still.

He expected to hear a slight humming of the "deadly field," but he noted only the muffled silence of the damp evening. It would be curfew in another couple of hours, but already this felt like the dead of night.

Jones could clearly make out the bright green grass blades, luscious and alive, all of them perfect, shimmering. Was it an illusion? A hologram? Everything he had been told, layer upon layer of rumor said that these patches were deadly disintegrators to peel a man down to the bone in a flash of infinite pain.

Jones had seen one, only one contradictory statement on The Net, and he had never been able to find it again. Nathans was sure someone else was tampering with The Net, covering up the real explanation behind the grass patches, and Jones felt confident that Nathans was probably right. But couldn't it be just as likely that someone— someone who could indeed tamper with The Net—had planted a fake *explanation* for Jones to see, to lure him into—

"Give me something to throw," he said over his shoulder, slamming the door on his fear.

The other Elite Guard looked around and cursed under his breath. "I can't see a damn thing with this helmet." Oddly, he took off his gloves instead, and Jones could see that the other Guard was black as well; he almost thought to comment on it but decided not to. The Guard crunched his heel on the street until one of the decorative cobblestones loosened. He pried it out with the blade of his heater-knife and tossed the cobblestone to Jones.

"Quiet, now," Jones whispered.

"It's your show. Does it make you feel important or something?"

Jones hesitated at the comment—why did the other Guard want to mock him?—but decided to ignore it.

The other Guard had not seemed impressed either by the mystery or by Jones's enthusiasm about the KEEP OFF THE GRASS patches. "What's your name?" Jones had asked.

"I'm not going to tell you, that's for sure. I'm not in a trusting mood tonight."

"I'm Jones," he said, puzzled and dismayed at the other Guard's attitude. Jones did not ask about it, though; as long as he helped out when he was needed, the man's problems were his own. At least if he was an Elite Guard, it couldn't be all bad for him.

Underhanded, Jones tossed the cobblestone into the deceptive patch of grass. He expected to see a flash of light, to hear some sound, but the stone simply fell *through* the grass, swallowed up without a trace. A second later, he thought he heard a muffled *thunk* as it struck something below.

Jones stood up and withdrew his heater-knife, suddenly wishing he had something longer, a stick or a pole. He looked around, but saw nothing else. Resigned, he leaned down over the low barbed fence, stretched his arm out as far as it would go, and touched the tip of the knife to the shimmering grass.

The dark helmet hid his unconscious cringe. With his fingertips he held onto the pommel, ready to let go at any second. The blade vanished into the grass up to its hilt. Looking closely, Jones thought he could almost see a shadow of it through the grass blades. He pulled the knife back out, completely intact.

Final test. He looked back at the other Elite Guard, who had taken one reluctant step closer to watch.

Jones slowly reached his hand out in front of him—the left hand, just in case—and touched the grass. He felt a strange disorientation as he watched his fingertips disappear, but he felt nothing, no pain, not even any change. Hesitant, he withdrew his hand, flexed his fingers, and then recklessly pushed it back through the grass patch up to the wrist.

He stood then, holding his hand up like a trophy and showing the other Elite Guard. "Let's go. I was right."

"Hooray for you."

They anchored their ropes to the street above, and threw down the ends, watching as the strands vanished into the imaginary grass—but now it only looked odd, not frightening. They uprooted barbed the fence from the stones and tossed it aside. Jones grasped the rope and eased himself backward until the green illusion and the darkness below engulfed him completely. As he hung, hooked onto the ropes with special clips on his armor, he looked back up and had the eerie sense of staring through the other side of a mirror.

"I'm all right," Jones called, "but I can't see anything."

He flicked on the vision enhancers embedded in his visor as he continued to descend. The rope twitched a little from above, and Jones saw that the other Elite Guard had begun his descent. As Jones looked around, the night sensors made the dimness turn greenish.

A few feet below them, a net had been strung out, anchored to the widely separated pilings. A net . . . to catch anyone who might go through the "maintenance openings," accidentally or on purpose? The strands appeared to be new, not more than a couple years old.

Jones scrambled the rest of the way down to the end of his rope and stepped off onto a crossbeam. Beyond, deeper under the Metroplex, he could see strings of mysterious lights, but he waited for the other Guard before going to investigate. Together they made painfully slow progress on the narrow and delicate walkways; Jones heard his companion swearing to himself. Only occasionally did they encounter a catwalk wide enough for them to move at a steady speed.

"How do they walk on these things?" Jones commented after he had almost lost his balance. "Or maybe these are just for the repair-rats?"

The other Elite Guard grunted and made no further comment.

When they reached the lights, both of them stopped in puzzled amazement. A network of sunlamps dangled down, tapping into the main electrical conduits of the city above.

Platforms were scattered about in a complex hierarchy. Boxes and crates of supplies hung suspended from the overhead girders. Small amenities such as books, jewelry items, and occasional treasured knickknacks implied that the place had been inhabited for some time.

But they saw no one. All around them stood the forest of pilings, crossbeams, girders; he heard the sounds of creaking ropes and the lapping of the ocean below. But everything was completely deserted.

"How many do you think live down here?" Jones whispered.

Looking around, his companion paused a moment as if assessing. "Fifty. Maybe a hundred."

They searched farther but found only more silent clues—nothing conclusive. Jones checked his chronometer and signaled that it was time to go back.

As they emerged again onto the street, Jones turned and watched the other Guard crawl up through the hologram. Jones found himself fighting to contain his pride and enthusiasm. Some of the excitement crept into his voice. "Wait till we report to Nathans! He'll be very interested in all this."

The other Elite Guard finally broke his silence and stiffened in frustration, "Don't feel too smug that you've got Nathans's ear, smartass. You think you've been *selected* for the Elite Guard? Big deal!

"You're not here because of any special talent, not because you're the best. You're here—like we all are—because Nathans holds us over a barrel. He can do anything he wants. But he doesn't like killing unless it's absolutely necessary—that's his big flaw. If someone's in his way, he doesn't just get it over with. He finds a new way to use you instead."

Jones felt as if he was falling off a cliff into ice water. His tongue dried all the way to its root, and he could not answer. No! What did the other Guard know? He was too cynical, too pessimistic—Nathans probably didn't trust the other Guard as much, and he felt slighted. That must be it. He had to get back at Jones—it was all so petty. But another part of him admitted that the information was no surprise, no matter how meaningful Jones wanted his work in the Elite Guard to be.

His companion continued, "You're not important to him. You've been duped."

Jones stood like a statue, trembling faintly. He kept denying it to himself, but the knots in his stomach grew larger and larger; the thin ice of security began to crack under his armored feet.

The other Guard reached forward, almost as if to touch Jones's shoulder, but he stopped himself and let his hand fall back to his side. "Now that I've got that off my chest, let's go and make our report, like good little soldiers."

Sluggishly Jones followed, devoid of all self-confidence again.

39

"Where *is* he?" Nathans demanded of the empty room.

He blanked the Net screen and paced in a furious circle as Jones entered the High Priest's private chamber. Nathans turned to the Elite Guard and spoke in a distraught voice. "Less than an hour before the greatest Sabbat in history, and our High Priest isn't here! I haven't spoken to him all day, and now he won't acknowledge any of my direct messages!" He pounded three times on the keypad as if knocking on a door, then turned away in disgust.

Out in the adjacent main grotto, the neo-Satanists had begun to crowd in expectantly. Most of them wore robes that had been freshly cleaned and pressed. A week before, Nathans had transmitted a message describing the ultimate importance of the Walpurgis Night Sabbat, signing himself as "High Priest Van Ryman." But he had warned that only "those with no doubts, those with the most unshakable faith" should come—on peril of their own souls. The response had been overwhelming.

Nathans made a distasteful noise of dismay and then sat down again, putting his elbows on his knees. He looked up at the Elite Guard, and Jones could see that the man's eyes were etched with red threads.

"At least you're here," he said, frustrated. He got up, paced again, burning off nervous energy. "Well, what did you find? And take that damned helmet off!"

Jones answered, but his doubts about Nathans's ethics, his true reasons for choosing the Elite Guard, drained away the enthusiasm. He didn't want to look Nathans in the eye, afraid he might be tempted to demand answers to the accusations. Were they true? No matter how much Jones tried to convince himself, it all fit too tightly together. And if he did voice his doubts, Jones was terrified that Nathans would laugh at him.

"Yes, they're just holograms." In a flat voice he described the shadowy place. Nathans didn't seem to notice any change in the Enforcer's attitude.

"But you didn't find anyone?"

"No. No one."

"The plot thickens . . ." Nathans mumbled to himself, then he waved it away. He hurried back to stare at the Net screen, then paced again. "I can't worry about that just now. Where the hell is our High Priest?"

"One other thing," Jones dutifully added. "When I reported in, I found a message for you. Someone named Zia apparently escaped from the security wing of the main hospital complex this morning. They expect to find her soon."

Nathans frowned. "Zia? Why in the world would she want to escape?" He looked baffled, but he pushed aside the information with annoyance—it would wait until after the Sabbat.

Jones found himself gathering courage, about to speak up and ask Nathans if the other Guard had meant anything, when a signal came from the outer corridor. Even before Jones or Nathans could move to answer it, the person on the other side of the door entered the proper password.

"Who the hell—?" Nathans whirled, then smiled in relief. "Ah, it must be him."

Instead the grotesque Zia entered as the door slid open.

Jones looked at her and unconsciously took a step backward. He quickly fumbled to put his opaque helmet back on, self-conscious about his reaction.

Before Nathans could utter a startled comment, Zia turned and barked an order out to the corridor. "Danal! Command: Follow!" Her voice held a sneering tone of condescension.

Head down, the Servant sluggishly entered the chambers. He didn't look around him, didn't offer any resistance.

"I brought you a present, Francois Nathans."

In an instant Jones also recognized the Servant—Danal—the one who had rebelled, caused the riot, jumped into the KEEP OFF THE GRASS patch—

"Vincent!" Nathans clapped his hands in delight, then turned offhandedly to the Elite Guard. "Jones, leave us. I want to hear what he has to say."

At being dismissed so casually, Jones felt a startled anger and distaste wash over him again. *I want to hear what he has to say, too!* he thought. *You can't just send me away—you're supposed to trust* me, remember? (*You've been duped . . . you're not important to him,*) Jones hesitated a moment, but Nathans did not retract his order, wholly absorbed in the Servant. The Elite Guard stiffened and clenched his teeth.

"Give me your scatter-stun weapon, too, Jones. That one." Nathans took the weapon himself out of the Guard's armor, and pointed it directly at Danal. He did not let his attention waver, nor did he glance again at Jones.

The Elite Guard's nostrils flared in disappointed resentment, but the helmet hid it all. With some difficulty he kept control of himself. Without a word Jones strode out of the chamber, making Nathans scramble-seal the door himself.

Danal stood motionless, making sure that he appeared completely cowed by Zia. She played her part perfectly with a gloating zeal, but he knew it was only her eagerness to strike back at Nathans. She no longer seemed interested in preventing the massacre merely to save the other converts.

Nathans grinned in amazement as he stood up. "Well, I don't understand all the details of this situation." He came toward the Servant, keeping the scatter-stun pointed directly at Danal's head. His voice held unexpected warmth, almost as if he wanted to embrace Danal. "But I must say I'm very pleased to see you back, Vincent."

"He ransacked The Net," Zia explained. "And somehow got the idea that I was his Julia. He came to the hospital complex and 'rescued' me—but I brought him back to you."

"Zia, you've done remarkably well." Nathans flashed a glance at her from the corner of his eye, but did not take his attention away from the Servant. "I hereby promote you to Coven Manager—that should please you. We'll see to the details later. Why don't you go attend the Sabbat? I've got some extra robes stored in the wardrobe inset there. Take one, and please be sure the hood covers your face. Sorry about that, but it's necessary."

Anger flared in the woman's eyes and she seemed almost ready to refuse, but Danal made a small frantic gesture he hoped Nathans could not see, waving her away. Zia controlled herself and appeared appropriately submissive.

"Thank you, Master Nathans." Listlessly she rummaged

in the wardrobe until she found a maroon robe trimmed in black. "I'd really like to attend a Sabbat again. Especially this one." Without looking back, she draped the robe over her arm as she left. Watching her from behind, Danal felt an eerie shiver—she seemed so much like Julia, her walk, her actions. . . .

Danal kept a blank face, but he seethed inside. He had waited long for this moment of confrontation. He had planned carefully, but how could he have forgotten so many things? How could he have been so naïve, especially where Nathans was concerned? He had not considered that Nathans could hold him so completely at bay with a weapon, nor had he imagined the man would so quickly dismiss Zia. If only he had thought!

He had not at all expected to see an Elite Guard in the private neo-Satanist chambers. Why would a member of the Guild be here? A neo-Satanist convert? No, Nathans hated the Guild—he would never have allowed an Enforcer, especially not an Elite Guard, so close into his circle.

Unless there were schemes even deeper than Danal had ever suspected. . . .

Nathans nodded toward the weapon. "I'm sorry for this, Vincent, but I was watching when you killed my surrogate, you know. I'm amazed at how fast you moved. You'll have to explain that to me sometime, but right now I don't want to take any chances." Then his voice turned inward, with a deeper sadness that Danal almost believed was sincere.

"Ah, Vincent, I tried so hard to teach you—I gave you every chance to really understand what has to be done. You were supposed to be my successor. But you didn't learn. You haven't learned anything. Those two imposter Servants got through all your defenses with no trouble at all. That was a simple trick, Vincent—you should have caught it." He shook his head and then snapped his gaze back up to look at the Servant. "You didn't learn."

Danal allowed a beatific, all-knowing smile to fall on his face. This would be smooth, simple. He laughed, taunting Nathans with an invincible calmness. "I learned plenty of other things, Francois—things *you* don't understand. I've looked Death in the face—I know what happens beyond life, all the answers—because when my memories came back, I remembered that, too. All the way through."

Nathans remained motionless, but the Servant could see him mentally squirming. Before the man could respond, Danal pulled out a second surprise.

"I've already removed the imposter, got my revenge on the person who stole my identity. He's dead now, and he won't be helping you out tonight. The Van Ryman mansion is mine again."

Nathans paled and his mouth dropped open. Then he squeezed his eyes together as if to force a calm back upon himself. Danal could have taken him then, but made no move. He wanted to see the man defeat himself instead.

Nathans drew a deep breath and stared at the Servant again. Behind his eyes burned a cruelty that caused him to lash back out, as if he were revealing a great and painful secret. "The imposter was your own father. Stromgaard. You killed him—for real this time."

Danal remained unaffected, not letting Nathans get any satisfaction. He shrugged. "As far as I'm concerned, I killed my father years ago. Anything else is just a bad dream."

Then the Servant struck his third blow; with each successive one, Nathans's confidence crumbled further and further.

"There's so much you don't know, Francois, it's almost sad. While I've been in hiding, I discovered the truth about the Cremators, too."

Nathans's eyes lit with rage.

"I learned who they are, and why they do what they have to."

Furious, Nathans sprang to his feet, but the Servant jerked up his hand so violently that it almost startled the man into firing the scatter-stun. "Stop!" Danal snapped. "If you Command me to say what I know about the Cremators, I'll terminate myself immediately. I've already died—it doesn't mean anything to me." He narrowed his eyes. "Just wanted you to realize that I know about the Cremators, and you don't, and you'll never find out."

"Traitor!" Nathans whispered under his breath. "Several times over."

Looking shattered and impotent, Nathans fell back into his chair and stared at Danal. The Servant stared back. They waited, engulfed in absolute silence for a full minute. The man seemed to be warring with himself, fighting back distasteful decisions.

Nathans heaved a heavy sigh and closed his eyes. He seemed to be very tired, but maintained his control through a supreme effort. "You served your purpose. You've answered my question: it *is* possible to bring back memories and personality intact."

He cracked his knuckles. "But now you've killed our High Priest, Vincent. The Sabbat must go on, you know, especially this one. You're putting me in the awkward position of having to expose myself as the head of the neo-Satanists." He drummed his fingertips on the tabletop, keeping his other hand leveled rigidly, pointing the scatter-stun.

"But after tonight, I suppose it won't matter anyway." He smiled with a cold smugness. "Enough is enough, Vincent. I thought very highly of you once . . . but what you did to me, well, even I can't forgive some things." He stood up, backing toward the inset wardrobe. With one hand he shuffled among the garments blindly until he drew out a plain white robe, tossing it toward Danal.

"For tonight's Sabbat, you're going to replace our scheduled sacrifice."

40

"Danal—Command: Follow!" Nathans snapped.

The dark, towering ceremonial doors to the Sabbat grotto swung open slowly. The electric candlelight inside the chamber caught and reflected from the intricate carvings on the clonewood. Danal looked into the shifting masses of robed neo-Satanists, all eager to see blood—real blood or synBlood, it made no difference.

High-pitched organ music skirled through the air, without a melody. Somewhere a gong sounded. The crowd made droning sounds, but a hush rippled through them as their new High Priest appeared.

Without looking back at the Servant, Nathans moved gracefully forward, striding and swaying so that his magnificent black robe billowed behind him. The red trim flickered like blood in the shifting artificial torchlight. The man's bald head had been adorned with temporary tattoos of astrological symbols.

A wide aisle between the sections of stone benches led straight up to the altar on its raised platform. Some of the cultists pushed forward, struggling to get a seat on the stone benches near the front, where they could see better.

Danal's legs jerked him into motion. He strode after Nathans, obedient but defiant, head high with impenetrable confidence. Let Nathans worry about that. Though the white sacrificial robe covered his jumpsuit, Danal's skin tone identified him as a Servant . . . but his actions and attitudes marked him as human.

The blocky druidic altar stone huddled in the center of a large pentacle drawn with glistening red paint. Black candles, each as thick as his arm, had been set at the points of the star, and a circle drawn nine feet in diameter surrounded the entire design. Old bloodstains discol- ored the altar stone; manacles had recently been attached to its head and foot to hold an unwilling victim in place.

As Danal stonily walked past the hooded forms, he

saw no faces, only the mixture of colors on their robes—
Acolytes, Acolyte Supervisors, and Coven Managers.
Around him he could smell the gathered musk of tense
human beings. Some clutched their printed program leaflets, inspecting them; more leaflets lay crumpled and
scattered on the floor.

The grotto around him looked only superficially different from when he had been the High Priest a lifetime
before. The chamber had been expanded to accommo-
date more cultists, and fountains of sculptured poured-
stone had been installed all around the perimeter, painted
and molded to look like springs from a living cave wall.
White, foamy water gushed up with a sighing sound,
echoing in the chamber.

Danal could not say anything or make any call for
help. Nathans had been very careful, very explicit. "Command: You will be silent during the ceremony, unless I
specifically ask you to speak." Danal felt his vocal cords
go dead—it would do him no good to cry out now anyway. He had to have faith in his plan—not irrational Faith
like that of the neo-Satanists but a confidence in his own
abilities, a trust in Gregor and Rikki and all the Wakers.

He didn't move his head, but memories passed in front
of him. All the times when *he* had been here, roles
reversed, leading the willing sacrificial victim . . . all the
times *he* had stood over the altar in the black and red
robe, looking down at the trusting face as the crowd
waited—

Danal pushed those thoughts away, holding onto the
good times, even remembering Francois Nathans and the
stimulating discussions they had had when it had been no
more than food for thought. But when Nathans had
made the ideas real—then it had all changed. Vincent
Van Ryman had been too much of a coward to help put
those ideas into effect—that was how Nathans must see
it.

Danal felt a chill as a new idea came to him, haunted
him. For a long time Nathans had treated neo-Satanism
as a game, too, disappointed and amused at its surprising
success. He had done no greater damage than sanction-
ing the occasional voluntary sacrifices until Vincent Van
Ryman had betrayed him. Vincent: his student, his hope,
his apprentice.

And in his anger at that, Nathans had struck back.
Danal remembered his dumbfounded disbelief—even while

it was happening—that his mentor could do such a thing to him. Nathans had arranged for the murder of Julia, his first real victim; he had killed Vincent and brought him back, while letting Stromgaard masquerade as High Priest. And finally lost patience enough to arrange for the slaughter of all the neo-Satanists. Danal felt certain Francois Nathans would never have done that before Vincent had betrayed him.

But Danal would not accept that blame. He had shouldered too high a price already.

His obedient legs carried him up to the stage one step at a time. He felt like an animal being led to slaughter. The altar stone spread out in front of him, cold and waiting. The gathered worshipers crowded closer on the stone benches below . . . and Danal knew he wouldn't be the only victim.

Nathans turned to face the crowd, putting on an exalted expression as he muttered out of the corner of his mouth, "Danal—Command: Lie down!"

Unable to resist, and not wasting energy with the effort, the Servant turned around and slowly lay back, feeling the cool, rough texture of stone against the fabric on his back. The white robe fell open, showing his gray jumpsuit. He stared up and dizzily saw the papier mâché stalactites hanging down like knives from the ceiling of the grotto. For one disoriented moment he thought he saw the black tunnel of Death opening up for him again. He felt a strange new fear—would Death be the same the second time through? Or did he get only a single chance?

Danal thought about slowing everything down by viewing it through his microprocessor, making his last moments seem like years in subjective time, savoring life. But he decided against it. Not microprocessor speed now. No. This was real, and he would finish out his life in real time.

Nathans gestured, and two Acolyte Supervisors appeared from alcoves beside the altar platform. They took Danal's bloodless Servant hands and lifted them over his head to meet the manacles; the other assistant then chained his feet.

That wasn't necessary, Danal thought. *He could bind me as effectively with a Command phrase.* Nathans still didn't trust him. The Servant felt a warmth creeping inside. Nathans was afraid.

Before the appearance of the High Priest, one of the

ranking Coven Managers had led the neo-Satanists in the elaborate rituals listed in their Sabbat program leaflets, ceremonies that Vincent and Nathans had long ago designed using choreographers and cultural specialists. The crowd seemed sated with ritual now, brought up to a different fever pitch, waiting for something more.

Nathans raised his hands and the background noise dropped off as with the chop of a guillotine blade. The organ music ceased.

"Good evening, ladies and gentlemen, and welcome to the Walpurgis Night Sabbat!" he called to the crowd. "I am your new High Priest, and I come to you with a promise. I have such confidence in your faith, in the truth behind what we're doing, that *if you believe*—we, you and I, can bring Satan back among us with this one last sacrifice!" Coldly he swept his hand behind him to indicate Danal on the altar.

The crowd began to cheer and whistle.

"It will be tonight—I guarantee it!"

Danal tried to sit up, but one of the assistants firmly pushed his head back down. He could have resisted with his strength, but decided to play passive for the moment.

"You have followed all the rituals, read all The Writings, attended all the Sabbats. I'm proud of you. But tonight, this magic night, is Walpurgis Night, the greatest Sabbat of the year. All the stars and planets are in their ideal positions. Tonight, neo-Satanism will come to its climax, and you'll all be part of a new age. For the return of our Master!"

More cheering. Nathans strutted back and forth across the stage. He seemed tense, almost hyperventilating, but Danal thought he could see a well-hidden smugness in the man's bearing. Nathans refused to turn to meet Danal's eyes; the Servant couldn't tell if the man avoided looking at him out of guilt and anger, or if he had simply become too caught up in his role.

Then Danal realized something else, something that might have been useful had he not been under a Command of silence—he didn't think Nathans had ever killed before, not directly, not with his own bare hands. Danal wondered if the man would have the nerve to murder his former student, his apprentice.

"The time is now!" Nathans cried, and his voice cracked in its enthusiasm. "Are you ready?"

The resounding shout from the audience chilled Danal. "Rah hyuun! Rah hyuun!"

Nathans whirled and stepped back behind the altar. He was moving too fast; the Servant could tell he wanted to get this over with. The thought surprised him—he had expected Nathans to gloat, savoring the moment of his ultimate victory.

From a slot in the side of the altar stone Nathans snatched out the wide-bladed arthame, the jeweled sacrificial dagger. He held it up with both hands over his head.

The crowd shouted again. "Rah hyuun! Rah hyuun!"

Danal knew the pain would come, a bright flash of Death, but still he stared up at Nathans to the last. By the look in the man's eyes, he could see that Nathans didn't dare hesitate or else his doubts might win through. Nathans's expression seemed to be trying to soften, but he hardened it again, fighting back against his feelings. Danal could see infinitely clear droplets of sweat on the man's scalp, glistening like beads among the painted symbols on his head.

The audience fell completely silent, sitting motionless on their stone benches in hushed anticipation. Nathans cocked the blade and tightened his grip on the hilt until his knuckles whitened. "Ashes to ashes, blood to blood; fly to Hell for all our good!"

Then Julia stood up in the audience, shrugging down her hood and exposing herself as a blank-faced, bald Servant.

Startled and distracted cries broke from the worshipers.

Nathans flicked his gaze up, and his face contorted in angry surprise. "Who has brought a Servant here?" he bellowed, "To our most sacred ceremony!"

Scattered throughout the audience, the Wakers stood up. Only forty-three of them, but they were well dispersed among the hundreds so that the effect was increased. Gregor threw off his Acolyte Supervisor robe, crumpled it in his large hands, and threw it to the ground. He proudly displayed his gray jumpsuit.

"You don't want to lay a hand on him, Mr. Francois Nathans," Gregor shouted.

The other Wakers exposed themselves, standing up as gray-clad Servants. Nathans stood aghast, staring at the sudden appearance of the Servants—Servants! His mouth hung open just enough that Danal could see the depth of his shock. The ceremony had been interrupted—Danal convinced his Servant programming that Nathan's Command no longer bound him to silence.

"So many things you don't know, Francois," Danal spoke quietly as he lay helpless on the altar, but with a scorn he knew would cut deeply into Nathans's confidence. "I'm not the only one. I was your great experiment, your guinea pig. But all these other Servants awoke to their memories, awoke to themselves, without any intervention from you. They all remember, Francois. Dozens and dozens of them. Think of how many more must be out there, hiding. Remembering life and death because your resurrection process is flawed."

Nathans worked his mouth, but only a wordless whisper came out. Even without slipping into microprocessor speed, Danal sensed that all time had stopped. The crowd fell silent, confused, waiting for their High Priest to react. Danal lay back in chains, unmoving.

"One more thing, Francois," he continued slowly, savoring the words. "They're the Cremators. Awakened Servants whose goal is to stop you from creating more like themselves!"

That seemed to be the last straw for Nathans. His eyes became wild, giving him a hunted look. Helpless and frantically desperate, the man whirled back toward the secret rooms behind the altar platform and shouted—

"Jones!"

The Elite Guard watched, helplessly horrified, at his station in the spy alcove. As the Sabbat continued toward its peak, he felt sick inside, enraged and disgusted—he had *helped* Nathans in this? How many other things would be clear if he looked at them under a harsher light? He squirmed, sweating and wide-eyed, as Nathans prepared to make the sacrifice. He could not see the expression on the man's face, but Jones imagined any number of them.

Then when the Servant appeared in the audience—Julia! he knew it was Julia—he reacted as if someone had struck him a sharp blow. It was utterly incredible even to imagine that she could be here! His world began to swim around his senses again, as if the gears of the universe had just become unmeshed.

Julia!

What was she doing here?

Was this something Nathans had set up? To trap him even further?

"Jones!"

Stunned, he finally heard the frantic tone in the man's cry. Interminable hours of Enforcer and Elite Guard training overrode his thoughts for a moment, and Jones lurched into motion. He burst out of the alcove onto the stage, fully armored and bristling with weapons.

The crowd gasped again at the sudden appearance of the Elite Guard. Their fear of the Enforcers Guild had nothing to do with their belief in neo-Satanism. And their confusion sank in deeper.

"Kill the Servants!" Nathans cried automatically. His voice seemed to be losing its grip on the tone of authority, and it came out with undertones of a manic whimper. The High Priest looked down, as if oddly terrified of the Servant chained on the altar.

Automatically Jones snapped out one of his projectile weapons.

—waiting for the holographic images to come at him, simulated attackers—

Servants. He had done this all before. He turned, crouched, looked at the massed cultists, the scattered Wakers. But these Servants seemed alert, alive, aware of what Nathans was doing. And this was not the simulation chamber.

"Kill them!" Nathans stretched out his hand, pointing with the arthame, pointing at Julia.

—"You're not here because of any special talent, because you're the best . . . You're not important to him. You've been duped."—

"Jones!"

—"And who do you think runs the Guild, Mr. Jones?"—

Out in the crowd, Julia stood unlike the other Wakers. She did not seem to recognize him; she didn't seem aware of anything.

As the Elite Guard hesitated, Nathans finally let out a strange cry and snatched out the scatter-stun from the folds of his own robe, brandishing it. "Damn you! Do I have to do this myself?"

—"He finds a new way to use you instead."—

Jones turned calmly,

—You've been duped—

and pointed the projectile weapon directly at Nathans.

He took no time to acknowledge the man's suddenly startled expression before he fired one round into the High Priest's chest.

Nathans fell forward, still gripping the scatter-stun like a lifeline, and collapsed across the chained Servant on the altar, sliding slowly to the stage floor. His blood spilled into the center of the pentacle. . . .

Danal watched Nathans die with an overwhelming hollowness inside, as if his own synBlood were pouring out onto the stage instead. All the plans, all the anger—*all the pride, all the fascinating discussions*—the betrayal, the revenge—how could he possibly feel ambivalent after all that?

The two horrified Acolyte Supervisors fought through their paralysis and tried to rush toward Nathans's fallen body, but the armored Elite Guard snapped up his projectile weapon, pointing it at them. The two assistants scattered and ran. Many of the cultists let out an enraged outcry, rising to their feet. The Elite Guard seemed terrified by the threat of a mob and fired two projectiles at the ceiling. Chunks of papier mâché rained down, and the neo-Satanists quieted instantly, stunned and confused.

The Elite Guard pulled off his helmet, breathing deeply of the thick air. He blinked, looking shocked but defiant by what he had done. He dropped the hard black mask with a hollow clatter inside the pentacle next to Nathans's blood.

The lights in the Sabbat grotto flickered and went dim. A low, almost subliminal tone rumbled through the enclosed chamber, nearly beyond the range of human hearing. But Danal could feel it grinding in his bones; it made an unwanted shudder crawl up his spine.

Jones moved over to the Servant and fumbled with the chains, trying to find some way to free his wrists. He found a hidden catch, and one of the manacles snapped open. Danal sat up and looked into the face of the Elite Guard, the real face, unhidden, but the emotions he saw were buried several layers deep; Jones did not seem willing to let them surface just yet. The black man kept flicking his eyes out to the crowd, where Julia stoodunmoving.

Gregor started to shout something, but his words were engulfed by a ripping crash of sound that echoed through the chains of microspeakers embedded in the grotto walls—speakers which only recently had been used to augment the chanting of the neo-Satanists.

At the same instant a flash of laser light dazzled across hidden mirrors on the stalactites in a lightning web. A dull orange glow seeped in around the edges of the chamber, strongest on the blank wall of textured rock to the left of the altar. A foul-smelling smoke curled up from cracks in the rock. Sulfur. Brimstone.

Collectively the neo-Satanists let out a kind of awed gasp.

Immensely powerful words clawed at the air, like the sound of the universe tearing at its seams.

"YOU HAVE SUMMONED. AND I HAVE RE-TURNED."

Bright orange light stabbed through cracks in the rock wall as the stone began to shift and crumble, exposing a black cavern that seemed to extend to the gullet of the earth. Danal's eyes stung as sulfur fumes belched forth . . . and behind the smoke, in ghastly shadows, he saw something move, coming forward, taking shape.

The Servant's skin crawled, and the audience let out mixed cries of absolute terror and utter delight. They had forgotten everything else now, the Servants, the death of the High Priest—this was the main event.

A hulking demon, mammoth in size, with curved horns and cloven hooves—true to every nightmare and legend of neo-Satanism—emerged from below. Probing, it set one titan hoof forward with a *thump!* on the stage, and then it strode forward into full view, lashing its arrow-tipped tail and shattering the rock wall. A violent purple glare burned behind the demon's eyes as it surveyed the gathered worshipers. Deadly fangs filled its mouth as it snarled.

Amazingly, Jones seemed startled but unimpressed, and he muttered something that Danal couldn't hear over the frenzied confusion of the crowd. But the Servant wasn't listening anyway—his entire conception of reality rocked back and forth. Impossible! Nathans lay sacrificed within the pentacle. Had Stromgaard been right all along? Danal couldn't accept that, but the demon stood in plain view, real and tangible, not a hologram.

"You have summoned me! You brought me back. And I am grateful!" The monster ignored the Servant on the altar as Danal freed his other arm and frantically tried to loosen his ankles, fighting his horror. The demon spread his arms and bellowed to the neo-Satanists.

"Your faith has resurrected me. And I will grant your

greatest wish! All of you!" The creature drew in a roaring breath. "For all those who truly believe, return with me now—to the wonderful depths of Hell!"

The monster gestured to the fountains mounted along the walls. The bubbling foamy water suddenly spewed forth a brilliant scarlet, fluorescent, brighter even than arterial blood.

"This is my blood! Take. Drink. Drink deeply! And join me in Hell!"

"No, don't!" Jones said. He must have shouted, but his voice sounded utterly insignificant in comparison to the other. "It's poison!"

Nobody seemed to hear him. After an instant of stunned immobility, some of the awed people tentatively rose from their stone benches and glanced at the fountains.

"Drink!" the demon bellowed.

"This isn't real!" Jones cried, looking at them, appalled. "It's just an android."

A few people stopped and looked at him questioningly, but the awesome form of the monster reaffirmed their belief. Danal blinked, amazed but relieved to have a rational explanation, no matter how impossible, to clutch at. An android? Androids weren't feasible, but they were more believable than walking demons.

"Like a Servant. A machine—a trick!"

Jones made a determined sound and pulled out his riot club, striding forward. He struck the demon on the thigh, on the hip, reached up to batter its shoulder. The club made solid, wet sounds as it impacted, but the android took no notice of him and continued to survey the crowd, speaking its programmed summons.

"Come join me! Why do you hesitate? Do you not believe the evidence of your own eyes?"

"But it's just an android! A prototype, a trick!" Jones insisted.

The first of the worshipers—a chunky man with graying hair—reached the fountains. Breathless and enthusiastic, he plunged his head into the brilliant, glowing liquid, splashed, and turned to look at the others as he swallowed a mouthful . . . and died in retching convulsions a few moments later. His eyes almost burst from their sockets. Seeing but not seeing, more of them surged forward to drink.

"Hey, stop!" Jones shouted from the stage. Danal added his voice. Many of the neo-Satanists did hang back, frightened and uneasy, but the pressure from the others buffeted them forward.

"Drink! Join me!" Prototype thundered.

More cultists lay dead by the fountains, piling up, but others pushed ahead, some hesitant, some eager. Danal struggled with the last manacle, staring in cold horror at the cultists. Nathans had known exactly how they would react—he had selected them for their gullibility, and only the ones with the most unshakable faith would have come to the Walpurgis Night Sabbat. But how could they not see what they'd gotten into?

"It's only an android! Prototype!" Jones cried again, softer this time, his voice with the beginning edge of hysteria. "Look!"

He pulled out his heater-knife and stood in front of the demon. Reaching up, he sliced with the hot blade through the rubbery synthetic skin of Prototype's chest. The Elite Guard slashed across, and down, peeling the corner to expose tendrils of optic fiber, glowing power sources, cables, pulleys, servomotors.

With some self-protective mechanism the android swatted Jones, sending him sprawling. He skidded across the stage, protected by his armor, but he struck his head on the floor and sat back, dazed. Prototype, his innards exposed by the sagging flap of synthetic skin on his chest, turned back to the worshipers. They looked at him, disregarded what they did not wish to see, and continued to press toward the scattered fountains.

In the crowd Gregor moved frantically, trying to pull the worshipers away from the fountains. "Stop them! Wakers!"

The other Servants wrestled with the neo-Satanists. Many stopped by themselves, looking angry and confused after Jones's revelation, but the majority clung blindly to their faith and threw themselves at the scarlet poison. The Wakers struggled with them, but they were outnumbered dozens to one.

"I want to take *all* of your souls back to my realm! Join me! Drink my blood!"

Danal finally freed himself and swung down off the altar stone. He had no time to ponder, but many of the pieces fitted into place in the back of his mind. Prototype—yes, an android, a puppet for Nathans to use, but also an experiment to stretch the capabilities of Resurrection, Inc. And if Nathans had built Prototype, he would only have extended the technology already available to him—

"Prototype!" Danal shouted, "Command: Stop!"

In mid-sentence the android froze, arms upraised, fang-filled mouth open.

"Command: Be silent!" Danal stepped toward the towering monster. He looked up at the demon's face. "Take it back. Tell them to stop."

The Satan simulacrum lowered its gaze to look down at the Servant. Its curved horns glistened, but the bright purple glow of its eyes held no menace now.

"I cannot," the android said. "My programming specifies the words I must speak to the audience. I cannot deviate."

Danal wanted to scream in desperation at the demon, or break down in tears.

Then, unexpectedly, in the pentacle on the floor beside the altar stone, the body of Francois Nathans stirred and sat up.

The hands twitched, as if trying to orient themselves. The gaping hole in the man's chest began to trickle red blood once more, splashing anew across his High Priest's robe. Something had begun to pump again in place of a heart.

Danal felt a sensation of eerie horror as Nathans fumbled with his hands, grasped the edge of the altar stone, and hauled himself to his feet. Then Danal noticed the fine-lined scars on the man's bald scalp—scars that were better healed but otherwise similar to those that all Servants had. From the implanting of a microprocessor.

Danal gasped as he tried to say something, but his mouth felt too thick. Had Nathans been so frightened of dying, so obsessed with returning to life, to have a standby microprocessor implanted in his head? Ready to switch on after actual brain death? It had been perhaps fifteen minutes, maybe longer—not long, but enough. Without the resurrection process, without that long interim step, perhaps he had believed that his memories, his *self* would come back with him. It made a cold, logical sense—as if a simple time factor was the only thing that mattered.

Death doesn't work that way, Francois.

Dead Nathans sluggishly turned and saw Danal. His arm was rigid, still gripping the scatter-stun. He raised his arm. Danal couldn't move. But Nathans seemed only to be following a reflex action, flexing a muscle, and stood motionless and cold. His eyes didn't blink. His chest continued to bleed. The expression on his face was slack and cadaverous. Blank. Utterly empty.

Like Julia.

41

Aftermath. Holocaust. The words kept running through Danal's mind as he stood horror-struck, staring out into the silent chamber.

The worshipers had been too many, too intent upon destroying themselves. Those who refused to drink the poison now stood distraught and frightened, but few of them helped to stop their companions. The efforts of the Wakers alone did little against the tides of people.

Burly Rolf knocked down many of the cultists, sprawling them on the floor as fast as he could stride from one to another—arms swinging, shoulder tackling. Rikki was too small to do much more than distract and harry them, but still he kept a few away from the fountains. Laina became injured when she tried to wrestle with too many of the worshipers at one time; they turned on her, and only microprocessor speed saved her from being torn to pieces.

Stunned and concerned, Gregor knelt beside an old man convulsing in his last few moments. The leader of the Wakers looked deeply at the old man's face, and propped the man's head on his knee. His lips, teeth, and mouth were a brilliant scarlet, stained by the dye. Blotches of burst blood vessels spotted his face and hands. The dying man seemed to sense Gregor's presence and opened his eyes; his limbs jerked spasmodically.

"Why?" Gregor asked, begging for some kind of explanation that would make sense. "You could *see* it was poison. You *knew* the demon was just an android. Why would you do this? To yourselves?"

It seemed a rhetorical question, but the dying man somehow became lucid and gasped an answer, "Because I have Faith!"

It all stopped when Jones had finally roused himself and, conquering his own revulsion, snatched the scatter-stun from Nathans's dead-but-alive hand. The Elite Guard went through the neo-Satanists, stunning them all, dropping them in their tracks. . . .

Other than sobs from some of the Wakers and the nonsuicidal worshipers, the sacrificial grotto now felt silent and empty. The fountains continued to pour forth the bubbling red poison, but Rikki and Rolf had gone to find a way to shut them down.

Danal stood, feeling numb and cold like a ghost, then slowly walked down the steps to the main floor of the chamber. He left Prototype behind him, Commanded into silence and immobility on the stage . . . and the zombie Francois Nathans bleeding away his second life.

Though many of the neo-Satanists lay unconscious, crumpled across stone benches, nearly a full hundred had managed to poison themselves. Looking lost out among the fallen bodies, Jones remained motionless, without his helmet but still encased in the midnight-blue armor. His mouth hung open with a thread of saliva connecting his lips; his eyes stood wide open and staring.

By now Danal felt almost inured to seeing the bodies. Poisoned—Nathans would think of that. Now they were all perfect candidates for Servants. He felt a pang of sadness as he looked back at Julia, still clad in her Acolyte robe, blank and seemingly without a conscious will of her own.

Gregor saw his gaze and spoke by Danal's ear, startling him. "She stood up by herself. I was beside her, and we couldn't figure out what to do. I was going to shout or something. But when Julia saw you were going to be sacrificed . . . well, she stood up. By herself." A tone of wonder drifted into his words.

In quiet amazement Danal went over to the female Servant, afraid to ask. "Julia. Do you remember anything else?"

She stood in silence, but did not deny what he asked. Danal didn't feel his hope slip away so quickly this time. A faint mist, almost like the shadows of a tear, seemed to form over her eyes. He thought he noticed the faintest tremor in her lips.

"You'd better come over here, Danal," Laina said huskily, interrupting and holding her injured wrist.

Reluctantly the nurse/tech took him near one of the fountains, stepping over motionless robed forms on the floor. With her foot she pushed aside several of the dead cultists, revealing a slim female form clothed in a new Coven Manager's robe.

"Ah, no," Danal said as he knelt down, but his throat

298

was so dry he doubted if any words had come out. The Servant pushed aside the hood and tried to read an expression on the disfigured lumpy face, but he could not interpret her distorted death mask. Some of the fluorescent red wine she had drunk lay in a sticky trickle down her cheek. Strangely, Danal discovered he had new depths of grief within him.

"Zia," he mumbled, "you knew better. You knew so much better."

"Well, what do we do now?" Laina asked. "Who do we tell? The Enforcers?"

Some of the other Wakers looked at Danal, then Gregor, then Danal again.

"Nathans ran the Enforcers Guild," Jones muttered quietly, almost to himself, and then he strode back out into the main chamber among the fallen bodies, as if running away from what he had just said. Danal stared after him, wide-eyed.

"I'm not sure if I trust him completely," Laina muttered.

"He did help. And at a crucial time," Gregor countered.

"He's still an Elite Guard. But I'll keep an open mind." She frowned uncomfortably. "Choice of trust isn't exactly a luxury we can afford right now."

The unconscious neo-Satanists would begin to stir soon. The other Wakers forcibly kept all the nonsuicidal worshipers from leaving the chamber, though many wanted to run into the night and hide from the horrors before them. Only the threat of being caught out after curfew held them back. A few volunteered to help separate the living and the dead from the motionless forms crumpled on the floor.

"Excuse me, folks," Rikki interrupted, "but we have to figure out what we're going to do."

Danal pondered a long moment, and suddenly nothing seemed at all simple. They had defeated Nathans, effectively stopped neo-Satanism; they should have been having a victory party, but things . . .

"Tell our story, I guess. Put it on The Net for everyone to see, before it gets distorted. There's certainly enough evidence, enough proof, enough witnesses." His voice didn't contain a great deal of enthusiasm, and none of the others responded until Rikki finally spoke.

"Blaming all this on Nathans alone isn't going to work. You know that, don't you? These people lying poisoned, the tricks, the sham—somebody's going to find a scapegoat. And we all know what great scapegoats a bunch of spooky Servants would make.

"*And* in a few minutes we're going to be in a room full of revived fanatics. They'll be angry, or worse. They've already proven they're missing a few circuits in the CPU." He tapped his temple and made a face. "Any one of them can make us speak a confession or shut us up forever, with a single Command. We don't have any way to fight against it."

The others fell uneasily silent. Gregor looked down at the stained pentacle on the floor.

"Unless—" Gregor stopped, at a loss for words. Danal watched him in desperate fascination, and waited.

"I had an idea a long time ago, but it didn't seem worth trying. Now, maybe we have to." He swallowed, then shrugged. "Well, what about a paradox, something that might burn out your Servant programming? Like a Command you can't possibly obey."

"Do it," Danal said without a pause. He immediately knew what Gregor suggested. "To me."

"Now, wait a minute." Gregor raised his large hand. "Think about this—it could burn out your programming, or it could just as well put your mind into an infinite loop. Make you worse than *him*." He indicated the Nathans-zombie, silent and motionless. "We can't lose you, Danal. Your story is a key point in our survival."

Some of the other Wakers murmured, but Danal silenced them all. "We don't have time for philosophizing, Gregor. We've got to take our best shot. Before it's too late for us."

Placatingly he said, "Look, I'm not trying to be a martyr—I've done that once and it wasn't very pleasant. But keep in mind, all of you, that I'm not much of a hook to hang your hopes on if I'm bound by Servant programming.

"Look at it this way—the Wakers themselves are undeniable proof that Servants *can* get their memories back. If your paradox overloads me, you can still tell my story . . . you can even set me up as your scapegoat, if you like. Say I was burned out in my final battle with Nathans, and leave it at that. They'll believe it."

Gregor looked at the others for some kind of support, but all of them remained silent, ready to accept Danal's decision. Out in the main chamber, some of the unconscious neo-Satanists started to stir.

"Freedom of choice," Danal said. "The Command phrase takes that away from me, but right now *I* choose to take the risk." He sat down cross-legged on the floor, looking up at the big Waker.

Gregor's expression turned sullen but resigned. "I pray it works. Now, listen carefully and get this right." He drew a deep breath, then spoke sharply.

"Danal! Command: Obey no Commands!"

Obey no Commands. Simple enough.

But then he could not obey the Command that forbid him to obey Commands. Therefore he was forced to obey, which compelled him not to obey—

His conscious mind recognized the paradox and dismissed it as unsolvable. But the microprocessor and the Servant programming kept churning away relentlessly, forcing the problem around in circles in search of a logical conclusion . . . when it had none. Infinite loop. Danal could not move a muscle, and his vision spiraled in toward black as the Servant programming drew more and more of his resources to solve the paradox. His nerves and senses were shut down as extraneous input, irrelevant to the problem.

Once more Danal floated in a blackless void, with nothing, not even the perceptions and violent after-images of Death to join him. The time continuum passed by outside, but he was isolated from it, deprived of everything.

He felt buried alive, smothered by his sensory vacuum. *In between.* Between life and death and life again . . . for the second time. Out of the senseless silence came echoes of lost sounds, the growing hum, the unearthly chimes. The void closed up around him, took substance, and became the tunnel he had traveled once before. Danal knew consciously that this had to be a flashback again, another hallucinatory memory that became all too real in his state of mental siege.

But then a new thought, a new fear appeared, whistling through his thoughts. What if the paradox had claimed too much of him, demanded all his resources down to the last speck of energy? What if his synHeart stopped pumping, the artificial blood stopped flowing, the microprocessor did burn out and . . . shut down?

He did not fear the prospect of death again, but he did feel an almost crushing despair to think of all the things left to him, all the doors he had just opened up for himself, for the Wakers, for the future of Resurrection, Inc.

Around him appeared those other spirits again, nameless, formless, just behind his ability to perceive them— and yet he did know them, not their names, not their features, but *them*. Ahead, they pushed him gently along toward a great starburst of dazzling light, waxing pure and brilliant. The bright light welcomed him, pulsed, opened wider, sentient but like a pool of incandescent emotion. He began to remember, finally . . . this had happened before, and then—

And then the last great impenetrable wall rose up in front of him, blocking him off. The black barrier mocked him, unyielding, irresistible—reinforced by the paradox that burned through his brain, far away in his own body. But unlike when Gregor showed him how to view his death flashbacks by choice, Danal had no way to turn back now. No reality lay behind him, and he could go no farther forward.

He pounded on the barrier, shouting with all his spirit, begging, then angry, then in despair. He knew that on the other side of the impenetrable barrier lay either an escape back to reality or . . . beyond. He had to break through somehow, or he would be trapped in this hellish limbo for all eternity, whether it lasted an instant or a century in objective time. He had to go back and *live*, or go forward to Death, but he could not move one way or another.

The guardian spirits had dropped back to the edges of the tunnel, almost out of his perception. They would not help him. All things were bound by their own rules, their own power.

Then Danal knew, and he spoke his phrase with an evenness that belied his eagerness, "Command: Let me pass."

The wall began to fold and crumble and dissolve.

Danal blinked. Even turning his head slightly seemed an infinite effort; all his muscles had locked, petrified. He wondered blankly how long he had been away.

"Gregor!" Rikki cried. "He's coming back!"

The images finally made sense in front of his eyes, and Danal saw he had not moved. He still sat cross-legged on the floor of the altar platform, staring down at the pentacle. But everything else had changed. The other Wakers had gone, and only Rikki remained by him.

Gregor came running up the aisle, *running*, with a look of boyish excitement that made Danal want to laugh. He saw Laina coming, too, and even Jones wore an expression of relief.

"How long?" he asked. His own voice sounded like a madman's shout in his ears.

"More than an hour," Rikki answered, looking delighted. "All the neo-Satanists are awake now. Jones had to stun a couple of them again, but most are just dazed. All the fight's run out of them. See, it hasn't hit them yet—they don't seem to realize what they almost did. And the sad part is, most of them honestly think they've missed their big chance at salvation."

"Danal!" Gregor exclaimed and clapped both hands around the other Servant's shoulders. Danal felt several of his locked muscles pop free from their stiffness.

"Gregor . . ." he said breathlessly, "I broke through. The last barrier. I saw *all* my Death memories."

This took the big Waker completely by surprise, but he quickly reoriented himself. "And? What did you see?" Gregor clutched his own hands, and then a look of fear came across his face, as if he wasn't actually ready for the answers just yet.

"It was like . . . you know how we can never really describe the first death flashbacks? Because we just don't have any words? This was more than that, because I was surrounded by things that even my mind couldn't . . ." He struggled to express himself, "I had no framework for the perceptions. I don't remember any of it now, but I know I saw it." He paused for a moment as an even greater wonder grew on his face. "And I think—I think I saw Julia there. I'm not sure." Danal clenched his fist in exasperation. "I can't remember. The barrier's gone now, but I simply couldn't retain any of the experience. Not even while I was there."

He smiled, though, with a look of blithe amazement that seemed to surprise the others around him. "You'll find something there, too, Gregor. You'll know what I mean."

Rikki fidgeted, impatient and not showing much interest in Gregor's fascination. "But did it work?"

Danal looked at him blankly for a moment, wondering what he meant.

Exasperated, Rikki crossed his arms and snapped, "Danal! Command: Slap your face!"

Smiling, Danal reached forward instead to pat the boy Waker on both cheeks.